ALTAR OF EDEN

JAMES ROLLINS

An Orion paperback

First published in Great Britain in 2010
by Orion
This paperback edition published in 2010
by Orion Books Ltd,
Orion House, 5 Upper St Martin's Lane,
London WC2H 9EA

An Hachette UK company

A CIP catalogue record for this book is available
from the British Library.

Printed in Great Britain by Clays Ltd, St Ives plc

The Orion Publishing Group's policy is to use papers
that are natural, renewable and recyclable products and
made from wood grown in sustainable forests. The logging
and manufacturing processes are expected to conform to
the environmental regulations of the country of origin.

www.orionbooks.co.uk

To my sister Laurie
We all love you

And Babylon shall become heaps, a dwellingplace for dragons, an astonishment, and an hissing, without an inhabitant.

JEREMIAH, 51:37

And what rough beast, its hour come round at last, Slouches towards Bethlehem to be born?

W.B. YEATS

The study of Nature makes a man at last as remorseless as Nature.

H.G. WELLS

Acknowledgments

I've never been a firm believer in the adage 'write what you know.' What's the fun in that? Still, as a veterinarian, I also always wanted to feature a book with a *veterinarian* in the lead. Still, even in this case, that old adage doesn't hold true. I had to lean on many people to bring this story to life. First and always, I must acknowledge my critique group: Penny Hill, Judy Prey, Dave Murray, Caroline Williams, Chris Crowe, Lee Garrett, Jane O'Riva, Sally Barnes, Denny Grayson, Leonard Little, Kathy L'Ecluse, Scott Smith, Chris Smith, and Will Murray. And an extra big thanks to Steve Prey for all his great help with the maps. Beyond the group, Carolyn McCray and David Sylvian keep life out of my way so I can write. Dr. Scott Brown was instrumental with some of the medical details, and Cherie McCarter continues to be a wellspring of information (including an article about a snake born with a clawed leg . . . love that!). And a special thanks to Steve and Elizabeth Berry for their great friendship (and for Liz, since it's missing from this book, I thought I'd put it here: 'sluiced'). Lastly, a special acknowledgment to the four people instrumental to all levels of production: my editor, Lyssa Keusch, and her colleague Wendy Lee; and my agents, Russ Galen and Danny Baror. They've truly been the foundation under this author. And as always, I must stress that any and all errors of fact or detail in this book fall squarely on my own shoulders.

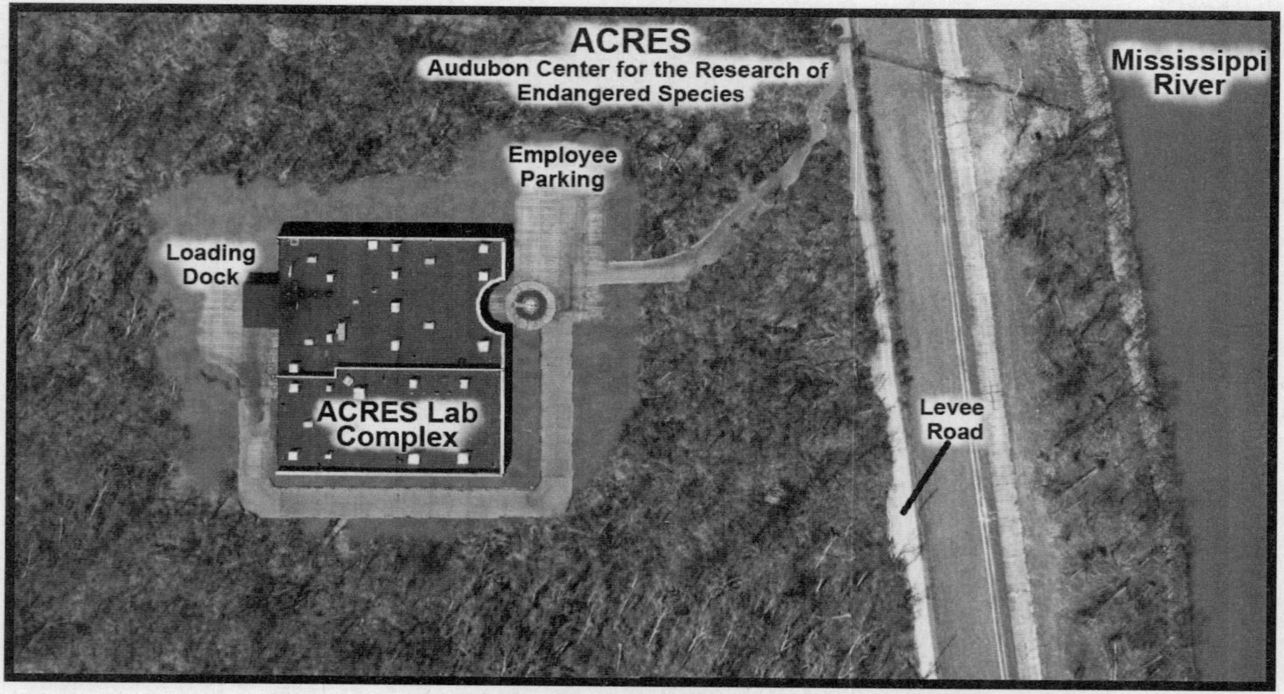
ACRES
Audubon Center for the Research of Endangered Species
Mississippi River
Employee Parking
Loading Dock
ACRES Lab Complex
Levee Road

Lost Eden Cay

Village Habitat

Mine Field

Barricade

Villa

Helipad

Cove

Private Marina

N
W   E
S

April 2003
Baghdad, Iraq

The two boys stood outside the lion's cage.

'I don't want to go inside,' the smaller one said. He kept close to his older brother and clasped his hand tightly.

The two were bundled in jackets too large for their small forms, faces swathed in scarves, heads warmed by woolen caps. At this early hour, with the sun not yet up, the predawn chill had crept down to their bones.

They had to keep moving.

'Bari, the cage is empty. Stop being a *shakheef*. Look.' Makeen, the older of the two, pushed the black iron gate wider and revealed the bare concrete walls inside. A few old gnawed bones lay piled in a dark corner. They would make a nice soup.

Makeen stared out at the ruins of the zoo. He remembered how it had once looked. Half a year ago, for his twelfth birthday, they had come here to picnic at the Al-Zawraa Gardens with its amusement park rides and zoo. The family had spent a long warm afternoon wandering among the cages of monkeys, parrots, camels, wolves, bears. Makeen had even fed one of the camels an apple. He still remembered the rubbery lips on his palm.

Standing here now, he stared across the same park with older eyes, far older than half a year ago. The park sprawled outward in a ruin of rubble and refuse. It was a haunted wasteland of fire-blackened walls, fetid pools of oily water, and blasted buildings.

A month ago, Makeen had watched from their apartment near the park as a firefight blazed across the lush gardens, waged by American forces and the Republican Guard. The fierce battle had begun at dusk, with the rattle of gunfire and the shriek of rockets continuing throughout the night.

But by the next morning, all had gone quiet. Smoke hung thickly and hid the sun for the entire day. From the balcony of their small apartment, Makeen had spotted a lion as it loped out of the park and into the city. It moved like a dusky shadow, then vanished into the streets. Other animals also escaped, but over the next two days, hordes of people had swarmed back into the park.

Looters, his father had named them, and spat on the floor, cursing them in more foul language.

Cages were ripped open. Animals were stolen, some for food, some to be sold at the black market across the river. Makeen's father had gone with a few other men to get help to protect their section of the city from the roving bands.

He had never returned. None of them had.

Over the next weeks, the burden had fallen upon Makeen to keep his family fed. His mother had taken to her bed, her forehead burning with fever, lost somewhere between terror and grief. All Makeen could get her to do was drink a few sips of water.

If he could make a nice soup for her, get her to eat something more . . .

He eyed the bones in the cage again. Each morning, he and his brother spent the hour before dawn searching the bombed-out park and zoo for anything they could scrounge to eat. He carried a burlap sack over his shoulder. All it held was a moldy orange and a handful of cracked seed swept up off the floor of a birdcage. Little Bari had also found a dented can of beans in a rubbish bin. The discovery had brought tears to Makeen's eyes. He kept the treasure rolled

2

up inside his little brother's thick sweater.

Yesterday, a larger boy with a long knife had stolen his sack, leaving Makeen empty-handed when he returned. They'd had nothing to eat that day.

But today they would eat well.

Even Mother, *inshallah,* he prayed.

Makeen entered the cage and dragged Bari with him. Distant gunfire crackled in short spurts, like the scolding claps of angry hands trying to warn them off.

Makeen took heed. He knew they had to hurry. He didn't want to be out when the sun was up. It would grow too dangerous. He hurried to the pile of bones, dropped his sack, and began shoving the gnawed knuckles and broken shafts inside.

Once finished, he tugged the sack closed and stood. Before he could take a step, a voice called in Arabic from nearby, '*Yalla!* This way! Over here!'

Makeen ducked and pulled Bari down with him. They hid behind the knee-high cinderblock wall that fronted the lion's cage. He hugged his brother, urging him to remain silent, as two large shadows passed in front of the lion's cage.

Risking a peek, Makeen caught a glimpse of two men. One was tall in a khaki military uniform. The other was squat with a round belly, dressed in a dark suit.

'The entrance is hidden behind the zoo clinic,' the fat man said as he passed the cage. He huffed and wheezed to keep up with the longer strides of the man in military fatigues. 'I can only pray we are not too late.'

Makeen spotted the holstered pistol on the taller man's belt and knew it would be death to be found eavesdropping.

Bari shivered in his embrace, sensing the danger, too.

Unfortunately the men did not go far. The clinic was directly across from their hiding spot. The fat man ignored the twisted main door. Days ago, crowbars had forced the way open. The facility had been cleaned out of drugs and medical supplies.

Instead, the heavy figure stepped to a blank wall framed by two columns. Makeen could not make out what the man did as he slipped his hand behind one of the columns, but a moment later, a section of the wall swung open. It was a secret door.

Makeen shifted closer to the bars. Father had read them stories of Ali Baba, tales of secret caverns and vast stolen treasures hidden in the desert. All he and his brother had found at the zoo were bones and beans. Makeen's stomach churned as he imagined a feast fit for the Prince of Thieves that might wait below.

'Stay here,' the fat man said, ducking through the entrance and down a dark set of stairs.

The military man took up a post by the doorway. His palm rested on his pistol. His gaze swung toward their hiding spot. Makeen ducked out of sight and held his breath. His heart pounded against his ribs.

Had he been spotted?

Footsteps approached the cage. Makeen clung tightly to his brother. But a moment later, he heard a match strike and smelled cigarette smoke. The man paced the front of the cage as if he were the one behind the bars, stalking back and forth like a bored tiger.

Bari shook within Makeen's embrace. His brother's fingers were clamped hard in his. What if the man should wander into the cage and find them huddled there?

It seemed an eternity when a familiar wheezing voice echoed out of the doorway. 'I have them!'

The cigarette was dropped and ground out onto the cement just outside the cage door. The military man crossed back to join his companion.

The fat man gasped as he spoke. He must have run all the way back up. 'The incubators were off-line,' he said. 'I don't know how long the generators lasted after the power went out.'

Makeen risked a peek through the bars of the cage door.

The fat man carried a large metal briefcase in his hand.

'Are they secure?' the military man asked. He also spoke in Arabic, but his accent was not Iraqi.

The fat man dropped to one knee, balanced the case on his thick thigh, and thumbed open the lock. Makeen expected gold and diamonds, but instead the case held nothing but white eggs packed in molded black foam. They appeared no different from the chicken eggs his mother bought at the market.

Despite his terror, the sight of the eggs stirred Makeen's hunger.

The fat man counted them, inspecting them. 'They're all intact,' he said and let out a long rattling sigh of relief. 'God willing, the embryos inside are still viable.'

'And the rest of the lab?'

The fat man closed the case and stood up. 'I'll leave it to your team to incinerate what lies below. No one must ever suspect what we've discovered. There can be no trace.'

'I know my orders.'

As the fat man stood, the military man raised his pistol and shot his companion in the face. The blast was a thunderclap. The back of the man's skull blew away in a cloud of bone and blood. The dead man stood for a moment longer, then flopped to the ground.

Makeen covered his mouth to stifle any sound.

'No trace,' the murderer repeated and collected the case from the ground. He touched a radio on his shoulder. He switched to English.

'Bring in the trucks and prime the incendiary charges. Time to get out of this sandbox before any locals turn up.'

Makeen had learned to speak a smattering of the American language. He couldn't pick out every word the man spoke, but he understood the message well enough.

More men were coming. More guns.

Makeen sought some means of escape, but they were trapped in the lion's cage. Perhaps his younger brother also recognized the growing danger. Bari's shaking had grown worse since the gunshot. Finally, his little brother's terror could no longer be held inside, and a quiet sob rattled out of his thin form.

Makeen squeezed his brother and prayed that the cry had not been heard.

Footsteps again approached. A sharp call barked toward them in Arabic. 'Who's there? Show yourself! *Ta'aal hnaa!*'

Makeen pressed his lips to his brother's ear. 'Stay hidden. Don't come out.'

Makeen shoved Bari tighter into the corner, then stood up with his hands in the air. He backed a step. 'I was just looking for food!' Makeen said, stuttering, speaking fast.

The pistol stayed leveled at him. 'Get out here, *walad!*'

Makeen obeyed. He moved to the cage door and slipped out. He kept his hands in the air. 'Please, *ahki. Laa termi!*' He tried switching to English, to show he was on the man's side. 'No shoot. I not see . . . I not know . . .'

He fought to find some argument, some words to save him. He read the expression on the other man's face – a mixture of sorrow and regret.

The pistol lifted higher with merciless intent.

Makeen felt hot tears flow down his cheeks.

Through the blur of his vision, he noted a shift of shadows. Behind the man, the secret door cracked open wider, pushed from inside. A large, dark shape slipped out and flowed toward the man's back. It ran low and stuck to the deeper shadows, as if fearing the light.

Makeen caught the barest glimpse of its oily form: muscular, lean, hairless, with eyes glinting with fury. His mind struggled to comprehend what he was seeing – but failed.

A scream of horror built inside his chest.

Though the beast made no noise, the man must have felt a prickling of warning. He swung around as the creature leaped with a sharp cry. Gunshots blasted, eclipsed by a savage wail that raised the hairs on Makeen's body.

Makeen swung away and rushed back to the cage. 'Bari!'

He grabbed his brother's arm and dragged him out of the lion's cage. He pushed Bari ahead of him. '*Yalla!* Run!'

Off to the side, man and beast fought on the ground.

More pistol shots fired.

Makeen heard the heavy tread of boots on pavement behind him. More men came running from the other side of the park. Shouts were punctuated by rifle blasts.

Ignoring them all, Makeen fled in raw terror across the bombed-out gardens, careless of who might see him. He kept running and running, chased by screams that would forever haunt his nightmares.

He understood nothing about what had happened. He knew only one thing for certain. He remembered the beast's ravenous eyes, shining with a cunning intelligence, aglow with a smokeless fire.

Makeen knew what he had seen.

The beast known as *Shaitan* in the Koran – he who was born of God's fire and cursed for not bowing down to Adam.

Makeen knew the truth.

At long last, the devil had come to Baghdad.

ACT ONE

FIRST BLOOD

Chapter 1

The Bronco crushed through the debris left by the hurricane and bounced off yet another hole. Lorna nearly hit the roof of the cabin. The car slid to the left on the wet road. She eased off the accelerator as she fought for control.

The storm had stripped vegetation, sent creeks overflowing their banks, and even floated an alligator into someone's swimming pool. Luckily the worst of the dying hurricane had struck farther west. Still, with such downpours, Mother Nature seemed determined to turn Orleans Parish back into swamplands.

As Lorna sped along the river road, all she could think about was the phone call. It had come in twenty minutes ago. They'd lost power at ACRES. The generators hadn't kicked in, and a hundred research projects were threatened.

As she rounded a final oxbow in the Mississippi River, the compound appeared ahead. The Audubon Center for Research of Endangered Species occupied more than a thousand acres downriver from New Orleans. Though associated with the city's zoo, ACRES was not open to the public. Sheltered within a hardwood forest, the grounds included a few outdoor pens, but the main facility was

11

a thirty-six-thousand square-foot research building that housed a half-dozen laboratories and a veterinary hospital.

The latter was where Dr. Lorna Polk had worked since completing her postgraduate residency in zoo-and-wildlife medicine. She oversaw the facility's *frozen* zoo, twelve tanks of liquid nitrogen that preserved sperm, eggs, and embryos from hundreds of endangered species: mountain gorillas, Sumatran tigers, Thomson's gazelles, colobus monkeys, cape buffalo.

It was a big position to fill, especially for someone only twenty-eight and just out of her residency. Her responsibility – the frozen genetic bank – held the promise of pulling endangered species back from the brink of extinction through artificial insemination, embryo transfer, and cloning. Yet, despite the weight of her responsibility, she loved her work and knew she was good at it.

As she raced down the long entry road toward the main facility, her cell phone chimed from the cup holder. She grabbed it and cradled it to her ear while driving one-armed.

The caller must have heard the line pick up and spoke rapidly. 'Dr. Polk. It's Gerald Granger from engineering. I thought you should know. We've got the generators working and isolated the power loss to a downed line.'

She glanced to the truck's clock. The power had been down for close to forty-five minutes. She calculated in her head and let out a sigh of relief.

'Thanks, Gerald. I'll be there in another minute.'

She flipped the phone closed.

Reaching the employee lot, she parked and rested her head on the steering wheel. The relief was so palpable she almost cried, almost. After taking a moment to collect herself, she straightened and stared down at the hands on her lap, suddenly aware of what she wore. She had fled the house in a pair of wrinkled jeans, an old gray turtleneck, and boots.

Not exactly the professional appearance she usually maintained.

Twisting to exit the Bronco, she caught her reflection in the rearview mirror.

Oh, dear God . . .

Her blond hair – normally primly braided – had been pinned back into a rough ponytail this morning. Several flyaways only added to her already disheveled appearance. Even her black-framed glasses sat askew on the bridge of her nose. At the moment she looked like a drunken college student returning from a Mardi Gras party.

If she looked the part, she might as well go all the way. She pulled out the pin holding her hair and let it fall around her shoulders, then climbed out of the truck and crossed toward the main entrance.

Before she could reach the facility's front doors, a new noise drew her attention: a heavy *wump-wumping*. She turned toward the Mississipi. A white helicopter skimmed over the tree line and headed in her direction. It was coming in fast.

As she frowned, a hand settled on her shoulder from behind. She jumped slightly, but fingers squeezed in reassurance. A glance back revealed her boss and mentor, Dr. Carlton Metoyer, the head of ACRES. Covered by the noise of the helicopter, she had not heard his approach.

Thirty years her senior, he was a tall, wiry black man with bushy white hair and a trimmed gray beard. His family had been here in the region for as long as Lorna's, tracing their roots back to the Cane River Creole colony, a blend of French and African heritage.

Dr. Metoyer shielded his eyes as he stared at the sky.

'We got company,' he said.

The helicopter was definitely headed toward ACRES. It swept toward an adjacent field and began to descend. She noted it was a small A-Star helicopter equipped with floats instead of the usual landing skids. She also recognized the slash of green across the white shell of the aircraft. After Katrina, most people in New Orleans knew that insignia.

13

It was one of the Border Patrol helicopters; fleets of such choppers had been vital to the rescue operations and security following the disaster.

'What are they doing here?' she asked.

'They've come for you, my dear. They're your ride.'

Chapter 2

Lorna's stomach sank as the helicopter lifted off – not so much from the motion as from sheer panic. She clutched the armrests as she sat next to the pilot. The growing roar of the rotors penetrated her bulky headphones. It felt like rising in an elevator. An elevator strapped to a rocket.

She had never been a fan of heights, hated air travel in general, and considered riding an airborne lawn mower the height of madness. She had only flown once in a helicopter, during an externship in South Africa conducting a census of African elephants in the lands bordering a preserve. Back then, she had prepared for that flight by downing a pair of Xanax tablets before the trip. Still, her legs had felt like warm pudding for hours afterward.

And today she'd had no warning.

Dr. Metoyer had only filled her in on the sketchiest of details as the helicopter landed. He had not even given her time to go inside and inspect her project's liquid nitrogen tanks. *Staff is already on it*, he had promised, adding that he'd check them himself and radio the details later.

Radio . . .

They were flying beyond any cell signal.

She risked a glance through the side window. The helicopter banked, giving her a bird's-eye view of the Mississippi. They were traveling downriver, roughly following the Big Muddy's course. The name was particularly apt follow-

15

ing the storm. The river was a chocolate brown, rich with silt, eddying and churning as it flowed toward the Gulf of Mexico.

They were headed out over the river's delta, where all that alluvium – silt, clay, sand, and soil – deposited and pushed out into the Gulf, forming over three million acres of coastal wetlands and salt marshes. Not only was the region environmentally significant, home to a vast and complicated ecosystem that traced its roots back to the Jurassic period, it was also commercially significant. The area supplied the United States with a large percentage of its seafood, and almost 20 percent of its oil.

It was also a weak link in the nation's border. The maze of islands, twisting waterways, and isolated fishing docks made the delta a sieve for smugglers and traffickers of all sorts. The Department of Homeland Security had designated the region a high-level threat and reinforced the New Orleans station of the Border Patrol.

According to her boss, the Border Patrol had been searching the area following last night's storm surge. It was common for smugglers to work under the cover of storms to bring in drugs, guns, even human cargo. Early this morning, a team had discovered a trawler beached on one of the outlying islands. After investigating the ship, they'd made a call to ACRES.

Much of that call remained a mystery, even to Dr. Metoyer. He had not been informed about the nature of the request, or why Lorna in particular had been asked to make this trip.

Despite her trepidation about air flight, a smoldering anger was building. She had projects in jeopardy over at ACRES. What was she doing flying out into the middle of nowhere? Her anger grew, stoked by her anxiety. What was going on? Why ask for her in particular? She knew no one in the Customs and Border Protection service.

The only answers lay at the end of this flight.

The radio built into her earphones crackled. The pilot

pointed toward the horizon. He wore a green uniform with shoulder patches marking him as part of the Border Patrol's Air and Marine unit. He had introduced himself, but she hadn't caught his name.

'Dr. Polk, we'll be landing in a few moments.'

She nodded and stared forward. The dense emerald of the swampy marshes broke apart below into a tangle of islands and peninsulas ahead. Farther out into the Gulf, a dark line near the horizon marked a row of larger barrier islands that helped protect the fragile marshes and coastal swamps.

But they weren't going that far.

She spotted a shiny white boat moored by one of the small islands. *Finally.* As they descended toward it she also noted an old fishing trawler rammed into the beach. It had struck hard enough to topple a few trees and ride halfway up onto the island. It plainly had been shoved there by the storm surge.

The helicopter dropped fast. Her grip tightened on the armrests. She had read that a majority of air crashes occurred during takeoffs and landings. Not a statistic she wanted to bear in mind at the moment.

Within a few yards of the water, their descent slowed. The rotorwash beat the waves flat. Then, as gently as a goose landing on a still pond, the chopper's floats settled to the water. A few flicks of some switches and the whine of the rotors began to slow.

'Please stay seated,' the pilot said. 'They're sending a Zodiac out for you.'

His nod out the window drew her attention to a small rubber pontoon boat that pushed off from the island and shot toward them. Moments later, a crewman dressed in the same Border Patrol green helped her out of the helicopter and into the Zodiac.

She dropped onto a bench of the pontoon boat, both relieved yet still carrying a hot coal in her belly. She shaded her eyes as they headed toward shore, searching for some answer for the mysterious and sudden summons.

The morning was already growing warm as the sun broke apart the clouds and opened blue skies. The day promised to grow into one of Louisiana's steam baths. And she was okay with that. She took deep breaths to steady herself, taking in the brackish odor of leafy decay, wet moss, and muddy salt water.

To her, it was the smell of home.

Her family had lived in Louisiana going back to the nineteenth century. Like all the old families of New Orleans, her history was as deeply ingrained as the lines on her palms. Ancestors' names and stories were as familiar as if they'd died only yesterday.

During the War of 1812, her great-great-grandfather, only seventeen at the time, had abandoned the British army during the Battle of New Orleans and made his home in the new burgeoning frontier city. He met and married the daughter of the de Trépagnier family and quickly made a small fortune by growing sugarcane and indigo on a hundred-acre plantation given as a dowry. Over the years, that fortune continued to grow, and the Polk family was one of the first to build in the oak-shadowed glen of New Orleans's Garden District. After selling the plantation, the family settled permanently in the district. Over the generations, the Polk mansion became respected as a gathering place for military generals, legal scholars, and countless men of science and letters.

The Italianate mansion still stood, but like the city, the Polk family had begun a slow decline during the twentieth century. Only Lorna and her brother still bore the family name. Her father had died of lung cancer when Lorna was a child; her mother passed away a year ago, leaving the siblings a mansion in ill repair and a pile of debt.

But the tradition of valuing education continued. She had gone into medicine and science. Her brother, younger by a year, was an oil engineer working for the state. For the moment brother and sister, both single, shared the family estate.

A grind of wet sand on rubber pulled her back to the present.

The small island, one of a series forming a chain back to the dense coastal marshes, was covered in cypress trees matted together by Spanish moss. It looked impenetrable beyond the edge of the beach.

But that's not where she was going.

'This way,' the Zodiac pilot said. He offered a hand to help her out of the boat, but she ignored him and climbed out herself. 'The FOS is waiting to speak to you.'

'FOS?'

'Field operations supervisor.'

She didn't understand the command structure of the Border Patrol, but it sounded like this was the guy in charge of the investigation. Maybe the one who had summoned her away from ACRES. Wanting answers, she followed the pilot toward the beached trawler. Having grown up along the river, she knew boats. The trawler was a small one, a forty-footer. Its starboard booms had been shattered by the collision, but on the port side, the long poles still pointed crookedly toward the sky. The shrimp nets were still tied down to the booms.

A handful of men, all in rough duty uniforms of the Border Patrol, gathered on the beach alongside the trawler. Some wore tan Stetsons, others green baseball caps. She also noted the holstered sidearms. One man had a Remington shotgun resting on a shoulder.

What was going on?

The men fell silent as she approached. A few pairs of eyes traveled up and down her form, looking little impressed. She kept her face fixed into something resembling a stern expression, but she felt her cheeks heat up in irritation. She resisted the urge to flip them all off.

Definitely a boys' club here.

The agents parted to reveal a tall man similarly attired in dark green trousers and a matching long-sleeved work shirt, casually rolled to the elbows. He finger-combed his black hair, damp with sweat, and secured a black baseball cap in place. But not before his blue-gray eyes also examined her from head to foot. Unlike the others, she sensed nothing lascivious in his attention, only sizing her up.

Still, she was glad when the bill of his cap shadowed those eyes.

He crossed to close the distance between them. He stood well over six feet tall, broad-shouldered and muscular without looking bulky. His carriage was of someone who knew how to lead with no need to dominate. Confidence, along with a feral edge, flowed from him.

He held out a large hand as he reached her.

'Dr. Polk, thank you for coming.'

She shook his hand and noted a long scar down his forearm, from elbow to wrist. Glancing up, she met his gaze. His complexion was a tanned olive, further darkened by black stubble over his chin and jaw. Her ear picked up his slight French Cajun accent.

So he was local to the area. In fact, there was something naggingly familiar about him – and then it struck her. She was about to demand an answer as to why she was brought here.

Instead, a different question stumbled out.

'Jack?'

His lips, full but definitely masculine, shifted to a harder line as he gave the barest nod. Her image of him similarly transformed in a sudden shift of perspective. The anger drained out of her, replaced with something colder and more uncomfortable. It had been over ten years since she'd last seen him. She had only been a sophomore in high school; he had been a senior.

Though she hadn't really known him well back then – in high school, two years was an insurmountable social gulf –

they had darker ties that bound them together. A connection she had wanted forever left in her past.

From the expression passing like a cloud over his face, he possibly wished the same. Either way, now was not the time to reopen those old wounds.

'Dr. Polk,' he said stiffly. His accent grew thicker, more husky. 'I called you here because . . . because I didn't know who else had the expertise to offer guidance about what we found.'

She straightened her back, going equally professional. Maybe that was best. She swallowed and stared toward the trawler, glad for an excuse to look away. 'What did you find?'

'You'd best see for yourself.'

He turned and led the way to the trawler. A rope ladder led up to the deck. He climbed first, clambering easily up. She was all too conscious of the hard strength in his legs and back. Once he vanished over the gunwale, one of his men secured the ladder's lower end, making it easier for her to climb.

At the top, Jack helped pull her to the deck. Two other men stood guard by a door that led to the lower holds. One of them passed Jack a flashlight.

'Sir, we've run a portable lamp down into the hold, but it's still damn dark down there.'

Jack thumbed on his flashlight and waved for her to follow. 'Careful of the blood on the stairs.'

His light revealed a dark stain along one side of the steps. Like something had been dragged down into the hold.

She suddenly did not want to go down there.

'We found no bodies,' Jack said, as if sensing her discomfort. Or maybe he was merely filling her in on the details of the case.

She followed him down the steps and along a narrow passageway.

'They kept them caged in the main hold.'

She didn't bother to ask what was caged. She already smelled the familiar musk of a rank kennel. She heard the shuffle of bodies, a rustling, a mewling cry, a sharp screech of a bird.

She began to understand why she had been summoned. Exotic animal smuggling was a billion-dollar-a-year industry, ranking just behind drug and gun trafficking. And unfortunately the United States was one of the leading consumers of such smuggled cargo, accounting for 30 percent of such sales.

She had read just last week about the bust of a major trafficking ring dealing in rare tigers. In that case, the Missouri couple wasn't bringing in the big cats for pets, but for *parts*. They were smuggling in tigers, then butchering them. Hides of leopards, tigers, and lions could fetch upward of twenty thousand dollars. But that wasn't all. Like some bloody chop shop, they were selling off all parts: tiger penises to be ground into aphrodisiacs, bones for arthritis cures. No part went to waste. Gallbladder, liver, kidneys, even teeth. In the end, such large cats were worth far more dead than alive.

She felt anger building as she followed Jack into the main hold.

A tall pole lamp lit the low-roofed space. Stainless-steel cages lined both sides of the long hold; larger pens in the back were still in shadows. She gaped at the size of the smuggling operation, certain now why she was needed here, a veterinarian specializing in exotic animals.

Jack turned and shone his flashlight into the nearest cage.

She stared inside – and knew she was wrong about everything.

Chapter 3

Jack Menard studied the woman's reaction.

Shock and horror widened Lorna's eyes. She covered her mouth with a hand. But only for a moment. After the initial surprise, he also recognized a glint of concern. Her eyes narrowed again, her lips drawn tight in thought. She moved closer to the cage.

He joined her and cleared his throat. 'What type of monkeys are they?'

'*Cebus apella*,' she answered. 'Brown capuchin monkeys, native to South America.'

Jack stared at the two who shared the small cage, squatting in their own filth, huddled and scared at the back of the cage. Their limbs and backsides were a deep chocolate brown, their faces and chests a softer tan, their heads capped in black. They were so small he could have cupped one in the palm of his hand.

'Are they babies?' he asked.

She shook her head. 'I don't think so. The fur coloring suggests they're adults. But you're right. They're way too small. Pygmy versions of the breed.'

But Jack knew that wasn't the most shocking aberration. With a quiet cooing noise, Lorna coaxed the pair to move toward the bars. Her coldly professional manner seemed to melt away, her face softening, relaxing. The pair of monkeys responded to her. Still hugging each other, they crept forward, clinging tightly. Not that they could ever truly be apart.

'Siamese twins,' Lorna said.

The two were joined at the hip – literally – fused together, sharing three legs but bearing four arms.

'Poor things,' she whispered. 'They look half starved.'

They came to the bars, plainly needing reassurance as much as sustenance. Their eyes were huge, especially in such small faces. Jack sensed their hunger and fear and also a trace of hope. He reached into a pocket and removed a granola bar. He ripped it open with his teeth, broke off a piece, and handed it to Lorna.

She gently passed it through the bars. One of them took it with its tiny fingers – then the pair retreated to share the prize, huddled around it, nibbling from both sides. But their eyes never left Lorna.

She glanced to Jack. For a moment he saw the girl he remembered from his school days, before he left for the Marines. She had dated his younger brother, Tom, during their sophomore year – and the summer thereafter. He shied away from that memory.

Lorna must have sensed this well of pain. Her face hardened, going professional again. She nodded to the other cages. 'Show me.'

He led her along the rows of cages, shining his flashlight into the shadowy recesses. Each enclosure held a different animal, some familiar, some exotic. But like the monkeys, they all bore some twisted abnormality. They stopped next at a large glass-walled terrarium that held a fifteen-foot Burmese python curled around a clutch of eggs. The snake looked ordinary enough until its coils slid more tightly around the eggs and revealed two pairs of folded vestigial legs, scaled and clawed, remnants of its lizardlike evolutionary origin.

'It looks like a severe form of atavism,' Lorna said.

'And that would be what in English?'

She offered him a small apologetic smile. 'Atavism is where a genetic trait, lost for generations, reappears in an individual.'

'A genetic throwback?'

'Exactly. In this case, a throwback to a time before snakes lost their limbs.'

'That's a mighty long *throw,* isn't it?'

She shrugged and moved on. 'Most atavism is caused by the accidental recombination of genes. But I don't think it was *accidental* here, not with this many cases.'

'So you're saying someone bred them this way on purpose. Is that even possible?'

'I can't rule it out. Genetic science has come a long way and continues to push boundaries. At ACRES, we've successfully cloned wild cats. We've even merged a fluorescent protein from a jellyfish to produce a cat that glows in the dark.'

'Mr. Green Genes. I read about that,' he said. 'In fact, it's one of the reasons why I called for you. I needed an expert on genetics and breeding. Someone to tell me who could have produced this bizarre cargo.'

He led her through the hold. A wire cage held a mass of winged bats the size of footballs.

'Vampire bats,' Lorna said. 'But they're ten times the size they should be. May be a form of primordial gigantism.'

Similarly a caged fox down the row was the size of a bear cub. It hissed and growled and threw itself against the bars. They quickly moved past, stopping briefly at a tall cage that held an ordinary-size parrot, but it had no feathers.

It cawed loudly, leaped to the front bars, and studied them while cocking its head back and forth. Jack had a hard time hiding his disgust. There was something so alien and *wrong* about its appearance.

Lorna just moved closer. 'When baby parrots first hatch, they're featherless or covered only with a light down. I don't know if this one's stunted into an infantile state, or if it's a throwback, too. In fact, it's theorized that birds are the closet living relatives of dinosaurs.'

Jack didn't argue. The creature – leather-skinned and beaked – definitely had a prehistoric look to it. But what really got him unnerved was the sharpness of its attention.

The bird leaped back to its perch, spouting a garble of Spanish. That aspect of the parrot – the ability to mimic – remained intact. It began to screech a string of numbers in English, its pronunciation and diction sounding perfectly human, if pitched slightly sharper.

'. . . *three one four one five nine two six five* . . .'

They continued onward, then Lorna stopped in midstep. She stared back at the cage as the bird continued to screech out numbers. It went on and on without stopping.

'What is it?' he asked.

'That parrot . . . those first numbers . . . I can't be sure . . .'

'What?'

'Three one four one five. Those are the first five digits of the mathematical constant pi.'

Jack remembered enough from high school geometry to know about pi, represented by the Greek letter π. He pictured the number in his head.

3.1415 . . .

Awe filled Lorna's voice as the parrot continued its numerological tirade. 'Pi has been calculated to trillions of digits. I'd love to find out if the numbers the bird is mimicking are sequentially correct. And if so, how long of a sequence the parrot has memorized.'

As the bird continued without pause, Jack noted a hush fall over the hold. The mewling, growling, even shuffling of the other animals grew quiet, as if they, too, were listening. Eyes, reflecting the light, seemed to stare toward them from the dark cages.

With a shake of his head, he moved on. He had a crime to investigate.

'What I really wanted to show you is back here.'

He led her to the larger pens at the stern end of the hold. One pen held a nursing lamb and its mother. But rather than curly wool, the animals' coats hung straight to the ground, more like a yak's pelt than a sheep's. But that's not what Jack wanted to show Lorna.

He tried to urge her on, but she paused at the next cage. The occupant of that pen lay stiffly on its side atop the hay floor, legs straight out, eyes wide and fixed, dead. It looked like a miniature pony, but the creature was no larger than a cocker spaniel.

'Look at its hooves,' Lorna said. 'They're cloven. Four toes in front, three in back. The earliest ancestor of the modern horse – *Hyracotherium* – was only the size of a fox and had the same digital division.'

She crouched to examine the dead body. The hoof of one toe had been torn away. Its head bore signs of fresh concussions, as if it had panicked and thrashed against the bars before it died.

'Looks like something scared it to death,' she assessed.

'I can guess what that might have been.' Jack headed toward the very back of the hold. 'This way.'

She followed. Irritation entered her voice, along with a thread of deeper anger. 'What were these people doing? For that matter, *how* did they do it?'

'That's what I hoped you could answer. But we have a bigger and more immediate problem.' They reached the last pen. It was large and heavily barred. Hay covered the floor, but no animal was in sight. 'We found the door dented and broken open when we came down here.'

'Something escaped?' Lorna glanced from the empty pen back toward the passageway and stairs, clearly recalling the blood trail.

'We need you to tell us what it was,' he said.

She frowned at him. 'How?'

He pointed as something buried beneath the hay shifted. A weak mewling followed.

Lorna glanced at him, her face shining with curiosity. He pulled the door and held it open for her to enter.

'Be careful,' he warned.

Chapter 4

Lorna ducked through the low door and into the pen. Inside, the space was tall enough to stand upright. Still, she kept slightly crouched. Most of the hay had been pushed and piled to the back of the pen. She studied the space with a critical eye. Her nose picked up the strong ammonia smell of old urine. She avoided stepping in a sludgy pile of scat, loose and watery.

Whatever had been caged in here had been ill.

The hay pile at the back shifted as something burrowed away from her. It backed into a corner and could retreat no farther. The mewling had stopped.

Lorna crossed, knelt, and gently picked the hay away. She spotted snowy fur with faint gray spots. A long tail lay tucked around the curled, frightened shape. Small feline ears lay flat against its head.

'A leopard or jaguar cub,' she whispered.

'But it's white,' Jack said by the doorway. 'Like some sort of albino.'

She stared at the cub's pinched blue eyes. 'No. Eye color is normal. Likely it's a form of inherited leucism. Where only the *skin* pigment is lost. Either way, it's definitely some type of panther.'

'I thought you said it was a leopard or jaguar.'

She understood his confusion. It was a common mistake. 'Panther's not really a taxonomic term. The genus *Panthera*

29

covers all the big cats. Tiger, lion, leopard, jaguar. And a white panther could be a version of any of those cats.'

'And which one is that cub?'

'From the skull structure and what I can tell from the faint spotting, I'd guess jaguar. But I can't be sure.'

Lorna knew that Jack needed more information. He must have suspected what was plain to her at first glance and wanted confirmation.

Out of the nest of hay, tiny eyes squinted up at her, poorly focused. They looked newly opened, suggesting the cub was only a couple of weeks old or maybe even younger. Additional juvenile features – stubby rounded ears, underdeveloped whiskers – supported her assessment of its newborn status. But what was throwing her off was its size. It had to weigh fifteen or twenty pounds, large enough to be seven or eight weeks old.

Even Jack must have recognized the disparity and what it suggested. 'And the age of the cub?'

'A week or two.' She glanced back at him. 'Extrapolating that would make an adult around four to five hundred pounds, more the size of a Siberian tiger. A typical jaguar weighs half that.'

'Another genetic throwback?'

She sighed. 'I'll need to run some tests to be sure, but first I'd like to examine the cub more closely.'

She carefully scooped the cub out of its nest. It squirmed and cried, but only weakly. She felt its bones; a pinch of skin revealed dehydration. She bit back anger at its mistreatment and cradled the cub to her belly. She did her best to calm and reassure the little fellow. From a glance at its genitalia, it was definitely a male.

She held the cub firmly, letting the panic beat itself out. 'Shh, it's okay, little one.'

One hand cupped his head while a finger gently and rhythmically rubbed under his chin. After a moment the cub leaned into her and let out a hungry cry. She allowed him to suckle on her finger.

Definitely a newborn.

As the cub attempted to nurse, she felt something in the mouth that shouldn't be there. At this age, young cats had no teeth, only gums to knead a milky teat. But her fingertip probed as the cub suckled. She discovered four teeth, fanged canines. While small and immature, they were still sharp and prominent – longer on top than on bottom.

And they shouldn't be there at all, not at this age.

The early presence suggested developmental dominance of this feature. It heralded a genetic expression of some significance. As the realization of what that might be sank in, she felt a trickle of dread along the back of her neck. She glanced over to the rest of the cages, settling on the dead pony.

No wonder it had died of fright.

She turned to Jack as she cradled the cub. 'We've got a bigger problem.'

'What's that?'

As she had extrapolated the infant's weight to estimate the size of the adult, she did the same now with its dentition. She knew what the early presence of these canine milk teeth might portend. She pictured fangs growing proportionally, upper fangs curving and extending beyond the lower jaw.

'This cub is something more than just an oversize jaguar,' Lorna warned.

'How so?'

She stood up, carrying the creature, and ducked out to join Jack. 'This is the cub of a saber-toothed cat.'

Chapter 5

Back in the brightness of the morning sun, Jack stood on the trawler's deck with Lorna Polk. She still cradled the jaguar cub. If the woman was right, they were looking for a massive cat, pale as a ghost, possibly with fangs ten to twelve inches long. She had gone on to explain how such fangs were not limited to the infamous saber-toothed tiger. According to her, many other prehistoric felines, even some marsupials, carried this genetic trait.

But a saber-toothed jaguar?

It seemed impossible. Still, he did not doubt her assessment. She had spoken at length about atavism and genetic manipulation and had supported her case soundly. Plus he had seen the other freakish animals caged down below.

He stared over the rail toward the coast. It was a dense mass of bottomland forests, marshes, and swamps, encompassing millions of acres of the Mississippi River delta.

It was also his home.

He'd been raised in the bayou, where family and clan held sway far more than any rule of law. His own family earned their income through shrimping and fishing . . . and through a few less-than-legal enterprises on the side. He knew how easy it was to hide out in the swamps, how difficult it could be to track something that wanted to keep out of sight.

Lorna stepped over to him. She'd been talking on the radio, making arrangements with U.S. Fish and Wildlife.

'They have a boat on the way,' she said. 'They're bringing portable cages and tranquilizers. I also talked to Dr. Metoyer over at ACRES. They're setting up a quarantine lab for the animals.'

He nodded. It had been decided to use the isolated ACRES facility as a base of operations. One of his men had found a steel trunk locked up in the captain's quarters. It held a laptop and some digital tapes. An expert on computer forensics was already en route from New Orleans to start working on the contents. Hopefully the archive held more than just the captain's stash of porn.

But before they abandoned the trawler completely, Jack still wanted more answers . . . specifically about the most pressing threat.

'Do you have any idea where this jaguar might have gone? Could it have drowned during the storm?'

'I doubt it. Big cats have no aversion to water, and jaguars are quite strong swimmers. And besides, these waters are shallow. It could easily have swum from island to island, taking rest stops along the way.'

'And you think it would have headed all the way for the coast.'

'Jaguars typically have territories covering a hundred square miles. These islands are too small. It would have kept going.'

'But what about her cub?' He nodded to the creature cradled in Lorna's arms. 'Would a mother abandon it so easily?'

'Not likely. Jaguars are very protective of their young. Nursing them until six months, mothering them until the age of two. But they're also practical. This cub is sickly. A typical litter for a jaguar is two or three cubs. I suspect there was another cub caged with this one. The mother took the stronger of the two with her, abandoning the weaker as a means of survival.'

'So she'll have a cub with her. That could slow her down.'

'It could also make her more dangerous. She'll aggressively

defend her last child.' Lorna's brow tightened with a new concern. She pointed to the blood trail on the stairs. 'Which raises another question. Where are the bodies? The ship's crew?'

'Not here, and not on the island,' Jack said. 'We searched. From the blood patterns, we figured the crew numbered four. Maybe the bodies were washed overboard.'

'Or they were dragged overboard.'

'Dragged? By the cat?'

'From the blood on the stairs, that body wasn't just washed away. The cat must've hauled it up from below.'

'But why?'

'That's a good question. Cats often hide their kills to protect the meat, even hanging them up into trees – but if that's not possible, they'll normally just leave the bodies to rot as carrion and move on.' Lorna frowned. 'The behavior here . . . it's not typical. If I'm right, it displays an unusual cunningness, as if she's trying to cover her trail.'

Lorna met his gaze. He saw the worry in her eyes.

'Maybe you're reading too much into it,' he offered. 'The tropical storm blew to near-gale forces last night. Maybe the cat and the bodies were all swept out into the Gulf by the tidal currents.'

'There's one way to find out.'

'How?'

Lorna waded from the Zodiac onto the sandy beach of the neighboring island. She left her boots in the boat and rolled her pants to her knees.

Jack followed at her side, his attention on the hump of sand and tangled cypress trees ahead. He went barefoot, too, but he kept his boots laced over one shoulder in case he had to venture into the dense thicket that crowned the island. He also carried an M4 carbine assault rifle over his other shoulder. If the cat had survived the storm, it had likely already reached the coast, but he wasn't taking any chances.

At Lorna's suggestion, he had piloted the Zodiac from the trawler to the closest neighboring island.

'The cat would have come here first on its way to the mainland,' Lorna insisted as she climbed up the beach. 'We need to look for any telltale pugmarks.'

'Pugmarks?'

'Paw prints. We should search above the high-tide mark. Also watch for scat, urine, scratched trees.'

'I know how to track,' Jack said. 'But what if the cat swam past this island?'

'Then we search the next one. She couldn't have gotten too far before needing to rest. Fight and flight take its toll. Adrenaline eventually gives out. She'll have needed a place to catch a breath.'

They began to circle the island, keeping to the high-tide mark in the sand. They scanned the beach in silence. The day's heat had grown to a stifling blanket. Only a few clouds remained from last night's storm. Sweat rolled down his back and pooled at his belt line.

'Over here,' Lorna suddenly said.

She hurried away from the water, heading up the sand to where a large cypress shadowed the beach. Spanish moss draped and formed a curtain. Some of it had been ripped away as if something large had torn through its mesh.

'Careful!' Jack warned and grabbed her arm. He pulled her back and raised his rifle. 'Let me check it out first.'

He edged to the tree. With his rifle leading the way, he poked through the rent in the moss. He scanned the bower below, then the limbs above. It looked clear.

Lorna spoke at his shoulder, not heeding his command to hang back. 'Look at the sand near the trunk.'

The ground had been churned up, but he noted a single distinct paw print pressed deeply into the sand. They crossed together into the shadows. Jack kept watch for any sign of movement around them. In such a heightened state of alertness, he was all too conscious of Lorna's shoulder against his side, of the smell of her hair, of her skin.

'The thing is huge,' Lorna said as she knelt down. 'From the size of this paw, I may have underestimated its weight.'

She splayed out her hand over the print. The paw was easily twice as big.

'So it definitely survived,' he said.

'And it's headed to the coast.'

Jack stood up and clutched his rifle. 'Even after the storm, the delta will be full of fishermen, campers, hikers. We'll have to evacuate the area. Put together a hunting party while we still have daylight.'

Lorna joined him. 'You'll have a hard time finding the cat during the day. It'll find a place to hole up and sleep. Your best chance is at dusk, when jaguars usually begin their hunt.'

He nodded. 'It'll take that long to put a team together anyway. Trackers, hunters, people who know the coastal region of the delta. I'll bring along my SRT.'

She glanced at him for explanation.

'Special Response Team.' Jack nodded to the white patrol boat moored off the other island. 'The Border Patrol's equivalent of Special Forces.'

'In other words, Border Patrol commandos?'

'They're good men,' he said a bit too defensively, only realizing afterward that she was gently joking with him.

Flustered, he turned away.

A flurry of activity was going on across the water. The Fish and Wildlife boat – a foil-supported catamaran – had arrived and anchored offshore. The wardens and border agents were busily ferrying cargo from the trawler's hold.

'Let's get back over there,' Lorna said.

Jack heard the desire in her voice, plainly anxious to oversee the off-loading herself. She had left the jaguar cub on his boat, cradled in an empty fishing tackle box.

They were wading toward the Zodiac – when the fishing trawler exploded.

Chapter 6

Knee-deep in water, Lorna watched in horror as the trawler's hull shattered outward in a blast of fire and smoke. Its wooden fishing booms went sailing high, trailing flaming nets. Debris scattered over the island and out to sea.

Along with bodies.

She covered her mouth.

How many had been aboard the trawler?

Burning planks and wreckage rained down upon the two anchored patrol boats. Shouts and screams echoed over the water. Smoke roiled high into the blue sky.

Jack grabbed her arm and dragged her toward the Zodiac.

They climbed into the pontoon boat and shoved off. Jack yanked on the outboard's starter, and seconds later, they were flying across the waters. He had the radio to his ear. She listened to his end of the conversation.

Confusion still reigned, but command filled his voice. 'Call back that chopper! Let emergency services know we're coming in with wounded.'

Across the way, the broken husk of the trawler smoldered on the beach. The other two boats circled the nearby waters, searching through the floating wreckage and flaming pools of oil. Survivors fished bodies out of the water.

Jack opened the throttle and shot the Zodiac back to the island.

Lorna pointed to a figure rising out of the surf. It was one of the Border Patrol agents. He struggled to his knees, cradling one arm. Blood ran down his face from a scalp wound. He looked stunned, in shock.

'Jack! Over there!'

He responded and swung the Zodiac in the man's direction. They sped over and collected the injured man. It was the agent who had passed Jack the flashlight earlier. His arm was broken, clearly a compound fracture from the white bone poking through his sleeve.

Lorna held a fistful of rags to his forehead, stanching the bleeding.

'Where's Tompkins?' the man asked, bleary-eyed. 'He . . . he was still on the upper deck.'

They searched the waters. The wounded agent tried to stand in the Zodiac, but Jack barked for him to stay seated.

Lorna noted Jack squint toward the beach one last time and away again. Only then did she spot a body sprawled near the tree line. Smoke steamed from his burned clothes. A dark stain flowed into the sand. The body was missing an arm and half its skull.

Jack met her gaze as he swung around. She read his expression.

Tompkins.

Lorna felt tears swelling – not in grief but at the senselessness of it all. 'What happened?' she whispered to herself.

Still, Jack must have heard her as he cut the engine and let the Zodiac drift up against his patrol boat. The pontoons bumped them to a stop. 'A dead man's switch,' he answered cryptically as men scrambled down to help carry the injured agent up to the deck of the boat.

Another replaced Jack at the rudder of the Zodiac, ready to continue the search for survivors. Jack was needed above, to take command. Lorna followed him up the ladder.

The open deck had been converted into a triage hospital. The uninjured tended to the wounded. Some sat up; others were flat on their back. She also noted one form covered over with a tarp.

Without being told, Lorna headed to the emergency medical kit on the deck. She began to administer first aid, using her medical skills as best she could, moving from patient to patient. Shortly thereafter, a Coast Guard rescue helicopter and a Life Flight air ambulance flew in and began loading the most critical cases.

Word slowly spread of the number of casualties.

Three dead.

A horrible number, but it could have been worse.

The Border Patrol boat began its journey up the Mississippi, followed by the Fish and Wildlife catamaran. A newly arrived Coast Guard cutter remained behind to secure the area and keep it cordoned off until a forensic team could sweep the wreckage.

Lorna stood by the bow rail, letting the wind cool the sweat from her brow, but it did little to ease the tension or shock. Amid the chaos, she had focused on her work, staying professional, turning her full attention upon a laceration, a concussion, a broken bone. It was a crutch she used to get through the morning. The remaining injured were now stable and monitored by a Coast Guard doctor.

Once she was no longer needed, the weight of the tragedy settled over her. She hugged her arms around her chest. *What if I'd still been in the hold with Jack . . . what if we hadn't gone to the island?*

She suddenly sensed someone behind her and glanced back.

Jack stood a few steps away, as if unsure if he should disturb her.

She appreciated his civility, though it irritated her a little, too. Did he think she was that fragile? She nodded to him to join her. She wanted answers, some explanation that would allow her to sleep at night. She hoped he could give it.

He came forward. 'I'm sorry for dragging you into this. If I had known—'

'How could you have known?' She turned to study the shoreline as Jack joined her at the rail. A long stretch of silence followed as each tested their footing with the other.

'What do you think happened?' she finally asked. 'The explosion. Earlier you had a theory. Something about a dead man's switch.'

He made a noncommittal sound at the back of his throat. 'We'll need a demolition expert to confirm it. But while you were working here, I inspected the wreckage. Looks like the fuel tank exploded. Maybe triggered by some sort of fail-safe.'

'Your dead man's switch.'

He nodded. 'Someone else knew about that boat. The cargo had to come from somewhere, had to be headed somewhere. After the storm, when no word reached that other party, they must have triggered the fail-safe by radio.'

'To destroy the cargo.'

'And cover things up.'

His words reminded her of her other responsibility. 'The animals . . . how many made it?'

'Unfortunately, the team only had time to ferry off a handful of the animals before the explosion. The parrot, the pair of monkeys, the lamb. They also managed to salvage that clutch of python eggs. But the snake and all the rest were lost.'

'We also have the jaguar cub.'

'That's right. I hadn't forgotten. Despite all that happened, there's another survivor to worry about.'

'The cub's mother.'

'She's still out there somewhere. As soon as we hit New Orleans, I've got to arrange a search party.'

'And in the meantime, I'll set in motion the genetic studies necessary to figure out exactly what happened to those animals, try to ascertain who might have been capable of all this.'

'Good. I'll call tomorrow to see what you found.'

He began to turn away, but she grabbed his arm.

'Wait, Jack. I can have everything set up at ACRES before nightfall.'

His brow crinkled in confusion, not understanding the implication behind her words.

'I'm going with you tonight,' she said.

His crinkles failed to smooth. If anything, they grew deeper.

She sighed in exasperation. 'When you go hunting for the cat, I'm coming along.'

He stared hard at her, his features turning granite. 'No. There's no need for you to come. It'll be too dangerous.'

Anger warmed through her – and a part of her appreciated feeling anything after so much death. She took strength from that.

'Look, Jack. I've hunted big game before. I'm an expert marksman with a tranquilizer gun.'

'So am I – and I'm not talking about a tranquilizer gun. And I know the bayou better than you.'

'And I know big cats better than *you*.'

'Lorna—'

'C'mon, Jack. Be reasonable. If I were a man, would we even be having this conversation? You told me that you were going to put together a team of experts: trackers, hunters, your Special Response Team. I'm offering you *my* expertise.'

He looked ready to argue, but she refused to back down – and not out of pride.

'I know big cat behavior better than anyone south of the Mason-Dixon Line.' She stared him square in the eye. 'My knowledge could save someone's life. You know that. Or is preserving your male ego worth someone dying over?'

She knew those last words weren't fair. Her anger had gotten the best of her. Though before she could take her words back, Jack turned away.

'Be ready by dusk,' he said and stalked off.

Chapter 7

Hours later, Lorna stood inside the isolation ward of the veterinary hospital at ACRES. Power was back up. The overhead lights shone brightly off the bank of stainless-steel cages climbing one wall. The ward had been commandeered in order to quarantine the animals recovered from the trawler.

Only five left . . . along with the clutch of eleven python eggs.

Dressed in scrubs, she cradled the jaguar cub in the crook of her arm and held a bottle of milk. It suckled and gnawed at the rubber nipple, eyes closed. A low growl flowed whenever she jostled him too much. Hungry little fella. It was his third bottle of milk since arriving here six hours ago.

She had spent most of her time here and was glad to do it. After all the death, there was a balm in spending time with the animals, to get them settled, examined, and fed. As always, she drew comfort and consolation in caring for her patients.

As a scientist, she understood why. There had been thousands of studies of the human–animal bond, how petting a cat lowered a person's blood pressure, how visiting dogs got bedridden hospital patients to respond and revive. While no one could quite explain this bond, it was real and quantifiable.

But for Lorna, it ran even deeper than that. When

surrounded by animals, she felt more herself, more alive, even her senses seemed more acute: noting the milky smell of a puppy's breath, the coarse feel of a cat's tongue on the back of her hand, the rumble of a frightened dog, more felt under her palm than heard. She had always been that way, going back to childhood. From third grade on, she knew she wanted to be a veterinarian. And over time, while other colleagues grew jaded, her bond only grew stronger.

As Lorna continued to feed the cub, she walked the bank of kennels. The conjoined monkeys shared a middle cage. The two were clutched together, asleep, nestled in a warm pile of towels. She noted the small white bandages over their elbows where they'd collected blood samples and run intravenous fluids to hydrate the mistreated pair. A steel dish in a corner held a pile of monkey chow, along with slivers of fresh bananas.

Lorna had already reviewed the medical file hanging on a clipboard below the cage. Their blood chemistries and CBC were unremarkable. Mild anemia and elevated liver enzymes, most likely from prolonged malnourishment. But despite the terror of their new surroundings, the pair had eaten well after their initial tests.

She noted that someone had already filled in the space for the patients' names. They had scribbled in *Huey and Dewey*.

She smiled. So much for professional detachment. But she could hardly complain. She rocked the cub in her arm like a baby. She had named him Bagheera after the panther from Kipling's *Jungle Book*.

Still, despite the endearment of names, the facility had a mystery to solve concerning these animals. Someone had gone to some effort to produce this bizarre cargo. Blood had been shed to cover it up. But why and to what end – and more importantly *who* were they?

Lorna sensed that answers were locked within these animals. Shortly after arriving, each had undergone a thorough physical exam, including a full-body Magnetic Resonance

Imaging scan. The MRI data was still being compiled by a new computer-modeling program, which used the data to produce three-dimensional images of all internal organs. She was anxious to see the results.

What other genetic abnormalities might they find?

At the back of the ward, a hay-lined run held the small lamb, a little girl. She lay in a pile of straw, looking forlorn without her mother. Large brown eyes stared at Lorna as she passed. She was worried about the lamb. So far she had refused to nurse off a bottle.

Before Lorna could ponder other ways to get the lamb to suckle, a loud irritated squawk drew her attention to the final patient. She turned to the last survivor of the trawler. An avian expert on staff determined the bird to be a male African Grey parrot, a species from the rain forests of West and Central Africa. Though without any feathers or plumage, that identification remained far from certain. The judgment was based on the bird's characteristic white irises. Set against black pupils and gray-green skin, the color pattern made the eyes excessively expressive.

She knew he wanted out of the cage. The parrot had already escaped once. Shortly after arriving here, he had used his beak and claw to flip the door latch and swing it open. They found the bird atop the bank of cages, screaming whenever anyone came close. They'd had to use a net to capture him and return him to his kennel, its door securely locked now.

'Sorry, Charlie,' she said as she stepped closer.

The parrot leaped to the front of the bars and flashed its eyes, black pupils waxing and waning in anger.

'Igor!' the bird screamed at her in an eerily human voice. *'Igor . . . good, Igor . . . Igor, Igor, Igor . . .'*

Lorna realized what he was trying to communicate. She smiled. 'So my little man, you're Igor.' She stressed the last word, clearly his name.

His eyes stopped flashing. The bird cocked his head back

and forth, studying her more quizzically, like someone debating whether to share a secret.

The name was disturbingly fitting. Igor was Dr. Frankenstein's deformed assistant. Someone out there had a black sense of humor.

The parrot turned his head to the side, staring at her with one eye. '*Want to go. Go away. I'm sorry.*'

A chill crept through with his words. She knew psittacine species, which included all parrots, had a brain-to-body ratio equal to that of chimpanzees. Parrots were the smartest of all birds with the cognitive capacity, according to some studies, of a five-year-old child.

Igor's nervous words reminded her of the famous case study of Alex, an African Grey parrot owned by Dr. Irene Pepperberg, a professor of psychology at Brandeis University. Alex wielded a vocabulary of a hundred and fifty words and showed an amazing ability to solve problems. He could answer questions, count numbers, even understood the concept of zero. And more than that, the bird could also express his feelings quite plainly. When Alex had been left at a veterinary hospital for a surgical procedure, he had pleaded with his owner: *Come here. I love you. I'm sorry. I want to go back.* Igor's words here in the isolation ward echoed eerily that same cognition and understanding.

Curious, she moved to place the jaguar cub back into its cage. The cub had finished the bottle and was already contently half asleep.

Igor continued to watch her, tracking her as she returned Bagheera to a woolen nest of blankets. Once she had the cub settled, she crossed back to the parrot and leaned closer.

She spoke softly. 'Hello, Igor.'

'Hello,' he mimicked back and climbed up and down the bars, still clearly nervous with his new surroundings.

She struggled to think of a way to help calm him – then remembered her visit to the trawler's hold and had a sudden inspiration. She slipped a PDA out of her pocket and keyed up the calculator. She pressed the icon for a familiar Greek letter.

Once ready, she asked, 'Igor, what is pi?'

The parrot froze on the cage door, eyed her again, then hopped back to his wooden perch. He stared at her with one eye, then the other.

'C'mon, Igor. What is pi?'

He squawked again, his head jogged up and down a couple of times, then he began a familiar recitation. '*Three one four one five nine two six five . . .*'

His head continued to bob with each number, rhythmic and regular. She stared at her calculator's display. It was the mathematical constant pi. The number sequence was correct. The parrot's nervous shivering slowly settled as he continued, passing beyond the number of digits on her PDA's display. He sank low to his perch and crouched over his claws, clearly finding some solace in the concentrated repetition, like someone knitting or an old man working a crossword puzzle.

He went on and on, slipping into an almost hypnotic rhythm.

She lost count of the number of digits he spouted.

It had to be well over a hundred.

She didn't know if the continuing sequence was just nonsense, but she planned on repeating the test at the first opportunity. She listened for several minutes in stunned silence, recognizing she would need pages and pages of the mathematical constant to see if the bird was correct.

How long a sequence has he memorized? And who taught him?

Before she could consider this further, the door to the isolation ward pushed open with a soft pop of its double seals. Igor immediately fell silent. She turned as the lanky figure of Dr. Carlton Metoyer strode into the ward.

'Carlton,' she said, surprised by the director's unannounced visit. 'What are you doing down here?'

He offered her a warm, fatherly smile. 'I see you've finished feeding *Bagheera*.' He stressed the cub's new name, his eyes dancing with amusement.

She inwardly groaned. She had only mentioned the cub's name to her research assistant, but as always, word traveled quickly across ACRES. She felt a flush warm her cheeks. She was supposed to be a postdoctoral fellow, not a preteen with a new kitten.

'His belly's full,' she said. 'At least for the next couple hours. Then he'll be crying for his bottle again.'

'That should give the lab enough time to finish their genetic analyses.'

'What's been done so far?'

She was anxious for any news. After arriving at ACRES with the animals, she had spent all her time stabilizing the debilitated animals and assisting in the collection of blood and tissue samples. While she had performed the physical exams, the DNA samples had vanished into the main genetic lab – Dr. Metoyer's exclusive domain. The director was world-renowned for his pioneering work on cloning and interspecies embryo transplants.

'We've barely scratched the surface,' Carlton said. 'But an initial chromosomal assay has already revealed an intriguing quirk. We're repeating the test right now, but I wanted to come down here and fetch you. It's something you should see for yourself.'

He motioned and headed toward the door. He was clearly enthused about something and that excitement passed to her.

She followed, practically vibrating with curiosity. As she left she glanced back and spotted Igor staring back at her, perched again on the door. He had returned to his shivering.

She heard him whisper behind her.

'Want to go home.'

Chapter 8

Lorna hated to close the door on Igor's plaintive plea, but she had a bigger mystery to solve. Still, a pang of sympathy coursed through her, dulling the sharp edge of her professional interest.

As the isolation door clicked shut, her boss was already halfway down the hall, moving with long, purposeful strides. He had been speaking, but she caught only the last bit.

'. . . and we've already started PCR tests to begin amplifying the key chromosomes. But, of course, DNA sequencing will take most of the night.'

She hurried to close the distance with Carlton – both physically and mentally. Together they headed down another hallway and reached the double doors to the suite of genetic labs that occupied this wing of the ACRES facility.

The main lab was long and narrow, lined on both sides by biohazard hoods and workstations. The latest genetic equipment filled shelves and tables: centrifuges, microscopes, incubators, electrophoresis equipment, a digital camera system for visualizing DNA, and racks of pipettes, glassware, scales, vials of enzymes and PCR chemicals.

Carlton led the way to where two researchers – a man and a woman – were crouched before a computer monitor. The pair stood so close together, both wearing white lab coats. They reminded Lorna of the conjoined monkeys, bonded at the hip just like Huey and Dewey.

'This is amazing,' Dr. Paul Trent announced and glanced over a shoulder as she reached them. He was young, thinly built, with wavy blond hair combed behind his ears, looking more like a California surfer than a leading neurobiologist.

Paul's wife, Zoë, stood next to him. She was Hispanic. Her black hair was bobbed short – shorter than her husband's – framing wide cheekbones, lightly freckled. Her lab coat did little to hide the generously curved body beneath.

The two were biologists from Stanford, wunderkinds in the field, earning their degrees before their mid-twenties and already well regarded professionally. They were in New Orleans on a two-year grant researching neural development in cloned animals, studying the structural differences between the brains of cloned specimens and their original subjects.

The pair of doctors certainly had come to the right place.

ACRES was one of the nation's leading facilities involved with cloning. In 2003, they had been the first to clone a wild carnivore, an African cat named Ditteaux, pronounced *Ditto* for obvious reasons. And in the coming year, the facility was about to begin the commercial cloning of pets as a method to raise funds for their work with endangered species.

Zoë stepped back from the computer monitor. 'Lorna, you have to see this.'

Lorna moved closer and recognized a karyogram on the screen. It showed a set of numbered chromosomes lined up into a chart.

Karyograms were built by using a chemical to trap cell division in its metaphase stage. The chromosomes were then separated, dyed, and sequenced via digital imaging into a numbered karyogram. Humans carried forty-six chromosomes, divided into twenty-three pairs. The monitor showed twenty-eight pairs.

Definitely not human.

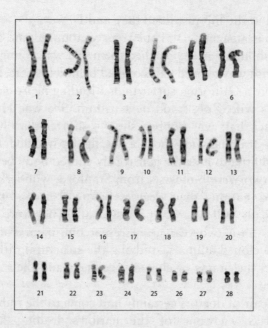

Carlton explained, 'We built this karyogram from a white blood cell from one of the capuchin monkeys.'

From the general excitement, Lorna knew there remained another shoe to drop.

Paul spoke up, his voice was full of wonder. 'Capuchins normally have a complement of twenty-seven pairs of chromosomes.'

Lorna stared at the karyogram on the screen. 'But there's twenty-*eight* here.'

'Exactly!' Zoë said.

Lorna turned to the facility's director. 'Carlton, you said you still wanted to repeat the test. Surely this is a lab error.'

'It's under way, but I suspect we'll confirm the original findings here.' He nodded to the computer.

'Why's that?'

Carlton leaned forward, grabbed the computer mouse, and toggled through another five genetic maps. 'This next karyogram is from the conjoined twin of the first monkey.

Again twenty-eight chromosomal pairs. Same as the first. The next studies are from the lamb, the jaguar cub, the parrot, and this last is from the Burmese python.'

The python?

Frowning, she glanced across the lab to where an incubator housed the clutch of snake eggs. In his desire to confirm what she was beginning to suspect, Carlton must have opened one of the eggs to get at the developing embryo inside and obtain its DNA sample.

'Pythons typically have thirty-six pairs of chromosomes,' Carlton continued. 'A mix of micro- and macro-chromosomes.'

Lorna read off the screen. 'There are thirty-seven here.'

'That's right. One pair more than normal. Like all the rest. That's why I'm sure we'll get the same results when we run the genetic studies again. It's beyond statistical probability that the lab came up with the same error six times in a row.'

Lorna's mind reeled as she struggled to come to grips with what this implied. 'Are you saying that each of the animals from the trawler is showing the same genetic defect? That each is carrying an extra set of chromosomes?'

Such genetic abnormalities occasionally occurred in humans. A single extra chromosome caused a child to be born with Down syndrome. Or there was Klinefelter's syndrome, where a male was born with two X chromosomes, forming an XXY karyotype. And in rare instances, some people were born with an extra *pair* of chromosomes. Abnormalities this severe usually resulted in early death or severe mental retardation.

She frowned at the screen. None of her animals exhibited such debilitation. The confusion must have been plain on her face.

'I don't think you're understanding the full thrust of what we're saying,' Carlton said. 'This extra pair of chromosomes isn't the result of a genetic error. It didn't come about from a random mistake in cell division in a sperm or egg.'

'How can you be so sure?'

Carlton manipulated the mouse and flipped through the six karyograms again. He pointed to the last chromosome pair on each of the studies.

'The specimens from the trawler aren't just carrying an extra set of chromosomes,' the director continued. 'They're carrying the *same* ones.'

Only now did Lorna recognize that the *extra* pair of chromosomes in each of the species looked identical. As the implication sank in, understanding began to slowly well up. It felt like a tide shifting the foundation under her.

Impossible.

Carlton poked at the computer screen. 'That is not an error of nature. That's the hand of man. Someone put that extra pair of chromosomes in all these animals.'

'Who . . . ?' Lorna mumbled, unbalanced to the point of feeling dizzy, but also oddly excited by it all.

Carlton turned to her, his bushy gray eyebrows resting high on his forehead. His wide eyes shone with raw curiosity. 'The bigger question, my dear, is *why*.'

Chapter 9

Deep in the bayou, Danny Hemple's father waded through the reeds. 'You're trying my last nerve, boy. Sometimes you're as useless as tits on a bull.'

Danny didn't argue. He knew better. At seventeen, he was nearly as big as his father, but not even half as mean. He'd once watched his dad beat a man bloody with the handle of a hammer, payback for short-changing him on his share of a fishing haul.

At the moment Danny watched his father drag a crab trap out of the muddy reeds. It didn't belong to them. And it wasn't some old barnacle-encrusted trap that had been long abandoned. It looked brand-spanking-new with a fresh line, buoy, and legal tag still attached.

His father used a pocketknife to cut the line and tag away. He slogged through the reeds with his prize. Danny spotted a dozen or so good-size Louisiana blue crabs scuttling within the stolen trap.

'Boy, get your thumb out of your ass and move the damned boat closer. We don't have all day.'

His father wore waders held up by suspenders as he worked through the shallows. Danny poled the boat closer to him. It was a half-rusted airboat that'd had its fan removed and replaced with an old outboard Evinrude. This close to the muddy bank it was too shallow to use the engine – and it would be too noisy anyway. What they were doing could get them in big trouble with the state wildlife guys.

Storms like the one last night wreaked havoc on the thousands of crab traps staked along the waterways near the Gulf. Surges ripped them from their moorings and cast them deeper into the surrounding swamps.

Like throwing out free money, his father had often quipped.

Danny had joked with his friends that it was more like casting pearls before swine. He had made the mistake of repeating that joke within earshot of his father. Danny's nose still had a knot from that old break.

'Come get this already! There's at least two more.'

Oink, oink, Danny thought sourly to himself and poled forward.

Once close enough, he took the trap from his father's arms and added it to the four already stacked in the boat. It was good haul, and as much as he might despise what they were doing, he understood why. At eight dollars a pound for claw meat and twice that for jumbo lump, they might clear close to a grand for the afternoon's work. Not to mention reselling the crab traps back to the same people who once owned them.

Scavenging like this wasn't lost on the Fish and Wildlife guys. If the wardens didn't haul you to jail and fine your ass, they held out an open palm for their cut of the bounty. The price for doing business out here, they explained. But that wasn't the worst danger. There were other hunters like Danny's father. Fights broke out over territories, sometimes leading to bloodshed. It was said the alligators out here were well fed.

Aware of that threat, Danny kept a watch on the bayou around him, though mostly with his ears. It was hard to see much farther than twenty yards in any direction. All around, forests of cypress and sweet gum dripped with mosses and vines and shut out the world. Branches laced over the narrow canal.

He listened for the trebling whine of a warden's airboat or the growl of another scavenger's outboard engine. So far all he heard was the whine of mosquitoes and the warbling calls of swallow-tailed kites as the birds swept through the branches overhead.

Danny wiped his brow with a handkerchief and stuffed it back in his pocket. The day's heat seemed trapped under the branches. Even the shade offered little relief. To make things worse, the crab pots had begun to stink.

But what could he do?

With no choice, he poled after his father, keeping along the edges of the reeds. They were deeper into the bayou than they normally searched. And out later than usual. Danny knew why his father was taking such a risk. His little sister's leukemia had relapsed. With his father between jobs, they had no health insurance. The storm had been a godsend. So Danny didn't begrudge his father's gruff manner for once. He recognized the worry and shame that lay behind it.

'I think there's another trap over there, Pop.'

Danny pointed his pole toward where a small branch of the canal dove into deeper shadows. A single white buoy floated in the current near the entrance.

'Then go get it while I free this one. Line's all tangled in some roots.'

As his father cursed behind him, Danny sank his pole into the water and punted his boat toward the side channel. The narrow waterway was covered in a layer of water lilies and wound itself into a dense tangle of forest. It looked more like a tunnel than a creek.

He had to work the boat into the channel to reach the stray buoy. A loud splash gave him a start. He turned to see a raccoon swimming across the main channel. It paddled quickly away. Danny scowled at it. Normally the vermin were not that frightened of people. And it was a foolhardy flight to begin with. Many a raccoon ended up as a snack for a hidden alligator.

Before he turned away, a second coon leaped from a branch, sailed far out, and splashed into the water. He puzzled at their panic.

'Whatcha lookin' at!' his father called at him. 'Hurry it up already.'

Danny frowned and returned to the task at hand. He leaned down and grabbed the buoy. He hauled it up and drew in the line. He felt the weight of the submerged trap. From experience, he knew it was a good haul. He braced his legs for balance and hauled the trap out of the water. Crabs packed the wire cage. A smile spread over his face as he calculated the value of the catch.

He dragged the trap into the boat and stacked it with the others. As he shifted to pole out of the side channel, a flash of white drew his eyes deeper down the waterway. He pulled a low-hanging branch out of the way. A tangled knot of four buoys floated about fifty feet away.

All right . . .

He used the branch to pull him and the boat deeper down the channel, then poled the rest of the way. Though focused on his goal, he kept a watch for any suspicious logs on the banks or any telltale peek of a scaly snout. Alligators often nested in such secluded channels. He didn't overly worry. Only during mating season did bull alligators grow aggressive and females attack anything that approached their nests. Besides, like his father, he had a holstered pistol at his hip.

He reached the cluster of buoys and was about to lean over and begin untangling them when he saw that their lines trailed toward shore. He spotted the cages abandoned at the edge of the water. Each was mangled and torn open, as if dropped into a wood chipper. He saw no sign of crabs.

His first thought was that some bull alligator had gone for an easy meal, but a cold finger of dread traced his spine. In all his years, he'd never seen an alligator attack a crab pot. And considering how heavy the traps were, it took something big to drag them to shore.

But if not an alligator . . .

He swallowed hard, his mouth gone dry. He straightened and poled away, retreating down the channel. He remembered the pair of raccoons hightailing it away. Something had spooked them, maybe something more than a kid in a boat. He stared back at the mangled cages, all too conscious of the stinking cargo sharing his boat.

He poled away faster.

A loud *crack* of a branch wheeled him around. His heart jackhammered into his throat. A thick tree branch crashed down and landed across the waterway, cutting off his escape.

Bushes rustled on the opposite shore – as if something had leaped out of the tree and landed on the far side. Danny dropped his pole and snatched for his pistol. He fumbled with the snap securing the weapon.

The rustling retreated, going fast.

Danny never caught sight of it, but he sensed something large and stealthy. Frozen in place, he strained his ears, worrying it might circle back.

A sudden shout almost toppled him out of the boat.

'Boy! Put your dick back in your pants and git back here!'

Only then did Danny realize the direction of the rustling. Where it was headed.

No . . .

Eldon Hemple knew something was wrong. He knew it before he heard his son's terrified scream.

'DAD!'

Eldon had hunted the swamps and bayous since he was knee-high to his own father, and his instincts were honed to a sharp edge. The sudden stillness was the only warning. It felt as if the sky were pressing down, like before a big storm.

He stood ankle-deep in the shallows, buried in a thicket of reeds and palmettos. He lowered the crab trap back in the water and freed his pistol. He turned in a slow circle, staring without blinking. His body screamed for him to run, a primal urge. He fought against it, not knowing the direction of the danger.

He strained to listen – for a splash, for the snap of a branch – some warning. Terror squeezed his chest. Fear not so much for his own life, as for his son's. He rode the boy hard, but he loved him even harder.

Then he heard it. Behind him. A harsh cough. Not like a man, but more like the chuffing of some beast. A low growl followed.

He swung an arm blindly behind him and fired, popping off a sharp series of blasts. At the same time he ran in the opposite direction, toward the deep water.

'Danny! Get outta here!'

He crashed through the reeds. Razor-edged leaves cut his face and bare arms. If he could get to deep water, dive into the channel . . .

Behind him, something crashed through the palmettos. Only then did he realize the cough and growl had been purposeful, meant to flush him out.

The reeds broke around him. Open water lay ahead. He bunched his legs for a leaping dive – but something massive struck his back, pounding him facedown into the shallow water.

All air was knocked from his lungs. Knives cut into his shoulder and back. He fought to get his arm around, to fire blindly over his shoulder. He managed one squeeze, the gun near his ear. The blast deafened, but not enough to miss the hissing scream that followed, full of blood and fury.

A shadow fell over him, blocking the sun.

He felt hot breath on his neck. Jaws clamped onto the back of his head and shoved his face under the water and into the boggy mud. He felt pressure in his skull, a moment of piercing pain, a crack of bone – then nothing but darkness.

Danny heard the gunshots, the piercing scream of rage, the call for him to flee. He knew he had only moments. Bobcats and bears hunted the Louisiana wetlands, but whatever had made that cry was far larger and had no place among its swamps and bayous. The hairs rose all over his body, vibrating to that scream.

He grabbed his pole and propelled his boat away from the main channel. It was the only direction open to him. The fallen tree limb blocked his way. It was far too large and tangled to move on his own. And he knew he had no time to struggle with it. He had to get as far away as possible.

As he poled, he listened for more gunshots, a blistering shout, any sign that his father was still alive. But the bayou had gone quiet. Even the mosquitoes seemed to have grown more hushed.

He dug the pole into the bottom mud and shoved. He passed the spot with the mangled crab pots and continued deeper into the maze of hillocks and dense stands of cypress. He didn't know this section of the bayou. All he knew was that he had to keep moving.

The weight of the pistol helped keep him breathing. He had shoved the gun into his belt, not trusting he could free it from its leather holster in time.

Just keep moving . . .

It was his only hope. He needed to reach open waters, maybe even the Gulf itself. But he realized he was headed in the wrong direction, north instead of south. He had no hope of reaching the Mississippi, but small settlements lay between here and the Big Muddy. If he could reach one, raise an alarm, stir up men . . . *men with lots of guns . . .*

Time slowly passed, measured by the pounding of his heart. It felt like hours, but was probably less than one. The sun hung low on the horizon. At some point noises returned to the swamp: the croak of frogs, the whistling of birds. He even welcomed the buzzing clouds of mosquitoes. Whatever monster hunted the swamps must have decided not to give chase.

The thin channel opened at last into a small lake. He poled into the center of it, glad to see the shoreline retreat around him. But the sun had dropped below the tree line, turning the lake's surface into a black mirror.

It was in the reflection that Danny caught a flicker of movement along the shoreline. Something white flashed silently through the forest, keeping mostly out of sight.

He grabbed the pistol from his waistband.

A deadfall along one edge of the lake allowed him to catch his first glimpse of the beast. It looked like a pale tiger, only sleeker and longer of limb, balanced by a long tail. It carried something limp and pale in its bloody muzzle. Danny feared it was some bit of his father, an arm, a leg.

But as he kept his gaze locked over the barrel of his pistol, he saw it was a large cub, carried by its scruff.

Before the cat disappeared back into the forest, it stopped and glanced back at Danny. Their eyes locked. Its muzzle rippled back and exposed fangs that looked like bony daggers. A hot wetness flowed down Danny's left leg. A trembling shook through him.

Then, in a flicker, the cat vanished back into the forest.

Danny remained with his pistol still pointed. After a full minute, he slowly sank into the center of the boat. He hugged his knees to his chest. He sensed the big cat had moved on, but he wasn't going anywhere. He would rather starve than ever move closer to shore.

As he watched the forest around him, he could not shake the memory of the creature's gaze. There had been nothing bestial in those eyes, only calculation and assessment. It had seemed to be judging him, deciding what was needed to reach him.

In that moment Danny knew the broken tree limb had not blocked his way by accident. The cat had done it purposefully, to separate the two men. It had gone after his father first, recognizing the greater threat, knowing its other prey was trapped and at its mercy. With Danny snared as surely as a crab in a pot, he was easy pickings for later.

Only something had drawn the beast off.

Something more troubling than a boy in a boat.

Chapter 10

Jack crossed over the swinging bridge. He didn't bother with the moldy rope rails that lined both sides. He didn't look down – though several wooden slats of the bridge had long rotted and fallen away. He carried his weight with the easy balance of the familiar.

Ahead, his family home rested on one of the small islands in Bayou Touberline. The land was really no more than a hillock pushing out of the black water, fringed by mats of algae and edged by saw grass. The house sat on the crown of the island, a ramshackle construction of rooms assembled more like a jumbled pile of toy blocks. Each marked additions and extensions built as the Menard clan had grown over the past century and a half. Most rooms were now empty as modern life lured the younger generations away, but the core of the ramshackle structure remained, a sturdy old stacked-stone home. It was there his parents still lived, well into their seventies, along with a smattering of cousins and nieces and nephews.

An old fishing boat listed by a dock near the side of the house. It still floated – more by the sheer will of his older brother than any real soundness of keel. Randy sat on a lawn chair at the foot of the dock, beer can in one hand, staring at the boat. Bare-chested, he wore knee-length shorts and flip-flops. His only acknowledgment of Jack's arrival was the lifting of his beer can into the air.

'So we're going hunting,' Randy said as Jack reached him. 'Did you call T-Bob and Peeyot?'

'They got word. They'll be here' – Randy stared at the lowering sun, then belched with a shrug – 'when they get here.'

Jack nodded. T-Bob and Peeyot Thibodeaux were brothers, half black Cajun, half Indian. They were also the best swamp trackers he knew. Last spring, they had helped find a pair of drug smugglers who had abandoned ship in the Mississippi and tried to escape through the delta. After a day on their own, the escapees were more than happy to be found by the Thibodeaux brothers.

'What are we hunting?' Randy asked. 'You never did say.'

'A big cat.'

'Bobcat?'

'Bigger.'

Randy shrugged. 'So that's why you came here to fetch Burt.'

'Is he with Daddy?'

'Where else would he be?'

Jack headed toward the house. His brother was in an especially sour mood. He didn't know why, but he could guess the source. 'You shouldn't be drinking if you're coming with us.'

'I shoot better with a few beers in me.'

Jack rolled his eyes. Unfortunately his brother was probably right.

Reaching the house, he swung open the door. He hadn't lived here in over a decade. He had his own place near Lake Pontchartrain, a fixer-upper he bought after Katrina. He entered the front parlor. This was home – more home than anywhere else. The smell of frying oil competed with a black mélange of spices. Over the ages, the odor had seeped into the very mortar of the stones, along with wood smoke and tobacco.

He flashed back to his mostly happy childhood spent in

this bustling, chaotic, loud mess of a family. It was much quieter now, like the house was half slumbering, waiting to wake again.

A call reached him. *'Qui c'est q'ça?'*

'It's me, Dad!' he called back.

To find his father only required turning his nose toward the heaviest pall of pipe smoke and following the soft, scratchy sound of zydeco music. His father was in his study down the hall. A stone fireplace filled one wall; the rest held shelves stacked with books.

'There you are, Jack.' His father made a half gesture toward rising out of his recliner.

Jack waved him back down.

He settled back with a sigh. His father was nearly crippled with arthritis. His once robust frame had withered to bone, knotted at the joints. He probably should be in a nursing home, but here was where he was the most content, with his books, his music, and his old hunting dog, Burt, the last of a long line of bloodhounds. The dogs were as much a part of the Menard family as any brother or sister.

The black-and-tan bloodhound lay by the cold hearth, sprawled across the cool stone, all legs and ears. At thirteen years, he had gone gray in the muzzle, but he remained strong and healthy and had a nose like no other.

A nose Jack wanted to borrow for the night.

His father tamped some more tobacco into his pipe. 'Heard you're taking the boys out to do a little hunting.'

Burt lifted his head, ear cocked, responding to a welcome word. His tail thumped once, almost a question, asking if he'd heard right. His nose might be sharp, but his hearing was fading.

'That we are,' Jack answered them both.

'Good, good. Your mother cleaned and oiled your rifle. She's out back with your cousin, hanging the laundry.'

Jack smiled, picturing the old woman taking apart his rifle and delicately cleaning each part. As a Cajun woman, she could probably still do that with her eyes closed. In her prime, his mother had been the best shot in their family. She had once pegged a bull gator from the kitchen window when it shambled out of the water and stalked straight for his kid brother. Tom had been playing too close to the water's edge, left unattended by Jack when he was supposed to be watching. She had placed one shot straight through the gator's eye, dropping it dead in its tracks. After scolding his younger brother and tanning Jack's backside for his dereliction of duty, she had simply returned to the dishes.

The memory dimmed Jack's smile. She had done her best to protect all of them, as fierce as any loving mother, but in the end she couldn't protect them from themselves. On the way down the hall, he had passed the bedroom shared by him and his brother. No one used it now. It had become little more than a shrine. Tom's awards and trophies still adorned the shelves, along with his collection of shells, books, and old vinyl records. There was little left of Jack in that room. He'd been shouldered out by grief and memory.

His father must have noted something in Jack's face. 'I heard you saw that girl today. The one who . . . who dated Tommy.'

He started to ask how his father knew that; then he remembered this was bayou country. Word, especially gossip, swept faster through the swamps than any storm. He now understood the rather cold reception and surly attitude from Randy.

'She's helping with a case. An animal smuggling ring. Nothing important.'

Jack felt his face heat up, embarrassed not only by the half-truth now, but by a larger untruth buried in his past. His brother's death had been attributed to a drunken accident. Lorna had been driving. That much of the story was true. Few people knew the rest. Lorna was blamed, given a slap on the hand, mostly because of Jack's testimony in private with the judge. His family, though, had never forgiven her.

'She seemed like such a nice girl,' his father mumbled around his pipe.

'They were just kids,' Jack offered lamely. He had promised never to tell anyone other than the judge the truth.

For both their sakes.

His father stared at Jack. The shine in those eyes suggested his father suspected there was more to the story.

A call from the other end of the house shattered the awkward moment. 'Jack!' his mother shouted. 'Where are you? I packed a cooler for you and the boys. Got a basket full of cracklin's and boudin, too!'

'Be right there!'

His father's heavy gaze tracked him as he left the study. He let out a sigh as he reached the hall. As he stepped out his cell phone vibrated in his pocket. Glad for the distraction, he brought the phone to his ear.

It was Scott Nester, his second-in-command with the CBP. 'We found someone who saw that damned cat.'

'Who? Where?'

'A kid in a boat. He took potshots at one of our search helicopters to get its attention.'

'Are you sure it's our target?'

'Oh yeah. Described a big white cat with big teeth. Says the cat killed his father. We've got a search team looking for the body.'

Jack's fingers tightened on the phone. 'Did the boy see where the target was headed?'

'North, he thinks. Toward the Mississippi.'

'Where exactly was the boy found?'

'You got a map?'

'I can get one.'

Scott passed him the coordinates. After a few more instructions, Jack hung up and hurried over to where his brother stored a set of nautical charts in a cupboard near the back door. It was crammed full of fishing gear, tackle boxes, and all manner of hand-tied lures. He stabbed his thumb on a stray hook as he dug out a map of the delta.

With chart in hand, he pinched away the stubborn lure and wiped the blood on his shirt. He crossed to a table, unfolded the map, and used a pencil to mark the location where the boy in the boat was rescued – or as best he could with the old chart. A couple years of shifting sands and repeated flooding blurred the details of even the region's best maps. Still he was also able to pick out the island where the trawler had gone aground. He drew a straight line between the shipwreck and where the boy was found.

The path aimed due north. The same direction the cat had been headed. Jack extended a dashed line north from the boy's location. He ran it all the way until he reached the Mississippi. The line ended at the small river town named Port Sulphur. He marked an X on the map. He knew the town. It'd been almost entirely wiped out by Katrina. Some homes had been washed a hundred feet off their foundations.

Leaning back, Jack studied the map.

Randy pushed through the back door and joined him. 'T-Bob and Peeyot just got here in their canoe.' He pointed to the X drawn on the map. 'That where we're going?'

'That's where we're starting. We'll gather everyone in Port Sulphur and head south into the bayou.' He stared at the dotted line. The saber-toothed cat had to be hiding somewhere along that path.

'So what's holding us up?' his brother asked and clapped him on the shoulder. '*Laissez les bons temps rouler.*'

Jack folded the map. Before he could follow his brother's advice and 'let the good times roll,' he had one more thing to do, to honor a grudging promise.

'I have someone to pick up first.'

Chapter 11

Lorna never got back to raking her yard after the storm.

By the time she climbed the stone steps to her home in the Garden District, it was late. The sun hovered near the horizon, casting heavy shadows off the magnolias and towering oaks. Storm-swept leaves and crinkled blossoms formed a Jackson Pollock painting across her overgrown lawn, along with a few broken tiles blown from the roof. A dry stone fountain topped by a moss-frosted angel stood in the center of the yard.

She sighed at the sorry state of the family mansion.

Paint bubbled and peeled across the porch. Its Italianate columns were chipped. Even the carved mahogany front door took an extra hard tug to pull it open, its frame warped from a century of passing seasons.

She struggled with the door now and fought it open. The house was dark. Her brother was troubleshooting a problem at an offshore oil platform in the Gulf. He wouldn't be back until tomorrow.

Just as well.

She flipped on the entryway light. A wooden staircase rose on the right side and climbed to a second-story landing and from there up to the third-story level. Overhead, a massive chandelier imported from an eighteenth-century French château hung down through the stairwell. Half the bulbs were dark. It took a feat of engineering to change the bulbs and polish the crystals.

She dropped the heavy case she was carrying by the door, wondering if she had time to draw a hot bath. Back at ACRES, she had changed out of her scrubs and back into her worn jeans and shirt. She longed to shed the soiled clothes and run the hottest bath the old water heater could manage. Maybe with bubbles and a single glass of Chardonnay. A girl could dream.

It would be a long night, and tomorrow would be a busy day at ACRES. She had done all she could there for now. Critical tests were still processing and wouldn't be finished until the morning. She was especially interested in the DNA analysis of the extra pair of chromosomes shared by all the recovered animals. Who had been performing these experiments and why? Answers could lie in the genetic codes of those strange chromosomes.

Before she could reach the stairs a phone jangled from deeper in the house. She hurried across the entryway to a hall table. It must be Jack, though she was surprised he wasn't calling her cell phone. Her heart beat faster, anxious to hear about the plans for tonight's hunt. But as she lifted the phone her heart sank – more than it should have – when she heard her younger brother's voice. It was Kyle, calling from the oil platform.

'Lorna, just checkin' in. Making sure the house is still standing.'

'At the moment it is. Can't promise anything beyond that.'

Her brother chuckled. He must be bored. As usual, they spoke more on the phone than at the house. When together, they tried to maintain a measure of privacy for each other, which wasn't hard in a home with seven bedrooms and five baths.

'I left a message earlier,' Kyle said. 'Figured you must've been called into work. Didn't want to bother you there.'

'You could've called. Though it's been a crazy day.' She gave him a thumbnail version of what had happened.

'Christ, that's really odd.'

'I know. We're still doing some lab tests—'

'No, I meant that Jack Menard called you into the investigation. That must have been uncomfortable.'

She took a moment to respond. *Uncomfortable* was a pale description of the storm of emotions that had run through her: guilt, sorrow, shame, anger, and something deeper, something hidden but shared between them. She pictured Jack's storm-gray eyes, the way his stare seemed to strip her to the bone. Not even her little brother knew the truth about that bloody night.

'At least you're done with him now,' Kyle said.

She found her voice again, but only a shadow of it. 'That's not exactly true. I'm going to help him search for the escaped jaguar.'

'What do you mean by *help?* To offer professional advice?'

'That, and I'm going with him on the hunt tonight.'

Stunned silence followed, then a hard outburst. 'Are you plumb nuts? Why?'

She glanced back at the black case by the door. It held a disassembled tranquilizer rifle. 'I want to make sure we capture the cat alive.'

'Screw the cat. You're going into the swamp with a member of a family that would just as soon feed you to a gator.'

She couldn't explain why she had nothing to fear from Jack. 'I'll be fine. It won't be just the two of us. There'll be a whole search team. There's nothing to worry about.'

'Don't go, Lorna. Or at least wait until I'm back tomorrow. I can come with you then.'

'No. Jaguars are nocturnal. She'll be hunting tonight. It's our best chance to catch her before anyone else is killed.'

'Lorna—'

Her phone chimed in her pocket. 'I've got another call.'

'Wait until I'm back,' he said in a rush before she could hang up.

70

'I'll talk to you in the morning.' She clicked the receiver down and fished out her cell phone. 'Dr. Polk here.'

'Are you ready?' It was Jack. His brusque manner instantly set her on edge. She heard the familiar whine of a helicopter in the background.

'Of course I am.'

'Can you meet us at the dock behind the Audubon Zoo?'

'I can be there in fifteen minutes. What's the plan?'

'We'll pick you up by chopper. I have everyone gathering at Port Sulphur.'

She heard the tension in his voice, sensing something left unsaid. 'What's wrong?'

'We've had a sighting. Your cat attacked someone earlier. Out in the middle of the bayou. We found the body a few minutes ago, up in a tree, wrapped in Spanish moss. Skull was crushed, an arm ripped off.'

Lorna felt the breath knocked out of her. They were already too late.

Jack pressed. 'One last time. My team can handle this on our own. There's no reason for you to go.'

She stared again at the gun case in the hall. Jack was wrong. She now had *two* reasons. She still wanted to capture the cat alive, but its behavior now worried her, made her even more anxious to track it. The jaguar hadn't holed up as she'd hoped. It was on the move – but to where?

'Jack, I'm going. Arguing will only cost us time. The faster we track this cat the fewer lives will be in danger.'

He sighed heavily over the line. 'Be at the dock in fifteen. Not a minute later. Like you said, we've no time to waste.'

He hung up.

Lorna hurried to the front door. There would be no hot bath. She snatched her case and tugged open the front door. Already the sun had sunk to the horizon. It would be dark soon.

As she rushed down the front steps a trickle of doubt ran through her.

What am I doing?

Her brother's concern, Jack's warning . . . she had pushed them both aside, but their worries had taken root in her, found fertile ground. She was a veterinarian, not a big-game hunter.

Still, she didn't stop moving. She headed for her brother's Bronco parked at the curb. She had hesitated once before, let fear intimidate her, and it had cost a boy his life.

Not this time . . . and not ever again.

Chapter 12

As the sun began to set, the marine helicopter banked away from the Mississippi River and out over the small town of Port Sulphur. From the air, there was not much to distract Lorna from her mode of transportation. If she kept this up, she might even get used to air travel, but her sweaty palms and shallow breathing defied any such accommodation now.

To offset her fright, she concentrated on the passing landscape below, marking landmarks, estimating how long she had to remain airborne.

Below, Port Sulphur was easy to miss, covering less than six square miles, protected by a weathered and battered levee system. It had once been a rugged company town serving Freeport Sulphur, but in the nineties, after drilling and refinery operations had shut down, the town had begun a slow decline, waiting only for Katrina to write its epitaph. A twenty-two-foot wall of water had swept through the town, all but wiping the place away. Of the three thousand or so residents, only a small fraction had returned to their flooded homes.

If Lorna hadn't been studying the world below with such anxiety, she might have missed the place. They were past the town in seconds and over water again – a wide, shallow lake called Bay Lanaux. They began a fast descent. It had been a short flight, covering the forty miles as a crow flies from New Orleans in less than fifteen minutes. Short as it was, Lorna was still ready to get out of this bird.

Tense, she jumped slightly when Jack's amplified voice cut into her headphones. He sat up front with the pilot. She shared the back with two other CBP agents. They had told her their names, but she had already forgotten, her mind too occupied with keeping the helicopter flying by sheer willpower.

'We'll be taking a CBP boat into the canals south of the lake,' Jack explained. 'The boat will act as the base of operations for this mission. Two smaller airboats will flank our path, canvassing the smaller byways and channels to either side. And in case they're needed, we have a pair of canoes for tighter places.'

Lorna stared out at the gathered maritime force as the helicopter settled to its floats in the water. A second, larger helicopter lifted off from the lake. It had carried in more of Jack's team, along with some local talent. The CBP boat nearby looked to be the same one from earlier, an Interceptor-class craft made for inland or ocean travel. A pair of smaller airboats circled farther out, propelled by their giant fans, whisking swiftly over the water.

After they landed, chaos ruled as men and weapons were ferried from chopper to boats. Reaching the aft deck of the CBP boat, Lorna found herself mostly in the way, tussled by big, rugged men smelling of cheap aftershave, leather, and gun oil. Rough voices barked around her or burst with laughter.

She moved to a quiet corner, away from the tornado of testosterone.

Nearby, a half-dozen men in dark green shirts and trousers – Jack's Special Response Team – bustled about securing weapons: sidearms, shotguns, assault rifles. Night-vision goggles sat atop their helmets. No one was taking any chances.

Three other men dressed in hunting vests and jeans shared the back of the boat, but they kept to the other side, sitting atop overturned canoes. Lorna recognized the flat-bottomed dugouts to be Cajun pirogue. All three men – two black, one white – definitely had the rangy look of backwater Cajuns. One vaguely resembled Jack, maybe a relative. While dating Tommy, she had never met all of the Menard clan.

The final member sharing the boat came waltzing up, tongue lolling, tail wagging. It was a purebred bloodhound, but even the dog's manner was cocky with a happy-go-lucky glint in his eyes that was pure Cajun.

'Burt,' she whispered to herself as memories of happier times swelled through her. She might not have met Tommy's older brother, but she had been introduced to the family's best hunting dog.

Jack had mentioned bringing a scent hound along for the hunt, but she never thought it would be Burt.

Glad for a friendly greeting, she knelt to accept the dog's attention. He ambled up, shaking a bit of drool. She reached out a hand to scratch behind one of his impossibly long ears – but a sudden sharp shout froze them both.

'Burt! Git your butt back over here! Leave that *bonne à rien* alone.'

The dog glanced over his shoulder and dropped his tail. With a reluctant, almost apologetic glance at Lorna, Burt turned and returned to the trio by the canoes.

The one who had barked the order glared over at her. It was the man who bore a resemblance to Jack, probably related. Lorna didn't understand what he had called her – *bonne à rien* – but from the sneer in his voice, it wasn't a flattering term.

Jack had been talking to his second-in-command, but he swung around fast and came at the other. He grabbed the man by the collar of his flannel shirt and pulled him nose to nose.

'If I ever hear you talk to Dr. Polk like that again, I'll toss your ass overboard. Brother or not. She's here at my request. Stow that attitude or get off my boat.'

Lorna stared harder at the two. *Brother?* She studied the other man with new eyes. That would make him Randy, the older brother of Jack and Tom. He had been in jail when she and Tom were dating, incarcerated for a year after a drunken brawl in a pub on Bourbon Street. It didn't help that he had slugged an off-duty policeman.

Randy seemed about to argue, and even placed a palm on Jack's chest as if to shove his brother away. But he must've read something in Jack's face. His arm fell away. He took a step back and tried to shrug it off with a halfhearted acknowledgment.

'You're the boss, little brother.'

Not satisfied, Jack held him a moment longer, letting his intensity burn.

Randy finally sagged. '*Mais oui!* All right! I heard you!'

Jack let him go and glanced to Lorna in the same apologetic way as the hounddog. The brother returned to his friends. The trio retreated to the far side of the canoes. Once Jack finished with orders for his second-in-command, he joined Lorna.

'Sorry about that. C'mon. Before you cause any more trouble, let me show you the layout for tonight's search. See if you can offer any advice. That's why you're here, isn't it?'

She rankled a bit at his surliness, but she kept her mouth shut. She followed him toward the pilot's cabin of the boat. As he held the door for her, she was surprised to discover that the cabin was air-conditioned, almost chilly compared with the persistent heat of the evening. The sun had set, but the western sky still glowed a rosy orange.

He led her to a chart table. The only other occupant in the cabin was the ship's pilot, dressed like all of Jack's men in the CBP rough duty uniform, minus the helmet. The ship was already headed across Bay Lanaux. The trundle of the engine vibrated the deck through her hiking boots. The line of bayou forest stretched ahead of them, looking impenetrable and dark.

'Here's the route we're taking.' Jack placed a palm on a map clipped to the table. He ran a finger down a line drawn on the chart. 'After the storm, we estimate the cat made landfall near Bay Joe Wise, then headed due north.' His finger stopped. 'Here is where we rescued the boy. That cat covered a lot of ground in a short time.'

Lorna had already heard the details about that fatal encounter. She took a deep breath, glad to fall back on her professional background.

'Jaguars hunt a wide territory,' she started. 'That's why she's on the move. She's genetically wired to keep moving until she finds a spot that she believes will support her.'

'So she could keep moving for a while?'

'Definitely. This migratory trait is one of the reasons jaguars are endangered in the wild. Their native jungles and forests are being encroached upon and broken apart by man. With this strong drive to roam, the breakup of their forests is driving them into deadly encounters with people.'

She had read about an environmental project was under way to create a continent-spanning chain of wild forests, linked from Mexico to South America, a vast landscape through which the jaguar populations could expand and migrate freely. It was called the Paseo de Jaguar, or Path of the Jaguar.

She studied the map, trying to figure out this particular jaguar's *paseo*. There was one important clue.

'Let's not forget that she also has a cub,' Lorna pressed. 'So she'll be looking for a territory with a rich food supply, rich enough for *both* of them.'

Jack kept to her shoulder, studying the map alongside her. 'But where? If she continues north, she'll be passing between Adam's Bay and Lake Washington. That's deep bayou country. Where do we even begin to search?'

'We start with her food supply. The bayous are the perfect environment for a jaguar. They typically hunt along waterways. In fact, a large part of their diet is seafood. Turtles, fish, caiman.'

Jack turned at her. 'The kid we rescued said the cat had torn into a bunch of crab pots.'

She nodded. 'Jaguars are opportunistic carnivores. They'll eat anything. They can even bring down cows and full-grown horses.' She responded to the disbelief in his face. 'They're the perfect killing machine. Where tigers and lions rip out the throat of their prey, jaguars kill by crushing their prey's skull. They have the strongest jaws of any large cat. Evolved, it's believed, to help jaguars crack through the iron-hard shells of turtles.'

'If they like turtles, we've got plenty of 'em in the bayous. Terrapin, snapping turtles, and all manner of cooters and sliders.'

'Yes, but they're small and less abundant than our jaguar will need. With her body mass, she'll be looking for a dense and easily accessible food supply. She won't stop until she finds it.'

Jack suddenly stiffened beside her.

'What?' she asked.

He leaned closer to the map and ran his finger along the hand-drawn line. He also searched to both sides of the path. His finger stopped and tapped. A name was written under there: *Bayou Cook*.

Jack straightened and glanced to her. 'How sharp is a jaguar's sense of smell?'

'Extremely sharp. They're mostly nocturnal hunters, so they have to be able to track prey by scent.'

'How far do you think they could track a smell?'

'Hard to say. Depends on the source of the odor, its strength, the wind direction.' She shook her head. 'Lots of variables. Could be many miles if the conditions were right.'

'So if a place gave off a really strong odor and the wind was in the right direction, it could draw the cat. Even from miles away.'

'Sure. But it would have to be a scent that the cat recognized as a food source.'

'You said jaguars fed not just on turtles and fish, but also on caiman. The southern cousin of the American alligator.'

'That's right.'

'So if there was a concentrated source for such a meal, a place that really smelled strongly—'

'It would definitely draw her.'

Jack ripped the chart from the clips and carried it over to the boat's pilot. He pointed. 'This is where we're headed. Bayou Cook. Radio the airboats, let them know there's been a change in plans. We'll head directly over there.'

'Yes, sir.'

Jack returned, the map in his hand.

'What's at Bayou Cook?' Lorna asked.

'A tourist site. Draws sightseers year-round, mostly from the cruise ships that dock in New Orleans. You get a swamp tour, an airboat ride, and at the end, a visit to Bayou Cook.'

'What's there?'

Jack stared hard at her, certainty in his eyes. 'Uncle Joe's Alligator Farm.'

Chapter 13

Uncle Joe had no interest in children, but the camp groups brought in good money.

He stood on the front porch of his house with a tall, frosted bottle of Budweiser resting on the rail. The scorching day only seemed to grow hotter and damper as the sun faded away. It was like that out here. The first hour after sunset, the heat seemed reluctant to leave, overstaying its welcome. But slowly over the course of the night, it began to drain away, making it easier to breathe.

He enjoyed that time of night.

'Course, the beer helped, too.

He took a deep swig and stared across the thirty acres of his property. On the far side, a new campsite had been carved out of the neighboring stand of old-growth cypress forest. It was currently occupied by a troop of Boy Scouts from Baton Rouge, booked for the entire week. Campfires flickered among the tents, and strings of lanterns decorated the encampment. Songs echoed through the early evening, accompanied by the honking of bullfrogs and the occasional hoot from an owl or bellow from a bull alligator.

Between his log home and the campsite stretched the eight pools and pits of the alligator farm. He also had a bobcat exhibit and a shallow pond that held Gipper, a giant snapping turtle. The farm was crisscrossed with elevated walkways and observation decks.

He looked on with pride. It had cost him over half a million to expand the place from a single pond with a few breeding alligators to this singular attraction of the bayou. Last year alone, he had grossed three times his investment.

Of course, some of that money was under the table. As a conservator, he wasn't supposed to sell the alligators for skin or meat, but it didn't cost much to grease the palms of local enforcement agents to get them to look the other way. And for some wealthy anglers, newly hatched baby alligators were considered the best bait for bass fishing.

Across the farm, Joe watched a couple men patrol the walkways, rifles at their shoulders. They were the local militia he'd hired earlier today after hearing of some large cat sighted near the coast. He had been warned by radio to evacuate the area, but the Gulf was far away. And he would lose thousands in deposits and campsite rentals from the Scout troop alone if he evacuated.

Besides, the warning was just that: a *warning*, not an order. He hadn't let Katrina chase him off; he wasn't about to let some wildcat do the same. To justify his decision, he had hired four men from the parish's sheriff's department. In these hard times, everyone was looking for a little over-time.

Footsteps approached behind him. 'Papa, I'm off to feed Elvis.'

He glanced back as his daughter crossed the porch. She carried a cookie tray stacked with chicken carcasses. 'Not too many. We have a show scheduled for the morning for the campers. I want him hungry.'

'You can't starve the old fella,' she scolded him gently.

He waved her away, feeling a welling of love and pride for his only child. At twenty-two, Stella had been accepted to business school at Tulane. The first of his family to attend college. She was aiming for an MBA, but also took classes in environmental law. While his preservation efforts here at the farm were motivated by profit, she was a true conservation-ist. She knew about his under-the-table dealings, but she had a good head on her shoulders. This was Louisiana. Nothing got done without some backroom bargaining. And besides, many of his illicit profits went right back into the farm and its many conservation programs.

She climbed down the stairs to the first of the elevated walkways that crossed the ponds. Footsteps again sounded behind him, accompanied by a slight shaking of the deck. His wife joined him, wiping her pudgy hands on a dish towel. She took his beer bottle, shook it to judge how much was left, then pulled out a fresh bottle from her apron pocket and handed it to him.

'Thanks, Peg.'

She settled next to him and leaned her elbows on the rail. She sipped at the remains of his old beer. She was a large woman, but he liked her big. He was not exactly skinny himself, with his belly hanging farther and farther over his belt buckle each year, and under his LSU ball cap, his hairline was retreating just as quickly as his belly was expanding.

'I wish she'd wear more clothing,' his wife said.

He watched Stella cross toward the central pool. He understood his wife's concern. She wore cutoff shorts and a blouse tied around her midriff, exposing her belly. She hadn't even bothered with shoes. And she definitely hadn't inherited any fat genes from them. She was all muscle and curves, with long blond hair, like some Venus of the bayou. Joe was not unaware of the effect she had on the local boys. Not that she gave any of them the time of day.

In fact, it was long odds that he'd ever get the opportunity to change the name of his farm from Uncle Joe's to Grandpa Joe's. He suspected Stella's interests lay elsewhere than boys. She talked much too much about her friend at Tulane, a girl named Sandra who wore a biker's jacket and leather boots.

But maybe it was just a phase.

He took a big swallow from his bottle.

If only she met the right boy . . .

'C'mon, big fella, who wants a late-night snack?'

Stella stood on the observation deck over the largest of the farm's ponds. Her only illumination was a single lantern on a pole. The black water below merely reflected the light, hiding what lurked beneath its surface. She unhitched the gate in the fence with one hand while balancing the tray of chicken carcasses in the other. She had freshly slaughtered the four chickens herself. Blood, still warm, spilled off the tray and down her arm.

She grimaced and headed out onto the bare plank that extended over the pond like a diving board. She moved to the end and leaned over the water until she could see her own reflection in the pond.

There wasn't even a ripple, but she knew Elvis was down there. The bull alligator had been at the farm longer than any of them, one of the original inhabitants of the breeding pond when her daddy first bought the place. Since he'd been caught in the wild, no one knew Elvis's exact age, but a team of biologists guessed the alligator had to be close to thirty years old. The scientists had come here to collect blood samples from the pond's denizens. Apparently a protein found in alligator blood showed promise for a new generation of powerful antibiotics, killing even resistant superbugs.

But even the biologists hadn't attempted to approach Elvis. He stretched eighteen feet long and weighed well over half a ton. No one messed with Elvis. Past his breeding age, he had the pond to himself and liked it that way.

He was definitely spoiled.

She set down the cookie tray next to her and knelt at the end of the plank. Grabbing one of the bloody carcasses, she extended her arm out over the water. Droplets of blood fell and lightly splashed into the water below, sending out faint circular ripples.

She waited – but it didn't take long.

Across the pond, a new set of ripples formed a V and aimed toward her position. The tip of the alligator's snout was all that was visible. It glided smoothly toward her, unhurried but determined. Behind, a sashaying swirl marked the swish of Elvis's massive tail, still hidden under the water. It was that movement, almost sexual in its sway, that earned the alligator its nickname.

'C'mon, Elvis. I don't have all night.' She shook the chicken.

As if put off by her demand, he sank out of sight. All ripples died away. Stella tensed. Movement at the corner of her eye drew her attention across the pond. Caught for just a glimpse, something bright flowed through the forest, reflecting the moonlight, then vanished back into the darkness. She stared at the spot, already beginning to doubt she'd seen anything. The swamp was full of stories of ghosts, usually attributed to glowing swamp gas, what the Cajuns called *feu follet,* or *crazy fire*.

But this wasn't swamp gas.

She squinted for any other sign of it, concentrating with both eyes and ears – then an eruption blasted below her. Water fountained upward, along with the explosive surge of a half ton of armored muscle. Massive gaping jaws, lined by jagged yellow teeth, surged up toward her, close enough she could've leaned down and tapped the creature's nose.

Elvis could leap high out of the water, clearing even his hind legs. Stella dropped the chicken into those open jaws. They clamped shut with an audible *snap*. Gravity took over and dragged Elvis back down. He splashed heavily and sank away with his prize.

Stella dropped another two chickens into the water. Normally alligators needed movement to draw them to feed, but Elvis was accustomed to being hand-fed. He'd fish out the other two carcasses at his leisure. Minding her father's instructions, she left the fourth chicken on the tray.

Done with the feeding, she collected the cookie tray and turned to head back. A large shape blocked the gate. Startled, she fell back a step, almost tumbling off the end of the plank.

But it was one of her daddy's hired guns. He carried a shotgun, a military-grade twelve-gauge, over his shoulder and leaned on the gatepost. 'Done feeding the beast, eh? See you gotcha an extra chicken there.'

The man shifted so that the lamplight revealed the speaker. Ten years older, he was a bull of a man, though a bull that had gone to pot. He wore a dirty Stetson that did little to hide the greasy strings of his mud-brown hair. He sucked on a toothpick and spoke around it. One hand rested on a fat belt buckle shaped like a set of steer horns.

She scowled and headed toward the gate. 'Shouldn't you be patrolling? That's what my daddy paid you for.'

He leaned on a hip, completely blocking her way. 'Why don't you be a good girl and head on back to the house and cook *me* up some of that chicken, sweetheart.'

His gaze traveled up and down her form, as if he were interested in more than just chicken. Disgust churned up, but also a trickle of fear. She was all too conscious of her exposure – not just the amount of bare skin, but also her precarious perch on the plank.

She also knew this man well enough to fear him. Garland Chase – better known around these parts as 'Gar' because of his resemblance to the nasty snake-fish that plagued these swamps – was the sheriff's son, and everyone in Pasquamish Parish knew his daddy turned a blind eye to his boy's less-than-legal activities, including running his own protection racket. Stella's father volunteered a monthly stipend to the 'policemen's orphan fund,' paid directly to this asshole.

'My daddy's paid you plenty for the night,' she said. 'You can fetch your own dinner.'

Feigning more courage than she felt, she straightened her shoulders and headed toward the gate. She refused to let him intimidate her. He backed aside, but only a step. She tried to push past him, but at the last moment he blocked the way with a thick arm again.

He leaned in close. She smelled his breath. He had been drinking.

'What's wrong? Can't dykes cook?' he asked. 'Or is it your girlfriend who does all the cooking? What you need is a real man . . . someone to teach you how to fetch and carry like a good wife.'

Fear turned to fury in a heartbeat. 'I'd rather fuck Elvis.'

The man stiffened, his fat lips disappearing into a sneer. 'Maybe I'll throw you in there and you can try. Accidents happen all the time in the swamps.'

Stella knew this wasn't an idle threat. The man wasn't above such actions. Gar and his cronies were known to have caused *accidents* in the past. It was one of the reasons her daddy never missed a payment.

She shoved his arm out of the way, but he kept tight to her, his eyes gone dead mean.

At that moment the screaming started – loud, strident, and terrified.

They both turned.

It rose from the Boy Scout camp.

Chapter 14

Lorna sat by herself on the front deck of the CBP boat. It slid smoothly down a narrow canal, framed by ancient cypress trees. The low rumble of the engine had a lulling effect. She had not realized how tired she was until this quiet moment. She took what rest she could, staring out at the spread of the bayou.

Half a mile ahead, the sharper whines of the two airboats led the way. Their searchlights were will-o'-the-wisps in the darkness. Closer at hand, fireflies flickered in branches and flew in warning patterns across the channel.

She listened to the swamp breathe around her. The wash of water through cypress knees, the whispery rattle of leaves from an occasional ocean breeze, all accompanied by the heavy croaking of bullfrogs, the screech of an owl, the ultrasonic whistle of hunting bats. Beneath it all she sensed something timeless and slumbering about this place, a glimpse of a prehistoric world, a sliver of a primordial Eden.

'Are you hungry?'

The voice made her jump. She had been close to drifting off, lost in her private thoughts. She sat up, smelling something wonderful and spicy in the air. It cut sharply through the moldy mire of the swamp.

Jack approached. He had a helmet under one arm and a plastic bowl in the other. 'Crawfish gumbo. Hope you like okra.'

'Wouldn't be a southerner if I didn't.'

She took the bowl gratefully. She was surprised to discover a couple pieces of *pain perdu* floating in the stew. Her mother used to make it every Sunday morning: soaking stale bread in milk and cinnamon overnight, then frying it in a skillet. The smell would fill the entire house. She'd never had *pain perdu* served with gumbo.

She spooned up a piece questioningly.

Jack spoke, a grin behind his words. 'My *grand-mère*'s recipe. Try it.'

She tasted a chunk of the sodden bread. Her eyes slipped closed. 'Ohmygod . . .' The blend of heat from the gumbo and sweetness of the cinnamon came close to making her swoon.

The grin in his voice reached his face. 'We Cajuns know a thing or two about cookin'.'

He sat near her as she worked her way through the bowl. They kept each other quiet company, but it slowly turned uncomfortable. There was too much hanging between them, ghosts of the past that grew all too real in the dark swamp and the silence.

Jack finally broke the tension. As if needing to push back the darkness, he swept out an arm and captured a flash of light that flickered past. He opened his fingers to reveal a tiny firefly, gone dark, its magic broken, just a small winged beetle again.

'Where my *grand-mère* was a great cook, my *grand-père* was a bit of a medicine man. He had all sorts of homegrown remedies. Bathing in pepper grass to soak away aches. If you had a fever, you slept under the bed. He used to crush fireflies and mix them with pure-grain alcohol to make an ointment. Cured rheumatism, he claimed.'

Jack blew on the beetle and sent it winging away, again flickering and winking brightly.

'I still remember him walking around the house in his underwear at night with glowing goop smeared all over his shoulders and knees.'

A warm laugh bubbled out of her. 'Your brother once mentioned that. Said it scared him to death.'

'I remember. *Grand-père* passed away when Tom was only six. He was too young to understand. 'Course it didn't help that whenever we spotted some fiery swamp gas in the bayou, I'd tell him it was the ghost of *grand-père* coming to get him.'

She smiled as their two memories wrapped around each other, centered around Tom. Silence again dropped around them. It was the problem with keeping company with Jack. No matter what they discussed, they had their own ghost haunting them.

In that moment they could've let the silence crush them, drive them apart, but Jack remained seated. Plainly there was much left unsaid between them, left unexplained for years. His voice dropped to a breath, but she still heard the pain. 'I have to ask . . . do you ever regret your decision?'

She tensed. She had never talked about it aloud with anyone, at least not directly. But if anyone deserved an honest answer, it was Jack. Her breathing grew harder. She immediately went back to that moment in the bathroom, staring down at the E.P.T strip. As always, the past was never more than a heartbeat away.

'If I could take it all back,' she said, 'I would. And not just for Tom's sake. There's not a day goes by that I don't think about it.' Her hand drifted to her belly. 'I should've been stronger.'

Jack waited a half breath, clearly weighing how much and what to say. 'You and Tom were just kids.'

She shook her head slightly. 'I was fifteen. Old enough to know better. Before and after.'

She and Tom had made love in the garden shed at her house after a spring dance. They were stupid and in love, having dated for almost a year. They'd both been virgins. Their coupling had been painful and ill-conceived and full of misconceptions.

89

No one got pregnant the first time.

After she missed her period, followed by confirmation with a pregnancy test kit, that particular misconception was shattered. The full weight of reality and responsibility came crashing down on them. They'd kept silent about it, a terrifying secret between them that wasn't going away. Over the next month, she had practically cleaned out a neighboring town's drugstore of its test kits. She prayed on her knees every night.

What were they to do?

She wasn't ready for a child, to be a mother. Tom was terrified of how their parents would respond. She had also been raised Catholic, had her first Communion at the St. Louis Cathedral. There seemed no options, especially if her parents learned the truth.

Tom had suggested a solution. In the neighboring parish, there was a midwife who performed abortions in secret. And not the clothes-hanger sort of deal. She had been trained at a Planned Parenthood clinic, taking that skill, along with some black-market tools and drugs, and setting up a makeshift clinic out of an old house in the delta. The midwife ran a booming business. And it wasn't just scared teenagers, but also cheating spouses, rape victims, and anyone who needed to keep a secret. There were plenty of those in southern Louisiana. The region had an unwritten rule: as long as you didn't talk about it, it never happened.

And in the end, that was the true power of the bayou. Under its dark bower, secrets could be drowned forever.

But it was a delusion to think such secrets truly died. Someone still had to live with them. And often what was thought gone forever rose to the surface again.

Jack read the pain in the woman's posture, the grief shining so plainly in her face. He should've kept his mouth shut. It wasn't his place to question her, to drive this stake through her heart. When it came to this story, he had his own burden to bear. Maybe that's why he was here, to find some way to forgive himself.

Jack spoke into the quiet. 'Tom never said a word about the pregnacy. Not even to me. We were sharing the same bedroom, so I knew something was wrong. He got all sullen and quiet, walked around the house like he was waiting for someone to hit him over the head. It wasn't until he called that night, half drunk, sobbing . . . perhaps seeking absolution from his older brother.'

Lorna turned to him. She had never heard this part. 'What did he say?'

Jack rubbed at the stubble on his chin. It made too loud a scratching sound, so he dropped his hand back to his lap. 'You were with the midwife at the time. While he was waiting, he slipped off to a nearby backwater moonshine bar and got drunk.'

She stared at him, waiting for more. He knew she was well familiar with *that* part of the story already.

'I could barely understand him,' Jack continued. 'He got you pregnant. That much was clear.'

'That wasn't all on him,' she added.

He nodded, moving on. 'Tom was racked by guilt. He was sure he had ruined your life. Sure that you would hate him. But more than anything, he felt like he had pressured you into going out there. That it was the wrong choice. But now it was too late.'

She glanced back to him. 'I knew he was scared . . . like I was. But I didn't know he was that tortured. He kept that locked away.'

'It's the Cajun way. *Joie de vivre*. Sadness is supposed to be bottled up, especially for the men. Probably why Tom got drunk. Couldn't keep that up without some anesthesia.'

She frowned. 'When I came out and found him slurring and weaving, I got so angry. I was in pain, half drugged on sedatives, and there he was, drunk. I yelled at him, lit into him good. We had planned on going to a hotel after the

91

procedure. My parents thought I was sleeping over with a friend. It was all planned. But after I found him in that state, I figured we would have to spend the night in the back of his truck, wait until he sobered up.'

Jack heard the catch in her voice and knew why. 'But Tom hadn't been drinking alone.'

'No.'

About that time, Jack had been racing across the parish on his motorcycle. After the drunken call, he knew his brother needed help. He certainly wasn't fit enough to drive.

Lorna's voice grew cold, distancing herself as much as possible from the memory. 'Tom had already passed out in the back of the truck by the time they came. They pulled me out of the rear bed. Had me on the ground before I even knew what was happening. I fought, but they pinned me down. They had my jeans down to my knees, tore open my blouse.'

'You don't have to go there, Lorna.'

She seemed deaf to him. 'I couldn't stop them. I still remember the bastard's stinking breath, fuming with alcohol. His laughter. His hands tearing at me. I should've been more careful.' Her voice cracked, and she visibly trembled.

'They were predators,' Jack said. He pushed against the guilt he heard in her voice. 'They probably scouted regularly around that makeshift clinic. With women already half drugged, they found easy marks. Who would report an attack? These were women sneaking off for a secret abortion at an illegal clinic. Their silence was practically guaranteed. The bastards probably plied Tom with cheap moonshine so he'd be out of the picture. Leaving you alone and vulnerable.'

'But I wasn't alone.' She turned to him, her eyes shining in the darkness.

Jack had arrived at that exact time, skidding to a stop on his motorcycle in the parking lot. He spotted them at the edge of the woods on top of Lorna. A blood rage had filled him at the time. He flew into the group of them, but he tempered his fury with calculation. With three against one, he needed to make an example, to unleash such a savage attack that it would cow the other two. He ripped the bastard off of Lorna, twisted his arm until bone snapped and a scream followed. He then pounded the man, half animal in his savagery, breaking the bastard's nose, his cheekbone, knocking out his front teeth.

Still, he had the wherewithal to tell Lorna to run, to get in the truck and hightail it out of there. He didn't know how many others were out there, if they had any friends nearby who would be drawn by the fight.

While he fought, Lorna had hesitated by the truck, hovering by the door. He'd thought she was paralyzed by fear.

'Get moving, you stupid bitch!' he had screamed at her, words he still regretted, both for their cruelty then and for the consequences that would follow.

She had jumped into the cab and, with a roar of the engine, flew off. While beating the man under him to a bloody pulp he watched her fishtail out of the parking lot and onto the narrow winding road that led through the bayou. At the time he didn't know his brother was passed out in the open truck bed. Only later, after the accident, did he learn the truth. She had lost control in the dark, miscalculated a turn, and ended up plowing into a tree.

The airbag saved her.

Tom was found fifty feet away, facedown in the water.

Lorna recognized the haunted look in Jack's eyes. She remembered little after the accident. The next days had been a blur to her.

In the end, the fallout of that night was typical of Louisiana justice. Deals were struck behind closed doors. She was convicted of a DUI, though not alcohol-related as everyone suspected following the tox screen on Tom's body. He had a blood-alcohol level four times the legal limit. Her DUI was based on her impairment while under the effect of a sedative, a detail kept out of the newspapers to spare her parents any additional humiliation.

Jack had also testified behind closed doors as to *why* she had been driving. At the same time he was also up on assault charges.

She was ashamed that she never really knew what had happened to him after that. He had simply vanished.

'Where did you go?' she finally asked. 'After the courthouse?'

He sighed and shook his head. 'The man I beat up, the one that attacked you, he came from a well-connected family.'

Lorna sat stunned. She struggled to shift her view of the past to match his words. Shock, then anger, burned through her. 'Wait. I thought no one knew who he was.'

During the attack, she hadn't gotten a good look at her assailant. And out in the backwoods, people kept their mouths shut.

'I was railroaded,' Jack explained. 'Looking back now, I recognize that they feared prosecuting me outright. It would expose the attempted rape – a crime that in the backwaters is often dismissed as boys being boys, but no one wanted to test that theory. And besides, you hadn't been raped, so why stir the pot?'

Jack must have felt her go cold next to him. 'Those were *their* words,' he said, 'not mine. Either way, the case never went to trial. Still, they couldn't just me let go. His family had pull. Mine didn't. We had a long history of trouble with the law. As you might remember, Randy was already locked up for assaulting a policeman. They made veiled threats against his life if I didn't cooperate, if I didn't keep my mouth shut. So I was given a choice: go to jail or join the Marines.'

'That's why you left?'

'Had no choice.' He kept his eyes purposefully away. 'And

to be honest, I was happy to leave. I was the one who sent you flying away in that truck, ordered you to leave. How could I face my family? And when I did return home after two tours of duty, I found it easier to remain silent. To let the dead rest in peace.'

Lorna understood that all too well. Even at her house, the matter was never discussed openly again by her family. *If you didn't talk about it, it didn't happen.*

They sat for a long spell in silence, but it was no longer as heavy, or as haunted. Footsteps finally interrupted.

Jack's second-in-command joined them. She had been introduced earlier. Scott Nester was from Arkansas and still carried a bit of hillbilly drawl in his voice, but his attitude was all professional.

'Sir, we still haven't raised anyone at the farm on the radio. How do you want to proceed? I can call the chopper to have them head out there.'

Jack stood up, the warmth and intimacy evaporating as he assumed the mantle of responsibility. 'The farm was told to evacuate. Maybe that's why no one's answered. Have you been able to confirm that they left?'

'I have Kesler still making calls.'

From Jack's expression, he was still weighing whether to call in the chopper. She wasn't sure that was a good idea. She lifted her hand. 'That much noise from a helicopter, the blaze of its searchlights . . . if the cat's nearby, the commotion might drive it off. We could lose this opportunity.'

Jack considered her advice, then checked his watch. 'We should reach the farm in another five minutes. The chopper can't get there much faster. Still, Scotty, go ahead and call the pilot. Make sure he keeps that bird's engine hot. We don't want – '

He was cut off by the pounding of boots. Another agent ran up. He looked barely older than a teenager.

Jack faced him. 'What is it, Kesler?'

'Sir, I just fielded a call about the farm.'

'Did they evacuate?'

'No, sir. I don't know, sir.'

Jack stared hard at the man, willing him to calm down.

He took a gulping breath. 'After making several calls, I received one back. From the local chapter of the Boy Scouts. According to the call, a group of scouts was headed to the farm this morning, to camp there for the week.'

Lorna's heart sank into her belly.

'No one's heard from them since.'

Chapter 15

Stella ran across the elevated boardwalks toward the camp-site. Children's screams continued to burst out, sharp and sibilant, but they were now punctuated by the deeper shouts from scoutmasters and chaperoning parents.

Her bare feet slapped against the boards, followed by the harder pounding of Garland Chase's boots. He swore a blue streak next to her, a walkie-talkie pressed to his lips.

'Get everyone over to the camp!' he hollered.

More fleet of foot, she reached the cleared section of old-growth forest first. Lanterns were strung on lines. A few campfires glowed. Tents dotted the open ground in an array of colors and sizes, from an old army-surplus pup tents to elaborate gazebos purchased from the local REI. There were also piles of kayaks, fishing gear, and empty sleeping bags strewn about like the skins of shedding snakes.

She ran up to one of the scoutmasters, a robust fellow whose belly strained his khaki uniform. His face was a sweaty crimson. 'What's wrong?' she asked.

The screaming rose from the far side of the camp, but it seemed to be already subsiding.

'Just some spooked kids,' the scoutmaster said with a scowl. 'They were out gathering firewood. Claimed they saw a swamp monster. Came running back screaming bloody murder. After all the campfire ghost stories, it was like throwing gasoline on fire. Got all the kids running and hollering, half in real terror, half in play.'

Gar swore under his breath. He had his shotgun clutched in one hand, the other rested on a knee as he leaned over, huffing and gasping from the sprint. 'Goddamn kids . . .'

'Sorry,' the camp leader said. 'We'll get 'em back under control. Put 'em all to bed. There won't be any more trouble.'

One of the scouts arrived. Redheaded and freckled, he looked to be around eighteen. Probably an Eagle Scout acting as the scoutmaster's assistant. He dragged an eleven-year-old boy by an elbow. 'Here's one of the kids causing all the trouble.'

The boy wore swimming trunks and a Gryffindor T-shirt. His eyes were huge, glassy. He trembled with fright – not because he was in trouble. Instead, his gaze remained fixed on the forest.

The scoutmaster grabbed his chin and made the boy face him. 'Ty, look at the ruckus you've caused with your silly story. Do you want me to send you home right now? What would your parents think about that?'

The boy strained against the grip holding him, near panic. Whatever had happened out in the swamp, this kid believed it was a monster.

Dropping to a knee to get eye level with him, Stella reached over and freed the boy from the older men. She kept hold of his shoulders. 'Ty, tell me what you saw.'

He again glanced toward the forest, then to her. 'I didn't get a good look.' His voice was a scared whisper. 'It was all white. Saw it leap over the water and back into the woods. We hightailed it out of there.'

'Probably just a deer,' Gar said with a dismissive sneer. 'Little bastard's just scared of the dark.'

The boy's shaking grew worse at Gar's threatening manner. Stella scowled, silently telling the bastard to shut up. The boy had seen something. *But what?* She remembered catching a fleeting glimpse of something herself in the woods, a ghostly shape that seemed to capture and hold the moonlight.

'It was big,' the boy said. 'Lots bigger than a deer.'

'How big?' she asked.

'Like a . . . I don't know . . .' He swept his arms wide. 'Least as big as a small car.'

Gar snorted and shouldered his shotgun.

Stella stood up. A coldness ran through her. Without missing a beat, she turned to the scoutmaster. 'I want you to gather all the children and head over to my house.'

She pointed to her parents' two-story log cabin. Built stoutly of cypress logs, it had ridden out Katrina safely. She wanted everyone under cover, not out in the open.

'What are you talking about?' the scoutmaster asked. 'Why?'

She took a deep breath. Earlier in the day, she had taken the call herself about a big cat loose near the coast. The details had been sketchy, except for one detail. The cat was said to be huge. She did her best to keep panic out of her voice.

'There's been a report of a large jaguar loose in the bayou,' she said. 'Escaped from a shipwreck along the coast, far from here, but let's not take any chances.'

The scoutmaster looked stunned. 'Why wasn't I told about—'

By now, Gar's team had arrived. The men came puffing up, rifles in hand. Gar seemed to draw strength from their numbers. He lifted an arm. 'Now let's all calm down. I heard about that report, too. Big cat or not, there's no way a jaguar covered that much ground in a single day. So let's not get all riled up just because some kid jumps at his own shadow.'

The scoutmaster looked unsure. The camp was his responsibility.

'I'll send some of my guys out to take a look,' Gar assured him. 'If there's anything in the woods, they'll find it.'

His men grinned, readying their weapons.

'You do that,' Stella said. 'But I'm still moving the campers over to the cabin.'

Gar looked ready to argue – then simply shrugged. 'Fine. I'll go with you. Make sure there's no other trouble.' He glared at the boy, then turned and ordered his men to sweep the neighboring forest.

Stella swung back to the camp leader. 'Get all the children together. As quickly and quietly as possible.'

He nodded. In a matter of minutes, children and adults were gathered into neat groups. En masse, they set off across the farm, traversing the boardwalks. Kids chattered excitedly. Adults looked worried or annoyed.

Stella led them, with Gar trailing behind. As much as she despised the man, she appreciated his shotgun at her back. She kept watch on the forest to either side. Nothing seemed amiss. Bullfrogs croaked, fireflies flickered, and mosquitoes buzzed and dive-bombed. Still, she felt a prickling along the nape of her neck, as if something were staring at her out of the dark forest.

She was relieved to clamber up the stairs to the family cabin. The home was large, and though it would be cramped, it should hold everyone. Her parents met her on the porch.

'What's happening?' her father asked. 'What's all the commotion?'

Stella related what she knew.

With a crinkled brow of concern, her mother wiped her hands on her apron, then waved to the children. 'Let's get everyone inside. I can make a big batch of hot chocolate.'

Stella kept to the porch as a parade of children filed into the house, following her mother like a gaggle of goslings. Many faces were pinched with worry, while others grinned at the excitement of it all.

Her father joined her. 'You made the right call, Stell. Peg will get those young'uns settled. But what're the odds that cat really is out there?'

Gar climbed up to the porch. 'Don't matter none. My

boys are scouting the woods. If that cat's out there, they'll take care of its sorry ass.'

'I hope you're right.'

'Hell, it's only a damn cat.'

As if summoned by his words, a shape dropped out of the dark forest on the far side of the ponds. It landed on one of the boardwalks and stood dead still, crouched low to the planks, practically filling the space. Its eyes reflected the moonlight, staring straight at them.

'Holy Mother of God . . .' Stella's father gasped out.

Gar fell back a step, while scrambling his shotgun to his shoulder.

'Don't!' Stella warned.

Gar fired. The blast deafened, smoke flowed from the barrel. It was a stupid potshot, a panicked knee jerk. There was no way he could hit the cat at that distance. Gar expelled the smoking cartridge and one-handedly pumped in another load. But he was already too late.

The beast's long tail swished once in agitation, then in a burst of muscle, it swung around and dove back into the forest.

'Everyone inside,' her father said. 'Gar, call your men back. We need every weapon here to protect the kids.'

Out in the woods, a spat of rifle blasts cracked. A single bloodcurdling scream followed. The three of them remained frozen on the porch. The dark forest went silent. Even the frogs had gone quiet.

Gar kept his cheek pressed to the butt of his shotgun.

'Joe!' Stella's mother called from inside.

'Into the house,' her father ordered.

As they began to retreat, a new noise sliced through the quiet: a sharp whining. It came from the other side of the house, where the farm's dock and fuel station jutted into a deepwater channel.

'An airboat!' Stella said.

Someone was coming.

Hopefully with lots of guns.

101

Uncle Joe waded across the great room of the cabin through a sea of children sitting on the floor or huddled in small groups. Wide eyes stared at him. Scoutmasters called out questions, but he was deaf to them. He focused on the large stone fireplace that filled the back wall. To either side, wide windows looked out toward the rear of the house, toward the docks.

He led his daughter and the sheriff's son across the room.

Gar headed to one window with his walkie-talkie at his lips, shouting for someone to answer him.

Were any of his men still alive out there?

He and Stella moved to the other window, taking up a post shoulder to shoulder. Inside the cabin, they could no longer hear the whine of the airboat. He reached the window and stared out. There was no sign of the boat, only the lights of the dock reflecting off the black water.

What if it wasn't headed here?

He had no way to radio out. After the storm, they'd been having trouble with the shortwave, a common problem whenever the temperature ran through such extremes. Humidity condensed inside the equipment, wreaking havoc with their reception. The warning call had barely been audible. The radio had shut down completely after that. He'd been meaning to fix it but hadn't gotten around to it.

He studied the waterway, the only channel into or out of the farm.

The canal was narrow and twisted, but he'd had it dredged deep enough to accommodate the larger tenders that ferried cruise-ship passengers to the farm. To either side, the forest had been groomed to look especially picturesque. The underbrush had been cleared to accentuate the size and majesty of the old-growth cypresses. Flowering plants, strategically placed, added to the beauty, as did the manicured beds of water lilies along both shorelines.

'There!' Stella burst out and pointed.

A sharp light bloomed into existence far down the channel, flickering between trees.

'Two of them!' Stella said, noting a second glow. 'They must be heading here!'

'Stay by the window. I'll go down to the dock.'

'Daddy, no. At least wait until they're closer. And take Gar with you.'

He hesitated. The first airboat appeared around a bend in the canal. It sailed in a smooth arc, propelled by the giant fan at its stern. Its searchlight speared straight at the cabin, blinding them. He lifted a hand to shield against the brightness.

As the airboat raced at full speed toward the dock, the second appeared behind it, riding the wake of the first. Rising and falling, its light played wildly.

The only warning was a sharp gasp from his daughter.

He blinked against the glare, catching sight of something large leaping out of the woods and flying high. It struck the pilot of the lead airboat and ripped him out of his seat. Pilot and cat went crashing into the water on the far side, splashing into a bed of water lilies. Before the first wave even washed up onto the bank, the cat bounded out of the shallows and back into the woods. A body floated on its stomach in the water. Its head bobbed farther out in the lilies.

'Daddy!'

Stella pointed back to the empty airboat. Momentum carried it like a missile straight toward the dock.

'The fuel tank!'

The airboat hit the dock at full speed. Its nose shot high as it flew up over the edge. Its underside struck the upright fuel pump and tore it from its stanchions. Gas sprayed as the boat landed atop it, sliding with a scrape of metal on metal. A pole toppled over, shattering an electric lantern.

Sparks danced across the deck.

Oh no . . .

Joe held his breath.

The other airboat, sensing the danger, tried to turn. It twisted broadside, pushing into its own wake, trying to brake and turn, to get away.

Too late.

A flash of fire, and the explosion ripped high. Joe shoved into his daughter and toppled them both away as the glass in the cabin's windows blew out. Heat and smoke pounded inside. Sharper screams cut through his ringing ears. He turned to see a flaming dock timber shatter through a window in the kitchen. He heard a rattle of more debris rain over the roof.

He knelt up and crawled back to the window.

The world was on fire. Even the canal was burning with pools of flaming oil. Smoke choked and swirled. He spotted the second airboat crashed upside down at the edge of the channel, tossed there by the blast.

Stella joined him and tugged on an arm. 'The house is on fire!'

She pointed to the kitchen. Flames had spread from the flying timber. He glanced up and spotted curls of smoke in the open rafters, along with a telltale glow. The roof had caught fire, lit by the rain of burning debris.

'We have to get the kids out of here!' She turned and called through the cacophony of screaming children. 'Gar! Help us get everyone out!'

But the man was already retreating on his own. Blood dripped down his face, cut by broken glass. He shoved kids out of his way and cracked the butt of his shotgun into a parent's face who tried to stop him.

'Gar!'

Stella made a move to chase after him, but he'd already reached the front door and fled through it.

Joe grabbed his daughter's elbow. 'You and Peg get the kids moving. I'm going for the gun case upstairs. Check with any of the adults. If anyone knows how to handle a firearm, send them to me.'

Stella stood frozen for a moment, scared and half in shock.

'Honey, take the kids back to the campsite. Get those fires blazing brightly.'

Something broke inside her, freeing her. She nodded. Her eyes focused on him more fully. 'Daddy, what are you fixin' to do?'

'Don't worry. I'll be right behind you. If we're going to survive, we'll need every weapon we can find.'

A loud *crack* echoed above. A section of roof opened, raining fiery ash into the room.

He shoved his daughter away from him. 'Go!'

Chapter 16

A whirlwind of fire swept into the sky.

Aboard the CBP boat, everyone froze for a stunned beat. As the explosion echoed away, Jack grabbed his second-in-command by the arm. 'Call the chopper! Now!'

Jack spun toward the pilothouse. The boat continued down the canal, chugging toward a bend in the channel. Ahead, the firestorm collapsed, leaving behind a ruddy glow that shone through the forest. He caught an oily whiff of fuel in the night breeze. He flashed back to the exploded trawler.

Was this another booby trap?

He dismissed that as unlikely. Only a handful of people knew his team was on its way to the alligator farm. Still, he wasn't taking any chances.

'Throttle down!' he called to the pilot as he entered the cabin. 'All ahead slow.'

He joined the man at the wheel.

The engine's growl dropped a full octave. The boat's prow lowered as their course turned into a glide. The pilot hauled on the wheel and guided them around the bend in the river.

Jack swore at the sight ahead.

The world was on fire.

'Sir?' the pilot asked.

'Full stop.'

At the end of the channel sat a large log home with a

wide dock below it. The smoldering wreckage of an air-boat lay amid the fiery ruins of the pier. Jack struggled to understand. Had the pilot lost control of his craft and rammed the dock? He couldn't put it past an airboat pilot. They were generally a cocky lot, daredevils of the bayous.

The second airboat rested upside down on the bank of the canal, nose buried half in the trees, likely tossed there by the explosion. In the glow of the fires, he spotted bodies in the water.

Scott Nester burst into the cabin behind him. 'Chopper's on its way.'

Jack barely heard him and pointed to the canal. 'Get swimmers overboard. We've got men in the water.'

Scott vanished back out again. Jack followed at his heels. His second-in-command shouted orders. The smoke had grown thicker, oilier, falling like an axed tree over the boat.

At the end of the canal, the log house continued to burn. A section of its roof collapsed with a plume of fiery ash. The fire had already begun to spread into the surrounding forest, licking quickly through the shrouds of moss-laden trees.

'Jack!'

He turned to find Lorna at his side. Her face was pale, her eyes huge. 'I heard screaming.' She pointed toward the inferno. 'Sounded like children.'

Jack pinched his brow in concentration, straining to hear past the crackling roar of the fire. He heard nothing, but he trusted the certainty in Lorna's eyes. He remembered the report of the missing scouts. If there were kids out there, his team had to find a way around the flames.

But how?

He dared not bring the big boat any closer. The conflagration completely cut off the way ahead, and with every gust of wind, the flames swept wider into the forest. He studied the dark swamp. This region of the bayou was a maze of sinuous waterways, most too narrow for the ship's Zodiacs.

But maybe not for something smaller.

Jack turned and spotted Randy and the Thibodeaux brothers. They had kept their posts by the pair of pirogue canoes. If they moved quickly enough, the canoes could be used to circle around to reach the farm.

'Randy!' Jack headed toward his brother, gathering men as he crossed the deck. Each canoe could hold five or six people. 'Get those canoes overboard. Now!'

Randy needed no further instructions. He matched Jack's gaze, understanding immediately. He flicked his cigarette into the water and turned to the Thibodeaux brothers. 'You heard my little brother.'

They moved swiftly, literally tossing the canoes over the side. Water splashed, and the boats bobbed back up. Ropes kept the canoes from drifting away.

Off to the side, men donned helmets and slung assault rifles and shotguns, then clambered down into the flat-bottomed skiffs. There was little chatter. Jack's team responded whip-fast to his orders.

'Coast Guard's been alerted,' Scott said at Jack's shoulder. 'We've got more boats and choppers on the way.'

He nodded. 'Take command of the boat here. I'll need you to coordinate rescue operations.'

'Understood.'

Jack's eyes momentarily caught on Lorna. She stood with her arms crossed, radiating irritated patience. She didn't want to be left behind, but she also recognized she was out of her league.

He turned and climbed over the edge of the boat. T-Bob and Peeyot took one canoe, along with three of Jack's team. Jack joined his brother and two men in the second boat.

The plan was for the canoes to head in opposite directions. It was the best odds for discovering a way around the fires. The Thibodeaux brothers' boat was already heading east, their paddles slicing cleanly into the water. Jack took a position at the prow of Randy's canoe. His brother manned the stern and guided their direction with a thick wooden paddle. They turned toward the western bank, aiming for a narrow tributary that spilled away from the main channel and flowed into the deeper bayou.

Jack lowered a pair of night-vision goggles over his eyes. Ahead, the dark swamp snapped into finer detail. The goggles used the latest technology, known as sensor fusion, combining the image intensification of ambient light with the heat differentiation from infrared. The only negative was their narrowed view. The goggles required constant panning to maintain a decent range of perception.

As the canoe pushed into the side channel, Jack absently glanced toward the fires. He bit back a curse as the brightness and heat of the flames blazed through his sensitive goggles, blinding him. He tore his gaze away, and to his relief, the boat drifted into the darkness under the trees.

His eyes slowly readjusted. The world focused back into phosphorus shades of green. Ahead, a few fireflies flickered like camera flashes in the dark. But off to his right, the world still shone brightly, as if a sun were rising to the south.

Jack kept his gaze fixed forward. They needed to find a way around that rising sun – before it burned them all.

Lorna watched Jack's canoe vanish into the darkness. The CBP had been left with a skeletal crew. Jack's second-in-command stood with a satellite phone pressed to the side of his face. The boat's pilot set about securing an anchor to keep the craft from drifting too close to the growing firestorm. In just the few minutes it took to off-load Jack's team, the flames had already grown higher and stretched wider.

She hated to be left behind, but at least she wasn't the only one. Burt sat on his haunches at her side. The hound leaned against her, commiserating at being abandoned. Jack had needed all the room in the tiny canoes for his team. No room for Burt. She felt a shiver in the dog's body. The fire and smoke had him nervous.

109

She patted his side. 'Don't worry, Burt. Jack will be back soon.'

A tail thumped the deck twice, acknowledging her but still not happy.

Splashing drew her attention to the stern.

A Border Patrol agent leaned over the edge of the boat and helped two swimmers roll a body onto the deck. It must be one of the airboat pilots. Even from steps away, Lorna saw the man was dead.

Burt stood up, but Lorna held a palm in front of his nose. 'Stay.'

The dog obeyed but remained on his legs.

Lorna crossed to see if she could be of any help.

The agent called down into the water to one of the swimmers, 'What about Jerry?'

Lorna guessed that was the name of the other airboat pilot.

The swimmer kicked up higher. 'Dead.'

As proof, he lifted a gruesome object and placed it atop the deck. It was a severed head. Shocked, Lorna fell back a step.

'Fan blade,' the swimmer guessed and made a slicing motion across his own throat. 'We'll retrieve the body next.'

The swimmer slipped back into the water to join his partner.

Lorna wanted to run, but she held pat. With only a glimpse of the decapitated head, she already knew the man's death had not come from a whirling fan blade.

Swallowing back her squeamishness, she approached closer and dropped to one knee. She avoided looking at the waxen face, the open eyes. Swamp water pooled under the head, tinged red against the white deck. She concentrated on the neck wound. It was not a clean cut. Instead, the wound had a ragged edge.

Not what one would expect from fan blade.

She reached out and used a fingertip to gingerly tease up

a flap of the torn skin, noting the pattern of the rip.

'Ma'am,' the agent said. 'Maybe you shouldn't be touching that.'

She ignored him. It took all her effort to maintain a dispassionate professionalism. In her role as a veterinarian, she had performed hundreds of necropsies and pathology exams. This was no different – or so she kept telling herself.

She leaned closer. The cervical vertebrae C3 and C4 had been crushed, pulverized under great force. A full five inches of white-gray spinal cord draped from the ruined column, like wire stripped from a cable. Only a tremendous force could have ripped the head from its body in such a manner.

Lorna swallowed hard. While working in Africa, she had come across the carcasses of antelope and gazelles freshly killed by lions. Examinations of those remains had revealed similar wounds, characterized by savage ripping and pulling.

'Ma'am,' the agent tried again.

Lorna stood up. The world darkened at the edges as her certainty grew. She stared at the forest. The firestorm was not the only danger out there.

Not by far.

She turned and hurried toward the man left in command here. 'Agent Nester!'

He was still on his satellite phone, but he must have recognized the urgency and terror in her voice. He lowered the phone, cupping his hand over it for privacy. 'What is it?'

'You have to radio Jack,' she said in a rush. 'Warn him. And the other boat.'

'Warm them about what?'

'The cat . . . that monster we came hunting. It's already here.'

Chapter 17

T-Bob kept to the front of the boat while his younger brother guided at the back with a paddle. With his eyes half closed, T-Bob listened to the bayou. He didn't need fancy goggles to hunt like the two Border Patrol agents who shared his canoe. He smelled their aftershave, the starch in their clothes.

He had no use for the pair.

T-Bob had been born in the bayou – literally birthed in a canoe like this one. He had hunted these parts since he could first walk. The bayou was as much kin to him as his own brother.

As they headed through the swamp, he listened to the forest around him. Night in the bayou was a noisy time. He heard the bullfrog, the owl, the twitter of nesting birds. To either side, saw grass and reeds rustled as his brother glided their canoe through the dense growth. Closer at hand, the whirring of mosquitoes buzzed his ears.

In the distance, he still heard the hungry grumble of fire eating wood, but it had grown muffled as they paddled deeper into the forest. Still, the heat and smoke continued to drive animals outward. A pair of marsh hares burst out of the reeds and bounded across the creek. A moment later, a red deer followed, flagging her white tail at them.

T-Bob studied their passage.

The animals weren't in full panic, so the flames must still be a ways off. From the path and direction of the fleeing creatures, he kept track of the fire's edge.

T-Bob had full confidence he could find a way around the flames. He tested the water with a fingertip, judging currents, and guided his brother with hand signals. He avoided channels that seemed too stagnant, knowing they'd only dead-end into a pond or pool. Instead, he kept to the flowing water and aimed them in a sweeping arc around the fires.

As he helped turn the canoe into a new stream, a strange odor struck his nose. Though it was faint, it was still like a slap in the face. The smell of the swamp was as familiar as his wife's slim body. He knew every exhalation of the bayou, no matter the season or the weather. His nostril crinkled. What he smelled had no part here.

He lifted a hand and formed a fist. Peeyot turned his paddle and slowed the canoe to a gentle and silent stop.

'Why are we—' one of the men asked.

T-Bob silenced him with a glare and an upraised hand. With the goggles in place, the agent looked more like an insect than a man.

Stupid *couyon*.

T-Bob turned his attention to the dark forest. He let the others keep watch with their high-tech gadgets. His senses were sharper.

Something had passed through here.

But was it still around?

T-Bob again let his eyelids drift lower, listening with his entire body to each splash, chirp, crackle, and rustle. A picture of the bayou formed in his mind's eye. As he sank deeper, he discerned a funnel of sound off in the distance, shaped both by noises and silences: a series of plopping frogs, the sudden interruption of a woodpecker's tapping, the chittering flight of a squirrel.

Something was out there and on the move.

Slowly, furtively.

It was heading toward the fire, rather than away.

113

Coming toward them.

T-Bob pointed, and his brother shoved off the muddy bottom of the stream. He glided the canoe expertly down the indicated channel. T-Bob no longer avoided the flames. He aimed their canoe straight toward the heart of the inferno. It was their only chance, to vanish into the fire's heat and smoke and hope the hunter didn't follow.

But for that to succeed, they needed to move swiftly and silently.

Behind him, a radio squelched loudly – then a voice called. 'Team One. Report in.'

The Border Patrol agent placed a hand on his radio, but T-Bob stopped him from unclipping it and shook his head. The four in the boat went dead still, eyes staring outward. They waited a long breath.

Except for the fire's rumble, the swamp had gone silent around them.

'I'm getting no answer from Mansour's team,' Scott reported in.

Seated stiffly in the canoe, Jack was about to reply when a spat of rifle fire echoed across the bayou. It sounded as close as the next tree, but he knew it had to have come from at least a mile off.

They had their answer.

Lorna was right. The cat was here.

Jack lifted the radio. 'How long until the chopper gets here?'

'ETA in five.'

'Have it sweep to the east. Toward where the others went.' He remembered Lorna's concern about the helicopter's lights, rotorwash, and engine scaring off the jaguar. He prayed it would work. 'Tell the pilot to keep low to the tree line. Maximum noise.'

Randy called from the back of the boat. 'What's going on?'

Jack kept the radio to his lips. 'And, Scotty, watch yourselves over there. Get everyone back on board.'

'Already done. We're watching both shorelines. Are you heading back to the boat?'

Jack felt the eyes of the other men on him. 'No. We'll continue on. Try to circle past the fire and offer support to whoever's trapped at the farm. They may need our fire-power with that cat on the loose.'

'Aye, sir. Understood.'

Jack lowered the radio.

Randy spoke from the stern. 'So we're going on?'

He nodded. 'We're almost around the fire.'

Jack stared through his goggles. The heat and glow of the inferno were plain through the trees. He hated to turn his back on the Thibodeaux brothers and his other teammates, but it would take them longer than five minutes to retreat out of the swamp and even longer to track the other canoe's path on the far side of the canal.

Jack pointed to a wider flowing stream heading due south. If it ran relatively straight, they could use it to skirt the edge of the fire and reach the alligator farm.

Randy sighed and shoved off. The two other men paddled. The canoe glided into the channel, and they were off again. Jack tracked the encroachment of the forest fire.

Unfortunately, the channel grew narrower and tree limbs lowered, until it felt like they were traveling through a chute, made even more pronounced by the tunnel vision of his goggles. Jack crouched low, and still low-hanging branches batted at his helmet and beards of moss slapped his face.

Randy swore behind him.

But at least the fires stayed to the east of them.

Unfortunately the stream grew more tortuous, taking sudden twists and opening into stagnant side pools. Fireflies swirled in the night, creating luminous silver-green clouds through his goggles.

Half blinded by a swarm, Jack did not see the branch. It smacked him in the face and clawed at his cheek. He shoved it out of the way, only then realizing his mistake.

The branch was soft, covered in cloth.

The body fell out of the tree overhead and crashed atop the canoe. Limbs tangled; men shouted in surprise and horror. Jack ripped off his goggles and yelled for everyone to calm down.

The corpse draped half in the water, facedown, over the edge of the canoe. It was missing a leg, a hand.

Randy pointed a paddle ahead.

Jack twisted. The glow from the nearby fires lit up a gruesome sight. Another two bodies hung in the trees like macabre Christmas decorations. As he stared, thick droplets of blood splashed into the water.

Jack glanced past them. About twenty yards away, a fence crossed the stream, sealing it off. A sign hung there. Though it was dark, he could still make out the red lettering.

NO TRESPASSING.

It had to be the outskirts to the alligator farm.

They'd made it. Confirming this, Jack heard people shouting off in the distance. The roar of the fire obscured any words. But Jack discerned brighter voices among the tumult.

Children.

'Keep moving!' Jack said.

His two men dumped the body overboard. Paddles splashed, and the canoe glided forward, passing under the draped bodies. A cold drop stuck the back of Jack's hand. He stared down at the splash of crimson, then back at the bodies. The positioning of the dead men so near the farm seemed too purposeful, as if they'd been left as a warning, the cat marking her territory.

Exactly how smart was this beast?

Chapter 18

Stella yelled to be heard above the scared cries and sobs of the children. 'Spread the campfires in a circle around us! Stoke them high!'

'Why are we staying here?' one den mother asked. 'The fire's spreading. We'll be trapped.'

Stella noted other eyes staring at them. Many of them hadn't seen the big cat or how quickly the monster moved. If they tried to escape on foot, it would pick them off one at a time.

'The campsite is open space,' Stella shouted. 'The wind is heading the other direction. And even if the fires circle us, we have access to water to soak ourselves. But just in case, we should start wetting down bandannas, be ready to cover noses and mouths against the smoke if the wind shifts.'

'She's right,' her father said, nodding to her. 'We're safest if we stick here.'

He was covered in soot and sweat. He had been helping the men and older boys with setting up the protective ring of fires. Her mother was with some of the other women, keeping the younger children corralled together, trying to stave off panic.

'Someone's coming!' a man yelled, pushing up to them but pointing back at the farm.

Stella and her father turned. Three figures stood on one of the boardwalks on the far side of the breeding ponds.

Smoke wafted over them. The fire raged nearby.

Where had they come from?

A fourth man climbed over one of the border fences and joined the others.

'Are those Gar's men?' her father asked.

'I don't think so.'

Stella squinted. A gust of wind cleared the smoke for a second. Three of the men wore uniforms, had helmets. They all carried weapons. 'Look like the military.'

They definitely weren't Gar's cronies.

In fact, she had seen neither hide nor hair of Garland Chase since the fire. After fleeing the burning house, he had hightailed it toward the radio shack near the edge of the farm. It sat on the highest ground, its roof bristling with antennas. Gar must have decided to hole up there, the coward likely barricading himself inside.

On the other side of the farm, the four men had gathered and now pounded across the elevated walkways. They headed straight toward the campsite. The closer they got, the more sure Stella grew about her initial assessment. The men wore combat uniforms and carried assault weapons. As they ran, they guarded both sides of the boardwalk as if expecting to be attacked.

Did they know about the giant cat?

In less than a minute, the four men came running up. Her father and the scoutmaster met them. The leader of the combat team stood a head taller than the others. He studied the camp with a calculating eye.

'Agent Jack Menard with the CBP,' the man introduced himself.

So he was with the Border Patrol. As her father gave a thumbnail version of their story, she noted a patch on his uniform. It bore the symbol of a rearing Pegasus with three lightning bolts and the encircling words: *Special Response Team*. They were the elite of the Patrol.

'We have a boat on the far side of the fires,' the man

said. 'Even if it could reach here, it's too small for this many people. But a Coast Guard rescue unit is on its way with helicopters and boats. Once they're here, we can begin ferrying everyone to safety. But it'll take time. We'll need everyone to stay calm.'

Her father lowered his voice. 'You should know that there's some sort of white tiger out there. One hell of a big monster.'

A nod. 'We know. Didn't you get the evacuation warning?'

Her father glanced sheepishly at her, then down.

'Doesn't matter,' the man said, not bothering to scold. *Water under the bridge,* his expression seemed to say. He even clapped her father on the shoulder. 'You've done a good job setting up a perimeter fire wall. If we stay alert and keep weapons ready, we'll be okay.'

Her father's back drew straighter. Stella studied the agent with new eyes, appreciating how he didn't browbeat her father and avoided demoralizing him during such a tense time. Recriminations could come later. For now, the agent wanted everyone focused.

No wonder this man was a leader.

Agent Menard passed on a few orders to his men, then unclipped a radio from his belt. She hovered a step away, eavesdropping.

'We've reached the farm. But there are over sixty people here. Men, women, children. Have you heard from the other team?'

As he listened she noted his fingers tighten on the radio.

His voice cracked, bright with anger, thickening his Cajun accent. 'She's gone and done what?'

Lorna headed overland through a section of bottomland forest. Two Border Patrol agents flanked her: Garcia and Childress. Ahead of her trotted Burt. The hound's nose was buried in the marsh grasses. The dog ran with his tail high.

She carried her assembled tranquilizer gun stiffly in front of her. It was a .50-caliber Pneu-Dart rifle loaded with a clip of five 1.5cc darts containing etorphine hydrocloride, known as M99, a highly potent neuroleptanalgesic. A single drop could kill a man. Five milligrams was enough to drop a rhino. Still, once darted, the drug took time to send an animal into a catatonic state.

So she was happy to have Garcia and Childress at her back with their assault rifles.

The three of them had left the CBP's Zodiac tied up on to the eastern bank of the channel. Minutes ago, they'd all heard the sporadic gunfire from the team on this side of the canal. Then nothing since. They'd kept watch on the forest through night-vision goggles, but there had been no sign of the other team.

Still, during that vigil, Lorna had spotted something of interest out in the swamp: a heat signature about fifty yards back into the bayou. The shape was indistinct. She couldn't be sure, but it looked too large to be a raccoon. She watched it for a full minute. It didn't move and seemed nested at the foot of a large cypress. Finally the silhouette rose and stretched its back, forming a characteristic feline arch, that seemingly boneless curve so typical of cats. It turned a few times, then settled back down.

Could it be the jaguar's cub, the sibling to Bagheera back at ACRES?

It could explain why the big cat had turned so aggressive. The mother wasn't only defending territory and food supply, but also her child. No wonder she attacked the Thibodeaux boat first. That team had been unlucky enough to pick this side of the channel, where the cub was hidden.

It all came down to the cub.

If they could capture it, get it back to the boat, they'd have the perfect bait for its mother, a way to lure it away from the assaulted team – that is, if the men were still alive. And if not, they'd still have a tool to control the jaguar.

And that's just what she had argued with Scott Nester.

Control the cub, you control the mother.

It was worth the risk of a fast search. She had insisted on coming along, warning Jack's second-in-command that she'd jump overboard and swim to shore if necessary. As they readied the Zodiac, Scott had tried to radio Jack for authorization. But there'd been no response, so Scott finally relented, just as concerned about his teammates' fate.

Still, his instructions had been firm to Garcia and Childress. 'There and back. If it runs off, you don't pursue.' He had pointed at Lorna. 'Drag her back by her hair if she gives you any trouble.'

So they moved swiftly through the forest. They aimed toward the large cypress. But there was no way to move without any noise. Within a few steps, Lorna watched the cub's silhouette slip behind the bole of the tree, alerted to their presence.

Was it still there or had it run off?

Generally cubs tend to stick to their nests, even in the face of danger. She recalled a nature documentary in which an entire litter of lion cubs was killed by a cobra, simply because they feared leaving their den. With any luck, the cub was still there.

As Lorna hiked, she caught the barest whisker of a heat signature through her goggles. The cub was still behind the tree, but it looked ready to bolt. She dared not try tranquilizing it. The darts were too potent for something so small.

But she couldn't let it get away.

'Burt . . .'

The hound stopped, one ear cocked back, listening, but he kept his nose fixed ahead. He didn't need any goggles to pick out the cub. Lorna had to trust that the hound was typical of hunting dogs in the area, trained like most to hunt raccoons.

And there was only one sure way of catching a raccoon.

'Go tree him, boy,' she commanded.

Burt lunged ahead, running low, spearing through the grass. He angled to the side, circling out and around. He wasn't about to let his prey escape into the deeper woods.

As Lorna had hoped, the cub stuck to its instincts. It didn't want to leave the spot where its mother had left it, but it also recognized the threat in Burt. Reacting on pure feline instinct, the cub shot up the cypress.

Burt hit the tree, letting out a loud bawl, announcing his success.

They all took off at a run toward the treed cat.

Lorna hated to terrify the small creature, but she also recognized the necessity of its capture.

And quickly.

The dog's barking was surely already drawing the big cat in their direction. Lorna reached the tree first. 'Quiet, Burt.'

The hound bounded about the trunk, excited, tongue lolling, but he obeyed and stopped his bawling.

The cub was perched on a limb overhead. Barely newborn, it hadn't been able to climb too high. Huge eyes, glassy with fear, stared down at them. It hissed a warning, its coat bristling out in all directions.

Lorna had brought along a thick red fire blanket, carried over one shoulder. She set down her rifle, unfurled the blanket, and tossed it like a net over the cub. The weight and the surprise rolled the cub off its perch. Tangled in the blanket, it fell, but Lorna caught it in her arms. It squirmed and fought inside the bundled blanket, but like its sibling it was malnourished. It didn't have much fight.

She hugged the cub through the blanket, trying to stifle its panic with a calming pressure. From inside came a plaintive mewling. The sound tugged at her heart.

Poor thing.

'Ma'am, time to go,' Garcia said.

He and his partner held their rifles tight to their shoulders. They all strained to listen for any telltale sign of an angry mother barreling toward them. Instead, a different noise intruded: a heavy *thump-thumping*.

They all turned to the north. Lorna winced as the bright lights flared in her goggles. It had to be the helicopter Jack had called down from Bay Lanaux. One-handed, she pushed the goggles to her forehead. Darkness enveloped her, and the brightness dissolved to a dot in the sky. The chopper was still a half mile off, but the noise grew louder with every heartbeat.

'Let's go,' Garcia pressed.

Lorna reached her free arm and grabbed her rifle from the grass.

As she straightened, she found herself staring at a pair of large eyes deep in the forest, reflecting the meager light, glowing in the dark.

She froze.

A deep growl flowed from Burt.

Then, in a blink, the eyes vanished.

She backed away in a hurried stumble.

'What's wrong?' Childress asked.

'Run!'

Chapter 19

Lorna clambered from the Zodiac up into the boat. She was winded. Her heart pounded in her throat. Reaching the open deck, she gazed back toward shore.

Why hadn't the big cat given chase?

Overhead, the helicopter hovered. Its rotors pounded down at them, shaking the leaves and branches of the tree line.

Though they had reached the boat with their precious cargo, she knew they were all far from safe. The tree line was only ten yards off. The cat could easily leap that distance from a dead standstill.

Garcia and Childress recognized this danger, too. As soon as their boots hit the deck, they spun with their rifles up and pointed toward the shore.

Burt hopped up from the Zodiac and sniffed at the blanket-wrapped parcel in Lorna's arms.

Scott Nester joined them. He had to yell to be heard. 'You found the kitten?'

'Cub,' Lorna corrected. 'And its mother.'

Scott stared at the dark bank. Nothing moved. 'Garcia? Do you see anything?'

'Nothing but friggin' fireflies.' The man kept alert, but the taut tension in his shoulders loosened. 'Maybe Dr. Polk only saw some reflection off the water. Childress and I didn't see anything out there.'

'She's out there,' Lorna insisted. It hadn't been refracted starlight off water. Those glowing eyes still burned in her memory, bright with a cunning intelligence.

'If you're right,' Scott said, 'then she'll stick close, knowing we have her cub. That should keep her away from the men out there.'

Lorna read the unspoken caveat in the man's worried expression.

If any of them are still alive.

Lorna hiked the cub higher in her arms. It had settled, the warmth and darkness lulling it into submission. She stared out at the dark woods.

Why hadn't the cat come after them? Lorna sensed it wasn't the noise and blaze of the hovering helicopter that held her back. She'd had no fear of attacking the airboat and its pilot.

The cub squirmed, seeking a more comfortable spot. While this cub wasn't as sickly as the one they'd recovered from the shipwrecked trawler, it was still in poor shape. Had the mother known that and given up on the cub? Was that why she hadn't given chase?

Lorna refused to believe that. The mother had gone to great lengths to protect her child thus far. She would not give up so readily.

So then where was she? What was her plan?

Another five minutes passed. Still, there remained no sign of her. The helicopter made a sweeping pass, its searchlight spearing the dark forest below.

Scott retreated to the far side of the boat, talking and coordinating with the Coast Guard on his satellite phone. The rescue force would arrive on site in another ten minutes.

Burt curled on the deck, his nose tucked under his tail. The dog seemed little concerned – and that worried her. The wind blew out of the east. If the cat's scent was in the air, Burt should still be wired, pacing the deck, whining.

'She's gone,' Lorna mumbled.

Behind her, Scott's voice grew agitated. She turned as he lowered his radio and hurried over to Lorna.

'Jack radioed in. The cat's been spotted over at the farm. Why isn't it here? I thought you said she'd stay by her cub.'

Lorna turned and stared toward the burning cabin, digesting the new information. The helicopter swept past, stirring hot smoke over the channel, yet careful not to fan the flames toward them. Still, fiery ash rained over the boat and sizzled into the water.

'I'm sending the chopper Jack's way,' Scott said. 'See if it can't chase that monster away from the children.'

Despite the heat, Lorna went cold. *Children*. Slowly she sensed an inkling of the cat's intent. She thrust out an arm.

'Give me the radio. I need to speak to Jack now!'

Jack inspected the circle of fires. They completely surrounded the campsite. Randy kept in step beside him. They both carried their rifles. Jack had everyone retreat into the center of the camp's tents, as far from the edge of the bayou as possible. Only those with weapons kept guard near the flames.

Still, they only had seven men.

Not enough to keep a perfect vigil on the forest.

With the fires blazing high, Jack's night-vision goggles were useless. The surrounding old-growth forest remained a dark, impenetrable wall. The cat had been spotted briefly by one of Jack's men. But it was gone before he could even shift his rifle into position.

'Fucking ghost' were the words used to describe it.

Randy spoke at his side. 'She's playing with us. Like a cat with a bunch of mice.'

Jack knew what his brother meant. The jaguar had proven to be a skilled hunter. She wouldn't have allowed herself to be spotted so easily. It was as if she were testing them.

Something felt wrong about this.

His teeth ached with tension of it all.

'Over here!' a man shouted on the far side of the

encampment. It was one of the scoutmasters. His rifle blasted.

Other men scrambled toward his position.

Some fired blindly.

Randy made a move to follow, but Jack grabbed his arm. 'No!'

Maybe it was his years of hunting the bayou, or his two tours playing cat and mouse with insurgents in Iraq, but Jack recognized that they were being set up.

He scanned the forests to either side. Randy understood, mirroring his action, his rifle poised and ready at his shoulder. But there was too much ground to cover for just the two of them.

Jack spotted the danger too late.

On the far side of a tent to the left.

A boy had been carrying firewood – a camp chair broken into kindling – toward the stockpile near one edge of the tents. He had stopped, half turned toward the sound of the gunshots. Behind him, a large shape burst out of the forest. In one bound, the cat hurdled the fires and landed within their secured area.

The attack was so fast, the boy didn't even have a chance to scream.

The cat grabbed him by the back of the shirt, spun off one paw, and leaped back over the fire and into the woods with the child.

Jack had his rifle up and pointed, but he had hesitated for a fraction of a heartbeart, afraid he'd hit the child, an instinctual reaction. And the wrong one. The boy was dead either way.

At his waist, his radio kicked in. 'Jack! Come in!'

He would've ignored the call, but the voice was Lorna's, and she sounded panicked. He snatched the radio and lifted it to his lips.

'What is it?' he barked, unable to hold back his frustration and anger.

'The cat! I think she's going for the children.'

Jack let out a shuddering breath. 'You're too late. She already attacked and killed a boy.'

'Killed? No, Jack, that's not what—'

From the forest, a sharp cry echoed out. Jack lowered the radio. It had to be the boy. His wails continued to echo out of the darkness, rising and falling in raw terror.

But at least he was still alive!

Relief fired through Jack, but also worry.

Why was the boy still alive?

Jack remembered Randy's description of the cat and the mouse, which suggested one grim answer.

Cats played with their food before killing it.

As Jack listened, the screaming went on and on.

Lorna heard the cries through the radio's open channel. That was enough. She turned and shoved the radio at Scott. 'Call the chopper back.'

The helicopter had begun to sweep toward the farm.

'What for?'

'I need to get over there! With the cub!'

Scott frowned but he didn't argue and lifted the radio. He shouted into it. Seconds later, the helicopter retreated back toward the boat. He lowered the radio.

'We can't land the chopper on the deck,' Scott said. 'They're going to drop a harness. It's a short hop over the fire to the farm.'

As realization struck her, Lorna felt instantly ill. Her blood drained to her feet. Her stomach tried to follow.

'They can haul you all the way up into the helicopter,' Scott explained. 'But it'll be quicker if they don't have to. They can simply ferry you in the harness.'

As she pictured swinging by a wire, the helicopter returned with a pounding sweep of its rotors. She looked up. Spooling from a winch by the chopper's side door, a thick cable lowered down a yellow rescue harness.

She suddenly regretted her rash decision. She hadn't fully

thought this through. It was bad enough flying in a chopper while *inside* the cabin.

The harness arrived, swinging and bobbing. Garcia grabbed it and hauled it toward her. She fought not to back away. It took all her will to simply hold her ground.

Scott took the blanket-wrapped cub as Garcia helped her into the harness. He slipped it over her head and under her arms, then cinched it tightly. 'Are you okay?' he asked.

As answer, she pointed. 'Pass me my rifle.'

Childress retrieved the tranquilizer gun from the deck. With a bit of effort, she awkwardly slung it over her shoulder. Once she was ready, Scott passed the cub back to her. She hugged it to her chest.

Scott gave her a questioning thumbs-up.

Not trusting her voice, she merely nodded.

Satisfied, Scott backed a step and twirled his arm over his head.

The engine above gunned harder, and the harness suddenly dug into her armpits. Her legs lifted off the deck. She kicked, anxious to touch ground again. But it was too late. The helicopter climbed while, at the same time, the winch retracted several yards of the cable.

She stared down as the boat dropped away under her. She tore her gaze away. She wanted to close her eyes but knew that would terrify her even more. Ahead, the log home still blazed. The roof had long caved in, leaving behind a smoldering frame. Smoke poured upward, licking with flames.

The helicopter climbed higher, aiming to fly over the ruins. She didn't think they'd make it. The pilot must have thought the same. The winch hauled her up farther. Then they were over the inferno.

The chopper's blades cut through the smoke and swirled a searing tornado around her. She held her breath and finally closed her eyes. The heat scorched as if she were flying over the mouth of a volcano. She hugged hard to both the harness and the blanket-wrapped cub.

Seconds later, they were clear. The temperature plummeted. She took a tentative breath of clear air and squinted her eyes open. The view below was peppered by black ponds. Wooden walkways, platforms, and bridges filled the spaces in between, along with a few tin-roofed outbuildings. On the far side of the ponds, a circle of fire lit the dark bayou. People clustered in its center.

The campsite.

The helicopter banked in a gentle arc toward the encampment. Momentum swung her outward on the cable. Wind rushed over her. For just a moment she felt a flush of exhilaration – but only for a moment.

Movement drew her attention directly below.

A man burst out of one of the smaller shacks, an outbuilding sprouting a tangle of antennas. He pounded across the walkway below. He waved a thick black shotgun in one hand and cupped his mouth with the other, shouting. The roar of the helicopter drowned out his words. He must've heard the chopper and thought it was the Coast Guard rescue force.

Frantic that he was ignored, the man ran faster – too fast. He finally spilled over his own legs and went sprawling hard onto the planks. She watched his shotgun strike the boards. Even through the engine's howl, she heard the gun blasts. A staccato series of slugs strafed out of the smoking muzzle.

Then the helicopter lurched above her, bobbling in the air.

Like a hooked trout on a line, she rocked and jerked in the harness.

Clutching for her life, she craned up. Oily smoke poured from the back of the helicopter. An unlucky round must have struck something vital.

The chopper tipped on its nose and began a fast descent, trailing flames now.

Lorna stared down as the world rushed up at her.

They were going to crash.

Chapter 20

Jack watched the helicopter plummet out of the sky.

Below its undercarriage, a figure swung in a rescue harness. From the flag of blond hair, Jack knew it was Lorna. The helicopter fought to slow its descent, wobbling wildly, rotors faltering. The pilot had the wherewithal to aim the craft away from the encampment, avoiding the gathered children.

Banking to the west, the chopper swung toward the bayou, dragging Lorna with it. She hung thirty feet below its floats. As the aircraft dropped, she struck the boardwalk hard and skidded across the planks on her back, dragged by the crashing helicopter.

But she wasn't hauled far.

The chopper crashed into the forest just beyond the farm's border. Spinning rotors sheared treetops, then the blades broke away and catapulted deeper in the bayou. Jack waited for an explosion, but only a thick cloud of smoke rolled into the sky. The hard-fought descent and cushion of the swampy bower must have blunted the impact.

'Bolton! Reese!' Jack turned to his teammates, bellowing to be heard above the cries and screams from the camp. 'Check on the pilot!'

As they took off Jack sprinted toward the nearest bridge, followed at his heels by Randy. He'd lost sight of Lorna.

Across the farm, a man staggered to his feet, backlit by

flames. He stumbled forward, heading in Lorna's direction, too. He carried a military-grade shotgun. It looked like an AA-12, a combat auto-assault weapon used in urban warfare, capable of chewing apart a steel oil barrel at thirty yards or blasting through walls.

Jack had seen the man fall, followed by the accidental burst from his gun. Must've been running with his finger on the trigger. Goddamn yokel had more firepower than he could handle. He'd seen it often enough in the backwaters.

The bigger the gun, the bigger the ego.

Jack dismissed the jackass and searched for Lorna.

Was she still alive?

Lorna lay on her back, dazed, ears ringing. She must have blacked out for a moment. She rose up on an elbow and heard screaming nearby. As if she were waking from a nightmare, it took her half a breath to remember where she was. She remembered twisting on her back as she hit, protecting herself as best she could as she was dragged. Still, her entire backside felt as if someone had taken a belt sander to it.

A shadow fell over her and growled. 'Jeezus H. Christ! Are you all right?' The nasal tone in his voice pitched higher. 'I didn't mean to shoot. It was an accident, I swear. If you hadn't gone off and kept flying away . . . I mean, didn't you goddamn see me?'

His words were harsh, graveled, more accusation than concern, as if what had happened were all her fault. But there was something else about the voice. Maybe it was the situation: on her back, dazed, woken into a nightmare.

Past and present blurred around her.

The shadowy shape dropped next to her, loomed over her. His face was sculpted out of darkness. He reached for her.

'Don't move.' It sounded like a threat. 'You're all tangled up.'

Still, she pulled away.

132

Something about that voice . . .

All of a sudden it struck her like a blow to the gut. The voice, even the shape of the silhouette leaning over her. She knew this man. Gasping in shock, she scrambled back, as if trying to escape a past that had haunted her for over a decade. She became further snarled in the helicopter's cable and her harness.

'What's wrong with you?' The speaker stepped forward, turning slightly to face the approach of pounding boots, his face lit by the fires.

She stared, shell-shocked. She recognized that man's features: the crooked nose, the fat lips, the piggish eyes. Memory crushed her. An empty space filled inside her with color and noise. In her ears, she heard her own sobbing, her cries to stop, felt again the humiliation and terror. She must've blocked it all away, pushed it deep down with everything else. Traumatized, she had somehow convinced herself that she'd not gotten a good look at her attacker.

She was wrong.

Here was the man who'd tried to rape her ten years ago, whose attack led to Tom's death.

'Lorna!'

She jumped at the call of her name. It was Jack, running toward her, coming to the rescue like before, blurring past and present even further.

Still, Lorna didn't take her eyes off the bastard in front of her. He seemed to shrink and drop back into the shadows as Jack came running up with his brother.

Jack hurried to her side, not even giving the monster a second glance. He dropped hard to his knees. 'Lorna, don't move!'

Though the words were the same as a moment ago, she heard no threat this time, only heartfelt concern in Jack's voice.

'I'm okay,' she said to him, then repeated it for herself. 'I'm okay.'

She grabbed his arm. He helped her up and out of the harness. Over his shoulder, she watched her attacker retreat away, heading across the farm.

'It's him,' she said.

Jack noted where she stared – then stiffened next to her in recognition. His face became a thundercloud.

Randy swore sharply. 'Shoulda known. Garland Chase. Sheriff Gumbo's inbred bastard. Who else would go and shoot half-cocked like that?'

Lorna clutched Jack's shoulder, finally putting a name to a nightmare. *Garland Chase.* Her voice rang with a mix of certainty and disbelief. 'He's the bastard who attacked me. The night Tommy died.'

Randy turned sharply toward her.

'I know,' Jack whispered.

Randy squinted. 'What're you two talking about?'

Jack's brother knew nothing about that night. His family had grown to hate her, to blame her, the same family she'd once hoped would be her own. She began to tremble, perhaps still half in shock from the crash.

Jack took her in his arms and held her.

She didn't resist. She felt the strength in his arms and something indefinable, a warmth and closeness long missing from her life. In his arms, she realized for the first time the true depth of her loss that horrible night – not just the loss of an unborn baby and a young lover, but also an entire family, a future full of love and warmth.

She'd lost it all that night.

Yet, with that recognition came no sorrow. Instead, anger, hot and bright, surged through her. Lorna was done with secrets, sick to the bone of them. She pushed out of Jack's arms – and fully out of that old nightmare. This wasn't the past. She wasn't a scared half-drugged teenager any longer.

She looked around her and spotted her tranquilizer gun. She stalked over to the rifle, picked it up, and hurried ahead.

Fire still blazed down her back with every step, but the pain helped focus her.

Jack came alongside her. 'Lorna, what're you thinking of doing? He's not worth it.'

She burned him with a glare. 'Of course he's not worth it. I'll deal with that bastard later. Right now we have bigger problems.'

She searched to either side of the boardwalk, backtracking along the path on which she'd been dragged. When she hit, she'd lost hold of the blanket and the cub. Both went flying out of her arms on impact. But where had they gone?

She rounded another pond – a breeding pond from the looks of it – and spotted a flash of crimson below, near the water's edge. Beyond the rail, a grassy bank ringed the pond. The fire blanket and its cargo had rolled halfway into the water.

Lorna set down her rifle, ducked under the rail, and dropped below.

Ahead, the blanket squirmed. A plaintive mewl sounded. The motion sent ripples across the pond's mirror. Out on the water, black logs drifted closer, drawn by the motion. A scaly-ridged pair of eyes rose like a submarine's periscope from the water.

A pair of boots struck the grassy mud behind her.

Jack.

She kept her focus on the pond, on the blanket, and rushed forward. She reached the bank in four steps. The blanket shook as the trapped cub struggled to escape the water.

If it got loose . . . ran off . . .

A hem of the blanket lifted. She spotted a tiny white muzzle, whiskers. Lorna lunged forward, sliding on her knees in the mud. She grabbed the blanket and scooped up the cub.

'Gotcha . . .'

She leaned back, pulling the cub to her chest. She rolled to her feet and straightened – when water exploded from the pond's edge. An alligator burst out, jaws wide, fish-belly–white maw and yellow teeth flashing in the dark.

Lorna jerked back, but she was too slow.

The jaws snapped with enough force to shatter bone. Teeth caught the trailing edge of the blanket and ripped it out of her grip. The beast surged back and tossed its leathery head. The blanket went flying, and the cub got hurled along with it. The small cat hit the grass, rolled, then pounced back to its tiny paws. It took off like a flash of lightning away from the pond.

No . . .

Lorna knew she'd never be quick enough to catch it again. If it reached the open bayou –

– but Jack dove across its path. Like a tight end catching a fumbled football, he snatched the panicked cub in mid-flight. He rolled with the cat clutched to his belly. As he came to a stop, shadows stirred under the boardwalk behind him.

'Jack!'

An alligator surged out of the darkness, barreling on four legs toward the man on the ground. Jack would never gain his feet in time. The gator lunged toward him.

'No, you don't, leatherface!'

A dark shape dropped down from above and landed on the alligator's back. Randy whooped and used his weight to pin the creature down, sprawling on top. The alligator twisted and rolled, but Randy kept hold. Lorna dodged out of the way as the pair came wrestling past. Before they hit the water, Randy rabbit-kicked with both legs into the gator's belly. The armored creature went flying, tail whipping, and splashed far out into the pond.

Lorna hurried and helped Randy up. More leathery logs floated toward them. It was time to get out of here.

She grabbed the sodden blanket from the water. And it was a good thing she did.

Jack was on his feet and struggling with the feral cub. Panicked and as large as a medium-size dog, it clawed and ripped at him, shredding his uniform's sleeves. But he refused to let go, his face clenched in pain.

She rushed to him with the blanket held wide. 'Give him to me!'

Jack gladly shoved the squirming mass of claws and needle-sharp saber teeth at her. She wrapped the cub again and bundled it up. The three of them hurried back to the boardwalk and climbed up onto the planks.

'Why is that little monster so important?' Jack asked as he stood. Blood rolled down his arms and dripped from his fingertips.

Lorna started to answer – then the words died in her throat. While turning to explain, she happened to glance down the boardwalk toward the forest's edge.

The answer to Jack's question crouched at the end of the boardwalk. It was a mountain of muscle, claws, and fangs, far larger than she had expected. It practically filled the boardwalk. The jaguar stared straight at Lorna.

A primal fear gripped her chest, making it hard to breathe. *How long had she been there?*

Moonlight and firelight washed over the cat's snowy fur. From its snarling jaws hung a small boy, limp and lifeless, caught by his scouting vest. According to Jack's radio message, the boy's name was Tyler.

Was he dead?

Then the boy's arm lifted weakly.

Still alive . . . thank God . . . but plainly in shock . . .

Jack swung around. He raised his rifle, but hesitated. Tyler still lived, but a shot that failed to drop the big cat immediately would likely result in the boy being mauled to death.

'Don't,' Lorna warned.

She stepped ahead of Jack. She parted the blanket to reveal the cub, hiking the little fellow higher.

C'mon, you know what you really want . . .

Still staring at her, the jaguar lowered the boy to the

planks, but kept one paw on his chest, pinning Tyler down.

'Lorna . . .'

She kept her gaze fixed forward, recognizing the preternatural intelligence in those eyes. 'I know what I'm doing,' she whispered back to Jack.

At least, she hoped she did.

Chapter 21

Gar lay flat on his stomach, trying his best not to be seen. His shotgun was trapped under him, but he feared shifting to free it.

Ten seconds ago, he'd been trotting back toward the safety of the radio shack. He and his buddies had stashed a case of Budweiser in there and had been taking turns during the day to slip inside and wet their whistles. What could it hurt? Gar had never really believed the story of a monster cat loose in the bayou. Christ, how many tall tales had he heard about the swamps over the years, many coming from his own mouth?

Figuring it was easy money, Gar had been more than happy to lounge around the farm, drink a few beers. He even emptied a couple of the campers' wallets, pilfered from unsupervised backpacks.

All in a day's work.

But now everything had changed.

While fleeing across the farm, he'd spotted a flash of white out in the forest, flowing straight at him. Reacting instinctively, he had turned and hopped over the boardwalk gate and onto the plank on the far side. The timber stuck out like a diving board over a pond. He had dropped flat to the board – and just in time.

The huge cat had bounded over the border fence and landed on the boardwalk twenty yards from him.

He continued to hold his breath, stifling a cry of terror. Under his bulging gut, he felt every nail head and knot in the wood. His bladder quivered, threatening to let loose. But he didn't move.

It would be death to be seen.

Voices drew his attention to the other side of the board-walk. He watched the woman from the helicopter cautiously ease toward the cat. She held a bundle of blankets up in her arms. Behind her, he recognized the Menard brothers – Jack and Randy. Even through his terror, a twinge of hatred burned in his chest. Jack had once broken his nose, knocked out his two front teeth. Gar had wanted him dead at the time. But instead his daddy got the bastard shipped off to Iraq.

Now Jack was back.

At the moment Gar was plenty happy about that. Jack had an assault rifle pinned at his shoulder, aimed toward the cat.

Kill the fucker, Gar silently cursed at him.

But Jack didn't shoot.

And Gar could guess why. He'd also spotted the boy. The cat crouched lower over the little snot-eater.

Shoot already, damn it!

The blond woman stopped a few paces past Gar's hiding spot. She dropped to one knee and placed the blanketed bundle on the planks. With her back to him, he couldn't make out what she was doing.

Something with the blanket . . . and under the blanket.

Why didn't the monster attack her?

She finally straightened and retreated back toward Jack and his brother. 'Go on,' she mumbled under her breath as she passed Gar's hiding spot again. 'Come get your baby.'

On the other side of the boardwalk, a low growl flowed from the cat – felt more in the gut than heard with the ears. It took one pace forward, then another, abandoning the unconscious boy. It slinked forward, low to the ground. Its tail swished in clear agitation, whipping side to side. Muscles bunched and trembled. Its lips pulled back into a silent snarl, baring huge-ass fangs.

As it came closer Gar tried to press harder against the planks. His bowels churned with a slippery queasiness. Cold sweat soaked his clothes.

Why wasn't the bastard shooting?

Lorna held a hand up, urging Jack to hold his fire. Jaguar skulls were the thickest of all large cats, necessary to support the strength of their powerful jaw muscles. Even at close range, a shot to the head might only glance away, and a nonfatal shot would turn their standoff into a bloodbath. She had to trust that the cat wanted to protect her last child, to make this trade.

Her cub in exchange for the boy.

Lorna gambled all her hopes – and their lives – on the fact that the cat hadn't slain the child.

The jaguar crept forward. Its eyes shone a tawny gold. Most felines had slitted pupils, but not jaguars. She watched the cat's pupils stretch wider, thrumming with adrenaline.

Lorna shifted from foot to foot, keeping the cat focused on her. Steps away, the jaguar reached the blanket, close enough for Lorna to catch a whiff of the muskiness of its wet pelt. It massed before her, a wall of savage intent, beautiful and terrifying at the same time. Large eyes shone with that preternatural intelligence again, studying her. The cat shifted closer, muscles bunching and rolling under the fur like a tidal prehistoric force.

If Lorna reached out a hand now, she could almost touch it.

A part of her wanted to – to prove it existed, to commune even for a moment with something that did not belong in this world. In the shine of those eyes, she sensed a bottomless depth, something more than *cat* staring out at her.

Then the moment broke.

Until now, the cub at her feet had been silent, but it caught a whiff of its mother. The cub scrabbled in the snarl of blankets, trying to wrestle itself free.

The mother glanced down.

Not good.

Lorna needed the mother's attention focused on her. She stamped her foot. The jaguar hissed and crouched lower, eyes darting back up to Lorna.

That's right. Keep looking at me.

The cat swatted out a huge splayed paw. Yellow nails caught the edge of the blanket. Then just as quickly the cat jerked her paw back. A black dart flew from the paw's pad and spun away into the night.

A moment ago, while setting down the cub, Lorna had jammed two tranquilizing darts between the planks of the boardwalk, the needles pointed up. She had hoped that the big cat might step on one of them, stabbing and injecting herself. Without being accompanied by a gunshot or a stinging impact, the needle prick might be ignored.

Or so she prayed.

The cat growled low and harsh. Before Lorna could even step back, the jaguar lunged forward. Panicked, shocked at its speed, Lorna tripped backward and fell hard onto her backside. But the cat ignored her. The mother grabbed both the blanket and her cub in her teeth, then spun around in a blur of fur and muscle and bounded back toward the cover of the forest.

Lorna knew that in another ten minutes the tranquilizer would melt away the cat's consciousness, sending her into a catatonic state. After that, it would be safe to track the jaguar and collect her unconscious body.

Lorna allowed herself a moment of relief, letting out a long-held breath. They'd done it –

– then the *crack* of a gun made her jump and flinch. Ahead, a flash of crimson exploded from the jaguar's left haunch. The impact caught the cat in mid-leap. Knocked around, the jaguar landed on her side and slid right next to the boy's slack body.

Lorna swung to Jack and his brother, but they looked just as startled.

'Take that, you motherfucker!' a harsh call shouted in triumph.

She twisted around to see a figure rise from beyond the boardwalk, seeming to hover in midair over the neighboring pond. It was that bastard Garland Chase. He had his shotgun up. He fired again and again.

The cat writhed with the impacts. But this was no bobcat. She was bloodied, but far from incapacitated. To the side, Lorna spotted a pile of white fur on the wood. The cub. Knocked loose by the fall and crushed under its mother's bulk, it lay limp and lifeless, its neck twisted wrong.

The shotgun blasts grew wilder as the man realized the cat was not down. A section of the wood railing exploded beside the jaguar. The cat burst toward them. In a blood rage, confused by the blasts and the pain, the cat attacked the closest targets. It leaped straight at Lorna, Jack, and Randy.

The sharp retort of a rifle blast deafened her left ear.

She ducked instinctively but noted the right orbit of the cat's eye shatter away into a cloud of blood and gore. The jaguar's attack halted in mid-lunge, as if hitting a wall. Her massive bulk dropped to the boards, legs splayed out.

Lorna started to straighten, but Jack grabbed her shoulder with one hand. He stepped past her, the muzzle of his rifle smoking. He approached the cat warily, his gun still up. Randy covered him.

But the cat was clearly dead.

Both mother and child.

A cry drew her attention over the rail of the boardwalk. A gate led out to a plank extending over the neighboring pond. It was the hiding spot from which Garland Chase had shot at the cat, endangering everyone. But the man was gone – no, not gone.

'Help me!'

She gained her feet and spotted Garland hanging from the plank's end by his fingertips. In his panic, he must have lost his footing.

To the side, Randy hurried past the cat to check on the boy. The gunshots had stirred Tyler out of his stupor. The boy pushed up groggily.

Lorna unlatched the gate. 'Jack, I need a hand over here.'

He turned – just as water erupted out of the black pond below.

A scaly shape lunged upward, jaws wide. Yellow teeth clamped onto one of Garland's kicking legs. He wailed as the bulk of the giant alligator ripped him from his perch. Flailing, Garland and the alligator crashed back into the water.

Lorna rushed down the plank. Below, the water churned as the gator rolled and shredded its prey. A pale hand swept into view then vanished again.

Jack joined her. He pointed his rifle, but there was no clear shot. The black water hid the fight below.

Across the pond, a voice called out. 'Elvis! No!'

A young woman stood atop an observation deck on the far side. She dove over the railing and into the water.

'What is she doing?' Jack asked. He lunged forward, clearly intending to dive in after her.

Lorna clutched his arm. 'Wait.'

The woman clearly worked here. She had called the gator by name. Lorna knew some alligators learned to recognize their handlers, even coming when called. Other trainers sometimes swam with their gators.

As the woman disappeared, the waters grew calmer. The frenzy died away. Moments later, she reappeared, dragging a slack figure by the collar. A greasy crimson sheen followed in their wake.

Blood.

'Help!' the young woman hollered.

Behind her, the alligator surfaced in the pond. The specimen had to be over fifteen feet long. From its jaws, a pale limb protruded, a leg torn away at the knee. Content with its prize, the alligator drifted away.

Lorna turned and hurried toward a set of steps that led down to the pond's bank. Below, the girl struggled to haul the victim's body out of the water.

Jack followed at Lorna's heels.

'I need your belt!' she called back to him.

As much as she hated to do it, she had to save the bastard's life.

Chapter 22

Hidden in the bayou, Duncan Kent sat in an ebony-hulled jet boat. He sucked on a cherry Life Savers. Four other men, all equipped in body armor, shared the craft with him. Another boat, a twin to his, floated twenty yards to his right. The team, ten in all, had been handpicked by Duncan. They were the elite of Ironcreek Industries.

Duncan studied the alligator farm through a pair of night-vision binoculars. Since sunset, the two boats had run dark through the swamps. The only light in Duncan's boat was the small GPS unit held in his other hand. He had used the device to track the specimen from the coast. Each beast of the Babylon Project had been tagged with an electronic marker.

The plan was for a quick kill and extraction, to take down the jaguar during the night and leave no trace behind. As luck would have it, the first part of his mission had already been accomplished. He stared through the binoculars at the cooling bulk of the great cat. It was a significant loss, but not a fatal one to the Babylon Project.

He recalculated his mission objectives as he watched a small group labor around an injured man on the ground. The man writhed in agony, while another sat on his chest. A blond woman set about cinching a makeshift tourniquet around a severed limb.

Duncan lowered his binoculars. His team had arrived too

late. Even with the tracker, it had taken too long to home in on their target.

No matter.

With the cat dead, the body would have to be secured. But not now, not with the Coast Guard on its way. He would have to bide his time, discover where it was taken. Still, bile burned in his gut. He had warned the CEO of Ironcreek about the risks of transporting specimens during a tropical storm, but his warning had fallen on deaf ears. His superiors were on a tight timetable. The specimens had been headed to Ironcreek headquarters in Bethesda, Maryland, to demonstrate the viability of the Babylon Project.

It was essential to Ironcreek's future. When it came to private military contracting, competition had grown fierce. With wars being fought on two fronts – Iraq and Afghanistan – the business of supplying men, supplies, and new technologies for the battlefield had grown into a multibillion-dollar industry. Ironcreek competed with Raytheon, AirScan, Dyn-Corp, and many others for government contracts. The key to thriving in this environment was to carve out a unique niche, to supply a service or product unlike any other.

Where outfits like Blackwater specialized in security and protection services, Ironcreek Industries concentrated on research and development for the military. In fact, their main competition wasn't from other private outfits, but from DARPA itself, the U.S. Defense Department's R&D agency.

Already the government was moving forward with various bioengineering projects, treading too heavily into Ironcreek's territory. DARPA was wiring rats and sharks with cerebral implants, learning to control them like biological robots. They were inserting electronic chips into insect larvae, so moths and flies would mature with the chips grown *inside* them. The list went on and on. The latest had DARPA dabbling into the genome itself, to find ways of enhancing performance through direct genetic manipulation.

To survive, Ironcreek needed a leg up in this burgeoning industry. They found it in Iraq within a biological weapons facility hidden in the heart of the Baghdad Zoo, a laboratory Ironcreek learned about from intelligence tortured out of an Iraqi military scientist. They had paid well to keep that intelligence secured within their own circles.

Duncan had been the one sent over to secure the research and any viable specimens. He had paid for the bounty with his own flesh. Written across his body in scars was proof of the project's viability. On the left side of his face, four ropy scars ran from the crown of his head to his chin. After a week in a coma, it took nine surgeries to rebuild his nose, fix his broken jaw, and screw in dental implants. Damage to his salivary glands and ducts left him perpetually dry-mouthed, alleviated somewhat by sucking on lozenges and hard candies.

More scars mapped his body – but not all of them were physical. Some nights he woke with his sheets tangled, soaked with sweat, his lips snarled in a scream of pain and terror. Memories of that morning in Baghdad – of the beast leaping on him, tearing into him – marked him as surely as any scar.

The creature had once been a chimpanzee. If it hadn't been half starved and debilitated by neglect, Duncan would not have survived. Still, he had given his blood for this project. He wasn't about to see it exposed and destroyed. Not when they were so close.

He recognized that there were problems, like the recent aberrations that had begun to arise at the test station on Lost Eden Cay. But when it came to success in the market-place, speed often outweighed precaution. *Safety first* was the motto of the spineless.

Duncan lifted an arm and waved it in a circle. The quiet burble of the boats' water-jet engines grew sharper as the boats turned away and fled back toward the extraction point.

'Sir?' his second-in-command asked, filling that one word with both respect and meaning.

What's the plan now? he was asking.

Duncan pocketed his GPS unit. 'The surviving specimens are still locked up at that animal research facility by the river.'

In order to safeguard Ironcreek's interest and limit exposure, the test subjects would have to be either secured or destroyed. He checked his watch and calculated a time line. They were running out of night, but he dared not waste another day.

'We'll hit it tonight,' he said. 'A surgical strike before sunrise.'

In his head, he began formulating an attack strategy, but his second-in-command had one more question.

'Sir?'

Once again, Duncan knew the query behind that one word and answered it. 'No survivors.'

ACT TWO

BABYLON RISING

Chapter 23

Lorna stood on her front porch. Sunrise was only a couple of hours away. She should be bone-tired, but the opposite was true. She was wired, still running on adrenaline from all that had happened during the night.

A step below her, Jack waited.

He had driven her from the New Orleans Border Patrol station, where she'd finished giving a statement. The campers were all safe, treated for some minor burns and smoke inhalation. The boy seized by the jaguar had been evacuated by a Life Flight air ambulance, as had Garland Chase. The man had lost a lot of blood, along with most of his left leg to the alligator, but he'd live.

The Coast Guard had wanted to shoot the gator, but Lorna had argued against it, explaining how the gunshots and fire had riled the beast, causing it to lash out with a million years of defensive instinct. The farm owner's daughter – the one who dove in and rescued Garland – looked ready to throw herself between the Coast Guard sharpshooter and the gator.

In the end, Elvis lived.

Unfortunately the same couldn't be said about the jaguar and her cub. Their carcasses were airlifted to ACRES. The animals' deaths were a tragic loss, but Lorna had also watched three men's bodies hauled out of the forest, their skulls crushed, their throats ripped out. The cat was a man-eater, a remorseless killing machine, too dangerous to be allowed to live.

Still, not all of the aftermath was tragic. The pilot of the crashed helicopter had survived, found in the wreckage with a broken arm and collarbone. Likewise, a lone pirogue had paddled into the park, appearing on the opposite side of the farm. The Thibodeaux brothers – thought lost to the cat – had survived their encounter, along with Jack's two teammates. T-Bob had had enough swamp savvy to abandon the canoe and retreat his group up a pair of tall cypresses. From the high vantage point and hidden from the cat, he'd taken potshots to drive her off.

Lorna pictured the mother's limp bulk rising into the air, hauled aloft in a cargo net. She was anxious to get back to ACRES, but Jack had insisted she fly with him back to New Orleans aboard a Coast Guard chopper to give a statement. Afterward, he offered to drive her home, then to the docks to retrieve her Bronco. She wanted to grab a change of clothes and head directly out to ACRES.

'I'll wait here,' Jack said from the porch step.

He stood in his undershirt. His uniform top had been shredded and bloodied by the cub's frenzy. His left arm was bandaged from wrist to elbow.

'Don't be stupid. Come inside.' She nodded to his arm. 'You're already seeping through your gauze. I've got a first-aid kit inside. I'll put on a fresh wrap before we head out. It'll only take a few minutes.'

He tried to hide his injured arm. 'I'll be fine.'

'Cat bites and scratches shouldn't be taken lightly,' she warned, and she certainly had the scars on her arms to prove it. 'Did they give you any antibiotics?'

'A prescription. I'll pick it up in the morning.'

She rolled her eyes. Clearly the Coast Guard medical team knew nothing about feline injuries – but then why would they? There weren't a lot of feral cats on the high seas.

'Are you allergic to penicillin?' she asked and turned to

the front door with her keys.

'No.'

'Cats carry a form of *Pasteurella* in their mouths, a toxic and septic bacterium. I've seen animal health technicians lose fingers and parts of hands from neglected bite wounds. Antibiotics must be started immediately. I have some Augmentin inside. I always keep a supply in case I need to self-medicate.' She glanced back to Jack. 'But you didn't hear that from me.'

He finally relented and climbed the last step to the porch. She tugged open the door, flicked on the light inside, and led him into the foyer.

'The kitchen's in back.' She pointed. 'I'll grab my kit and meet you there.'

She climbed the stairs to the upper landing, taking the steps two at a time. Her abraded back protested, but she didn't slow. *Definitely wired.* She retreated to the hall bathroom and opened the medicine chest. Rows of prescription pill bottles lined the shelves, along with various toiletries and sundries. She grabbed the bottle of Augmentin and shook it. *Plenty still left.* She also snatched a fresh roll of gauze, hydrogen peroxide, and iodine.

As she closed the medicine chest she caught her reflection in the mirror. Her hair was a scraggly mess, half plastered to her skull. Her clothes had fared even worse. She wasn't a vain woman, but there were limits even for her. She abandoned the medical kit into the sink and turned to the tub. She twisted on the shower, waited for the steam to rise, then climbed in fully clothed. She let the water run over her for a full half minute. With her eyes still closed, she stripped to the skin, let the blistering-hot water scald over her, then finally climbed back out and toweled off.

In another few minutes, her hair was brushed loose to her shoulders and she'd hurried to her room naked and changed into a fresh pair of jeans and white tank top. Retrieving the medical kit, she headed downstairs.

She found Jack sitting at the kitchen table, his back to her. His head was hanging, half drowsing from his posture. She hated to disturb him and paused in the doorway.

For just a moment she flashed back on Tom. As she caught Jack in half silhouette, the family resemblance was uncanny. Relaxed with his guard down, Jack looked ten years younger. She could see the boy hidden behind the hardness of the man, almost a ghost of his younger brother.

He must have heard or sensed her presence. His head jerked up and toward her, his face going stony again. Still, his Cajun accent drawled softly, huskily.

'Lorna . . .'

The one word flushed goose bumps along her arms. His gaze traveled sleepily up and down her body, taking in her new clothes. If not so exhausted, he might not have been so brazen about it. Under his raw gaze, a warmth traveled deep into her belly and settled there.

Discomfited, she hurried to the table and dumped the medical supplies down, then crossed to the sink to get a glass of water for him to take with the antibiotics. She was glad to have her back to him as she turned on the tap.

Get ahold of yourself already . . .

Glass in hand, she turned back around. 'Better take two pills. Then let me check that arm.'

As he shook out the pills into his palm, she pulled up a chair and laid out the fresh gauze and a bottle of Betadine. He craned back to swallow the antibiotics. She noted the pinpricks of blood that stained his undershirt.

'Did anyone treat the wounds on your chest?' she asked.

'They're just scratches.'

Annoyance burned away the residual discomfort of his close presence.

'Take off your shirt,' she said.

'They're nothing.'

She waved at him. 'Don't argue.'

He gave her a tired sheepish look, then, in one pull, shed

his shirt. His bare chest and belly were crisscrossed with shallow scratches. The movement and pull of cloth set a few to bleeding again. No one had bothered to clean them.

She sighed. 'There's a full bath with a shower off the sleeping porch in back. I want you to take hot water and soap to any and every wound from that cub.'

'We don't have time—'

'Doctor's orders.' She stood up. 'There are clean towels in there. I'll get you a fresh shirt. My brother's about your size.'

He looked ready to argue, but she pointed her arm.

'Go. I'll make a fresh batch of coffee and warm some leftover beignets.'

That seemed to satisfy him, and he headed off toward the bathroom.

She pulled out a teakettle and a French press to make coffee. As the water heated she picked up the phone and punched in the number for ACRES. She called the genetics lab, figuring someone was still there.

The line picked up. The voice spoke in an impatient rush. 'Dr. Trent here.'

'Zoë, it's Lorna.'

In the background, she heard the neurobiologist's husband, Paul, talking animatedly about RNA transcription errors. She also recognized Dr. Metoyer's muffled voice but couldn't make out his words. None of them had left. They were pulling an all-nighter, too.

'I was just checking in,' Lorna said.

'Then you'd better stop checking, *chica*, and get that butt of yours over here! You're missing all the fun. And I can use a little estrogen here.'

She smiled at her colleague's excitement. 'Had to pick up a few things from home. I should be there in the next hour. Is the DNA analysis finished?'

Zoë's voice grew more serious. 'Not yet. Should be done by the time you get here. But the MRI data finished compiling. The results showed some strange neurological anomalies.'

157

'What do you mean?'

'It's too much to go over on the phone. Oh, and just so you're prepared, about an hour ago we performed a series of EEGs on your animals.'

Electroencephalograms?

'What? Why?' Irritation dulled her initial excitement. Lorna felt protective of the recovered animals. They had been traumatized enough. 'Any live testing should have waited until I was on the premises. You all know that.'

'I know, I know. But the procedure was noninvasive. We'll explain it all when you get here.'

'I'll be right over.' She hung up the phone, knowing her last words sounded as much a threat as a promise.

The teakettle whistled for her attention. She packed the French press with a chicory blend from Café du Monde and allowed the simple routine to resettle her thoughts.

Down the hall, she heard the bathroom door pop open. Jack returned with his hair wet and his skin almost steaming. He came in barefoot, wearing only his work trousers and a towel over one shoulder.

'I heard talking as I was drying off. Everything okay?'

'Will be once I get over to ACRES. Something's got them all worked up.'

Jack nodded to the table. 'Then this can wait. I can take care of all of this after I drop you off—'

'Sit.' She pointed a cup of hot coffee toward the table. 'Sugar? Cream?'

'Black will do.' He sank reluctantly back into his seat.

Lorna checked the scratches and bite wounds, satisfied that he'd scrubbed them clean. 'This'll sting.'

She painted the marks with Betadine, noting his skin flinch with each touch, but the deeper underlying muscle never moved and his breathing never changed its steady rhythm. She felt an impulse to press her ear to his chest, to listen to his heart, to monitor that rhythm, too, but she restrained herself.

The only other reaction from his body was a flush along his neckline and a hardening of his abdominals, as if he were preparing to take a blow to the stomach. She suspected it wasn't all from the pain. Confirming this, he shifted self-consciously.

As she worked in silence, she noted several old ropy scars across his left shoulder, neck, and down his back. Without meaning to, she allowed one finger to lightly trace one of the scars.

'Shrapnel from an IED,' he explained matter-of-factly. 'A roadside bomb.'

'Sorry. I didn't mean . . .' Her hand dropped away, and her face heated with embarrassment.

She finished her ministrations and replaced the bandage on his arm.

When she glanced up, she found him staring her full in the face. His eyes were like a wolf, raw and unreadable. He leaned closer. For a moment she thought he was going to kiss her, but instead he reached to the cup of coffee on the table.

'Thanks.' He stood up. 'You said something about a new shirt.'

'That's right,' she stammered out, feeling stupid for forgetting – *and for stammering*. 'I'll get one from my brother's room.'

She was happy to flee the room. She wiped her damp hands on her jeans. She blamed the fine sheen of perspiration over her body on the night's humidity. Or maybe it was just the exhaustion, weakening her guard. Or maybe it was the boy she'd noted in the slumbering man. An echo of Tom, of long nights in each other's arms.

She might have forgotten, but her body had not.

She dragged a clean T-shirt from her brother's dresser and hurried back to the hallway where Jack waited. He tugged on the shirt. She was wrong about Jack being the same size as her brother. The shirt was a tight fit and clung to his shoulders and chest.

159

'Ready?' he asked as he shoved his feet into his socks and boots.

She nodded and pulled open the front door, glad for the cool night breeze on her heated face.

Out of the shadows in the front yard, a hard shout called to her.

'Where the hell do you think you're all going?'

Chapter 24

At the shout, Jack pulled Lorna behind him, an instinctual reaction. He crouched, feeling exposed under the porch lamp, blinded by its glare. Towering oaks and bushy magnolias shadowed the dark walkway. Movement drew his eye below. A figure stalked up from the front gate.

Lorna stepped back into view. 'Kyle? What are you doing back? I thought you were stuck on that oil rig for another four days.' Lorna turned to Jack and explained under her breath. 'My brother.'

'I told you on the phone I was coming back early.'

'And I told you that wasn't necessary.'

'Well, I wasn't about to let you go hunting in the swamps by yourself. And it looks like I got here just in time.'

The figure climbed the steps and into the porch light. Jack sized him up. Lorna's brother had the same sandy-blond hair as his sister – in his case cropped short on the sides and longer on the top. From the looks of it, he hadn't shaved in days and had worn the same cargo shorts and loose polo shirt for just as long. He had a wiry physique, like a coiled spring – though at the moment wound a bit too tightly. As the kid gripped the porch rail, Jack noted that his fingernail beds and the wrinkles of his knuckles were black with ground-in oil. The only thing darker was the kid's demeanor as he eyed Jack with a hard suspicion.

'I told you not to come,' Lorna said. 'The hunt's already

over. You came all the way back here for nothing.'

'Then where are you two going?' Kyle stood a step below, blocking the way.

'Over to ACRES.'

'Both of you?'

Lorna glanced to Jack. 'No. He was just taking me over to fetch the Bronco. It's over by the dock near the zoo.'

Jack cleared his throat. 'Or I could take you directly to your lab. Be faster, and I wouldn't mind hearing firsthand what your colleagues have figured out about those animals. Might be important to the investigation.'

Lorna nodded. 'I'd like . . . I mean, that would be fine.'

Kyle narrowed one eye and studied him. 'You're Jack Menard, aren't you?'

He nodded.

Kyle turned back to his sister. 'Then I'm going with you.'

'Don't be stupid. Get some sleep.'

'If he's going' – Kyle stabbed a finger at Jack – 'then I'm going. Someone needs to chaperone this date.'

'It's not a date.' Lorna's face flushed, more angry than embarrassed. 'I can damn well take care of myself.'

'What? Like the *last* time you took off with one of the Menard brothers?'

Lorna's eyes widened, shocked by his words, struck dumb. Jack had to restrain an urge to slam a fist in the kid's face.

Kyle seemed to recognize he'd overstepped himself and back-pedaled. 'Sorry. That was a stupid thing to say.'

He hurriedly climbed the last step and joined his sister, as if shortening the distance could temper his words. He touched her arm, but she turned away. He followed, matching her step for step.

'After what those Menards put you through,' Kyle said more softly as his anger bled away to raw concern. 'I don't want you hurt again. That's all I was saying. I'd cut off my right arm to protect you. You know that.'

She sagged under his assault. 'Of course I know that,

Kyle. But in this case, you don't know what you're talking about.' She glanced over at Jack. 'I trust him.'

Something in her face more than her words steeled through Jack. He found himself standing a bit straighter. At the same time he remembered her fingers on his skin, warm and soft.

Kyle looked between the two of them, then shook his head. 'I'd still like to go with you. I won't get any sleep till you're home anyway.' His tone was more conciliatory and plainly worked better on Lorna. 'And I promise I won't cause any trouble.'

'Fine. But we're leaving right now.'

'That's okay by me.'

He stepped aside, and Lorna led the way back to the street. Kyle kept pace next to Jack. Though the kid had taken a more mollifying tone with his older sister, Jack read the continuing suspicion in his glance as they headed out. Kyle was clearly keeping his guard up – and Jack respected that. Lorna's brother only wanted to protect her and didn't care whose feathers he ruffled.

They all piled into the service truck and headed out. Jack placed a quick call to his own brother about the change in plans. Randy still had Burt and had been waiting at the station for them to head back home together.

'Then I'll just meet you at that zoo place,' Randy said and hung up before Jack could argue.

Lowering the phone, Jack glanced sidelong at his passenger. Lorna shared the front seat with him. He could tell she was lost elsewhere. Her eyes had crinkled at the corners, her mind already working on the mysteries surrounding this case, the woman becoming the doctor again.

Kyle leaned forward, intruding between them. 'So what's up with these damned animals anyway? What's so special about them?'

Lorna muttered, still lost to the moment. 'That's what I'm trying to figure out.'

Chapter 25

An hour later, Lorna sat before a thirty-inch wide-screen LCD computer monitor in the genetics suite. Multiple windows were open on the screen, but she studied the one in the center. A three-dimensional image of an avian brain rotated on the screen, compiled from the Magnetic Resonance Imaging scan done on the African Grey parrot named Igor. A neighboring window showed a photo of the reptilian-looking featherless bird.

'What are we looking at?' Jack asked behind her.

Zoë Trent answered him, standing on her other side. 'Something remarkable.'

The neurobiologist shared the small conference room with them off the main lab. Her husband, Paul, was still out there reviewing the DNA analysis on the aberrant chromosome.

'What's wrong with this bird?' Kyle asked.

Her brother sat on a stool beside the small birdcage that held Igor. The parrot sat sullenly, hunched low to the perch. The bird was nothing like the bright and attentive fellow he had been earlier. Also watery droppings covered the bottom of his cage.

Diarrhea due to stress.

A knot of annoyance burned in Lorna's gut. Her colleagues should have waited until she returned to perform those extra tests. The health and well-being of the facility's animals were her responsibility. And that duty extended to the animals rescued from the trawler. The creatures had already been through enough. They didn't deserve to be treated like guinea pigs here, too.

'How come this ugly guy doesn't have any feathers?' her brother asked.

Lorna answered without taking her eyes off the screen. 'First, he's not *ugly*. Second, we think it's a genetic throwback, a lost trait that's surfaced again.'

'Weird.'

She didn't argue with that. It was weird. Everything about this was strange. 'Just keep him company. He's spooked. Talk to him.'

Parrots were social creatures and found solace in companionship.

Kyle shrugged and leaned closer to the cage. Her brother lowered his voice to a gentle coo. 'So who's an ugly bird? Not you.'

Igor cocked an eye quizzically at Kyle and responded with a soft clucking, the avian equivalent of a chuckle.

Like Lorna, her brother always had a way with animals. And despite his quick temper, he had a big heart, which might explain his volatility. He felt things deeply, and she knew how much he loved her, sought to protect her. With their father passing away when they were children, he had always taken on the role of the man of the house – and even more so after their mother had died. She both loved him for this effort and bristled against it, but in the machismo world of the South, it was an all-too-common family dynamic.

Jack drew her attention back to the computer. He leaned a hip on the desk. 'So what's so remarkable about this MRI scan?' he asked Zoë. 'Why insist Lorna see this first?'

The neurobiologist pointed to the monitor. 'It'll help explain why we didn't wait before performing the electroencephalograms.' Her voice took on an apologetic tone, but it didn't appease Lorna.

165

She studied the rotating image. The brain looked like most birds', and in fact it was not that much different from a mammalian brain. On the screen, the spinal cord bloomed into a medulla, a cerebellum, and a cerebrum that was divided into two hemispheres. She noted something strange almost immediately: five distinct darker objects appeared to be embedded between the hyperpallium and mesopallium layers of forebrain, the avian equivalent to the human neocortex. They were crisp and hard-edged, appearing almost crystalline in structure.

She rotated to get a top view of these odd densities. The five formed a perfect pentagram within the neurological tissue.

'What are they?' she asked.

Instead of answering, Zoë reached and tapped a button on the keyboard. The parrot's brain vanished and was replaced by another. 'This is the brain from one of the capuchin monkeys.'

Lorna pictured the conjoined twins as she leaned closer to the screen. The same strange densities were lodged within the brain tissue of the monkey. She revolved the image. *The same number and lodged in the equivalent morphological locations.* Even the pattern was the same. *A perfectly symmetrical pentagram.*

Despite the warmth of the room, a chill edged through her.

Zoë shifted closer. 'We found these same odd intrusions in all the animals recovered from the trawler. I can show you the other scans.'

Lorna shook her head, trusting her colleagues' assessment. 'Are they implants?'

'We don't think so.' Excitement welled in the neurobiologist's voice. 'We think they might be natural features.'

'Natural?'

'That's right.' Zoë shifted the computer mouse to zoom down on one of the densities. 'Look closer. See how there's no scarring around the intrusions like you'd expect from a surgical implant. Also there's no granulation tissue walled around it like you'd see from an embedded foreign body.'

'Then what are they?'

Zoë shrugged. 'That's what Dr. Metoyer wants to know. Jon Greer over in pathology is attempting to dissect one from the dead cub's carcass so we can study it. He's also taking multiple brain biopsies around the intrusion.'

'Biopsies?' Jack asked. 'Why?'

Zoë circled a finger around the abnormalities on the computer screen. 'The neurological tissue appears to be *denser* within the zone of the intrusions. Dr. Metoyer wanted to confirm a supposition that this region is made up of more densely packed neurons.'

Lorna wanted to know, too. She remembered the glow from the jaguar's eyes, its cunningness. Even the parrot's ability to recite the mathematical equivalent of pi. More neurons translated to a richer synaptic environment, which meant more computing power to be tapped. This discovery could explain why the animals seemed especially hyper-intelligent.

Zoë straightened and ran a hand through her short black hair. 'Now you know why we wanted to perform those EEGs. We were so excited. We couldn't wait.'

Lorna slowly nodded. By studying the electrical patterns of the brain, they were looking for any change in functionality associated with these intrusions. 'What did you find with the EEGs?'

'At first nothing. Each animal's brain-wave patterns seemed normal enough, each as unique as a fingerprint. There seemed to be no common ground.'

Rather than disappointment, Zoë's face shone with amazement. Lorna knew there was another shoe still to drop. Zoë glanced over to Igor's cage.

Lorna followed her gaze, then back to the neurobiologist. 'What?'

'I'll show you.' Zoë sidled next to her and tapped rapidly at the keyboard. 'I'm going to display the set of four EEGs we took from the parrot, the two monkeys, and Bagheera, the cub. For simplicity's sake, I'm only going to show a single lead from each animal.'

The readings appeared on the screen.

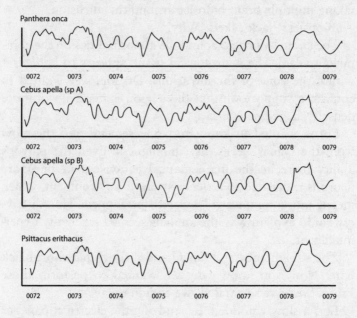

Zoë glanced over to Lorna with one eyebrow cocked. She read her colleague's question. *Can you see anything weird here?*

It took Lorna only a second. She pointed to the two center tracings. 'These two runs are nearly identical.' She read the labels and scrunched her brow. *Cebus apella. Specimens A and B.* 'Those readings came from the conjoined twin monkeys.'

Zoë nodded. 'That's right. At first we thought it might be a mistake. Perhaps the electrode net placed on one monkey was picking up the electrical pattern from its twin. Or maybe because they were genetic twins, their brain activity also matched. Just to be sure, we brought all the animals up here and retested them.'

She tapped at the keyboard and another four leads were displayed. 'This is what we got when all four specimens were in the room at the same time.'

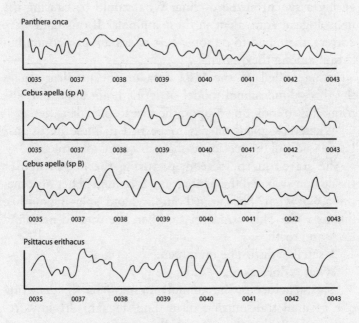

Lorna leaned closer, running each lead with the tip of a finger. Amazement grew. *Impossible.*

Jack spoke next to her. 'They all look roughly the same.'

'We ran the leads for a full ten minutes each. They continued to stay synchronized.'

Lorna struggled to comprehend what she was seeing.

'Afterward,' Zoë said, 'we took the other animals back to their ward. Except for the parrot here. We tested Igor again with the others gone. His EEG returned to its original unique pattern.'

Lorna stared over to the parrot and her brother. 'Are you saying that when they're all together, their brain-wave patterns somehow slip into perfect synchronization?'

'That's what seems to be happening.'

How could that be? She had heard of women in dorms who would begin to menstruate in unison when housed together – but that was due to pheromones in the air, triggering a synchronized cycling. What could be causing the neurological equivalent in these animals? If this data were correct, there had to be some sort of stimulus or communication among the animals.

Lorna pulled up the MRI data on the monitor. Again the three-dimensional model of Igor's brain appeared. She rotated it to look down upon the five strange densities.

'Whatever's going on has to be tied to these intrusions,' Lorna said. 'All the specimens share this common structure.'

She stared at the screen, picturing the net of denser tissue that spanned the pentagram. It reminded her of something. But what? She cupped out her hand, splaying her five fingers wide. Then it dawned on her. She rotated her hand back and forth.

'A satellite dish,' she mumbled.

'What?' Zoë asked.

'The structure in the animal's brain. What if it's acting like a small transmitting dish? Emitting an ultralow frequency signal that the others pick up and somehow triggers this synchronization.'

Zoë frowned, caught between disbelief and possibility.

'Are you talking about some form of telepathy?' Kyle asked, eyeballing the parrot with suspicion.

'No.' Lorna spoke faster. 'At least not exactly. For the EEGs to match, something has to be triggering it. It can't be hormonal or pheromonal. They're different species.'

'Plus the reaction time is too fast,' Zoë added, her disbelief fading.

Lorna nodded. 'But a weak electrical signal could trigger

it. Just enough to flip a switch in the brains of all four animals.'

'But what could be powering it all?' Jack asked. 'I don't see any battery.'

Zoë answered him. 'No battery is needed. The brain's an electrical organ, producing energy known as action potentials by pumping chemicals into and out of neurons. The average brain produces a continuous ten to twelve watts of electricity. Morning, noon, and night. Enough to power a flashlight.'

'And certainly enough to transmit a low-grade signal.' Lorna stared at the MRI model and swallowed.

A new voice spoke by the doorway. 'Which, of course, begs another question, my dear.'

Lorna turned to find her boss, Carlton Metoyer, leaning in the doorway. *How long had he been listening in on their conversation?*

'What question is that?' Zoë asked.

He stepped into the room, wearing a crisply pressed lab jacket, ever the southern gentleman, even when up all night. 'Dr. Polk has just offered us an intriguing solution as to *how* these brains are linking up. Which raises an even more dynamic question.'

Lorna understood and asked that question aloud. 'Why?'

Why were these animals linking up?

Chapter 26

Duncan sat alone in a truck parked outside the entry road to ACRES. He had the window rolled down and listened to the nighttime chorus of frogs and crickets. Off to the left, the Mississippi River whispered muddily as it swept alongside the levee road. A soft wind stirred the thick humid air, making it almost breathable.

With his night-vision scope fixed to his face, he studied the facility on the far side of the levee. The place was dark, except for a few lighted windows on the first floor. His earpiece registered the call signs of his team as they reached their various positions around the building. While waiting, Duncan kept watch on the one road into and out of the facility.

He didn't want any surprises.

His second-in-command finally reported the all-ready. 'On your signal.'

'Have you confirmed the number and identity of the civilians?'

'Seven. One is a Border Patrol agent, and we should assume he's armed.'

'Make him a high-priority target. Remember, we need one of the scientists to interrogate off-site.'

'Understood, sir.'

They needed to gauge how much the researchers had learned about the Babylon Project – and more important, if any word had spread. After that, the subject would be eliminated and the body disposed of. There were plenty of hungry sharks in the Caribbean.

Duncan studied the facility one last time. His team had the place surrounded and locked down. Incendiary charges would cover their tracks afterward. At first light, an animal rights terrorist group would e-mail and claim responsibility for the attack. Nothing would be traced back to Ironcreek Industries.

With everything ready, he lifted the radio to give the order to move in – when suddenly lights flared behind his truck. The flash stung through his night-vision scopes. He tore off the goggles and glanced to the rearview mirror.

A truck rumbled around a far bend in the river road. Its headlights swept around the corner and speared Duncan's parked truck. He lowered his radio and waited.

Suspicion rankled through him.

At this hour and in these remote parts, he had not expected any traffic.

While he watched the vehicle approach he popped another Life Savers in his mouth. Pineapple. He grimaced at the flavor. Not his favorite. Still, he sucked on the candy. As he waited he judged the threat level and recalibrated his plans.

Once the truck was close enough, he saw that it appeared to be a beat-up Chevy, held together mostly with rust and old gray primer. It sidled toward his position.

Keep moving he willed it.

As if obeying him, the Chevy swung wide, preparing to pass around, but a flare of crimson bloomed from the rear as the truck began to brake. The vehicle slowed and settled to a stop beside Duncan's truck with a wheezy sigh of its engine. The driver leaned toward the open passenger window and pushed up the brim of a ball cap. He wore a hunting vest over a stained T-shirt.

'Need a hand, buddy?' he called out. His accent was

thickly Cajun, just a swamp rat out late.

Duncan shifted the pistol on his lap and inwardly grimaced.

The jackass just had to stop . . .

Duncan tilted toward the window. The driver flinched at the sight of his scarred face, one not easy to forget. There could be no witnesses. He lifted his gun to the window –

– but a black-and-tan hound suddenly lunged up from the truck's rear bed. It bayed loudly at him, like an angry bullhorn.

Startled, Duncan jerked back with a strangled gasp. Old terror crackled through his ribs. He flashed back to another time a beast had caught him by surprise.

The driver turned and hollered at the dog. 'Burt, shut your piehole! I can hardly hear myself think.'

Duncan's heart pounded in his throat.

Oblivious of his reaction, the driver swung back toward him. 'Mister, you don't happen to know if there's some zoo place out here, do ya? My fool of a brother was heading over—'

Terror turned to fury. Angered at being caught off guard, Duncan yanked up his pistol and thrust it through the window. As he pulled the trigger the dog launched out of the truck straight at him.

He flinched as the gun went off. Blood splattered against the other windshield. The driver grabbed the side of his head, yelling a loud *'Fuck!'* and dropped out of view.

Duncan swung toward the attacking dog, but the hound twisted in midair, struck the side of his truck, and fell between the two vehicles.

Across the way, the Chevy's engine suddenly revved and gears popped. The truck bounced away, careening wildly back and forth as the driver drove blindly from his hiding place.

Duncan shoved the door open, leaped out into a shooter's stance, and emptied his entire clip at the truck. The Chevy veered sharply to the left, not slowing down. It leaped off the levee road and went airborne over the steep edge.

He ran after it while ejecting the dead clip and slapping a fresh one into his pistol. He watched the truck's front end hit the stony embankment below and flip upside down into the storm-swollen Mississippi River. The current spun the vehicle as it quickly sank.

Duncan kept watch, gun pointed. He waited a full two minutes. No body came thrashing to the surface.

Screw it.

With no time for a more thorough search, he swung away. Even if the man survived, Duncan's team would be long gone before the bastard could alert anyone.

Red-faced, with his heart still thudding, he returned to his truck. He watched for any sign of the dog, but the hound must have high-tailed it away. At the truck, he grabbed his radio off the front seat. He was done here. He lifted the radio to his lips.

'All positions. Move in. Take this place down.'

Chapter 27

'Igor, tell me what pi is,' Lorna said as she leaned by the birdcage, taking Kyle's place. 'What is pi?'

The others gathered behind her. The parrot stared at her with one eye, then the other. Following her brother's gentle attention, Igor had straightened out of his sullen hunch. But there remained a dullness to his gaze unlike his earlier verve.

Carlton stood at her elbow. 'Lorna, what are you doing?'

'Testing something.' She waved her boss back. 'Everybody clear away.'

As they retreated she moved closer, lowering her voice to a soft, soothing whisper. 'C'mon, Igor . . .'

'Igor,' the bird mimicked tentatively.

'Good, Igor. Who's a good bird?'

'Igor!' he squawked more brightly, and hopped from foot to foot on the perch.

'Good boy. Now tell me what pi is. You've done it before. Pi.'

On the computer nearby, Lorna had pulled up a full page of the mathematical constant: 3.141592653589793 . . .

The parrot bobbed his head. *'Three . . .'*

'That's right. Good, Igor.'

'One . . . four . . .'

He was doing it again, but then things began to fall apart. *'Eight . . . seven . . . round . . . triangle . . .'*

Igor cocked his head almost upside down, eyes squinted to slits, as if struggling to remember.

'Lorna?' Carlton pressed. He glanced at his wristwatch, losing patience.

She turned. Instead of being disappointed by Igor's poor performance, she grew more assured. Still, she wanted to confirm her hypothesis. 'Zoë, would you mind running down and fetching Bagheera? And, Paul, can you bring up the capuchins?'

The two neurobiologists nodded and rushed off.

Lorna faced Carlton. 'Earlier – both at the trawler and down in the ward – Igor was able to recite pi to hundreds of digits. Back then I didn't have time to double-check his recitation, but the bird was correct to at least a dozen digits.'

'I remember that, too,' Jack said, supporting her.

Carlton shrugged. 'I don't understand. It's simple mimicry, is it not? Nothing more. What are you trying to prove?'

'I think it's more than mimicry. You posited the question *why* these animals seem to be synchronizing their brain waves. I think I might have the answer.'

She noted Jack staring at her. She took strength in the intensity of his interest and attention. But what if she was wrong?

A few moments later, Zoë and Paul returned with charges in hand. Zoë carried Bagheera like a baby in a blanket. The cat stared out at them with bright-blue eyes. The two monkeys clutched Paul's lab coat with both hands and feet. He gently cradled them under an arm, while wearing a goofy smile, like a proud papa.

Lorna asked Carlton, 'Once the animals were brought together, how long did it take for this synchronization to occur?'

'I'd say a matter of seconds. Half minute at most.'

Satisfied, Lorna turned back to the birdcage. *Let's try this again.*

'Igor, what is pi?'

The bird's posture had gone straight again, fully attentive, his eyes brighter, staring hard at Lorna.

'What is pi?' she repeated.

Igor flashed his pupils at Lorna and began a recitation with that eerily human voice. This time there was no hesitation. *Three, one, four, one, five, nine, two, six, five . . .*

Kyle, seated by the computer, followed on the screen. Her brother's eyes got huge. 'By golly, he's right.'

As Igor continued to recite the numbers his eyes drifted closed – not with squinted concentration, but more like contentment. *. . . three, five, eight, nine, seven, nine, three . . .*

Everyone remained silent. Lorna's boss drifted closer to Kyle and followed along on the screen.

Igor performed for a full three minutes, passing beyond the hundreds of numbers displayed on the screen.

Lorna watched Carlton's face shift from skepticism to awe. He finally took off his glasses and polished them with a handkerchief. He shook his head. 'I concede. His memory is amazing.'

'I'm not sure it is *memory*,' Lorna said as Igor continued. 'I think he's actively calculating it.'

Carlton looked ready again to scoff – then something seemed to dawn in his eyes. 'You're thinking . . . the synchronization . . . that it goes beyond physicality and into *functionality*.'

She smiled and nodded.

'What's that mean?' Kyle asked.

Zoë moved closer. She stared down at the cub in her arms. 'Then they're not just linking up to synchronize – '

Her husband finished her thought. ' – they're networking together at the functional level.'

Kyle shrugged heavily, still not understanding. Jack also moved closer to Lorna, wanting to know more.

She explained. 'A brain is really an organic computer. And most of the time its vast network of neurons and synapses are inactive, a large resource of untapped computing power.

178

I think the transmission dish – the one inside their heads – is functioning as a network router, linking the computing power in each animal's brain. Each one has full access to tap into the dormant resources of the others' organic computer. Basically these animals are forming a crude computer network, linked wirelessly.'

'But how can that be?' Jack asked.

Before anyone could answer, the buzz of a cell phone interrupted the discussion. Carlton gave an apologetic look and answered it. He listened for a moment, then said, 'Thank you, Jon. We'll be right down.'

Lorna's boss closed his phone and faced Jack.

'It seems our resident pathologist might have an answer to your question, Agent Menard.'

Jack had experienced his share of dead bodies, but there was something particularly macabre about the pathology suite at ACRES. The windowless room was as large as a basketball court. Drains and floor traps crisscrossed an expanse of cement floor. Huge stainless-steel tables lined the center of the room lit by surgical lamps. Overhead ran a pulley-and-chain system for moving the carcasses of large animals into and out of the place. The air reeked of formaldehyde and an underlying hint of decay.

On the whole, the space had a feel of a giant slaughter-house.

The promise of answers from the facility's pathologist had drawn everyone down here.

Off to one side, the intact carcass of the female jaguar covered one table, but they all gathered by another. It held the dissected remains of the young cub. The tiny body was splayed out like a frog. Its cavities had been hollowed out. Parts floating in labeled jars: heart, kidney, spleen, liver. But the most gruesome sight was the cranial cavity: sawed open and empty.

The brain rested on an instrument tray at the head of the

179

table. The organ's gray surface glistened moistly under the halogen lamps.

Jack noted Lorna staring at the hollowed-out carcass. The violation and needless loss of life clearly troubled her, but the pathologist drew her attention.

Dr. Jon Greer waved everyone closer with a thumb forceps. 'I thought you should see this in person.'

Jack did not necessarily appreciate this consideration, but he kept quiet.

Using the forceps and the edge of a scalpel, the pathologist peeled back the top layer of the brain and exposed a deeper layer of the cerebrum. The tissue looked much like the rest of the organ, except for what appeared to be four tiny black diamonds reflecting the light. The indentation for a fifth marked the firm flesh.

'I teased out one of the inclusion bodies and did a couple of quick tests. Let me show you.'

He moved to a neighboring table. On a plastic tray rested one of the black diamonds, only this one had been sectioned into four pieces. Greer used tweezers to pick up a shard. He moved it over to a pile of material that looked like coarse ground pepper.

'Iron filings,' the pathologist explained.

As the shard passed over the pile, a few metallic granules leaped and clung to the sliver.

Greer glanced to the others. 'I believe what we're dealing with – what's lodged in these brains – are dense aggregates of magnetite crystals.'

'Magnetite?' Jack asked. No one else looked particularly surprised. Lorna's brother merely looked ill and like he'd rather be anywhere but here. 'Like magnets?'

'Sort of,' Lorna said.

Zoë explained. 'All brain tissue, including our own, has magnetite crystals laced naturally throughout it. Crystal accumulations can be found in the cerebral cortex, the cerebellum, even the meningeal layers that cover the brain.'

Lorna nodded. 'The magnetite levels in avian brains are even higher. It's believed that these magnetic crystals are one of the ways that birds orient themselves to the earth's magnetic field during migrations. It's how they get to where they're going each year without getting lost. It's also found in bees, fish, bacteria, and other organisms that navigate by internal compass.'

'Then why do we have it in our brains?' Jack asked.

Lorna shrugged. 'No one knows.'

'But there are theories,' Zoë interjected. 'Newest research suggests that biomagnetism may be the foundation for life on this planet. That magnetism is the true bridge between energy and living matter. For example, piezoelectric matrices can be found in proteins, enzymes, even DNA. Basically *all* the building blocks of life.'

Lorna lifted an arm and cut her off. 'Okay, now you're losing even me.'

'Regardless of all that,' Greer interrupted, 'we've never seen this level of magnetite in any animal. Nor such precise symmetry and pattern of deposition. I took the liberty of examining the inclusion under a dissecting microscope. The structure is composed of smaller and smaller crystals, breaking down into tinier and tinier identical parts.'

'Like fractals,' Kyle said.

'Exactly,' Greer said.

Jack had to refrain from scratching his head. *What were fractals?*

The pathologist continued: 'But those magnetic inclusions or nodes are only half the story.' He led them back to the exposed brain. He used the tip of his tweezers to draw lines from one magnetite inclusion to another. 'Each node is linked by a microscopic web of crystals, from one to the other, forming an interconnected array. And wrapped throughout this webbing is a dense region of neurons.'

'As would be expected,' Dr. Carlton Metoyer said.

The others turned to the head of ACRES.

Carlton explained. 'It's been proven that magnetic stimulation of the brain results in the growth of neurons and new synaptic connections. If this magnetic array formed during embryonic development, the low-grade and constant magnetic stimulation would produce a richer region of neurons locally.'

Jack remembered the earlier discussion. 'And this would make the animals smarter?'

'Individually . . . to some degree. But it also adds validity to Dr. Polk's theory of some wireless interconnectivity. More neurons, more electrical stimulation locally. If I had to hazard a guess, I'd say the transmission triggering the synchronization is electromagnetic. A weak EM pulse shared among the animals.'

Lorna shook her head, struggling through it all. 'There's still so much more we need to know.'

'Then I'll let you all get back to your own research,' Greer said, 'but there's one last thing.'

'What?' Carlton asked.

The pathologist shifted to the other side of the table. Another tray rested there. A tiny object lay inside. It was clearly man-made. A plastic capsule the size of a pea. Through its clear surface tiny electronics were visible.

'I thought you'd like to see one of the microchips embedded in the animals.'

Lorna crinkled her brow. 'Microchips? Are you saying they're tagged?'

Greer turned to her. 'MRI scans showed each animal had such chips implanted under the skin. We had thought they were I.D. chips used to mark each animal, like they do for dogs and cats. But I compared this one to the tags used here on our animals. This baby is much more sophisticated. It's packed full of electronics.'

'Can I see it?' Jack asked.

The pathologist picked it up and passed it over. Jack studied it closer. Though he couldn't tell much without further study, his internal radar buzzed a warning. From the complexity and degree of miniaturization, it looked military grade.

Maybe a transponder . . . or a GPS tracker . . .

As he thought that, the lights suddenly extinguished. The windowless room fell into pitch darkness. Everyone held their breath, waiting for the emergency generators to kick in.

Finally, Carlton snapped peevishly, 'I thought we had the power glitch fixed.'

Jack tensed. His internal warning system went from a low buzz to a full Klaxon of alarm. He remembered his assessment a moment ago.

A tracker . . .

He pictured the explosion at the trawler. Someone had been attempting to cover their tracks. But not all of those tracks had been obliterated.

Some led here.

Certainty grew inside him. 'It's not a power outage,' Jack said coldly into the darkness. 'We're under attack.'

Chapter 28

In the darkness, Lorna stumbled away from the necropsy table and hit a warm body. Arms caught her, held her. She knew it was Jack by the musky mix of sweat and iodine.

Light bloomed on the far side of the table as Zoë freed her cell phone and used the light of the screen to push back the darkness. The phone wasn't good for much else. The storm had knocked out the area's cell tower – not that they had good service here anyway.

They all gathered closer to the phone's glow like moths to a flame.

Carlton stood with his hands on his hips, maintaining his usual aplomb. 'Agent Menard, what makes you think this is some form of attack versus a power glitch?'

Jack answered swiftly and forcefully. 'Until I know better, Dr. Metoyer, I'm assuming the worst. Whoever firebombed that trawler could be coming after the remaining animals. That chip removed from the cub looked like a tracking tag, one that could lead them here.'

'That's a stretch, Agent Menard,' Carlton dismissed. 'Besides, who would go through so much effort?'

Lorna felt the tension in Jack's body, which had gone rock hard. He still hadn't let her go. Her brother eyed her with a dour expression. Under Kyle's judgmental gaze, she finally slipped out of Jack's arms on her own.

'Maybe we should listen to the agent,' Zoë said as she

retreated next to her husband. 'Take precautions. What could it hurt?'

All faces turned to Jack.

'This room has no windows,' he said. 'Which means it's a blind spot to any surveillance of the facility. Just to be cautious, everyone should stay here while I check out what's going on.'

Greer spoke up. 'What about just leaving?' He pointed to the far side of the room. 'There's a service ramp that leads out from here.'

'No. They'd have the place surrounded by now. The exit would be watched.'

'Then what do we do?' Zoë asked, her fear growing as large as her eyes.

'For now, you all hole up down here. Is there some place to keep out of sight, maybe barricade?'

'The walk-in cooler,' the pathologist said. 'But there's no way to lock it from the inside.'

Kyle spoke up. 'Let me look at it. After spending four years in engineering school, I should be able to finagle a way to secure it from the inside.'

Jack nodded. 'Good. Then everyone else grab weapons. Scalpels, knives, scissors, syringes, whatever you can find and retreat there. I'm going to make for my truck. I have a rifle and a shotgun in a lockbox out there.'

Greer had found a pair of emergency flashlights, clicked one on, and passed the other to Jack. 'In case you need it.'

The group began to disperse under the pathologist's direction, gathering anything sharp.

Lorna followed Jack out of the circle of light and into the gloom as he headed toward the door. A small battery-powered 'Exit' sign glowed weakly above the doorway ahead.

'What about my tranquilizer gun?' she said. 'The one I went hunting with. I dropped it back at my office. It's closer than going outside.'

She didn't want Jack confronting some assault team while totally unarmed.

He nodded. 'Good idea.'

'I'll go with you.' She knew Jack would argue, so she pressed. 'It takes skill to safely load the syringe cartridges with M99.'

And it did. Just a few drops could kill a man in seconds.

Still, he seemed ready to balk.

'I'll go just as far as the office,' she promised. 'It's only one flight up. Then I'll head straight back here.' She passed him and reached the door before he could stop her. 'C'mon. Let's go.'

She pulled open the door, but he blocked her from stepping out. She was ready for him to push back, to refuse to let her go. Instead, he slipped out ahead of her.

'Keep behind me. No talking.'

She followed his broad back into the hallway. As the door closed the hallway went pitch-black. Jack reached and fumbled for her hand. His grip was huge, rough with calluses. But his hard hold helped settle her in the darkness. He led her in the direction of the nearby stairwell.

Why doesn't he use his flashlight?

They reached the dark stairs and began to ascend. Faint light filtered as they neared the first-floor landing. Windows let in some meager glow from the stars. After the pitch darkness below, even this little bit of illumination was welcome.

He continued down the hall. Her office and lab were only a few doors down. Halfway there, a muffled crash echoed, sounding like it came from the front of the building. Her fingers tightened on Jack's hand. No one else was supposed to be here.

Jack hurried toward her office door. He pushed it open, swung an arm out, and scooped her into the room ahead of him. She rushed inside as he softly closed the door. Framed against the frosted glass of the door's window, she saw him lift a finger to his lips.

186

She hurried to her desk, bumping her knee against it in the dark. She had left the rifle case on top of her desk. She fumbled for it, undid the latches, and quickly assembled the two halves. Marines might be able to break down their weapons in the dark, but not her. She struggled for a breath, but finally the stock snapped into place.

Behind her, Jack kept watch on the door.

She grabbed two syringe cartridges and plucked the vial of M99 from its velvet-molded compartment in the case. It was stupidly dangerous to attempt this in the dark, but she had no choice. She might not be able to assemble a rifle blindfolded, but she had years of experience with needles and drug bottles. She quickly filled the two syringes and loaded them into the rifle.

As she turned Jack's silhouette slipped back from the window. Through the frosted glass, darker shadows swept past out in the hallway, eerily silent. She had not even heard a footfall. One shadow stopped outside the door.

Lorna froze, holding her breath. Her heart pounded against her ribs.

Then the shadow moved on. She could guess where they were headed. The kennel ward lay in that direction. Still, they would be disappointed when they got there. They'd find mostly empty cages. While the lamb was still down there, the other rescued animals were up another level on the second floor, still caged in the genetics lab after Lorna's testing.

But how long would it take to find the others, especially if the intruders were using electronic trackers? Would the devices even work inside?

After ten seconds, Jack crossed to her, moving unerringly in the dark. She tried to give him the rifle, but he pushed it back into her chest. His words were a breath against her ear. 'Stay here. Stay hidden.'

He squeezed her fingers tighter to the rifle, communicating silently.

She understood.

The game had changed. What was a possibility before was now a terrifying reality. They were under siege. He refused to leave her unarmed while alone. From the firm grip on her fingers, this was one argument she wasn't going to win.

He didn't wait for any acknowledgment and moved back toward the office door. He eased the door open and slipped out. Once in the hall, he pulled the door silently closed.

Lorna stared at his silhouette out there, suddenly not wanting him to leave. But Jack had no choice. His shadow retreated, heading in the opposite direction from the intruders.

But how many more were out there?

Jack hated leaving Lorna alone, but he dared not wait. He hurried down the dark hall toward the nearest exit. He should never have allowed her to come with him. The others, locked up in the cooler, had the best chance of avoiding any encounter with the assault team. And he didn't harbor any delusions that these were ordinary thieves. These were professional killers, likely with military backgrounds.

His mind ran over their potential objectives, and he didn't like the conclusions he came to. Clearly this nighttime raid was a cleanup operation, a continuation of what was started with the trawler's explosion. The primary objective had to be the collection and elimination of the remaining animals. But what then? How *extreme* was the order, how *thorough* a cleanup was necessary to cover their tracks?

He feared the truth.

As he reached the end of the hall, a set of swinging double doors led out to the main lobby and the front entrance. He knew better than to attempt to exit that way. He remembered how swiftly and silently the team had moved down the dark hallway. The intruders had to be employing some form of night-vision equipment, and someone was surely guarding all the exits.

Knowing that, he wanted to get as close to the parking

lot before abandoning the cover of the building. Any open window would do.

Still, he wanted to know what he faced.

He edged to the double doors. A pair of narrow, wire-reinforced windows allowed him to spy into the shadowy lobby. The main entrance – a set of glass doors – lay directly opposite his position. He saw no movement, no suspicious shift of shadows inside or outside.

But he wasn't fooled.

He began to turn away, then stopped. If it hadn't been so dark, he might have missed it. In the center of the lobby, half hidden by a sofa, a small blinking red light drew his eye. The waxing and waning glow illuminated a five-gallon steel canister on the floor.

The hairs on the back of his neck shivered at the sight.

Bomb . . .

Jack pulled back and swallowed his fear. At least he had his answer concerning the ultimate objective of this raid. The assault team wouldn't be satisfied with just eliminating the animals.

This was a total clean sweep.

No one was meant to survive.

Jack pictured the others hidden in the building, both those below and Lorna locked in her own office. He had felt the tremble in her body as he whispered for her to stay. She had put her trust in him, a trust now proven to be sadly misplaced. Holing up here would only get them all killed, blown up during the firestorm to come.

He had only one choice.

If it was a war they wanted . . .

Turning back to the swinging door, he shifted his weight to one leg and kicked out with the other. The door swung open, and he tossed the flashlight into the lobby while flicking it on with his thumb.

The blazing light tumbled in a wheeling arc into the pitch-dark lobby.

Jack trusted that whoever was watching this door was using night-vision scopes. He didn't have a flash-bomb to blind naked eyes, but the sudden burning flare of the flashlight through the night-vision scopes would achieve the same end: to momentarily blind any spying eyes, while at the same time drawing attention to the lobby.

Jack turned on a heel and headed to the side of the hallway, to a window that led out toward the parklike grounds between the building and the parking lot. If this was going to be a war, he needed weapons.

He yanked the window open, punched out the screen, and climbed into the bushes just outside. He ducked into cover. The distraction would only buy him a minute at most.

It would have to be enough.

He shoved through the bushes and sprinted toward the dark parking lot. Off to the side, in the direction of the front door, he heard a muffled order crack out, angry, pissed.

Jack kept low as he ran, praying the others kept their heads down, too. Especially Lorna.

But he made a mistake, underestimated his opponent.

A sharp detonation blasted behind him. Startled, he tripped on the wet grass and fell headlong. He caught himself and shoulder-rolled to the side. He stared back toward the building. Fire and smoke spat out the front of the facility. Broken glass rained down as far as Jack's position.

He sat in the grass, stunned. They'd blown the bomb. He had only hoped to distract the others while he fled the building. Blinded, they must have feared an escape out the front door and overreacted, triggering the bomb. It was overkill, like swatting a fly with a wrecking ball.

From this response, Jack knew two things about the leader of this assault team. The bastard was ruthless and determined.

Jack rolled back to his feet and set off for his truck.

If they were to survive, he would have to be the same.

Chapter 29

Duncan approached the fiery ruins of the facility's main entrance. He had a gas mask held in place as he pushed through the smoke. The heat seared his face, clearly defining where nerve-dead skin ended and healthy tissue started. He evaluated the damage ahead.

The incendiary charge had sent a ball of fire and superheated air through the front of the building. Flames licked through the toxic smoke, but the charge's concussive force was only moderate. Glass had blown out, and a part of the drop ceiling had caved in, but structurally the building remained intact. Duncan had studied the schematics of the facility. The place was built like a concrete bunker, meant to withstand hurricanes and floods. It had been a calculated risk. One charge would not knock it down.

That's why Duncan had ordered another ten charges set around the building. His goal was not to *blast* the facility to the ground, but to *burn* it down to the foundation. Already the fires from this single charge had spread into the second level. He hadn't planned to prematurely set off the charge. But the sudden flare of light in the lobby had blinded him. Even ripping off his night-vision goggles hadn't dimmed the flash. It felt as if his retinas had been permanently burned. Angry and fearful that the scientists were making a break for the main exit, he had reacted on impulse and blown the charge to plug the hole here.

No one could be allowed to escape.

Reaching the doors, he stared into the fire-ravaged lobby. Smoke, swirling soot, and collapsed debris made visibility difficult. One of his men had already dismantled the building's sprinkler and alarm systems. He searched for bodies, for whoever tried to make a break for the exit.

Half the lobby was covered in the collapsed drop ceiling. If there were bodies under there, he'd never know. Satisfied that no one could have survived the firestorm, he retreated.

Luckily this facility was remote and isolated. He doubted anyone would have spotted the brief fireball rolling into the sky. Still, the premature explosion upset his timetable, shortened it. With fires spreading, his team would have to clear out of the building sooner than projected.

Once clear of the smoke, he crossed back to his second-in-command. The man had a hand pressed to an ear, clearly listening to a report from the team inside.

Duncan waited for him to sign off, then asked, 'What's the word?'

'The team reached the kennel ward. Found one of the animals. A sheep. We decapitated it as ordered. Team has the head and are moving out.'

'What about the others?' Duncan knew from the transponders that there should be at least another four specimens.

His second shook his head. 'No sign. Korey is splitting his team. Three men are heading down to the morgue. To attend to the carcasses recovered from the swamp.'

Duncan pictured the two cats.

'The other three are going to split up and canvass floor by floor, room by room. We'll find the others.'

Duncan slowly nodded. The order from Lost Eden Cay was to salvage what they could – specifically, the skulls of the specimens – and burn the rest. It seemed the problems on Eden had been growing worse. His superiors had little patience with the mishap here. Duncan needed to perform.

But it was more than that. It was a matter of pride. His blood and flesh had gone into the Babylon Project. He would not see it fail.

The animals were the intellectual property of Ironcreek Industries. What was in their skulls belonged to the company, and in turn belonged to him. He recognized that if his team couldn't find the missing animals, the flames would still claim them. Nothing would remain. Still, he wouldn't be satisfied until he had the heads of all the animals.

Plus there remained one other objective.

'What about the scientists?' Duncan asked. 'Have they secured at least one for questioning?'

Again that irritating shake of a head. 'No, sir.'

Duncan sighed and kept watch on the building. He hoped he hadn't inadvertently blown them all up, but either way, he'd know soon enough.

'Keep that net tight around the building,' Duncan said. 'If Korey's team doesn't flush them out of hiding, the fires soon will.'

Chapter 30

Lorna crouched low in her office. She clutched the rifle to her chest. Since the explosion, it was getting more difficult to breathe. Smoke rolled under the door and continued to fill the small space. Terror kept her breathing sharp and shallow. She fought back tears, not all of them due to the sting in the air.

She pictured Jack caught in the blast. She had no way of knowing if he was alive or dead. Either way, she was on her own. She had only two choices left to her: stay and suffocate or move and risk being caught.

It was really no choice.

But where to go?

She wasn't about to head out into the main hall. Any attempt to reach her brother and her colleagues in the pathology lab would mean crossing paths with the intruders. The others should be safe down there for the moment if they kept quiet. The walk-in cooler was the size of a double-car garage and steel-reinforced. It should withstand any smoke and fire for a while.

But that didn't apply to her.

She glanced over a shoulder. A second door at the back of her office led to her adjoining lab, where she spent most of her workday. From there, she could sneak her way, lab by lab, away from the flames.

But she knew she had to do one thing first.

Igor and the others were still up in the genetics lab, a floor above hers. She could not let them burn. There was a small service stair that led from this floor up to the next. She could reach it if she crossed her lab.

Still, a part of her only wanted to hide, to let someone rescue her. She fought against it, knowing it was born of shock, that such panic hadn't served her in the past, and it wouldn't now.

Move . . .

She slowly rose from her crouch, drawing some strength from the weapon in her hands. She wasn't totally defenseless.

Keeping a watch on the main office door, she retreated to the other. Once she was moving, the terror abated somewhat. She placed a palm against the lab door to make sure it wasn't hot. Satisfied, she eased it open and searched the lab.

Tables, benches, and biogenic equipment – microscopes, catheters, micropipettes, incubators, cell fusion units – filled the space, along with books and piled lab reports. One entire wall was filled by a double-door refrigeration unit, along with a bench holding a long bank of stainless-steel Dewar's bottles containing cryotubes of frozen embryos, sperm, and eggs of endangered species. It was her life's work: the facility's frozen zoo.

Despite her terror, a part of her feared the loss of all her hard work. It could be duplicated eventually, but it would take many years and not all of it would be recovered. She could only hope the fires didn't spread here and that the liquid nitrogen would keep the embryos frozen long enough for a fire-response team to arrive.

Unable to do anything else, she crossed the dark space and headed toward the service stair that led to the second floor. She strained to listen for any sign of the intruders. The pounding rush of blood in her ears made it hard to hear. She stepped carefully, one hand holding her rifle, the other reaching out as she moved through her lab. Luckily, she knew the place well enough that she could have crossed it blindfolded.

She reached the door that led up to the next level. Again she tested it. It was warmer than the one into her office, but still not hot. She was headed toward the fires, but it should take her only a few moments to rush up, grab the animals, and head back down and away.

She edged the door open, found the stairwell empty, and hurried up the narrow flight to the second floor. The genetics suite encompassed most of this level. The door into the lab was only a step away. Holding her breath and steeling herself, she rushed across and through the door. Once inside, she leaned back against the closed door.

She did it.

Across the dark and quiet lab, a soft questioning chirp called to her.

Igor.

The parrot knew she was here. She pictured eyes staring toward her out of the darkness. A slight chill danced over her skin. She remembered the strange intelligence the bird had demonstrated earlier.

She stepped away from the wall and shook away the chill. These were innocent creatures, cruelly used. And at heart they were still animals – only more so.

She crept cautiously down the length of the suite. Being on the top floor, the genetics lab was equipped with a few skylights, which lessened the gloom a bit.

She found Igor still in his cage in the conference room off the main lab. The cub and twin capuchins had been temporarily housed in transport cages, not much different from plastic airline carriers. The cages were used to temporarily hold and move various subjects undergoing testing.

Reaching them, she realized a dilemma. How was she going to carry them all? In their carriers, the cub and monkeys were no problem. But she'd need a third arm for Igor's cage.

Slipping into the conference room, she crouched by Igor's cage. 'Now be quiet,' she whispered, lifting a finger to her lip. 'Shh . . .'

He seemed to understand and matched her tone, uttering under his breath. 'Igor . . . help, Igor . . .'

That's the plan, little fella.

He must smell the smoke.

She unlatched the small door. She couldn't haul the cage, but she could carry the bird. Igor hopped up on the inside of the door, cocking his head back and forth. As she pulled the door open the parrot came with it, as if he knew her intent.

He climbed to a wobbly perch atop the thin door. She held out her arm. Without any prompting, he hopped from the door to her arm and scrambled up it, using his beak on her sleeve to tug up onto her shoulder. He quickly sidled next to her head.

She felt the tremble in his body. The explosion and smoke surely had him spooked. He plainly trusted her to get him out of here – and she intended to do just that.

With Igor balanced on one shoulder, she slung her rifle over the other. Out in the lab, she collected the two carriers. Bagheera had slunk to the back of her cage and silently hissed at her, mouth open, tongue curled, baring immature fangs. The two capuchins clung to the front of the cage, each with one arm. Small masked faces pinched out at her.

Her charges in hand, she headed back across the lab to the service stair. The carriers made her ungainly, especially with the rifle, but she had to manage at least as far as the main floor. Even if it meant setting them all loose out a window, she would. They stood a better chance out there than in here.

As proof, the smoke in the stairwell was already thicker, the air hotter. It was like climbing down a chimney.

She hurried, trying to move as quietly as possible. The animals also remained silent, as if sensing the danger. The only sound was a deep rumble in Igor's chest, almost like a moan. She only heard it because he was squashed up against her ear. She worried about toxins in the smoke. Birds were almost all lungs and air sacs and thus more susceptible to poisons.

She was happy to leave the stair and return to her lab. The room was cooler, likely due to the thawing frozen zoo. She noted a disturbing condensation in the air. She knew the cause. The liquid nitrogen used to keep her samples frozen was constantly evaporating, shedding gas. Normally this was ventilated out of the room. But with the power off, it was building up in here. Left unventilated, nitrogen would eventually displace the oxygen and become deadly.

Worried, she crossed to the lone window in her lab. She set the carriers down and cranked the window open. A river breeze blew in. Igor shivered. Claws dug into her shoulder.

'It's okay,' she shushed as she finished. 'We're going.'

She intended to head through Dr. Chang's biometrics lab, which neighbored hers, then to the veterinary suite at the back of the facility. She wanted to get as far from the flames as possible, then find a place to hole up and hide.

But that was not to be.

'*STOP!*'

The sudden shout made her jump. It came from behind her. Igor lost his grip and slid halfway down her shirtfront before catching hold with his beak. She reacted instinctively and grabbed Igor with both hands and tossed him out the window.

He fell like a frozen turkey. Without feathers, he couldn't fly. But it was only a short drop to the grass. Though she didn't see him land, she heard a tiny squawk of protest. She prayed it wasn't heard.

'*TURN AROUND SLOWLY!*' A shadowy shape stepped from the doorway to her office. Too distracted by the worrisome condensation, she hadn't noticed the open door. '*DROP THE WEAPON OR I'LL SHOOT!*'

It took her a moment to realize he meant the tranquilizing

rifle. She hurriedly shrugged it off her shoulder, let it clatter to the floor, and lifted her palms in the air.

She was trapped.

Chapter 31

Jack crouched behind a broadleaf bush. It had taken longer than he'd hoped to reach the parking lot. Sticking to cover at all times, he'd had to circle through the fringe forest to get here without being spotted. He dared not risk discovery until he was armed with more than his bare hands.

From his hiding spot, he stared toward his truck. It lay only thirty yards away – across open ground. There was no cover. He'd be totally exposing himself. To make matters worse, the parking lot was gravel. Without care, his boots would crunch loud enough to be heard across the Mississippi.

He had no choice.

Rising up on his toes, he shoved out between two bushes like a flushed rabbit and sprinted toward the truck. He expected to hear the crack of rifle with every step. But the night stayed quiet. With attentions focused on the facility, no one must be looking out here.

Reaching the edge of the lot, he skidded in the wet grass, then carefully stepped flat-footed across the gravel as quietly as possible. He crossed to the back of the agency truck and dropped out of sight.

He crouched, one hand on the ground behind the truck bed, and took a moment to collect himself. The truck was a Ford F-150 Raptor with a crew cab and custom-built shell in back. The weapons lockbox was in the rear compartment.

Before he could move, something wet and cold touched his exposed wrist. He jerked back with a noisy crush of gravel. A dark shape shimmied out from under the truck. It was a dog – a black-and-tan hound. A tail whipped back and forth behind it. It took him an extra moment before recognition struck him – followed by shock.

'Burt,' he whispered.

How could that be?

He struggled to make sense of it. He'd left the dog with his brother back at the station house. Then he remembered the phone call. Randy had said he was going to head over here rather than wait at the station. ACRES lay on the way back home.

So where was Randy?

Jack turned to the levee and searched along the private entry road that led from the river to the parking lot. He saw no sign of his brother's truck, and that beat-up Chevy was hard to miss. As he looked, hoping for some other possible explanation, Jack pictured Randy stumbling upon the assault team, blindly waltzing his ass into a firestorm.

Jack sank to a knee. His vision darkened at the edges as he recognized the truth. Burt wouldn't have left Randy unless he had no choice. The dog must have caught Jack's scent and retreated to the truck.

He covered his eyes as if that would shut out the truth.

God, no . . .

A part of him wanted to run out toward the road, calling his brother's name. But that would only get him killed, too. Burt slunk next to him, belly to the ground, his tail's tip tentatively wagging, a submissive posture, asking for forgiveness, for reassurance.

Jack reached a hand and rested it on Burt's flank. 'Good boy,' he mouthed quietly.

He had to get moving now – or he never would.

With his heart weighted like a stone, he climbed to his feet and used a key to open the security shell in back. There was no overhead lamp to alert anyone equipped with night vision. He climbed into the back, reached the weapons locker, and fumbled in the dark with another key to unlatch and pull the lid open.

Inside, the lockbox held his service weapon, a Heckler & Koch P2000 double-action pistol, along with his Remington 870 shotgun. He strapped on the pistol but ignored the shotgun. Instead, he reached for the third weapon inside. He'd confiscated it from Garland Chase: an AA-12 combat auto-assault shotgun. Set on auto, shooting three hundred shells per minute, it could shred his truck to shrapnel.

As his brother would describe it, it was *one mean-ass motherfucker*.

Jack remembered the explosion. He grabbed the weapon. The bastard running this assault might be ruthless, but he never met a Cajun with his blood up. Jack would teach the bastard what it meant to be hunted.

He hopped out of the truck, careful of the gravel, and patted his thigh, a silent command for Burt to follow. Out in the fields and bayous, he and Burt had always made a mean-ass team – and now they had the proper firepower to match.

'C'mon, boy. Let's go hunting . . .'

Chapter 32

With her hands in the air, Lorna faced the gunman as he came forward. He wore a heavy set of goggles over his eyes, obscuring most of his face. The lack of human features made him all the more menacing. Even more than the assault rifle pointed at her chest.

He waved her to the side with the tip of his weapon. 'Get back from the window!'

She obeyed and retreated to the side, bumping against a bench. He kept his weapon pointed at her and lowered himself to one knee beside the two plastic crates on the floor. He quickly peered into each one, then stood up.

He touched two fingers to his throat and spoke in a clipped, military cadence. 'Alpha One. I've secured one of the scientists. A woman. She has the animals. Two of them. She tossed another out a window on the west side.'

Lorna silently cursed. So he'd witnessed that.

There was a pause, then he spoke again. 'The bird. That's right. I'll check.'

He flipped up his goggles and touched a switch on his helmet. A lamp flared above his forehead. The brightness blinded her. With the rifle still pointed at her chest, he ducked his head out the window and quickly scanned the lawn and bushes outside the window.

Lorna held her breath.

He pulled his head back and stared back at her. With his

goggles off, he looked no more human. Under the helmet lamp, his face was all shadows and stubble, but his eyes shone at her, cold and merciless. She kept perfectly still under that predatory gaze.

But he ignored her and continued his radio communication. 'No sign of the parrot.' Another pause as he listened to orders. 'Yes, sir. Decapitate the specimens here. Collect the heads. Understood.'

Lorna went cold as he dropped his free hand to his belt and unsheathed a vicious-looking steel dagger. He lowered to a knee, but he kept those dead eyes on her.

He continued to speak into the radio. 'I'll wait for Takeo before moving the woman.'

The soldier – and there was no doubt he was a mercenary commando of some sort – ducked and pointed his helmet lamp into one of the crates. His dagger flashed menacingly in the sharp light.

As if sensing the threat, a frightened chitter rose from the capuchins.

Even past the thunder of her heart, a maternal surge of fury flooded Lorna. She rode that wave and burst forward. In her hands was a steel thermos. When the soldier had searched out the window, she had grabbed the bottle from the bench at her elbow and twisted the cap off one-handed behind her back.

She hurled the contents into the face of the soldier. Caught by surprise, he widen his eyes. The splash of liquid nitrogen struck him across the bridge of his nose. She twisted to the side as his gun reflexively fired. A flurry of rounds blasted past her. Glass shattered from shelves; plaster exploded.

Then gun and dagger toppled from his fingers. Both hands flew to his face. His corneas had been flash-frozen on contact. His eyeballs burst and wept down his face. Blind and in agony, he fell to his back, a scream strangled in his throat. She watched him gasp out a mist of condensation. He must have inhaled some of the liquid nitrogen as it

204

splashed, sucked it into his nose and mouth and down into his throat and lungs.

He writhed and clawed at his face and neck, struggling against the pain, fighting to breathe with frozen lungs.

Lorna held back her own stunned horror before it paralyzed her. She'd never killed a person before – and though the soldier still fought, she knew he was a dead man, a living corpse.

She stumbled on numbed legs past his agonized form and reached the two crates. She knew she didn't have much time. Others were on their way. She lifted one crate to the window, opened the gate, and upended the carrier. The two capuchins clung inside, scared and confused. She shook the cage, trying to dislodge them. One lost its grip and pulled its conjoined twin with it. The stunned pair tumbled into the dark.

Sorry, little ones.

She hated to abandon them, but their best chance of survival was away from here. She returned to the second crate and hauled it to the open window. Spooked by the gunfire, the frightened cub leaped out as soon as the gate was open.

She dropped the crate and retrieved her rifle. She considered going for the assault rifle, but the soldier writhed on top of it. She couldn't get any closer – both guilt and terror kept her back.

But there was one thing she still wanted. During his violent struggles, the soldier had knocked the goggles off his helmet. She picked them up off the floor and pulled them over her eyes. The dark room suddenly snapped into a green-phosphorus clarity.

Able to see in the dark, she considered hopping out the same window, fleeing after the animals, but she'd be exposed out in the open. The intruders were well equipped and likely had the grounds under surveillance. The small animals might escape that net. She would not. Her best chance of survival still lay inside, to keep hidden for as long as possible. With the animals free, her only responsibility was to herself – and the others still trapped below.

She fled her lab and headed toward the rear of the facility. Now able to see, she moved swiftly, with more confidence. She needed to reach the veterinary clinic, her domain.

If she could reach there, she had a plan.

Out front, Duncan listened to the garbled moans die over the radio. He had no idea what had happened to his man, the one who had found the woman and the animals, but he'd clearly been incapacitated in some manner.

Another of Korey's team came on the radio. His voice was raspy with static, but the anger came through clear. 'Fielding is down. Dead. No sign of the woman. Crates are empty.'

Duncan touched his throat mike. 'Find her.'

He closed his eyes for a moment and sucked on a lime-flavored Life Savers. If the crates were empty, she must have tossed the others out with the bird. The specimens were loose on the grounds.

Opening his eyes, he turned to his second-in-command, Connor Reed. He knew the man had been listening to the radio chatter. Connor's face was a hard mask. He ran a hand over the stubble of his red hair. The younger man had been with Duncan's unit going back to boot camp. He'd been the one who led the charge and blew away the mutated chimp that had mauled him in Baghdad.

'Who's on the west exit?' Duncan asked.

'Gerard is at the tree line with a sniper scope.'

'Go join him. Search for those specimens. Shoot anything that moves out there.'

'Yes, sir,' he said and ran off.

Duncan knew Connor would not fail him. The man was as brutal and unrelenting as a machine. Once let loose, he would lay down a swath of destruction. Two years ago, Connor had wiped out an entire Somalian rebel village – men, women, children, even the stray dogs – all to avenge a comrade who'd lost a leg to a roadside bomb. He'd get the job done here with the same ruthless efficiency.

As Connor disappeared around the corner Duncan's radio crackled to life again. 'Alpha One, Korey here. Reporting from the morgue.'

'Go ahead,' Duncan said. 'Have you secured the carcasses of the two cats?'

'Yes, sir. Their heads are on the way up. But we believe we've also discovered where the other targets – the scientists – are holed up. Found some sort of big meat locker down here. It's locked tight, but I thought I heard movement inside.'

Duncan brightened at the news.

'Permission to blow the doors, sir. Though I can't guarantee there won't be target casualties.'

Duncan understood the man's caution. They needed at least one of them alive. He weighed the risk of killing everyone inside and decided it was worth it. He knew there was at least one person still running loose. The woman. That was good enough.

'Do it,' he ordered.

'Yes, sir.'

Duncan returned his attention to the smoking ruin of the front of the facility. Fires burned deeper inside, glowing through the pall. No one was coming out this way, and Duncan had a man posted at the entry road.

It was time to end this.

He pulled out his sidearm. The heft of the Sig Sauer pistol helped weight and center his determination. He headed toward the least smoky window. There was a woman loose in there. Scared. On the run. Likely armed.

He smiled – or at least half his face did.

He didn't want her killed. At least not until he was done with her. Got answers from her. And maybe a little more besides.

With his scarred face, few women would give him a second glance, except in horror. And even fewer would ever satisfy him. Unless paid or at the point of a gun.

He headed for the building, determined to find this woman. The hunting would make the prize all that much sweeter. Afterward he would get all he could out of this woman.

Then put a bullet in her skull.

Chapter 33

Jack kept to the forest.

He wanted to move more quickly as he circled toward the rear of the complex. He had traveled out and around, intending to come at the place from the back. He knew any eyes would be focused toward the facility, not over their shoulders.

Still, he dared not make a sound. He forced himself to move silently, to place each foot with care. Burt shadowed him, moving just as quietly, recognizing that this was a hunt. Jack's heart thundered against such caution, urging him to run headlong back toward the facility, guns blazing.

Moments ago, he had heard gunfire, muffled and indistinct, coming from somewhere inside ACRES. He recognized the rattle of an assault rifle. He pictured Lorna bleeding, sprawled in death.

He fought against despair as he approached the southern side of the facility. From fifty yards away, he took a position under the low limbs of an old black oak, half shrouded by Spanish moss, and studied the building and grounds. The pathology lab lay to the rear of the facility, in the basement level. The others had holed up there.

But are they all still there . . . and what about Lorna?

He pictured her reacting to the fire. If she wasn't still in her office, the flames and smoke would likely drive her toward the back of the place.

Meaning everyone should be close by.

At least, he prayed so.

He studied the building more closely. A concrete ramp led down to a steel roll-up door, large enough to drive a Pershing tank through. The pathologist had mentioned the back entrance earlier.

Jack didn't intend to use that big door. Instead, he focused his attention on a smaller service entry beside it. As he recalled from the pathology floor's layout, the door led into a side office. That would be his point of entry.

Sliding back behind the oak's trunk, Jack knelt beside Burt. He dared not make for that door. Not yet. As sure as a catfish loved mud, there had to be at least one man watching the rear of the building. But where was he? With the woods dark as pitch, the bastard could be anywhere.

Jack gave Burt a scratch behind an ear. While Jack might not have night-vision gear, he had another way to extend his senses: one of the best hunting dogs in all the state of Louisiana.

'Time to flush out that bird.' Jack waved an arm and gave a soft command. *'Hup!'*

Burt took off like a shot. Since a pup, the hound had been taught to roust birds out of field and forest. Jack had trained him with clipped pigeons, and with the help of Randy and Tom, he'd established a flushing pattern with Burt, a precise zigzagging run that would clear a field of birds as efficiently as a lawn mower. The memory of training with his two brothers brought a pang of grief, as sharp as a knife to the belly.

He bit against that pain and followed down the center of Burt's switchbacking pattern. The hound ran the woods back and forth, pivoting exactly at the range of a decent rifle shot.

The river breeze blew in his face, perfect for hunting.

Jack followed, moving from tree to tree, listening to the dark wood. He tuned out the whispering rush of his dog running back and forth. Burt was twenty yards ahead – then he heard it.

A snap of a branch to the right. A heavy footfall. Someone turning.

Jack set his back against a tree and pinpointed the location in his mind's eye. He let out the soft whistle-chirp of a Carolina wren, one of the region's most common and vocal birds. Burt knew the signal and went silent. Jack pictured the hound dropping flat to the ground as trained.

He waited for a full minute, long enough for the guard to turn his attention back to the facility. Satisfied he'd held back long enough, Jack slipped around the tree, and with even more caution than before, he crept toward the location Burt had exposed.

The edge of the woods appeared ahead.

Starlight bathed the open grounds beyond, brighter than the dark bower of the woods. Silhouetted against that backdrop stood a darker shadow. A guard had taken a position at the edge of the forest, a sniper rifle at his shoulder. The weapon looked like an M21, a semiautomatic rifle. If anyone had come out that rear door or dared approach it, this lone gunman would've dropped them in a heartbeat.

Pistol in hand, Jack moved like a ghost through the woods, glad to have the wind in his face. The river breeze would help mask any scent and muffle any telltale noises.

Still, when Jack was two yards away, something must have prickled the hairs on the other's neck. The guard turned.

Jack moved fast. He dared not shoot. The crack of his pistol through the open air would be like a cannon blast out here. He lunged before the other could react. Jack twisted the weapon out of his startled grasp while sweeping the man's leg and dropping him to the ground. Jack followed him down, landing both knees square on his rib cage, squashing air out, preventing a scream.

Jack jammed the pistol under his chin and fired.

Like with a pillow, the skull and helmet muffled the blast to a harsh *pop*. Still too loud.

Fearing any response, he leaped up, whistled for Burt, and sprinted toward the building. He ran across the open ground and hit the ramp at full clip. He flew down it, half tumbling. He came close to running headlong into the steel roll-up door but caught himself at the last moment.

He twisted to the side entry. He tested the knob.

Locked.

He had expected no different – only hoped for at least a small break. It wasn't to be. He holstered his pistol and shrugged off the other weapon from his shoulder. The AA-12 assault shotgun was not a subtle weapon.

Then again maybe it was high time for subtlety to end.

He backed three steps and pointed the barrel at the door's dead bolt.

Before he could pull the trigger, a spat of distant gunfire erupted. Off to the west. From the clear ring of the blasts, the shots had come from outside. Jack glanced that way.

What was going on? What were they shooting at?

He turned farther and realized someone was missing.

Burt.

Jack went cold. The hound seldom broke his field training, not unless something really irresistible struck his nose: a dead fish, a rotting squirrel. To make matters worse, Burt loved to roll in those rich stinks.

As he listened the spat of gunfire died off.

The night went quiet again.

Jack turned back to the door. Unlike Burt, he didn't have the luxury of curiosity. Or subtlety.

He lifted the shotgun and fired.

Lorna heard something loud blast beneath her. She couldn't tell if it came from inside or outside. She'd been hearing periodic gunfire as she fled across the neighboring labs toward the veterinary clinic. Listening to the blasts, she was

212

glad she had opted to stay inside versus taking her chances outside. She never would have survived.

A part of her heart went out to the animals she had let loose.

Were they the targets of all this gunplay?

Knowing she'd done all she could, she continued until she reached the veterinary wing. The clinic was currently under renovation, with the surgical suite undergoing a much-needed update. Because of the construction, there were no animals housed here.

Lucky for that.

With rifle in hand, she pushed carefully into the main treatment room of the clinic. She stayed low, her senses stretching outward for any hidden dangers in the dark. The smell of fresh paint and wood dust struck her. Through her night-vision goggles, she made out the central exam station with an attached wet table and overhanging surgical lights. To the left, a bank of empty stainless-steel cages covered one wall, while the other side opened into a scrub area and the half-renovated operating room.

All seemed quiet.

She crept only a couple of steps into the room and turned to a smaller door on her immediate left, marked with posted hazard symbols.

She tugged it open. Inside stood a bank of green oxygen tanks. Five in total. The set of tanks supplied the clinic and other labs with its piped oxygen. She knew by memory which tank fed the surgical suite and unhooked its regulator from the wall – then twisted the valve to On.

A fierce hissing flowed from the open tank.

She left the others untouched.

Trembling with fear, she closed the door and retreated toward the operating room on the other side of the room – but not before first stopping to raid the veterinary lab in the corner.

She only had one last preparation to make.

But did she have enough time?

With the shotgun blast still ringing in his ears, Jack kicked open the outer door. The small office beyond barely had enough room for a work desk and filing cabinet. He moved quickly. To his right, a closed door led to the pathology lab. Directly ahead stretched an office window that looked out onto the open floor.

Jack noted a few wobbling glows out there.

Flashlights.

They speared toward the office, drawn by the shotgun blast.

Never stopping, Jack grabbed the desk chair with one hand and flung it through the window. Glass shattered. At the same time he dove to the door, shouldered it open, and rolled out into the cavernous room beyond.

He spotted two men standing ten yards away.

They were in full camo, with flashlights in one hand, pistols in the other. Drawn by the exploding office window, they were a fraction too slow in turning toward Jack.

Sweeping around with his shotgun, Jack pulled the trigger and held it. A barrage of shells sprayed out like a machine gun. The rounds blasted the two men across their midsections, ripping them nearly in half.

Flashlights went flying.

Not knowing how many more men were down here, Jack leaped for the cover of a steel equipment locker. He stared across the room toward the hall that led toward the walk-in cooler.

A glow came from that hallway.

As he watched, the light clicked off.

Damn it.

At least one more man was still down here.

Before he could even calculate a strategy, two shots fired. The pair of discarded flashlights went dark. The last man was a crack shot, taking out the last lights.

Not good.

Jack was now blind. He pulled back undercover.

As he did so he heard boots pounding across the cement floor, the ring of a heel hitting one of the steel drains. He blindly pointed his weapon and strafed in the general direction. The muzzle flash would give away his position, but he had no choice. He kept firing until the drum magazine emptied.

A sharp cry of surprise cut through the barrage.

Jack's ears strained as the echoes died away.

Was the man down?

Even as he thought it the steps resumed out of the dark, more stumbling, erratic – but they were heading *away*.

Jack dropped the shotgun and grabbed his pistol.

Across the room, a door opened and slammed closed.

The man had fled out of here.

Suspicion rang through Jack. These were trained killers, not cowards. What would make the man flee like that?

He stepped out of hiding and kept his pistol pointed toward the door – when the world exploded.

Chapter 34

Duncan listened to the muffled blast fade away. It came from a floor below. He had tried to raise Korey's team down there, but he'd gotten no answer.

Worrisome, but not his primary concern.

The place was surrounded. No one was getting in or out.

Duncan stood over Fielding's dead body. His face was a bloody ruin, his eyes gone, his lips blackened as if flash-frozen. Duncan had already noted the liquid nitrogen tanks in the room and could surmise what had taken place. Fielding must have underestimated the woman and let his guard down.

Stupid.

Duncan felt no sympathy for the man's agonizing death.

Another of Duncan's unit, an Asian-American named Takeo, came up behind him. 'Second floor is swept. No sign of the woman.'

Duncan didn't acknowledge him. He wasn't surprised.

Another teammate spoke by the lab door. 'Do you want me to go check on the others down in the morgue?'

That could wait.

'You're both with me,' he ordered.

With the place surrounded, nothing else mattered. He'd be out of here in two minutes. With at least one prize in hand. Then he'd burn this fucking place to the ground and be done with it.

'Where to, sir?' Takeo asked.

Duncan didn't answer. He had noted a stack of cards by the lab's computer. *Dr. Lorna Polk*. From his intel on this place, he knew she was the staff veterinarian. She ran this cryogenic lab and the veterinary facility. From the schematics, the veterinary wing lay toward the rear of this level, farthest away from the fires.

Panicked, she would've fled to a place of security, a place she knew.

Duncan stepped over Fielding's corpse and headed in that direction. He moved cautiously. The body was a good lesson. He would not underestimate Dr. Polk.

'Follow me.'

Jack picked himself up. The blast had knocked him off his feet. Across the dark lab, a fire glowed. It raged down the hall that led to the walk-in cooler. Smoke poured into the main room.

He gave the open pathology lab a quick scan and saw no sign of the assault team. But the man who had fled would alert others. Jack didn't have much time. He ran toward the fires.

As he rounded into the hall smoke choked the passageway ahead. Flames danced up the walls to either side. At the far end, the steel door to the meat locker had been blown off.

He heard a woman crying through the smoke. The assault team must have learned the scientists were holed up in here and had tried to blow their way inside. But someone had been heavy-handed with the C-4.

Jack rushed forward, heedless of the spreading flames.

As he sidestepped the blackened door an arm thrust through the smoke and stabbed at his face. Jack leaned back, catching a flash of silver as a blade passed in front of his nose.

'It's me,' he hissed out. 'Agent Menard!'

Through the pall of smoke, Lorna's brother appeared, holding a scalpel in one hand. His other arm was cradled to his waist. From the angle of his hand, he'd broken his wrist.

Kyle pushed forward, unapologetic about nearly blinding him. He had only one thought. 'Where's Lorna?'

Jack shook his head, and his heart sank. He had hoped she would've made it down here somehow and joined the others.

'I don't know,' he said.

'What do you mean you don't know?' Kyle looked like he was ready to lash out again with the scalpel.

'I left her upstairs, locked in her office.'

Jack moved past Kyle, drawn by a woman's sobbing. He had to get these people moving. Inside the cooler, he found the neurobiologist, Zoë Trent, kneeling over her husband. He lay on his side in a pool of spreading blood. A thick steel pipe pierced his chest, impaled through by the force of the blast.

The man wasn't moving, wasn't breathing.

The pathologist, Greer, knelt on the other side, a finger to the man's throat. He glanced to Jack and shook his head.

A cold fury flashed through him.

Kyle spoke at his shoulder. Guilt rang in his voice. 'If I hadn't locked this place up so tightly . . . if they didn't have to blow it . . .'

'Then you'd all be dead,' Jack said and knew it to be true.

Carlton Metoyer stood over Zoë, his face sunken and much older. He tried to get her moving. 'He's gone, my dear,' he said softly. 'We must go.'

'Noooo,' the woman moaned and clutched her husband's hand.

Jack had no time for niceties. He stepped forward and bodily picked her up. She struggled against him. He carried her away from her husband and down the fiery hall. The woman's thrashing died down to a limp-limbed moaning. She hung on to him as if drowning – and maybe she was.

But Jack was in no position to pull her back.

Reaching the main floor, he passed her to Greer and Carlton. 'Get her out of here. Out the back. The way should still be clear for a few more minutes. Make for the woods and keep moving.'

They didn't argue, too shell-shocked and scared.

Kyle hung back as they headed away. 'My sister . . .'

Jack pointed after the others. 'Go. I'll find her.'

Still, he hesitated.

Jack shoved him after the others. 'Trust me. I'll get her,' he promised. *Or die trying.*

Lorna knelt at the entrance to the surgical suite. Wearing her night-vision goggles, she had a clear view across the treatment room to the entryway. She had been staring for so long her eyes felt dry and sandy. But she dared not even blink.

And it proved fortunate.

Without warning – not a footstep, not a whisper – the door swung open. Two shapes burst inside, staying low and splitting to either side, weapons at their shoulders.

A third followed, standing taller.

Something about his posture set her heart to pounding harder.

Lorna leaned out of direct sight and picked up the flint striker from the floor. She normally used the tool to ignite the Bunsen burner in her veterinary lab. Minutes ago, she had picked it up from the lab bench – along with the portable propane tank that fueled the burner. This far out, they had no natural-gas lines.

With her other hand, she lifted the loose air hose that rested in her lap. Normally the hose connected the anesthetic machine to the oxygen bib on the wall. She had disconnected the anesthetic machine but left the hose running up to the wall, where plumbed pipes ran from here to the oxygen tanks in the mechanical room. Afterward, she had spent two minutes backfilling that line with propane gas.

Lifting the hose now, she unpinched its end and raised the striker. With a fast squeeze, the flint scraped, spit out a spark, and ignited the leaking gas.

Flames spat out the hose end. She pinched it closed again and watched a blue flame shoot down the propane-filled hose. The glow rushed up to the wall bib and vanished away. She pictured the fire continuing, sweeping through the pipes, a flaming arrow headed straight toward –

The hissing drew Duncan's attention as soon as he stepped across the threshold. *Snake* was his first thought, jumping immediately to a bestial threat. But it came from the left, from behind a closed room plastered with a pair of hazard-warning emblems.

Blood rushed to his temples and pounded there.

Across the room, a tiny flicker of flame flared in his night-vision equipment. It could mean only one thing.

Ambush . . .

He didn't have time to warn the others who had flanked right and left. He lunged away from the hissing door, shouldering into Takeo. His other teammate stood directly in front of the door –

– when it exploded.

A blue fireball shattered the door off its hinges. It struck the unsuspecting man in the back, splitting in half. A secondary explosion followed. Duncan managed to roll Takeo's body between him and the blast.

Shrapnel blew, along with the tumbling clang of a green oxygen tank.

With the din still ringing, Duncan pushed Takeo off him.

The Asian man rolled to his knees, dazed, stunned. He turned toward Duncan as if looking for an explanation. Shrapnel peppered his face. Blood flowed. He was missing one ear.

Then the man slapped a hand to his neck.

His fingers removed a dart from under the angle of his chin.

A tranquilizer dart . . .

Deafened by the blast, Duncan hadn't even heard the shot.

Takeo's head fell back. He garbled something, choking up a thick white froth – then went rigid and fell back to the floor.

Before Duncan could move, something struck him square in the throat like a punch to the larynx. He scrabbled and knocked the dart off, furious at being caught off guard.

Despite his forewarning, it seemed he had still underestimated Dr. Polk. But there was nothing he could do now except curse her.

Fuck you, bitch . . .

Lorna watched the second man drop. She could tell he fought against the tranquilizer. But even a pinprick of M99 could be fatal. And she'd shot them both in the throat, where blood vessels were rich, and unloaded enough drugs to drop a rhino.

Still, she waited for thirty seconds until there was not even a twitch.

But she dared wait no longer.

Across the room, the flames spread, making the night-vision goggles a hindrance. She swept them off, cautiously stepped out, and headed toward the exit. She didn't want to risk being trapped here by the fire. She also wanted another weapon. Her rifle had held only the two cartridges. She was out of ammunition.

She crossed to the first man and scooped his rifle from the floor. It was heavy, muscular, and unfamiliar. She studied the weapon as she sidled past the second man – but as she stepped away, something snagged her ankle, jerked her leg, and flipped her face forward to the ground.

Duncan rose as the doctor's face struck the floor. She cried out and tried to roll over, dazed, her chin split and bloody. With a savage grin, he climbed on top of her, swung his Sig Sauer, and cracked the pistol's butt against the back of her skull.

Under him, her body went slack. Out cold. Only she wasn't playing possum like he'd been doing a moment ago.

In the end, who underestimated who, Dr. Polk?

Duncan rubbed his throat. It still stung from the impact of the dart. He'd likely be hoarse for days. But nothing worse. The dart had struck his throat mike, blunting the needle enough that it only lodged shallowly into a thick callus of scar tissue. Not a hard target, considering most of his neck was wrapped in leathery scars from that old attack.

He flipped her over. She was still breathing. Good.

He also noted she was quite the looker. And blond, just the way he liked them.

Satisfied with his trophy, he leaned down and hauled the woman up and over a shoulder. He clamped a hand on her buttocks to hold her and headed back through the facility, intending to vacate the building the same way he came in.

Riding on the adrenaline, he quickly reached the main hall. Smoke choked the passageway. Out there, he spotted a body in camo gear, sitting and leaning up against one wall.

A hand lifted as he appeared, beckoning. A voice croaked out to him. 'Sir.'

It was Korey, the assault-team leader.

The man had been down in the morgue, supposedly

blowing his way into a meat locker to fetch one of the scientists. Fat lot of good that did. He plainly screwed it up, leaving Duncan to take matters into his own hands.

Korey groaned and dropped his arm, too weak to hold it up. The man sat on the floor, in his own blood – and shit from the smell of it – holding a fist to a belly wound. It looked like he'd taken a cannonball through his gut.

'Help . . .'

Someone must have gotten the drop on Korey's team.

Duncan glanced back down the smoky hall, suddenly feeling eyes on him. It was time to get out of here. Ignoring the wounded man, he hurried to the open window.

He had what he came for. Fuck the rest.

Reaching the window, he hunkered down and climbed through the window with the woman. Once outside, he touched his throat mike and called up his second-in-command.

'Connor, prepare the team to move out.'

'Sir?'

'You have your orders. I'll meet you out front.'

He headed in that direction.

'What about the escaped specimens?' Connor asked. 'We've still not found them. These tracking transponders are shit in close quarters.'

That was true. The GPS was only good for pinning down a location to a quarter square mile or so. With so much forest and brush, it was a needle-in-a-haystack situation out there.

Connor continued. 'All we've spotted so far is some stray dog.'

Dog?

Duncan then remembered the hound from the Chevy, the one who'd startled him. Fire entered his voice. 'Did you kill the motherfucker?'

'No. Bastard ran off.'

Too bad.

'Then abandon the search,' he ordered with finality. 'Once clear, blow this place to hell.'

'Understood.'

He hurried toward the truck parked out front. Whatever pride had fueled his need to apprehend all the animals had cooled. He had a good enough trophy in his arms. The remaining animals were weak and immature. They wouldn't survive long on their own in the wild. And besides, he had what he needed for damage control. The woman could tell them what was learned here and who else knew. That should satisfy his superiors at Lost Eden Cay.

Then the woman would be his to dispose of as he pleased.

And he intended to be *pleased*.

Chapter 35

Jack knelt in the smoky hall beside a man bleeding to death. It was one of the enemy, maybe the very one he had shot earlier. The soldier hadn't gotten far. From the gaping wound in his gut, he didn't have long to live.

The soldier stared at Jack with glazed, pained eyes.

Knowledge of his death shone there.

Jack had seen it often enough in the battlefield. He placed his trust in that shine, knowing that in such moments absolution was often sought.

'There was a woman here,' Jack pleaded. 'Blond. A doctor. Do you know where she is?'

Jack had already wasted too much time. As he fled the lower level he was forced to balance between caution and panic. He feared stumbling headlong into an ambush – he would be no good to Lorna if he was dead. But he also sensed that time was running out.

Where could she be?

The man croaked a single word, never taking his eyes off Jack, as if needing even this tiny bit of companionship at the end. 'Captured . . .'

Jack tensed, biting back a curse. 'Where did they take her?'

The soldier struggled to answer, but his eyes rolled back.

Jack gripped the man's free hand. 'Where?' he begged.

Eyes fluttered back to stare at him. The man's head fell to

the left. He stared toward an open window. A slight breeze stirred the smoke there.

'They took her out?' Jack asked.

No answer. Jack reached to the soldier's chin and turned the man's face toward him. Open eyes stared blankly. The man was gone.

He gave the soldier's hand a final squeeze and shoved to his feet.

Following the only bread crumb left to him, Jack rushed to the window. He stuck his head out and searched the grounds. He saw no one. He quickly clambered out the window and landed in the wet grass. Off to the east, the sky was beginning to brighten.

He heard a truck engine roar to life from the front of the building.

Pistol in hand, he ran in that direction. His chest tightened with a cold certainty. The assault team was pulling out as dawn beckoned. And they had Lorna.

He reached the corner of the building and caught taillights through the smoke. A truck bounced out of the yard and onto the road heading toward the river.

Jack lifted the pistol, but he held back from firing.

He could just as easily hit Lorna.

Frustrated, he lowered his gun and sprinted toward the neighboring parking lot. The rolling smoke from the fires, which now licked up from the roof of ACRES, helped hide his flight.

He pounded across the gravel and reached his truck. He yanked the door, leaped inside, and keyed the ignition. Popping into gear, he smashed the accelerator. The engine roared and gravel spat out behind the spinning tires. The Ford leaped forward as Jack fought the steering wheel. He spun the truck, fishtailing in the gravel, and took off after the other.

He couldn't let them get away.

Ahead, taillights sped down the winding entry road.

Jack flattened the gas pedal to the floor. Steering one-handed, he lowered the side window and stuck out his pistol. He fired at the other truck, low, toward the tires. He didn't truly expect to hit them, but he hoped to get their attention, to startle them enough to either slow down or lose control.

He hit a pothole as he fired a third time, throwing his aim high.

The rear window of the other truck splintered with cracks.

Jack silently cursed. He had to be more careful.

Ahead, brake lights flashed for a second – then the truck sped faster. From a sunroof in the other vehicle, a figure climbed into view bearing aloft a rifle. Shots blasted back at him.

Jack ducked low but didn't slow. His windshield spattered with cracks. A slug puffed into the passenger headrest.

The other truck's brake lights flared again. The driver had to slow to make the turn onto the levee road that ran alongside the Mississippi.

Jack kept his boot pressed hard on the accelerator. If he could ram them from behind, send them sailing over the far side of the levee, he had a chance of stopping them.

The distance closed between them.

The other truck began to swing for the turn.

C'mon . . .

Jack urged more speed out of the V-8 engine.

Focused on the other truck, he almost missed seeing a man step from behind a tree alongside the road's shoulder. He lifted a grenade launcher to his shoulder and pointed it at Jack's truck.

Jack should have known that the assault team wouldn't leave their rear flank unprotected. They had posted some man at the entrance, someone with serious firepower.

This all flashed through Jack's head as he watched the rocket launcher fire, exploding with a spat of flame and smoke.

A spatter of thunder woke Lorna – so loud it felt like nails hammered into her skull. She cried out, as much in pain as confusion. She tasted blood. Her body was being thrown about as if she were on a boat in a storm.

It took her a long agonizing moment to realize she was in the backseat of an SUV. The thunder was gunfire, coming from a shooter standing next to her, halfway out an open moonroof.

She tried to lift her hands to her pounding head, but found them tied behind her back. She was thrown against the passenger window as the truck made a sharp turn onto the levee road.

Memory flooded back to her.

The attack, the bloodshed, the ambush in the clinic . . .

She stared out the window toward ACRES. Another truck barreled up the entry road, coming straight at them, looking ready to T-bone right into the side of this vehicle.

Lorna recognized the other truck. 'Jack . . .'

Then flames flashed by the side of the road, drawing her eye to a soldier standing there with a smoking weapon.

Jack's truck exploded. The front end jackknifed into the air, riding a fireball. It flipped onto its rear fender and toppled over onto its cab. Glass and fiery metal rained down.

The blast was so loud she didn't know she was screaming until it was over. Someone grabbed her shoulder and shoved her back into her seat. A hand slapped her face, momentarily blinding her.

'Shut the hell up!'

Through tears, she glanced one last time out the window. The SUV was speeding down the levee road. She could not see Jack's truck any longer. But a moment later, a muffled detonation erupted farther away from the road. A massive swirl of fire climbed into the dark sky.

ACRES.

She closed her eyes, too numb to scream. She pictured her

brother and her colleagues. She prayed they'd gotten out –
but even that hope was dashed with the hoarse words from
the driver.

'Connor, order Daughtery to do a final sweep of the area
before he takes off. Kill anyone still alive.'

Chapter 36

Deaf, Jack lay on his back in prickly brush. He had trouble focusing his eyes. The world swam in and out of focus.

Fires raged to one side. Smoke rolled over him, smelling of oil. He turned his head enough to see the fiery wreckage of his service truck on the road.

He remembered the soldier with the rocket launcher.

Jack had reacted on pure instinct as the weapon fired. No thought, just action. He had popped the door and thrown himself away from the truck. The blast wave still caught him and flung him like a rag doll through the air into the weeds.

Must have blacked out a bit.

He lay a moment longer, unsure if he could move. It hurt to breathe. Busted a rib at least.

Then he heard the heavy tread of boots, rushing his way.

Jack pawed around him for his pistol, but he had lost it. He struggled up despite the complaint from his beaten body. He would not die on his back.

A figure rose up before him. The soldier had traded his rocket launcher for an assault rifle. The weapon pointed at his face.

'You are one tough bastard to kill,' he growled.

Jack lifted his arms. He knew there would be no mercy, no use begging. Not that he would. Instead, with his arms up, he flipped the guy off with both hands.

This earned a respectful sneer. Still, the man leveled the rifle.

Jack kept his eyes open, ready for what was to come.

A loud *crack* sounded.

Jack frowned as the gunman fell face forward, blood spewing out his nose, and almost landed in Jack's lap.

Behind the soldier stood a wet dog of a figure.

'Randy . . . ?'

His brother tossed aside the thick tree limb he'd used to club the gunman. He glanced around, swiping a hand through his soaking-wet hair, then turned his attention back to Jack.

'So where's Burt?'

A half hour later, Jack and his brother still combed the woods around the burning building. They had to move with care. The firebombing had turned the research facility into a blazing torch. Lit by flames, shadows danced throughout the woods, making the search all the more difficult and nerve-racking.

Randy had explained about the attack on the road, being forced into the river. But you couldn't drown a Cajun that easily. He swam downstream a fair spell and crept back when he heard all the gunfire.

Traipsing the woods now, Jack couldn't ask for a better partner. The two brothers hadn't hunted together for years, but they fell into an easy and familiar stride with each other: one taking the lead, then the other, silently signaling, sticking to the darker shadows. Over the past years, a wall had grown between them, built by secrets and Jack's self-imposed estrangement. As they traipsed the woods, Jack recognized how much he missed the simple camaraderie of family, how quickly that wall could drop if he'd let it.

But for now, he had a job still to do. It wasn't just Burt whom the two hunted. They watched for any straggling members of the assault team.

Jack had confiscated the rifle from the mercenary Randy

had clubbed. Unfortunately, his brother had hit the man with all his strength and caved in the back of the guy's skull, killing him instantly.

'I was pissed,' Randy had explained. He told Jack about the roadside ambush, the crash into the Mississippi. 'Fuckers almost drowned my ass.'

The death was unfortunate. Jack would've liked to interrogate the man, to discover where the others had taken Lorna. With the soldier dead, he had hoped to find another replacement out here. But with the sun now rising, their search came up empty-handed. They had circled the entire facility. The attackers must have evacuated the area following the firebombing.

'Now what?' Randy asked.

'We find Burt and get the hell out of here.'

With the area secure, Jack cupped his mouth and whistled sharply. Randy did the same, calling out Burt's name. The fire's roar fought to drown their efforts. Jack circled out again, whistling and calling more boldly this time.

Halfway back around, a loud crunching and snapping erupted from the deeper forest. Jack tensed, raising his rifle in that direction.

Instead of the dog, their calls drew four others out of the woods.

Lorna's brother and her colleagues came stumbling forward. They looked haggard and ragged, but happy to see them.

That is, all except one.

Kyle came at Jack as if he was going to attack. His eyes searched to either side, then toward the smoldering fire. His voice was a tearful croak. 'Lorna . . . ?'

'No,' Jack assured him, but he didn't blunt the truth. 'She got out, but the others took her.'

'Took her?' he echoed.

Before Jack could explain, a baying howl rose from deeper in the woods to the west.

Randy brightened. '*Mon Dieu!* That's Burt!'

His brother set off into the forest. Jack followed, leading the others. He wasn't about to leave the hound here. With the sky brightening, someone would quickly spot the column of smoke pouring into the sky. An emergency response team would be closing down on the place with sirens blazing. By that time, he wanted everyone together – and on the same page.

As they crossed through the forest Kyle kept step with him, cradling his broken wrist. 'Why did they take my sister?'

'To interrogate her,' Jack said bluntly. 'To cover their tracks. They'll want to know how much was learned about those animals.'

Kyle grew pale. 'Then what?'

Jack glanced to him. The question didn't need to be acknowledged. They both knew what would happen afterward. Instead, he answered the question buried behind the other. 'They'll keep her alive at least for another day.'

Carlton joined him. 'How do you know that, Agent Menard?'

'Because this was meant as a surgical strike. To get in and out fast. It didn't turn out that way. With the deaths and all the mess here, they'll retreat as far as possible before questioning her. Likely to their base of operations, wherever that might be.'

'I'd guess somewhere beyond the U.S. border,' Carlton stated.

'Why do you say that?' Jack asked. He suspected the same, but he wanted to hear the doctor's estimation.

'What was done to those animals. The way they were treated. No lab on U.S. soil would be allowed to perform such abominations. But to circumvent such rules and regulations, American companies and corporations frequently set up clandestine labs just outside our borders. In Mexico, the Caribbean, South America. In fact, there are thousands of such unsanctioned labs around the world.'

Jack digested this information. He'd come to the same conclusion, mostly from the fact that the trawler had tried to enter the country through the bayou. It definitely had the feel of an attempted border crossing.

'So what do we do?' Kyle asked.

Jack faced the others, needing their cooperation. 'If we're right, Lorna's best chance for survival hinges on the kidnappers' continuing belief that we're all dead. They'll feel more secure, less panicked, if they think they're holding the only witness. Can you all do that?'

He got nods all around, even from Zoë. Her eyes were puffy and red, but also raw with fury. Her grief had turned to a hard anger.

'Over here!' Randy called. He had run ahead of the others, following Burt's bawl.

Jack hurried forward. He found the family hound circling a tall cypress, his tongue lolling, his tail high and proud.

Randy stood with his hands on his hips and stared up into the cypress. 'What the hell did that old dog go and tree?'

Jack looked up into the branches.

Something stirred there, then called down threateningly and stridently.

'Igor!'

Jack took a step back in surprise.

Movement drew his eye elsewhere in the tree. A pair of small brown faces peered down at him through clusters of cypress needles. A feline hiss rose from another branch.

Jack gaped at the animals, trying to fathom this discovery. He'd assumed they were all killed in the fire.

'Lorna . . .' Zoë said, her eyes widening. 'She must have released them before getting captured.'

Carlton stared up, both amazed and intrigued. 'Bonded, they must have stuck together out here.' He took off his glasses and rubbed his nose. 'I wonder if the terror of their flight bolstered that strange connection of theirs. Adrenaline flaming their neurons to a whole new level of synchronization.'

As the others spread around the tree Burt bumped into Jack's leg, wanting acknowledgment. Jack now understood what had drawn the hound off into the woods. He remembered Lorna had used Burt to hunt for the cub's littermate back in the bayou. And if Jack knew one thing about hounds, it was that they never lost their nose for a good scent.

Jack patted the hound on the side. 'Good boy, Burt. Good boy.'

Kyle was not impressed. 'What about Lorna? You've still not told us what your plan is to find her.'

'That's because I didn't have one.'

Kyle's face sank.

'But I do now,' Jack assured him.

For the first time since the power was cut off at ACRES, Jack felt a surge of confidence – not enough to wash away his bone-deep fear for Lorna, but it was enough.

'What do you mean?' Kyle pressed. 'How are we going to find her?'

Jack pointed up the tree. 'With their help.'

ACT THREE

BEASTS OF EDEN

Chapter 37

For once in her life, Lorna had no fear of flying. She stared at the sweep of sunlit blue water below the small plane. The sea stretched to the horizon in all directions, interrupted by a scatter of islands to the south. She felt no anxiety as the plane sped due south: no sweating palms, no palpitating heart.

She only felt numb.

Like a looped film reel, she kept picturing Jack's truck exploding, followed a heartbeat later by ACRES disappearing into a hellish fireball.

All dead . . .

While she should fear for her own life at the moment, she felt nothing, hollowed out and empty. Even the pounding in her head seemed a distant thing. A goose-egg-size knot had grown behind her left ear. A vague ringing persisted on that side.

Tinnitus, she diagnosed, secondary to the injury.

They'd offered her a minimal amount of medical care, but mostly they'd been on the move. Her kidnappers had driven her to a clearing in the bayou. As the sun rose a helicopter had flown her to a waiting ship anchored beyond the barrier islands in the Gulf of Mexico, then she'd been transferred onto a seaplane. They'd been in the air for over three hours, heading as near as she could tell into the western Caribbean, possibly toward Cuba.

She turned from the window as the man who had captured

her ducked out of the cockpit into the main cabin. The plane sat six passengers and was luxuriously appointed in leather with mahogany accents. Whoever was financing this operation had deep financial pockets.

The man with the scarred face joined her and her two guards. He had showered aboard the ship, and his hair was fixed by gel into a greasy look. She studied the scars over his face and neck as if reading a map. He'd been attacked by some animal. Maybe a lion from the severity of his old injuries. He had never introduced himself, but she had heard one of the men call him Duncan.

He didn't acknowledge her as he sat down next to a muscular man with a leathery face and red hair scalped into a military cut. He'd been assigned to watch over her. Not that there was much for him to do. Her hands were cuffed, but at least in her lap now. She had not offered any resistance. She was at their mercy, and so far they hadn't treated her too roughly.

She figured she'd learn more by being compliant than by screaming and thrashing. Still, as Duncan joined them, that hollowness inside her began to fill with a burning vitriol. It dripped like bile into her heart and spread.

The bastard sat down, ignoring her. He turned to the redheaded commando. 'Still no word from Daughtery. He should have reported in by now.'

'What do you want me to do?'

'When we get to the island, roust up some eyes and ears in New Orleans. I want to know what happened back there after we left.'

'Yes, sir. But you know Daughtery. Always a bit of a loose cannon. Probably ended up in the French Quarter. Got himself drunk on Bourbon Street and is sleeping it off with some whore.'

'If so, I'll cut off his left nut the next time I see him.'

'Might not make a difference. To rein him in, you'll have to cut 'em both off.'

Duncan acknowledged this by raising one eyebrow, as if seriously considering this option. He finally leaned back but looked little placated. His hard eyes gazed somewhere beyond the cabin of the seaplane.

She kept a sidelong watch on him, not trusting him.

He must have sensed her attention. Without moving a muscle, his gaze hardened on her.

With a sigh, he leaned forward. She noted the slack on the left side of his face, likely nerve damage. He reached into a pocket and slipped out a roll of tropical-flavored Life Savers and offered her one.

She shook her head.

He shrugged, popped one in his mouth, and sighed. 'You impress me, Dr. Polk.'

She tried not to flinch at the use of her name. She had no ID on her. He must have noted some reaction. His lips thinned to a ghost of a satisfied smile. He had purposely used her name to unsettle her.

It had worked.

He continued: 'By my estimation, you alone took out at least three of my men.'

She heard no anger in his voice, no threat of revenge.

'Impressive,' he said. 'And smart. I hope you'll prove as smart once we reach the island. My superiors and I will have some questions for you. Cooperation will be rewarded.'

And if she didn't cooperate, the threat was plain in his eyes.

Instead of further unsettling her, the intimidation only helped center her. She spoke for the first time. There was no use begging for her life. She knew it was forfeit. Instead, she wanted answers for the bloodshed and death.

'What's behind all this?' she asked. She tried to sound confident, but she had to struggle not to let a quaver enter her voice. 'The genetic changes in the animals, all you've done to cover it up . . . what are you all doing out here?'

Duncan took her questions in stride. A part of her

hoped he'd refuse to answer, but he showed no reluctance in responding, which unnerved her more than his threat a moment ago. If she had any question of surviving this ordeal, it was dashed by his candor.

'We call it the Babylon Project.'

Babylon?

He read the confusion in her face. 'Named for where it all began. In a word, we're involved in *biowarfare*. Or more specifically, I should say *bioweapon systems*. As you'll soon see, what you stumbled upon is merely a scratch on the surface of larger ambitions. When we're done, the way wars are fought will be forever changed.'

For the first time, true fear filtered through to her. This was no mere smuggling operation tied to a clandestine research project. It was much bigger.

Before more could be explained, the pilot came over the radio, cutting them off. 'We'll be landing in five minutes. Everyone buckle up.'

Lorna turned to the window again. The seaplane dipped toward the set of islands she had noted before. Most appeared to be sandbars supporting a tree or two. The grouping formed a gentle arc centered on a larger wooded island shaped like a dumbbell. They looked to be two islands that had fused together long ago by a bridge of sand and mangrove forest.

The seaplane dove toward the western half of the island. A deep cove scooped out an arc of white sand. Beyond the beach, a whitewashed villa climbed in a series of stacked tiers up a steep forested hill. A series of blue pools spilled from one level to the next. As the seaplane banked and angled for a descent into the cove, she got a bird's-eye view of the island's eastern half. It appeared deserted and untamed.

Thousands of such small islands and cays dotted the Caribbean. Many were privately owned and shifted national allegiances as easily and as often as one changed hairstyles. If someone wanted to set up a private research facility – one that was isolated and beyond the rules and regulations of modern society – here was a perfect place to do it.

The seaplane swept cleanly into the cove and dipped to the water. Fountains sprayed from the twin floats as the craft landed and glided toward a stone pier. Ahead, white sand sparkled against the blue water. Palms and mangroves shadowed the interior. A flutter of native doves took wing from the dense forest, disturbed by their approach.

It appeared to be paradise – but she knew it held a darker secret, a black heart kept out of direct view.

Lorna let out the breath she'd been holding.

She turned from the window to find Duncan studying her.

He lifted an arm toward the island. His eyes danced with amusement. The irony of his next words were not lost on her.

'Welcome to Eden, Dr. Polk.'

Chapter 38

Jack had returned to his workplace, towing the others with him. He had everyone sequestered in the computer lab of the New Orleans Border Patrol station house.

The red-brick facility had a long history, going back to the twenties, when the agency's main goal was to capture deserting crewmen and Prohibition-era smugglers bringing rum in from the Caribbean. But times had changed. As part of Homeland Security now, the station housed one of the most advanced surveillance and computer units in the country, employed to protect the borders against terrorists and their weapons.

As Jack paced the secure room, he rubbed his temples, trying to hold his head from splitting apart. Since he'd arrived here, his skin had begun to burn with a fever, and an ache smoldered deep in his bones, ready to catch fire. He had dry-swallowed three aspirins and waited for them to kick in. He didn't have time to be sick – and this tension wasn't helping.

'How long do we need to stay here?' Zoë asked.

Jack lowered his hands from his head. 'No more than a day.'

By that time Lorna's fate would be sealed. It would no longer be necessary to maintain the ruse that everyone had perished at ACRES. The first emergency response helicopter had arrived on scene a quarter hour after Jack had found Burt in the woods. He had been relieved to see the CPB emblem on the chopper's side. The station's helicopters were often first-responders.

Jack had waved the chopper down. He knew the pilot well and quickly explained the necessity to keep their fate under wraps. Afterward, Jack coordinated with law enforcement to maintain that blanket. Morning news shows were already reporting on the tragedy and the lack of survivors. Shortly after that, the local NBC affiliate received an e-mail claiming the firebombing was the work of a new animal-rights terrorist group.

It was surely bogus, likely planted by whoever orchestrated the assault. Still, it served Jack equally well. The terrorist angle had the news organizations chasing their own tails. No one questioned the lack of witnesses or survivors.

Afterward, Jack had moved everyone here.

Including Burt and the animals from the trawler.

Randy slouched in an office chair, his eyes closed, with Burt curled at his feet. The other animals were recovering from mild tranquilizers. Dr. Greer had removed their tracking tags under local anesthesia. The tags rested on a nearby table, secured in a copper Faraday cage to prevent them from being tracked. All except one that was being analyzed by a computer forensics expert brought in from the local FBI office. With magnifying glasses fixed to his face, he had deactivated the tag.

He also confirmed Jack's earlier suspicion. 'This isn't commercial grade. I'd say military or paramilitary. Either way, someone with money.'

As they waited for further details, Carlton joined Jack, cradling a mug of coffee in his hands. 'If your man is right, it confirms a suspicion.'

'What's that?' Jack asked, glad for the diversion.

'All that's happened. This is beyond a simple corporation sidestepping rules and regulations regarding animal research. This has the fingerprints of something larger. Possibly with government backing.'

'As in our government?'

Carlton looked upon him as if he were a naive child. 'Underground projects are financed all the time by the U.S. government, including grants from DARPA, the Defense Department's research-and-development agency. But you should know that over the past few years, rumors have persisted in the scientific community of projects so black that people disappear into them and are never seen again.'

'And you think we stumbled onto one of them?'

Carlton sighed. 'I don't know. But there's another worrisome trend. In regard to private defense contractors. I assume with your military background that you're familiar with Blackwater?'

Jack nodded.

Blackwater was a private corporate security force contracted by the U.S. government to serve in Iraq and Afghanistan. Basically they were mercenaries. Jack had worked alongside several members of Blackwater in Iraq. He had no beef with any of them, though there was a certain level of resentment among U.S. troops. Both armies fought in the same terrain, but the Blackwater mercenaries were both better equipped and better paid. In fact, most were former soldiers recruited after leaving the service. Even Jack had been approached and considered it.

Then the scandals broke out about Blackwater: testimonials of secret assassination programs, weapons smuggling, massacres of civilians, even the deaths of federal witnesses.

In the end, Jack had opted to protect the homeland here.

'Why bring up Blackwater?' he asked.

'Because the corporation earned over a billion dollars in government contracts since 2000. And they're only one of six hundred such firms operating in the two theaters of war.'

'I'm well aware,' he growled, urging the man to get to the point.

'Then what you might not know is that such contracting is no longer limited to just paramilitary firms – the scientific community has also been co-opted. Hundreds of research groups have hopped on the bandwagon. Large and small. And from what I've heard, the competition is not only fierce – but also cutthroat.'

Jack hadn't known about this detail. He pictured the animals, the assault force, the brutality.

'With such vast sums of money involved,' Carlton continued, 'the scandals of Blackwater are spreading like a virus through these scientific communities. Accusations of corporate espionage, vandalism, outsourcing of research to third-world countries to avoid regulations. The list goes on and on.'

Jack understood the doctor's concern. Such a description certainly fit with all that had happened.

A door swung open behind him. Lorna's brother had returned from the medical ward. His arm was in a plaster cast from hand to elbow. His gaze was glassy from pain killers.

Randy stirred and opened one eye toward Kyle. 'Great,' he mumbled under his breath. 'So one of the Polks has rejoined us. Guess that means someone's gonna try to kill me again.'

Kyle scowled at Randy. 'What're you talking about?'

Jack stepped between them. His head pounded. He didn't need any more aggravation, especially from Randy. Whatever wall had dropped between the two brothers out in the woods had risen back up in the light of day.

'Randy, just keep your mouth shut for once.'

His brother glowered and crossed his arms. 'I'm just saying, whenever Menards and Polks mix, someone in our family gets killed – or nearly killed in my case.'

Kyle's face went a deep red. 'So then what about my sister? You and your brother are here swilling coffee and stuffing your faces with doughnuts while she's still in danger.'

'There're doughnuts?' Randy asked, sitting straighter.

Kyle shook his head and turned his wrath on Jack. He

lifted his arm. 'I'm all fixed up. So what are we going to do about Lorna? You said you had a way of finding her.'

'Calm down. I do . . . or hope I do.' He glanced over to the computer forensics expert.

'How?' Kyle pressed. His voice lost its angry edge and took on a more plaintive tone.

Jack picked up the Faraday cage holding the surgically removed tags. 'With these.'

When the power had been cut off at ACRES, Jack had been examining one of the tags. As the lights blacked out, he had pocketed it for safekeeping, wanting to examine it in more detail later. But when he abandoned Lorna in her office, he did more than just leave her with the tranquilizer rifle.

'I planted one of these tags on Lorna. In her pocket.'

The tension in Kyle's face softened with hope.

'My God,' Zoë mumbled. 'You think we can use it to track her?'

'That's what I'm counting on.'

The forensic expert must have heard their talk. 'I think I can make it work,' he called over. 'It's definitely a form of GPS technology. If all the tags use this same technology, I should be able to find her. Though it might take a while. I'll have to hunt satellite by satellite.' He swung around to face them. 'It would be faster if I had some general idea where to begin looking.'

Jack contemplated all he'd learned from Carlton and his own suspicions. 'Mexico, or somewhere off the coast,' he guessed. 'Maybe the Caribbean. They wouldn't be too far. But definitely south of the U.S. border.'

Carlton nodded his agreement.

Kyle sagged again. 'That's a lot of territory to cover. I should know. The oil company I'm contracted with has platforms up and down the Gulf Coast.'

'That's good to hear,' Jack said. 'Because if I'm right, we may need to use one of those rigs as a base of operations.'

Kyle glanced at him. His eyes lost some of their glaze,

calculating and taking strength from the fact that he could be useful. Still, his main concern remained, and he mumbled it aloud.

'Is she still alive?'

Chapter 39

Lorna marched down the dock toward the villa. Behind her, the man named Connor gripped a pistol in his hand, but he didn't even bother pointing it at her.

What was the use? Where could she go?

They'd even taken her cuffs off.

Rubbing her wrists, she followed behind Duncan. The scarred man led the way toward a covered breezeway at the end of the dock. The air was fragrant with sea salt and the cinnamon scent of the mangrove forest. She noted a few beach chairs out on the sand and a row of yellow sea kayaks. It looked like any other island resort.

Until you looked closer.

At the edge of the beach, shadowed by the palms, stood men in camouflage gear with shouldered rifles. Up higher, an elaborate antenna-and-dish array covered the villa's roof, far more than necessary for phone and satellite television service. There was also an eerie silence here. No reggae music, no laughter, only the gentle wash of waves on the beach.

The atmosphere felt charged, as if a storm were brewing.

Maybe it was the tension in the face of the guard who met them at the breezeway. She noted a flicker of fear in his eyes as he pulled Duncan aside for a private conversation.

Waiting, Lorna stood on the dock under the baking midday sun. The ringing in her ear had disappeared, but the motion of turning her neck to scout her surroundings triggered a stab of pain from the goose egg at the back of her skull. Still, if she hadn't stopped, she might have missed it.

A blue tarp lay spread at the far end of the beach.

It looked like it covered some beach craft, except she saw Duncan glance that way, too. Only then did she notice the black stain running from the tarp to the water, like a trail of oil. But Lorna knew it wasn't oil.

Focused, she noted a pale white shape sticking out from under the sheet.

A human hand.

Duncan rejoined them. He faced Connor. 'They had another infiltration last night. It swam in. Killed Polaski. Wounded Garcia before it was shot.'

'How could it have caught them off guard? What about the tracking tags?'

'I don't know. I'm off to talk to Malik about that. He left word for me to join him in the lab.'

Connor pointed a thumb at Lorna. 'What about her?'

Duncan shrugged. 'Bring her along. Lock her up in one of the holding pens down there until I'm ready for her.'

They set off again, passing down the breezeway and across an expansive patio. The lounge chairs and teak tables were empty, except for a pair of dark-skinned men wearing lab smocks. One smoked a cigarette listlessly, holding the filter toward his palm in a European fashion. His companion sat with his head in his hands.

The villa's main floor was all windows that faced the cove. Heavy hurricane shutters had been closed over them, giving the place a barricaded feel. Passing through a pair of tall French doors, the interior was gloomy, but plainly luxurious: ivory damask curtains, furniture constructed from rough-hewn mahogany and rosewood, probably harvested locally, and limestone-tiled floors. All the hues were muted, with splashes of vibrancy from animal-print pillows and an occasional painting on the wall.

251

Duncan led them through the front pavilion and down a long hallway. When the doors and windows were open, the hallway must serve as an extension of the breezeway, carrying the tropical sea breezes deeper into the house. To either side of the main hall opened various rooms, including a kitchen where a trio of cooks prepared a meal.

The smell of baking bread and a simmering garlic stew stirred her stomach, reminding her of how long it had been since she'd had anything to eat. But they didn't stop for a snack. They headed straight back to where the hall ended at a library study.

It looked like something out of the British Museum, a tantalizing mix of leather-bound books and collected artifacts: conch shells, antique seafaring tools, including a sextant and windlass from a sailing ship. One wall displayed massive plates of fossilized seabeds, snapshots of an ancient world populated by trilobites, prehistoric fish, and sea fans.

A bear of a man met Duncan there, rising from a seat by a cold fireplace. He had been staring out a set of open windows. The man wore hiking pants and boots, along with a loose camo jacket. He appeared to be in his early sixties but remained well muscled, with salt-and-pepper hair and a face that sun and wind had polished to a tanned smoothness. He had the stamp of ex-military, probably navy from the sailing cap resting on the arm of his chair. But he carried himself with some sense of affluence, too.

Lorna guessed the man owned the villa. In fact, he seemed as much a part of this room as any of the artifacts.

He crossed and shook Duncan's hand, swallowing the scarred man's palm and fingers in his paw.

'Sir,' Duncan said, biting back his surprise. 'I hadn't expected you to be here. I thought you'd still be at the Ironcreek presentation in D.C.'

'Not much reason after losing our cargo.'

The older man glanced at Lorna. His only reaction was a deepening of a crease between his eyes. Then he ignored her.

She sensed he didn't give women much shrift. She had met her share of such men.

'I flew in this morning,' the big man explained. 'Just in time for the commotion here.'

Duncan sighed through his nose. 'I was just heading down to talk to Dr. Malik about the incident.'

'He's waiting for you.' The man lifted an arm to the wall of books and artifacts. 'We'll talk afterward.'

'Yes, sir.'

A section of the bookshelves slid open to reveal that the main hall continued past the library – and into the side of the mountain.

Lorna's heart beat faster. Connor nudged her toward the opening. She had no choice but to follow Duncan into the buried section of the complex.

The door sealed behind her with a dread finality.

Will I ever see the sun again?

Connor spoke, stepping closer to Duncan in a conspiratorial way. 'What's Bryce Bennett doing here?'

Duncan's voice was a black glower. 'Malik must have been keeping our boss informed about the problems here. I told him not to bother the boss, but that just proves you can't trust a raghead. Not even one on our side.'

Duncan continued down a short passageway. It dumped into a large circular work space, broken into stations, with additional rooms and passageways radiating deeper underground. White-smocked technicians worked at various stations. Some glanced at her – then quickly away again. It seemed the villa was a front for this underground complex, the perfect façade to hide what lay beneath it.

As she entered, she looked around. Much of the main room was nearly a match to Dr. Metoyer's genetics lab, only tenfold larger and better equipped. It housed an extensive array of thermocyclers, gel boxes, hybridization ovens, incubators, even a LI-COR 4300 DNA analyzer. There were also a bay of clean hoods and banks of shakers and centrifuges, and at the back, a full electron microscope suite and micro-array facility.

There was nothing this lab didn't have – and couldn't do.

The scientist in her grew jealous, while another part paled at how much all this must cost. And what it implied. Someone had spent a fortune to hide this lab beyond U.S. jurisdiction and control.

Duncan led her across the room and down another hall.

'Take Dr. Polk to one of the holding pens in back,' he ordered as he ducked through a side door. 'I need to have a word with Dr. Malik.'

Connor poked her in the back to keep her moving. As she continued a hall window opened on her left and revealed a view into a surgical suite. It was sparsely furnished with a stainless-steel table and overhead halogens on a dual swing arm.

A middle-aged man dressed in scrubs stood in the room. From his swarthy complexion and thick black hair, he looked Arabic or maybe Egyptian.

Duncan stepped into the room through another door. From the storm clouds building on the man's brow, he was not happy.

Lorna slowed, mostly because of what lay on the table.

Connor didn't press her. He was staring, too.

'How did this specimen get all the way over to our side of the island?' Duncan said, jumping straight in with no pleasantries. 'I thought you were constantly monitoring them.'

'We were,' the man said, irritated, matching the other's heated tone.

It had to be Dr. Malik. Lorna guessed he was the scientific head of this facility, while Duncan ran security. The two had clearly locked horns in the past.

Malik pointed to the table. 'The other specimens must have cut the tag out of this one. With something sharp. Maybe a stone ax. Let me show you.'

The doctor stepped to the side, allowing Lorna to see

fully for the first time what lay on the table. She covered her mouth in shock. Blocked by Malik, all she had seen before were legs and a lower torso. From the fur and small body, she had assumed it was an orangutan or some other great ape.

But as Malik moved out of the way, she knew she was wrong.

The arms were less furred, and the chest bore a clear set of bullet holes. But it was the face and head that made her gasp out loud. Matted, coarse hair framed a bare face with a protuberant jaw and maxilla, but not as prominent as an ape. It was flatter. Also the eyes were larger, rounder, the forehead taller and ridged.

Lorna had seen pictures of early man, of hominid species like *Australopithecus* or *Homo habilis*. The resemblance was unmistakable. What lay on the table was no ape.

She remembered the throwback traits seen in the animals from the trawler, a turning back of the evolutionary clock. Her vision darkened with the implication of what lay on the table. They weren't just researching with animals.

She turned to Connor and couldn't keep the disgust or horror from her voice. 'You've been experimenting on humans.'

Chapter 40

Jack stood in the office of his sector chief, Bernard Paxton. It had been Paxton who had handpicked Jack a year ago to lead the Special Response Team – though at the moment, he looked like he might be regretting that decision.

Paxton stood on the opposite side of his desk. He was in full dress uniform after speaking to the press all morning: navy-blue slacks with black piping and matching shirt. He'd oiled his dark hair and even donned his ceremonial 'Ike' jacket, but he left it unbuttoned and loose as he leaned over the desk.

A detailed map of the Gulf of Mexico was spread on the table.

Paxton tapped a finger on the map. 'That's where you picked up Dr. Polk's signal? From the tracker you planted on her?'

Jack nodded. 'Those are the coordinates. Lost Eden Cay. Somewhere in that cluster of islands.'

Paxton heard the hesitation in his voice. 'But you can't be absolutely certain.'

'We only caught a few seconds of signal – then lost it.'

Jack bunched a fist as he stood stiff-backed. The FBI consultant had finally picked up a signal off a military GPS 2R-9 satellite orbiting twelve thousand miles over the Gulf. The reading had seemed solid, strong enough to pinpoint a location about a hundred miles off the coast of Cuba. Then the reading had simply vanished.

'You lost the signal and never picked it up again?' his boss asked.

'Her kidnappers might have taken her inside. Somewhere blocked from satellite pickup. Or, according to the FBI guy, the kidnappers might be employing some form of local electronic jamming equipment, keeping the island locked down.'

Jack refrained from voicing one other possibility. He pictured Lorna's body being dumped overboard into the ocean. That would also block the signal.

Paxton sighed, expressively loud. 'Then that's unfortunate. This set of islands flies the Nicaraguan flag. We can't go storming their beach based on a ghost of a contact that we can't replicate.'

'Sir . . .'

Paxton held up a hand. 'It's beyond our jurisdiction. I can open diplomatic channels, begin a dialogue, but it'll take a day at least.'

A day we don't have, Jack thought and swore silently. He fought to keep in control. He wanted to pound on the desk, scream at his boss, demand an immediate response, but such an outburst would do more harm than good. He didn't want to get kicked off this case.

'Let me work my magic,' his boss continued. 'Give me a few hours to make some calls. In the meantime, have that FBI agent keep tracking that signal. If we can solidify that trace, it would help my case. In the meantime, Jack, get some rest. You look like shit.'

Jack felt like it, too, but didn't say so. His head pounded. His throat burned as a fever took hold. He had no time to coddle a flu or cold. Aspirin and antihistamines would keep him propped up at least for another day.

After that, it wouldn't matter.

'Grab a cot out back and take a nap,' Paxton said. 'That's an order.'

'Yes, sir,' he said and turned in frustration back toward the office door.

'Jack,' his boss called. 'I'll do everything I can.'

He nodded, knowing the man would. He headed back down to the computer room to give the others the bad news. Reaching the basement facility, he took a moment to compose himself, then entered. Faces turned hopefully in his direction. At the moment the only ones here were those who had survived the assault at ACRES.

Kyle stood up from a stool. 'When are they heading out to find Lorna?'

Jack didn't answer.

Randy read his brother's expression and understood. 'Motherfuckers . . . we're not going.'

Kyle glanced at Randy, then back to Jack. He visibly paled and sank back to his seat. The kid checked his watch. It had been five hours and twenty-two minutes since the rescue helicopter had found them in the woods. They all knew time was running out for Lorna – if it hadn't already.

A fire grew inside Jack, stoked as much by fever as by frustration. He read the despair in the others' expressions and refused to give in to it.

To hell with it.

He closed the door behind him and pointed an arm at his brother. 'Randy, get off your ass and call the Thibodeaux brothers. Tell 'em we're going hunting again.'

Randy stood up, a question forming on his lips.

Before it could be asked, Jack swung his arm to Lorna's brother. 'Kyle, you said you could get us on one of those oil platforms if we wanted.'

Kyle nodded and stood back up. 'Not a problem. When?'

'Now.'

Jack swiftly ran logistics through his burning mind. He knew a pilot and at least two of his Special Response teammates who could keep their mouths shut and would do what was asked of them. That should be enough. In fact, the smaller the strike force, the better. They had to get in under their radar and secure Lorna before anyone knew better.

Carlton stood with Zoë and Greer. The head of ACRES understood what was not being spoken aloud. 'The animals are about to be transported to the New Orleans Zoo's veterinary hospital. We'll go with them and keep our heads down. And we'll continue researching what we can over there.'

Zoë nodded. 'Paul . . .' Her voice cracked around her husband's name. 'He backed up our data to an off-site server. We'll be able to pick up where we left off.'

Carlton placed a comforting hand on her shoulder. 'We'll update you if we learn anything that will help.'

Jack gazed at the expectant faces staring back at him.

'Then let's get moving.'

Chapter 41

Standing in the holding pen, Lorna now knew what a pit bull on death row must feel like. Under the glare of stark bare bulbs, she studied her confinement. The rest of the subterranean laboratory had been as sleek and antiseptic as a modern hospital.

Not here.

The cell floors had been cut out of native rock and trenched to help wash down urine and feces. The walls were damp cement blocks, sealed by a chain-link gate. She stood in more of a dog run than a prison cell.

Without even a stool to sit on, Lorna paced the ten-foot-by-four enclosure. Another dozen identical runs ran the length of the low-roofed room. All of them were empty, but she could imagine the usual inhabitants. She ran a hand along the wall, felt the scratches in the cement. She remembered the dead body on the surgical table. From the high forehead and flat face, it had to have once been human, but like the animals from the trawler, it had reverted to some earlier form, a genetic throwback to a prehistoric form.

But to what end?

Duncan's description returned to her: *bioweapon systems*.

She had no explanation of what that meant but now knew with cold certainty that this outfit had moved beyond animal research into human experimentation. And isolated out here, who would question it or even know about it? It wouldn't even be that hard to find test subjects. The Caribbean area was rife with human trafficking. In poor countries like Haiti, people were regularly sold into slavery, sometimes by their own relatives. Authorities in the region knew about such trafficking, but they would look the other way for the right price.

She heard a door open across the room. Voices reached her.

'I put her over here.'

'Bring her out.' She recognized Duncan from his raspy, harsh voice. 'Malik wants to attend her interrogation. It seems her background as a veterinarian has intrigued Dr. Raghead.'

Lorna absorbed his words. Her hands went instantly damp. She moved away from the chained gate as the two men stepped into view.

Her bodyguard unlocked the gate with a key. Duncan stood back with his arms crossed. 'C'mon,' the man named Connor ordered. He didn't even bother with his holstered sidearm.

Lorna took a deep, shuddering breath. It took all her strength to obey. She didn't want to be dragged kicking and screaming out of the cell. For the moment she had no recourse but to cooperate.

Duncan fixed her with that dead gaze of his, his face a frozen mask of scar tissue and barely suppressed anger. Without a word, he turned and led them out of the kennel and back down to the main lab. Only now the circular room was empty. Except for Dr. Malik. He stood at one of the genetic workstations and turned as they approached.

Lorna hesitated at the threshold. Connor shoved her from behind. She stumbled into the room, close to falling on her face.

Malik scowled. 'Is that bloody necessary?' he scolded. His words had a British lilt to them, but the accent was plainly Middle Eastern. He waved to Lorna. 'Join me over here, Dr. Polk.'

Duncan accompanied her to the workstation while Connor hung back.

Up close, Malik appeared older than she originally estimated. Though his dark skin was unlined and his thick hair salted with gray, he had to be in his late fifties. He still wore the same surgical scrubs from before, but he had donned a starched white lab coat that reached to mid-thigh.

He motioned her to a chair. 'I must apologize for dragging you into all of this.'

She remained standing. Duncan grabbed her shoulder hard, guided her to the chair, and pushed her into it.

Malik's frown deepened, but he kept silent.

'Ask your questions,' Duncan said. 'Let's get this over with.'

Malik sighed. 'For the sake of the security of our intellectual property rights, I must ask what you and your colleagues in New Orleans learned from the specimens in your possession.'

Lorna could not look them in the eye. Her gaze dropped to the equipment around her. She took in the labels: Pure-Link Genomic digestion buffer, Novex zymogram gel kits, a Spotlight hybridizer. Behind Malik stood a stack of two incubators and an inverted microscope station with two micromanipulator controls for viewing and working with embryo dishes.

She recognized the setup as an in vitro fertilization lab.

Was this the origin of all the bloodshed and horror?

She lifted her face, only to have the back of a hand strike her hard across the mouth. Blood flew from her lips. The knot behind her ear rang with the impact, echoing the pain of the blow.

Tears welled in her eyes – less from pain than fury.

'That's enough!' Malik said.

Duncan ignored him and loomed over her. 'Answer his

262

questions or there will be worse.'

Lorna saw the promise in his eyes.

Malik began again, but Lorna cut him off, wiping the blood from her split lip. She had already decided not to withhold any information. What was the use?

'We found additional chromosomes in all the animals,' she started. 'And we discovered the structural changes in the brain. A network of magnetite crystals.'

'Impressive,' Malik said. 'Considering how little time you had with the specimens.'

'What else?' Duncan asked, the threat plain in his voice.

She didn't hold back. 'And we learned that the animals were somehow able to link up neurologically. And we came to believe this networking enhanced their intellectual capacity.'

Malik nodded, confirming what was conjecture before.

'That's as far as we got,' Lorna said.

'Who else knows about what you learned?' Duncan pressed.

Lorna guessed this was coming. It was the only reason she'd been dragged here, the only reason she was still alive. To discover if the information had leaked out of ACRES. Her only hope of staying alive was to shadow the truth.

'I can't say for sure,' she said. 'But we regularly back data up to an off-site server. It's done automatically.'

Malik looked at Duncan.

A half scowl twisted the commando's lips. 'Shouldn't matter. At least not immediately. With everyone dead, it will buy us a window of time to clean this up.'

'We'll still need it purged as soon as possible,' Malik said. 'Mr. Bennett will insist on it.'

'Where's the backup stored?' Duncan asked her.

'I don't know,' she answered truthfully. ACRES contracted with an outfit in Baton Rouge.

Duncan lifted his hand again, ready to test her veracity.

Needing to be convincing, she cowered back and protected her face. 'All I know is the name. Southern Compu-

Safe. But they have servers throughout Louisiana.'

She didn't know if that last bit was true, but if this bastard believed the data was bottled up at one site, he'd just order the facility blown up. In that scenario, she would not be needed. To live, she had to remain useful.

Duncan lowered his hand, momentarily believing her. His gaze went long as he weighed his options.

She had to direct those *options* as best she could. She continued, talking rapidly, allowing the terror buried deep inside her to shine out. 'The only way to access the stored data is through a series of security clearances. An employee ID password, followed by a series of challenge questions unique to each employee. But I have no idea how to gain access remotely.'

This last bit was true.

Duncan seemed not to hear her. His gaze remained fixed in that thousand-mile stare.

Malik spoke up. 'How long would it take to get a secure satellite uplink to this Compu-Safe? One that can't be traced back to us.'

Duncan spoke in a monotone. 'At least four hours.' He glared at Lorna. 'But it will only take a few calls to confirm if Dr. Polk is telling us the truth.'

Lorna wanted to shrink from that gaze, but she held firm.

'Then it seems we'll have her company for a bit longer,' Malik said. 'Which is just as well. I'd like to pick her brain concerning the trouble we've been experiencing in the field of late.'

'She doesn't need to know about that,' Duncan said.

'It never hurts to have a fresh perspective on a problem. And what can it hurt?' Malik lifted an eyebrow toward the commando. 'That is, unless you're worried about the security here. If you're afraid she might escape.'

Duncan's face darkened.

Lorna found herself warming to the doctor.

Until his next words.

'Besides, Dr. Polk and I will have plenty of time to talk as I prepare her.'

Something about that statement sent a chill through her. Even Duncan looked momentarily disgusted.

'Prepare for what?' Lorna asked.

Malik crossed and patted her on the shoulder reassuringly. 'A minor procedure. While we have you here, it seemed a shame to waste an opportunity to freshen our genetic stock supply.'

'What do you mean?' Lorna's stomach clenched around a knot of worry. She flashed to the body on the surgical table.

Malik patted her shoulder a final time and stepped from her side.

'Fear not. We're just going to harvest a few of your eggs.'

Chapter 42

Lorna held back tears as the technician stepped away, carrying vials of her blood in color-coded tubes. Nervous sweat dampened her body. She rubbed a finger along the bandage taped to the tender crux of her elbow.

The medical ward looked like a gynecologist's office from hell. A battery of ultrasound and surgical equipment surrounded her. The exam table she sat on reclined and had stirrups – but there was no padding, no attempt at comfort. It was all cold stainless steel. But most disturbing of all were the thick leather straps meant to secure a patient.

It confirmed her suspicions that most of the human subjects here were forced to cooperate, likely obtained from modern-day slavers, a booming business in the Caribbean. A shudder passed through her as she wondered how many women had been strapped here, forced to endure unimaginable violations.

Finally, her guard Connor came forward. 'Let's go.'

She didn't resist. She allowed herself to be manhandled off the table and toward the exit. It hurt to walk. Besides drawing blood, the technician had collected a painful bone-marrow biopsy from her hip. She felt the ache with each step, but she knew the worst was yet to come. The preoperative tests were to evaluate hormone levels, along with a genetic assay.

Pending those results, the stirrups and straps awaited her.

Connor kept hold of her elbow and marched her from

the room and through a door into an adjoining office. Dr. Malik sat behind the desk, writing in a chart. Behind him rose a bookshelf crammed with texts and journals. From the ragged and dog-eared look to the research library, the volumes weren't for show. Malik closed the chart as she was shoved into the room. He had a small pair of reading glasses perched on his thin nose and stared over them at Lorna.

'Please have a seat,' he said and waved to a chair. His focus shifted to her bodyguard. 'Sergeant Read, that will be all for now. I'll summon you when we're done.'

Connor didn't move and seemed ready to set down roots. 'Commander Kent said I should stay with the prisoner.'

Duncan had given those orders before leaving to investigate her claims about a backup of their research at Compu-Safe.

Malik let out a long sigh. 'That won't be necessary, but if it would make you happy, you can stand guard at the door.'

Connor scowled, looking ready to argue. His fingers tightened on her elbow.

Malik waved dismissively at the guard. '*Outside* the door, if you don't mind. Buried down here, there are no windows. Our guest won't be going anywhere. My office is as good as any jail cell.'

Connor's scowl deepened, but his fingers released their clamp. Lorna suspected his grip would leave bruises, maybe even fingerprints. He stepped back. 'I'll be right outside the door.'

Malik seemed to have already dismissed him. His gaze focused on Lorna. 'Dr. Polk, please have a seat. We have much to discuss. Some of which I suspect you'll find illuminating.'

Lorna was happy to accept his offer. After all that had happened and the ache in her hip, she didn't trust her legs. She sank into the seat and gazed around the rest of the office. To the left, the wall was covered with various LCD monitors, centered on a larger fifty-inch plasma screen.

Most were dark, though four showed various views of the subterranean facility, including the gynecology room.

He must have been watching it all.

Disgusted, she turned away.

Diplomas and awards covered the other wall. Lorna studied them, anything to help her understand the man behind the desk. Many of the mounted certificates were in foreign languages, including several in Arabic. She recognized one in French – *Université Pierre et Marie Curie* – and beneath it a credential from the *Centre National de la Recherche Scientifique*. This last was the largest research organization in France.

No matter his ethics, Dr. Malik was no crackpot.

'We should have your tests completed within the hour,' the man said and leaned forward. 'Let me explain what will happen from here. Just so there's no anxiety.'

Lorna couldn't tell if the man was being purposely dense about her situation or particularly cruel.

He continued: 'After the tests, we'll design a genetically specific combination of Lupron and Menopur, along with an experimental follicle-stimulating hormone. Normally it takes days before the ovary will be fit for harvesting eggs. But with the technique I've developed, it will require only a couple of hours. So we have time to talk.'

Lorna finally found her voice. 'What are you planning on doing with my eggs?'

'Trust me, they will be put to good use. We'll use them for a new embryo hybridization project we're about to start.'

'What sort of embryos?' Lorna pictured the body on the table.

'That's not an easy question to answer. And before we get to that, I must first be honest with you. I've reviewed your file.'

My file?

'With your background and experience in genetics and breeding, I could find good use for you here at my lab. It would be a waste to discard such a valuable researcher out of hand. And if you remain cooperative, there's no reason you couldn't remain on the island.'

'As a prisoner.'

'I'd prefer the word *colleague*,' Malik said. 'And it's far better than the alternative. Perhaps if you better understood our methodologies and goals, you'd have fewer qualms.'

She wasn't so sure about that, but she saw no reason not to hear the man out. The longer he was talking, the longer she remained alive.

'Go on,' she said, wanting to know anyway. 'What exactly are you all doing here?'

Malik settled back, as if satisfied with this concession – or maybe he merely liked to have someone to talk to. 'What are we doing? To even begin to answer that, we'll have to go back to the very beginning. Are you familiar with the book of Genesis?'

Lorna struggled past this odd non sequitur. 'As in the Bible?'

A nod. '"In the beginning was the Word, and the Word was with God, and the Word was God."'

Lorna didn't know what to make of this statement.

A twinkle entered Malik's eye. 'Excuse my bit of hubris. I must be overly affected by our supreme benefactor, Bryce Bennett. He's a deeply religious man. It's one of the quotes he often spouts in regard to our work here – and one of the reasons he chose this island for his facility. Lost Eden Cay.' Malik smiled inwardly and shook his head. 'Truly, how could he not locate it here?'

'I don't understand. What does all this have to do with your genetic experiments?'

'All in good time. First let me start with *my* definition of the grand beginning. The scientific basis of all creation. Bennett has his Word of God. I have something entirely rooted in the scientific method.'

'And what is that?'

'Are you familiar with fractals?'

Again Lorna was taken aback by the non sequitur. *What is this guy talking about?* Still, at the same time, she recalled hearing that word before. Her brother had used it in reference to the pattern of magnetite crystals found in the dissected feline brain. She knew something about fractuals, but nothing beyond the basics – and definitely not how fractuals were involved here.

She merely shook her head, wanting to hear what the researcher had to say.

'Ah, well, by definition, fractals are jagged, irregular geometric forms generated by a repeated pattern of that same shape. Or in other words, they're large shapes that can be broken down into smaller and smaller versions of itself.'

Lorna frowned. She remembered Jon Greer's description of the magnetite nodes in the animals' brains, how the matrix was made up of smaller and smaller crystals.

'I see you're confused. Let me show you what I mean,' Malik said and tapped at his computer keyboard. To Lorna's right, one of the monitors bloomed to life. 'All geometric shapes can be defined by a single algorithm or mathematical equation. Here's a rather simple one.'

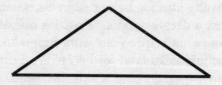

It was just an ordinary triangle.

Malik tapped again. 'But if you have the computer multiply it several times, adding one to another, it grows to this.'

On the screen, several of the triangles – positioned at various angles and on different planes – now formed a complex polygon. She shrugged, unimpressed.

'I know,' Malik conceded. 'Not much to look at, but let's

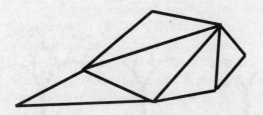

have the computer take that same triangle and repeat it a hundred thousand times, shrinking some, enlarging others, changing inclination, but basically just repeating the same triangle over and over again. Here is what you get.'

Lorna's eyes widened. 'It's forming a mountain range.'

'Exactly. A landscape composed of millions of repetitions of the same shape. In this case, triangles. This is how computers today generate such detailed backgrounds in movies and video games. Just countless repetitions of the same basic *algorithm* or *fractal* to produce a more complex one.'

'But what does all this have to do with—'

Malik cut her off. 'Because this phenomenon isn't just found in mountains and coastlines. It's found throughout the natural world. Take a tree, for example. If you look at the branching of any tree, it's just a repetition of the same basic pattern, unique to that species of tree.'

On the screen, she watched a simple shape appear: a single line with two branching offshoots, forming a Y. Then more and more Y shapes branched out from the first and multiplied into a fully dimensional tree.

'This same fractal basis of the natural world is found everywhere. From the structure of galaxies down to the tiniest snowflake, from the flow of ocean currents up to the shape of clouds in the sky. It's all around us and *in* us.'

'In us?'

'Fractals make up our bodies. They can be found in the growth of blood vessels, the pattern of alveoli in our lungs, the shape of our kidneys, even the branching of the dendrites in our brain. But it's so much more than that. When you look deeper, they're even in the way our bodies *function*. It's been shown that fractals define how we walk, the beating pattern of our hearts, the rates of respiration of our lungs. Likewise, scientists are now using fractal science to evaluate brain function, studying the fractal pattern hidden within EEGs. And they found it.'

Malik must have noted the look on her face and smiled. 'That's right. Some neurophysiologists are even coming to believe that the evolution of *intelligence* grew from fractals. That intelligence came about because of the repetitious growth of a smaller constant. In other words, there might be a fundamental fractal of intelligence, a primary seed from which all intelligence grew. Similar to that sprouting tree I just showed you. Can you imagine if we could harness that fractal, learn to control that power?'

Lorna thought back on the animals from the trawler and their strange intelligence. 'That's what you've been experimenting on. You're looking for that fractal?'

'Exactly. And we're close to a breakthrough.'

Lorna heard the raw desire in his voice.

Before Malik could explain further, a quiet knock on the door drew their attention. The lab technician who had drawn her blood entered. He was a stick insect of a man, all legs and arms, with a receding hairline that made his features look/squashed beneath that high forehead.

Loathing swelled at the sight of him, along with fear.

Were they already done with her tests?

'What is it, Edward?'

'Dr. Malik, I wanted to let you know that I've completed the scan on the subject.' His tiny eyes flicked to her, then away again. 'Both blood and marrow. I find no evidence of contamination.'

'Very good. How long until the hormone levels are back from the lab.'

'Half an hour.'

'Thank you.'

The man bowed his way back out of the office.

Malik folded his fingers atop his desk. 'That's good news. There should be no reason your eggs won't be perfectly suited for the next phase of our experiments.'

Lorna shied away from that reality and asked a question that was nagging her following the technician's pronouncement. 'What contamination were you searching for in my blood?'

'Ah, yes, well, with your exposure to the test subjects, we needed to make sure you weren't exposed to a nasty blood-borne protein that the subjects produce. A side effect of their alteration, I'm afraid. One we don't quite understand. A self-replicating protein that's produced in their blood but is toxic to us.'

'Toxic?'

'That's correct. The proteins appear to be benign in our altered specimens, but once transmitted to others, it triggers flulike symptoms. The protein spreads through the blood like a wildfire and crosses the blood-brain barrier. Once there, it hyperexcites the neurons to a dangerous extreme. Initially the excitement produces an amazing but temporary heightening of senses. Quite astounding actually. Better eyesight, smell, taste, touch. Across the board. Initially we researched a way to use this effect to enhance soldiers in the field. But in the end we had to give up.'

'Why?'

He shrugged. 'Unfortunately hyperexcitement of the neurons quickly burned out a subject's brain. No way to avoid it or cure it. Everyone infected died within forty-eight hours of exposure.'

Chapter 43

Jack's head pounded with each thrum of the chopper's rotors. The bright sunlight reflecting off the Gulf below didn't help. Even sunglasses did little to dull the stabbing brilliance.

Seated beside the pilot, he closed his eyes. Queasiness churned through him. He normally never experienced vertigo or motion sickness, but at the moment his stomach repeated every roll and lift of the helicopter. He pressed his damp palms against his knees. He swallowed back bile.

'Almost there,' the pilot reported through the headphones.

Jack opened his eyes and spotted the oil platform ahead. It looked like a rusted black dinosaur struggling out of a tar pit. The bull's-eye was painted on the helipad. Drill crews scurried like ants below.

Lorna's brother pushed forward from the backseat and leaned between Jack and the pilot. Jack twisted to face Kyle. The kid shared the passenger cabin with Randy and two of Jack's men: Mack Higgins and Bruce Kim.

Mack looked like the brand of truck he'd been named after. He was massively framed with a shaved head and prominent forehead that looked like the hood of a semi. At the moment he chewed on the stub of a cigar, unlit, as he studied the oil rig below.

His partner was a wiry Korean-American with lanky black hair that shadowed his dark eyes. With his olive complexion and boyish appearance, he looked like Bruce Lee's younger brother – and was just as good a fighter.

Jack had handpicked the pair and left his second-in-command, Scott Nester, to cover their asses back in New Orleans. Scott would also keep Jack abreast of any official response from Sector Chief Paxton. But otherwise, they were on their own out here.

Almost.

'Randy just heard from his friends,' Kyle said. 'Their boat is already heading south.'

Jack nodded. That would be the Thibodeaux brothers. The pair had borrowed a private charter boat from one of their cousins, normally used for deep-sea fishing in the Gulf. Once at the oil rig, the team in the chopper would split up. Jack would head out in a seaplane with his men, while Randy and Kyle would take the helicopter and meet the Thibodeaux brothers' boat.

The planned assault on the Lost Eden Cay would be a coordinated two-prong attack at dusk. Jack had studied nautical and satellite maps of the arc of islands. He had them both folded under his left thigh. He had planned on studying them again on the way out to the rig, but his pounding head and churning stomach discouraged it.

The plan was not a complicated one: get in, find Lorna, get out.

According to the satellite maps, the main villa lay on the western side of the island. As the sun set Jack and his men would lead an amphibious assault on the far side, where it would be darker, where eyes would be less likely to be watching. From a mile out, his team would do a sea-drop in scuba gear, their weapons in dry sacks. They would use personal tow scooters to swiftly propel themselves underwater to the island's eastern shore and head overland from there.

To hide their beach landing, Randy and the others would limp their charter boat into the villa's cove on the other side of the island, to draw attention away from Jack's team. The

Thibodeauxs had a cache of weapons, including rocket-propelled grenade launchers, loaded aboard the boat.

Jack hadn't bothered to ask how the Thibodeauxs had acquired such a mass of weaponry. He knew better than to inquire. The Thibodeaux family claimed roots that reached back to the eighteenth century, to a bloodline of Caribbean pirates that plagued the islands. And according to some stories, the Thibodeaux clan hadn't entirely shed their notorious past.

So Jack didn't care how the brothers obtained this cache of firepower, but he was glad they had. The charter boat would stand by out in the cove, feigning a blown engine, smoke pouring from the engine compartment, ready to come in guns blazing to aid in Jack's assault if necessary.

But one detail remained unknown.

Was Lorna still alive?

With all the flurry of preparations, Jack had kept himself distracted from his fears for her. But on the ride here, with nothing to divert his attention, a fire built in his gut. While it had only been a day since they first met at the trawler, she had found a place in his heart. Maybe it was their shared past, but it felt like more than that.

He pictured her seablue eyes, her sandyblond hair, bleached white by the sun at the tips. He recalled the way she chewed her lower lip when concentrating. The rare smile that broke through her serious demeanor like a flash of sunlight on a cloudy day. These memories and others popped like flashbulbs in his head. But he also remembered her from another lifetime: across a dark parking lot, on her back, shadows falling on her amid harsh laughter.

He had saved her back then – but he'd also failed her just as much.

With that last memory, a sudden fierceness choked through him, blinding him and pushing back the nausea. It was a ferocity that he'd never felt before in his life. He'd experienced fierce firefights and bloody ambushes in Iraq, but as he pictured Lorna a deep and primal well of savagery burned through him. He wanted to gnash things with his teeth, to grind bone, to rip things with his bare hands.

All to protect her – not as a boy any longer, but as a man.

Blind to all else, he jumped as the skids of the chopper struck the rig's helipad. He hadn't even noted their descent. Doors popped open, and the others piled out.

Jack remained a moment in his seat. He let the blood flow through him, felt it crest, then recede. He finally shouldered open the door and joined the others.

He didn't dismiss what he had felt, but he also would not let it rule him. He had a job to do. But a part of him also shied away from looking too intimately at the source behind that rage, to the tender emotion buried deep that had ignited it.

Now was not the time.

Not until she was safe.

Chapter 44

Lorna stood with Dr. Malik before one of the wall monitors. On the screen rotated a three-dimensional scan of a brain. It reminded her of the MRI done on Igor's brain. After all the bloodshed and fire, that seemed a lifetime ago. She tried to concentrate on Malik's explanation, but a pall of grief and defeat weighed her down. The doctor's words sounded hollow and distant.

'Here is the best image we could muster of the brain anomaly found in the test subjects.'

Malik pointed a finger at the five nodes on the screen, colored a distinct blue to distinguish them from the surrounding gray cerebral tissue. The number and pattern of the nodes were identical to those discovered during Igor's MRI back at her lab. But Malik's scan had much better resolution. Not only did the nodes stand out crisply, but so did the fine branching of magnetite crystals that connected the nodes together.

As it rotated, the pattern looked to have the same crystalline structure and shape as a snowflake.

'Are you familiar with fractal antennas?' Malik asked.

Lorna fought through her despair to answer. It took her an extra beat to croak out a 'No.'

'Do you own a cell phone?'

The strange question pierced the fog in her head. Curiosity focused her sharper. 'Of course.'

'Then you already own a fractal antenna. In the last decade, scientists have learned that antenna arrays patterned after fractals have an amazing ability to broadcast along a wider range of frequencies with a greater strength-to-size ratio. This breakthrough allowed manufacturers to shrink antennas down to microscopic sizes, yet still function like antennas a hundredfold larger. It's revolutionized the industry. That's the power hidden within fractals.'

Malik pointed to the screen. 'And that's what we're looking at here. A fractal antenna grown from natural magnetite crystals in the brain.'

Lorna studied the snowflakelike pattern and remembered her own crude analogy to a satellite dish. She also recalled the strange synchronization of EEGs. 'And it's this fractal antenna that allows the animals to link up neurologically.'

'Exactly. The pattern of magnetic crystallization seen here is definitely fractal in nature. The entire neural matrix is made up of the repetition of the same basic crystal shape.'

'Like the triangle multiplying into a mountain.'

Malik nodded. 'But this is only the tip of that mountain. Initially this scan was the best we could discern using standard techniques. Such methods only allowed us to look so far. Even zooming down with an electron microscope only revealed a crystal made up of hundreds of even tinier crystals. It was like with those Russian nesting dolls. Every time you thought you'd reached the smallest crystal, it would open up to reveal even smaller versions of itself inside. It went on and on – stretching beyond our ability to detect.'

Malik's voice cracked with frustration. Lorna remembered the raw desire in the researcher's eyes as he described his search for a fundamental fractal that was the root of all intelligence.

'No matter how hard we looked, the primary fractal kept retreating out of reach, growing smaller and smaller, eventually disappearing beyond where we could scan, down a spooky hole no one dared follow.'

Lorna pictured the white rabbit from *Alice in Wonderland* bounding down his rabbit hole.

'And though we weren't able to go down that hole, I could guess what was down there.'

Lorna's interest piqued sharper. 'What?'

'The strange world of quantum physics. Following fractals smaller and smaller, it eventually leads to the subatomic world. In fact, some physicists now believe that the science of fractals could explain away some of the spookiness of quantum theory. Such things like nonlocality and entanglement, how a subatomic particle can be at two places at once, how light behaves both like a wave and a particle. When you get that small, things get weird. But fractals may hold the answer to explaining it all.'

Lorna didn't see where this was going. Her impatience must have been plain to read.

'So let me show you what I learned myself from that research. Something practical, yet amazing. I scanned this same brain again, but this time, not looking for crystals, but for the magnetic energy produced by those crystals. Though I might not be able to *see* the physical crystals, I could still measure the electromagnetic signature from those invisible crystals.'

'Like the light from distant stars,' Lorna said.

Malik's eyes widened, caught by surprise. 'Yes, a perfect analogy. Though we can't see a sun or a planet, we can detect the light that reaches us.'

'So you repeated the scan looking for energy instead of crystals.'

'I did. And this is what I found.'

He pointed a remote control at the screen and pressed a button. The blue snowflake suddenly bloomed outward, becoming a cerulean storm within the specimen's skull.

Lorna gasped and covered her mouth in shock. 'It's everywhere . . .'

Malik smiled, proud of his discovery. 'Each node is like the seed of a fractal tree. The crystals spread outward into branches, then into tinier stems, and on and on.'

Lorna pictured the fractal tree she had been shown earlier, how a single Y grew into a three-dimensional tree. The crystals were doing the same in the brain, spreading outward while growing tinier and tinier at the same time until they were no longer visible with any scanning tool, but they could still be detected by the electromagnetic radiation coming off the hidden crystals, energy rising out of the subatomic world.

Malik waved her back to her seat by his desk. 'So I've shown you how far down this fractal puzzle burrows. How it roots down into the quantum world. So now let's consider the opposite: how far this fractal tree stretches *outward*. You already know these specimens are capable of linking up, of networking together.'

She nodded and understood where he was going. 'You believe by linking together, that same fractal tree is branching out further into the world.'

'Correct. The fractal tree is growing beyond the confines of a single skull. And growing stronger.'

Lorna remembered Igor reciting the mathematical constant pi.

'Which begs the question where will it end? If it can spread nearly infinitely down into the subatomic world, can it spread infinitely *outward*? If so, what might be the result? What level of supreme intelligence might be created?'

In her mind's eye, Lorna pictured the roots of this fractal tree disappearing into the world of quantum energy, feeding on that infinite source of power. Yet she also pictured those tree branches expanding ever outward. Maybe it was the earlier biblical analogies that had started this discussion that drew one last comparison from her.

'It's almost like the Tree of Knowledge. From the book of Genesis.'

Malik gave a dismissive snort. 'Now you're sounding like Mr. Bennett.'

Her voice grew firmer, drawing strength from certainty, fearful of what manner of intelligence would be born from this experiment. It made her go cold.

'You have to stop what you're doing,' she said.

Malik sighed as he sank into his desk chair, plainly disappointed. 'As a fellow scientist, I had hoped you'd be more open-minded.'

She was saved further admonishment by a knock on the door. The genetics technician stepped again into the room, bearing aloft a steel tray holding three large syringes.

Malik brightened again. 'Ah, Edward, are the hormonal tests completed?'

'Yes, Doctor. And I have the drug cocktail prepared for the subject.'

Malik's gaze shifted back to her. 'Then it seems we must continue our discussion a little later, Dr. Polk. See if I can't persuade you to look at this more rationally versus leaning on the Bible. But I guess that's expected when you're working on an island named Eden.'

Lorna placed a hand on her belly, fearing what was to come. Behind the technician appeared the familiar bulk of her bodyguard. Connor must have read the panic in her face. A hand settled to his holstered sidearm, discouraging any fight from her.

'After your injections,' Malik said, 'you'll want to lie down for at least a half hour. I'm afraid what's to come will not be pleasant. Accelerating the follicle stimulation of your ovaries can be a bit' – he chose his next word carefully – '*taxing*.'

Lorna's fear sharpened into a knife in her gut.

'Afterward we'll talk again. We'll have a couple of hours before your ovarian tissue will be ready for harvesting. Before that's done, I'll show you what we intend to do with your eggs.'

He waved her off. With no choice, Lorna stood up. It took an extra moment for her blood to follow. Her vision darkened at the edges.

Connor came forward and grabbed her elbow impatiently.

As she was hauled away she got one last look at the monitors on the wall. The brain scan continued to rotate on the screen, showing the magnetic storm raging within that skull.

Despite her terror about what was in store for her, a part of her went cold and determined at the sight – and its implication. God had banished man from the Garden of Eden for daring to trespass upon the Tree of Knowledge.

But what if man learned to grow his own Tree?

Where might it end?

She didn't know the answer. She knew only one thing for certain.

Someone had to stop them.

Chapter 45

'*Bon Dieu*. You don't look so good, little brother.'

Jack couldn't argue with Randy's assessment. He felt like someone had poured molten lead into his joints while leaving his skin to alternately burn or go damp with a cold sweat. He had drugged himself with some nondrowsy TheraFlu and hoped it would be enough to sustain him for another twenty-four hours.

'I'll be fine,' he said to Randy, as much as to himself.

His brother stood a few yards from a small A-Star helicopter as it warmed up its engine, rotors whirling up to full speed. The roaring whine cut like a rusty hacksaw into his skull. The chopper would be airlifting Randy and Kyle over to the Thibodeauxs' boat, currently steaming toward Lost Eden Cay.

Off to the side, Kyle stood with his arms crossed, anxious to get moving, one fingernail digging into his plaster cast, like a dog worrying a bone. He had wanted to join Jack's assault team, to go directly after his sister, but his broken wrist precluded him from accompanying them. Not that Jack would have let Kyle anyway. He needed men he could trust, men with military training in covert operations.

Still, Kyle looked ready to claw his cast off and join Jack's men. Mack Higgins and Bruce Kim waited a couple decks below, down by the wellhead with the drill crew. Even farther down, a seaplane floated at the foot of the offshore platform, ready to fly the assault team over to the island and dump them and their gear a mile offshore.

'You have the timetable?' Jack asked Randy.

His brother tapped a finger against his skull. '*Mais oui.* It's all in here.'

Jack didn't like the sound of that. He'd just spent the past half hour going over the assault plan in the office of the rig's geologist. For this to work, each group would have to act in perfect synchronization.

Kyle stepped forward and cast a scowl in Randy's direction. 'Don't worry. I have it all written down. We'll wait for your signal before approaching the island.'

Jack nodded, glad at least that someone good with numbers was going to be aboard the Thibodeauxs' boat. He had full confidence in Randy and his friends when it came to a down-and-dirty bar fight, but as to sticking to timetables, Cajuns seldom wore wristwatches.

Randy merely shrugged. 'Whatever. We'll be where we need to be.'

'And I'll make sure they are,' Kyle added.

Now it was Randy's turn to glower. '*Je vais passer une calotte,*' he threatened under his breath.

There was definitely no love lost between these two men. Jack hoped that old anger – buried deep between their two families – didn't boil up into a problem for this mission.

'Just get on board the chopper,' Jack said. 'I'll touch base by radio when we're in the air.'

The two men turned to the helicopter. They kept a wary distance from each other as they walked away.

Jack dismissed them from his mind and headed for the stairs that led down from the elevated helipad. He wanted to be out of direct earshot when the helicopter took off. His head pounded with each rising beat of the rotors as he climbed down the steep stairs. Finally sheltered from the rotorwash, he was assaulted again by the smell of oil and axle grease from the rig. The farther down he went, the worse it got, until he swore he could taste grease on the back of his tongue.

Fighting down a gag, he stopped on a landing that fronted the open Gulf. A fresh breeze blew in his face. He sucked down a few cold gulps to clear his head. As he did so the A-Star helicopter lifted off overhead and flew over the waters.

He watched the chopper swing south – then his cell phone vibrated in his pocket. *Now what?* He pulled it out and checked the caller ID. He didn't recognize the number, except it was a New Orleans area code. Unsure who it was, he answered it brusquely.

A familiar voice responded, as calm and gentle as if this were an invitation to high tea. 'Agent Menard . . . I'm glad I could still reach you.'

'Dr. Metoyer?' Jack let both his surprise and impatience ring out.

'I know you must be in a hurry,' Carlton Metoyer said, 'but I believe I have information that may have a bearing on your mission.'

Jack stepped back into the freshening breeze off the Gulf to listen. 'What is it?'

'It's about what was done to the animals. With all that happened back at the lab, we never had time to review our DNA analysis on that extra chromosome found in those animals.'

Jack recalled that Lorna had mentioned something about an extra chromosome. She believed it was the cause of the strange mutation in the animals.

'Once we got settled at the Audubon Zoo here, Zoë and I had a chance to run through those results. The chromosome proved to bear some shocking characteristics. Something you should know about.'

'Go ahead. But I'm pressed for time.'

'Of course, Agent Menard. Let me get to the point. I don't know how familiar you are with genetic code, specifically with *junk* DNA?'

Jack sighed, earning a flare of his stabbing headache. 'Biology was not my strong suit, Doctor.'

'No worries. This is Biology 101. As I'm sure you already know, DNA is a vast storehouse of genetic information. The human code is three billion letters long. But what you must understand is that only a very small percentage of DNA – three percent – is actually functional. The other ninety-seven percent is genetic garbage, basically baggage we've accumulated and been carrying around for millennia.'

'So why are we dragging it along?'

'Good question. Recent studies now suggest that not all junk DNA is pure garbage. Researchers have noted that specific regions of junk DNA match base pair for base pair with old viral code.'

Jack checked his watch, not sure where this was going.

Carlton continued: 'There are two theories of why we carry around this ancient viral code. One scientific camp says it's there to protect us against a new viral attack, basically genetic memory lying in wait until it's needed again. The other camp says it's merely old viral code that became absorbed into our DNA over the course of millennia. Literally the baggage of evolution. I've come to believe maybe it's both. Especially as these bits of viral code can be found in DNA across animal species, from the lowliest burrowing mole to us humans. It's like we're carrying these identical chunks from some ancient source and keeping it for some future reason.'

Jack heard an edge of excitement enter the doctor's voice. 'What's the point here, Doctor?'

'Yes, of course. I'm rambling. We've been studying the genetic code of that foreign chromosome, and Zoë had the brilliant idea to compare the sequence to various data banks, including the Human Genome Project. Within an hour, we had a hit.'

'What do you mean?'

'The genetic code of the extra chromosome. We found the exact same code already buried in our junk DNA – and not just ours but most animals'.'

'What?'

'The extra chromosome in these test subjects matches a set of old viral codes locked in *all* animal DNA, including our own.'

'Okay, but what does all that mean?'

'It means that animal kind – at least vertebrates – might have been exposed to this extra code before. Sometime in our evolutionary past. We dealt with it, and it became an inert part of our genome. Only now we've encountered it again. In *active* form.'

'Active?'

'I'll let Zoë explain. She has the better grasp on this.'

Before Jack could object, the phone was fumbled and a new voice spoke. 'Hi, Jack. Sorry to bother you.'

'How are you holding up, Zoë?'

'Okay. I just need to keep busy, to be useful.'

His ear picked up the strain, the tears hidden behind her words. It drew an ache from his heart, echoing his fear for Lorna. 'Tell me what you learned, Zoë.'

Her voice grew firmer, moving away from that well of grief. 'Before we left ACRES, my husband, Paul, had been studying the DNA, highlighting certain sequences of code, what we call genetic markers. It was plain what he suspected. The markers were unmistakable.'

'Unmistakable of what?' Jack asked.

'The markers clearly suggest this foreign chromosome is viral in origin.'

'Viral? Wait. Are you saying the chromosome is a *virus*?'

'We're coming to believe so. Most viruses invade a cell's nucleus, then hijack the host's DNA by meshing with it in some manner. It's why so many pieces of viral code make up our junk DNA. Only this virus doesn't only hijack a host's DNA. It became its own chromosome.'

Again Jack felt a sweeping chill. He began to get an inkling of why Carlton had called.

'We assumed someone had been genetically engineering

these animals,' Zoë continued, 'that they were taking foreign genetic material and artificially inserting it into these animals. The same way we can insert a glowing gene of a jellyfish into a mouse egg and breed mice that can glow. But it was an assumption we jumped to prematurely. After these results, it's possible that the animals might have been merely exposed to this virus, *infected* with it. They then passed the genetic code to their offspring, who were born with these strange changes.'

Jack now understood why he'd been called. He stared across the empty Gulf waters. No wonder the kidnappers chose an isolated island for their experiments.

'This virus,' he said. 'You think it might be contagious?'

'It could be. We don't know. We've already put the animals here in strict quarantine. But we thought you should know before you reached the island. To take precautions.'

'Thanks. We'll do that.' Jack was suddenly all too conscious of his flu symptoms, but he didn't have time to worry about it. He had a job to do.

The tromping of boots on the steel stairs drew his attention away from the Gulf. Mack Higgins climbed up to the landing. He still chewed on the stump of a cold cigar. His eyes widened at finding Jack there.

'Just a second, Zoë.' Jack lowered the phone and nodded to Mack. 'What is it?'

'Pilot says we're all fueled up.'

Jack nodded and lifted the phone again. 'Is that all you have, Zoë?'

'Only one last thing.' There was a long pause. Her voice came back brittle with anger and hurt. 'Find Lorna. Bring her home. And make those bastards who killed Paul pay.'

'I promise, Zoë. On both counts.' He hung up. Lowering the phone, he faced Mack. 'We set to go?'

'Pilot needs another ten minutes to run a final preflight check, then we'll have the thumbs-up. But you should know. I just got off the horn with Jimmy back at the station.'

Paxton's blowing a gasket over there. Knows we're AWOL and off the grid.'

Jack grimaced. It was bad news, but not unexpected. Paxton was no fool. Jack's venture threatened to get them all canned, if not tossed into prison.

'It's not too late for you and Bruce to head back,' he offered.

Mack grinned rakishly around his cigar. 'What would be the fun of that?'

Jack clapped him on the shoulder in thanks and motioned him back toward the stairs. 'What about word from the FBI agent? Any sign of Dr. Polk's GPS signal?'

Mack's demeanor darkened. 'Not a blip or a ping out there, boss.'

Jack swore inwardly. If only he had more proof that Lorna was out there . . . not just for Paxton, but for himself, too. As he headed down the stairs doubt began to fray the edges of his resolve. What if she wasn't even on the island? Or what if she was already dead? He swallowed back those fears. They would do him no good.

She had to be alive – and somehow he knew that to be true. But that didn't mean she wasn't in bad trouble. And unfortunately he felt that just as strongly, and that fear grew with every passing minute.

'We still bugging out of here in ten?' Mack asked.

Jack shook his head. 'No. We're out of here now.'

Chapter 46

Lorna must have passed out. One minute she was heaving bile into a bucket beside the treatment table, and the next she was on her back on the same table. Smelling salts passed under her nose. The ammonia smell felt like a kick to the face. She batted away the technician's hand.

What are they doing to me?

The ovary-stimulating drugs had been injected intravenously. Nausea swept through her even before the last needle had slipped out of her vein. She fought it for a full ten minutes, but eventually her stomach gave out. They must have expected that side effect and kept an emesis pan bedside. She filled it three times until she was left dry-heaving.

As the smelling salts brought her back around she struggled to sit up. The room spun.

'I'd lay down,' a voice said beside her.

She turned and recognized the broad-shouldered gentleman from the villa's study. Seated next to her, he still wore the same hiking pants and khaki vest. This was Bryce Bennett, the man behind the operations here. Up close, he appeared even larger. His tanned face looked like fine-grained leather, his blue eyes like pale ice.

He waved the technician out of the room.

'I had chemotherapy for lymphoid cancer ten years ago,' Bryce said, leaning forward. 'Got it from exposure during my years as a submariner. Back when soldiers were still watching atomic tests from the sidelines. So I know what you're feeling right about now. But you'll get your sea legs back in a few more minutes. At least the other women did.'

Lorna stared around. She was momentarily alone in the treatment room with the man. Not that she could do anything. She felt as weak as a newborn with pneumonia. But with each breath, she did feel her head clearing.

'What are you doing here?' she asked. She meant it to mean *why* had the big man bothered to come down here. But the single question encompassed so much more. Why were they putting her through this? What was the purpose of all of this?

He took her question literally. 'I came here after speaking with Dr. Malik. Something you said intrigued me. I thought we could share a few minutes before they're ready to continue the procedure.'

'What about?'

'About Eden.'

She didn't know what to make of that and remained silent.

Bennett sighed and leaned back in his chair. She noted a silver crucifix pinned to his jacket's lapel. It flashed as he shifted back into his seat.

'But let's start at the beginning. I started this project because of a paper produced by the chief scientific advisers of the Pentagon, a group calling themselves the JASONs.'

He lifted an eyebrow at her to see if she'd heard of them.

She merely kept her face blank, giving him nothing.

'Ten years ago, the JASONs fiercely advocated for the military to invest greater resources into what they all called *Human Performance Modification*. They were concerned that our enemies were getting the upper hand. Foreign powers were already doing pharmaceutical research into performance enhancement. Such drugs could produce troops who were smarter, stronger, and better able to handle the rigors of war. You can imagine the alarm bells that raised among the Pentagon top brass.'

Bennett chuckled at the thought. 'The advisers went on to warn the brass that the U.S. was falling way behind, and as a matter of national security, they recommended two things: to increase research funding and to monitor those foreign studies abroad. And believe me, following this report, money flowed – and it flowed in all directions. One of my competitors in the defense contracting business is already actively testing drugs as a way to improve memory and cognitive performance in troops.'

Lorna began to understand where this was headed. She pictured the brain scan back in Malik's office. She also recalled the description Duncan had used for the project: *bioweapon systems.*

'Following those guidelines, money also went into monitoring other projects abroad. It was during a coordinated attempt to co-opt foreign researchers as moles that we were approached by Dr. Malik.'

A door opened behind Bennett. As if summoned by his name, Malik swept into the treatment room. At his heels followed the chief of security. Duncan was red in the face, making his scars stand out more prominently.

From their demeanors, it was plain they'd been arguing.

Bennett turned to them. 'What's wrong?'

Duncan spoke first. 'We've lost one of the cameras in the compound.'

'It might just be a mechanical glitch,' Malik quickly added.

'Or it could be one of his creatures took out the camera. If they were smart enough to cut out the tracking device in order to sneak over here and kill one of my men, then they're smart enough to knock out a camouflaged camera.'

'What about the other cameras?' Bennett asked. 'What are they showing?'

'Nothing out of the ordinary,' Malik insisted. 'Their activity appears routine. No sign of any hyperaggression. I still say such outbursts are isolated aberrations and can be eradicated.'

'And I say we go in with assault rifles and purge the place.'

Bennett held up a hand. 'That would set us years behind. Duncan, have the security doubled at the gate between the two islands and send an armed team to check on that camera. We'll decide what to do from there.'

Lorna listened to this exchange in silence. Back in vet school, she'd learned that it was better to keep quiet and let the client do most of the talking. More information came out that way.

But Duncan didn't fail to note her presence. He glared at her as if this were all her fault. 'Sir, I also heard word from our computer tech. It looks like the New Orleans facility does indeed contract with Compu-Safe to back up their computers. There's a good chance their data was saved to an outside server. We're still tracking where that might be.'

'Keep looking,' Bennett growled. 'We can't risk losing our technological advantage.'

'Yes, sir.' Duncan headed away again.

Lorna was glad to see him go.

Bennett turned his attention to Malik. 'Doctor, you've arrived at an opportune time. I was just going over how the Babylon Project got started, how you sensed the winds were changing and threw your hat on our side of the ring.'

'Yes. Such a change also allowed me to continue my research, only this time with sufficient funding.'

'We call that a win-win situation,' Bennett said.

'Indeed.'

Bennett faced Lorna. 'Do you know why we call our work here the Babylon Project?'

She shook her head.

'Because it started in the biblical region of Babylon. Dr. Malik was already under way with his project twenty years ago, a secret weapons project hidden beneath the Baghdad Zoo. He was doing biowarfare research with a virus he discovered in a small Kurdish village in the mountains near Turkey. You may have heard of Saddam destroying Kurdish villages back in 1988. During that attack, he bombarded this village, too, and many others with mustard gas and Sarin nerve agent. He also bleached the local wells. All to cover up what they found there.'

'What did they find?' Lorna asked hoarsely, her throat sore.

Malik answered. 'All the children in the village had been born strangely *regressed* during the prior year.'

Lorna pictured the hominids and could guess what the doctor meant by *regressed*.

'The children were kept hidden by the superstitious villagers, believing their lands to be cursed. This certainty also grew after similar genetic abnormalities appeared in the village's goats and camels. Eventually word spread, especially when the adult villagers began to get sick, succumbing to strange fevers that left them hypersensitive to light and noise.'

Lorna recalled Malik describing a toxic protein.

'I was called in to investigate. I did DNA tests and found all the children bore a chromosomal defect.'

'An extra chromosome.'

'That's right. But it wasn't a chromosome. It was an invader. A virus that injected its own DNA into a cell nucleus and took up residence there.'

Lorna finally sat up. This time the room only spun a little. The nausea was also quickly receding, though a cramping ache had begun to throb in her lower back, likely rising from her drug-assaulted ovaries.

'A virus?' she asked.

'That's right. And from what we've been able to tell of its evolutionary origin, we've encountered it before.'

As proof, Malik went on to describe how remnants of this code still existed in our DNA, buried and dormant, just a fragment of junk DNA.

'In fact, this ancient exposure may be why all animal species carry some level of magnetite crystals in their brain. Like broken pieces of a mirror stuck in our head, a remnant left behind from this previous encounter millennia ago.'

Malik continued: 'But these villagers exposed themselves anew, along with their livestock, when they dug a new well, far deeper than they'd ever gone due to a decade-long drought. Once the water was flowing, they quickly contaminated themselves and their livestock with this virus.'

She understood. 'And this virus inserted its DNA, spreading through their cells.'

'It seems to concentrate in very active cells. Lymph, gastrointestinal cells, bone marrow. But also germ cells in ovaries and testicles.'

'And in doing so, it passed its DNA to their offspring.'

'Exactly right. But in the cells of adult animals, it remained dormant, inactive. It only switched *on* inside a fertilized egg. The virus began to express itself as the embryo grew, changing the architecture of the brain to meet its ends. In early embryonic development, it triggered the brain to form those magnetite deposits, and then it grew in a fractal manner in tandem with the developing brain.'

Lorna pictured again that fractal tree, spreading ever outward.

'The viral DNA also continues to produce proteins as an offspring grows. We believe the protein acts as a neurostimulator, basically keeping the neurons more excited, generating additional energy to power and maintain this fractal antenna. But it's this same protein that kills those who don't have the neurological capacity to handle it, those who don't have this magnetic architecture in their brains. Truly insidious when you think about it.'

'How do you mean?' Lorna asked.

'Maybe this deadly feature also serves an evolutionary advantage. A way for the new generation to wipe out the old.'

Lorna went cold at this possibility.

'Either way,' Malik said, 'we *do* know another effect of these proteins. Under electron microscopy, we studied the rest of the host's DNA. Specifically we examined the region of our junk DNA that corresponded to the virus's genetic code. This region was puffy and unbundled, suggesting active transcription and translation.'

'And what does that mean?' Bennett asked, scrunching his brow.

Lorna knew the answer. Her stomach churned – but not from the injected drugs this time.

Malik explained. 'Such an appearance suggests that ancient region of DNA had become active again. In other words, what was junk was no longer junk.'

'How could that happen?' Lorna pressed.

'I could go into detail about messenger RNA, reverse transcriptase, but suffice it to say that these proteins stimulated and awakened this ancient DNA. I believe that awakening this old code is one of the reasons these animals end up being genetic throwbacks. That by turning on the DNA carried in the genome for millennia, it somehow also dredged up each animal's genetic past, reawakening evolutionary features locked for millennia within that junk DNA.'

'Like some sort of genetic trade-off,' Lorna said.

Malik crinkled his brow at her, not understanding.

She laid it out. 'The virus triggers a leap *forward* neurologically, but to balance it out, there's also a corresponding evolutionary leap *backward*.'

Malik's eyebrows rose on his forehead. 'I'd never considered that.'

Bennett nodded. 'Hassan, maybe you were right about Dr. Polk. She might bring a fresh outlook to your problem.'

'I agree.'

They both faced her.

'If you're feeling settled enough to walk,' Bennett said, 'it's time you truly got a taste of Eden. And the serpent that plagues us.'

Chapter 47

Lorna followed Malik back to his office. Her legs wobbled with each step, and she came close to falling on her face after first sliding off the exam table. Bennett caught her and offered her his arm. She hated to take it, but the only other choice was to be carried there.

At least moving helped clear her head.

By the time she reached the chair in front of his desk, she felt strong enough to let go of Bennett's arm and move to the seat. The burning ache in her lower back had also dulled to a low throb. She sank to the chair as Malik took a remote and pointed it at the wall of screens.

'This is a live high-definition camera feed from the habitat we set up on the neighboring island. The animal reserve is connected to ours by a land bridge, but we've set up an electric fence between the two islands and maintain around-the-clock guards. The other island is a perfect test field for evaluating how this new intelligence manifests in a real-world setting.'

The center plasma monitor bloomed to life. The clarity was such that it looked more like a window into another world – and perhaps it was. The view opened into a clearing in a primeval forest. Crude, palm-thatched huts circled the edges, and in the center, a fire pit glowed with embers.

A pair of naked figures crouched near the pit. They were the size of large children, naked but covered mostly in fur.

The male rose to his feet as if sensing their observation. He searched around. His nose was broad and flat, his forehead high and prominent, shadowing his eyes. His jaw protruded, looking like it had been crudely sculpted, halfway between ape and man.

Despite her weakness, Lorna rose again to her feet, fascinated despite her personal repugnance concerning the research here. She recognized the creature. Here was a living example of the body she'd seen earlier. A hominid-like version of early man. As if wary, the male helped the female to her feet. Her breasts hung heavy. She held a hand to her belly, which bulged.

'She's pregnant,' Lorna said, surprised.

'Due any day,' Malik agreed. 'We're lucky to catch a view of the female. She normally stays hidden and only comes out at night.'

'I named her Eve,' Bennett said with a vague note of fatherly pride in his voice.

Malik rolled his eyes a bit at the conceit of his choice of names. 'She's the first of them to conceive in the wild. We've normally orchestrated all breeding via artificial insemination in the lab. We're very curious what sort of offspring she'll give birth to.'

'How old is she?'

'The male is eight, the female seven.'

The shock must have been plain on Lorna's face.

'The specimens mature at a very fast rate,' Malik explained.

Behind the figures, a large dark shape crept out of the shadowy forest. It kept low to the ground, padding on wide paws, tail straight back, ears laid flat. It stalked toward the unsuspecting figures. It was an ebony-furred version of the saber-toothed jaguar killed in the bayou. A juvenile, from the looks of it. Still, this youngster had to weigh over a hundred pounds, most of it muscle. Its eyes squinted toward the two targets – then in an explosion of muscle, it charged at them.

Lorna took a step back in horror.

The male suddenly swung around. The cat skidded to a stop and promptly rolled onto its back, baring its throat and wiggling happily on the ground. The female bent down, one hand supporting her lower back, and rubbed the cat's chin. A tender smile suffused her face. Her features were a more softly sculpted version of the male's. The cat's tail swished in contentment.

Bennett stepped to Lorna's side. *'And so the lion shall lie down with the lamb . . .'*

Malik explained less philosophically. 'They're all bonded. The habitat was established a year ago. At first there were a few deaths, but over time, the specimens established and grew into an interconnected family of sorts, connected, we suppose, by their mental affinity, sharing at a level we cannot comprehend.'

Lorna heard the longing in his voice – not out of any desire to experience it, but more out of a desire to understand and harness it.

As she watched, another three figures entered the clearing. One carried a crude spear, the other two hauled a small pig between them.

'We stock the island with deer and pigs,' Bennett said. 'To keep them fed.'

'They also have wild-growing coconut and mango trees and a freshwater spring,' Malik added. 'But other than that and the makeshift shelters, we've left them to fend for themselves. To see how they adapt, to coexist, and use their strange intelligence to solve problems. We set up weekly challenges and tests and evaluate their performances.'

Behind the trio of hunters, a pack of a dozen dogs burst out of the forest. Lean, with bushy tails and sharp ears, they looked like miniature wolves, each the size of a cocker spaniel. The dogs swept into the clearing, but rather than moving like a tumbling, riotous pack, there was a strange coordination to their movement. They gave the clearing one full run, then swept eerily to a standstill, dropping simultaneously to their haunches, like a flock of birds settling to a perch.

Another handful of hominids appeared from the huts, drawn out by the commotion. Lorna counted.

At least ten.

'It many ways,' Bennett said, 'this place truly is Eden. All God's creatures – great and small – living in harmony.'

Malik had a less biblical take on the matter. 'What we're seeing is a demonstration of fractal intelligence, where the whole is greater than the sum of its parts. We believe the group has developed a hivelike intelligence, where the individuals in the habitat act like one living unit. It may be why they haven't developed the ability to speak. They each know the others' thoughts.'

'And perhaps that's the way the world once was,' Bennett said. 'Before we were cast from Eden.'

Rather than dismiss the biblical analogies this time, Malik nodded. 'Mr. Bennett might be right. Perhaps what we're looking at is the source of the mythology of an earlier earthly paradise, the proverbial Garden of Eden. Various versions of that story persist in cultures around the world. Why is that? Perhaps it rises from some race memory of such a prior union. Just as we still carry magnetite crystals in our brain – fractured pieces of this old neural network – maybe we do somehow recall this earlier paradise.'

'And maybe it's *more* than just memory,' Lorna said, finding herself inadvertently caught up in the wonder of what she was seeing.

Malik turned to her for elaboration.

She nodded to the screen. 'For the past decade, animal researchers and human psychologists have been exploring the human–animal bond – the strange and deep affinity humans have for animals. No one really knows the source of this affinity. We do know it goes beyond mere affection or need for companionship. New studies show the human body *physically* responds to the presence of animals in a positive manner.'

'What do you mean by positive?' Bennett asked.

She offered some examples. 'People who own animals have lower cholesterol levels and a lessened risk of heart disease. Just petting a cat causes an immediate drop in blood pressure. Bringing companion animals into hospitals and hospices accelerates healing times and boosts immune responses in patients. Yet it remains a mystery *why* we have this bodily reaction.'

She pointed to the screen. 'Maybe that is the answer. Maybe more than just a race memory of Eden resides in us. Maybe our bodies *physically* remember it, too. Memory locked in both mind and body.'

'That's an intriguing view, Dr. Polk. And you may be right. Perhaps there remains some weak connection, some residual vibration from the fragments of magnetite crystals that persist, connecting us all together.' Malik sighed and frowned at the figures on the monitor. 'Still, it's the *body* part that has been plaguing us here.'

She understood, putting the details together in her head. 'The genetic throwbacks,' she said to Malik, then turned to Bennett. 'You mentioned the Pentagon's interest in the performance enhancement of humans. You still haven't gotten it right. With such mutational throwbacks, you can't bring your research forward.'

Bennett nodded. 'That's right.'

'It's the Holy Grail of our research,' Malik said. 'A human birth without turning back the evolutionary clock.'

'Does the Pentagon even know you're doing these human studies?'

Bennett shrugged. 'They know not to look too closely. It's why we shipped only animals on the trawler, to demonstrate our progress in order for our funding to continue flowing. We're so close to fully realizing our goal. Can you imagine if we could tap into this resource? Soldiers who are not only smarter, but with unit cohesion like no other army.'

'But that isn't our only obstacle,' Malik said. He stared grimly as the hunters tossed the pig onto the hot coals of the fire pit. 'It seems our Eden has its serpent, too.'

'What do you mean?'

'Let me show you.'

Malik pointed his remote at the other monitors that surrounded the plasma screen. Image after image appeared. Most were pictures of bloody wounds sustained by various men and women, some in white lab coats, others in worker's coveralls or khaki uniforms. But one screen played a video, filmed at night, hued in shades of silver. A shape – one of the hominids – bounded down a dark beach and leaped upon a guard smoking a cigarette. It tore at the man's throat with tooth and nail. The savagery was shocking. Even after the guard was down, the creature continued to claw at the man's face, ripping away a chunk of his cheek.

'That happened last night,' Bennett said.

'Bouts of hyperaggression,' Malik explained. 'They flare up with no warning, no provocation, no explicable reason. One of them might appear gentle one day but would suddenly attack a technician the next. It's one of the reasons we decided to isolate the colony to the far island. They were growing too dangerous to keep here. Our head of security would have preferred to destroy them, but there is still so much we can learn by studying them. From a safe distance.'

She pictured Duncan's map of scars. 'Is that what happened to his face? Was he attacked?'

'Duncan?' Bennett shook his head. 'He was injured much earlier, back when we were first salvaging specimens. Got badly mauled. Spent a week in a coma and countless hours under a surgeon's knife just to get back some semblance of a face.'

No wonder the bastard hates them so much, she thought.

Bennett continued: 'But that's the nature of the beast. I personally believe our aggression problem here at Eden

304

arises because our test subjects have an unnatural connection to wild animals. Such contact defiles God's plan. Corrupts what little bit of humanity remains in them. If we could purge that, we'd be better off.'

'And I can't discount that,' Malik added. 'There remains a feral edge to them that we can't tame. Maybe it does rise from this merging of animal and man. To that end, we've restricted our next phase of research to human studies only. It's why we need plenty of fresh genetic material.'

Lorna didn't like the sound of that. The ache in her ovaries reminded her *where* they would harvest the new genetic material.

'But we'd appreciate hearing any insight you might have in regard to the serpent in our midst,' Malik said. 'Mr. Bennett and I have already discussed utilizing your talents.'

Lorna suddenly sensed all this was some sort of test, a practical exam of her usefulness. To survive, she had to prove herself. If she failed at any point, her life was forfeit.

'Perhaps it would be best if you showed what we're working on now,' Bennett said.

In other words, part two of her exam was about to begin.

Lorna eyed the center monitor. The village was covering the pig with leaves and stones. She watched a version of Igor up in a tree, cutting down palm fronds with his beak. The sight of the featherless parrot reminded her of all she'd lost, of the hopelessness of her situation.

Something in the forest must have made a noise. Suddenly all eyes – dog, cat, bird, man – snapped in that direction, shifting like a single organism. The entire habitat froze in place. They all seemed to be staring directly at the camera, straight at her.

Her body went cold.

Malik placed a reassuring hand on her shoulder. As if that contact broke some spell, the village snapped out of its fixed focus and resumed their coordinated effort. But Lorna could not shake the menacing intensity of that attention.

'Don't worry,' Malik said. 'You won't have anything to do with them. That place is off limits. Isolated to their habitat, they've become progressively insular, dangerous to anyone outside their interconnected family. It would be suicide to step foot in there.'

Despite the danger posed, she could not stop staring at the screen. Still, she understood the security issue. Having been involved with the New Orleans Zoo, she knew the obstacles and challenges when it came to safely housing wild animals, especially predators.

She was glad someone was keeping a close eye on that place.

Chapter 48

Duncan stood on the stretch of sand that connected the two islands. He sucked on a cherry Life Savers, but not even the sweetness could dispel the bitter taste at the back of his throat. He hated to put his men at needless risk, especially when Malik couldn't recognize a failure when it was biting him in the ass.

Across the sand, a trio of his commandos approached the forest on the far side. They were armed with XM8 lightweight assault rifles outfitted with 40mm grenade launchers.

Duncan wasn't taking any chances.

He never did.

Malik had thought him overly paranoid when he designed the security measures to isolate the other island. A twelve-foot electric fence split the land bridge in half. Coils of concertina barbwire topped the gate and rolled out into the water. He'd also mined the seabed to either side with antipersonnel charges that would explode and shred the shallows with razor-sharp flechettes. Additionally, he'd tagged all the beasts over there and monitored their movements around the clock. There should have been no accidents, no surprises, certainly no deaths.

Duncan had seen the body on the beach. The man's face was gone, stripped to the bone. Staring at the mutilation, he had flashbacks about his own attack – and that only stoked his anger to a hot fire. Even his own men gave him a wide berth, seeing something in his face that scared them.

And he was okay with that. He wanted his men to remain wary.

Across the way, the trio of men vanished into the forest. Duncan listened to their chatter. He didn't have to be down at the beach, but he felt it was his duty. He wanted to be here in case there was trouble. He never sent his men into a firestorm that he wasn't willing to follow them into. It was why his men respected him, were loyal to him.

He listened to the men's chatter over the radio in his ear. They kept their talk to a minimum, but he wasn't satisfied. He touched his throat mike.

'Keep silent out there. Hand signals only. Sound out if there's trouble.'

He got confirmation from all three.

He resumed his pacing as he waited. Each minute dragged. His jaw muscles began to ache.

Finally, a new voice spoke in his ear. 'Commander Kent, the team is about to enter the blacked-out zone.' The speaker was posted back at the villa's security nest, monitoring all the camera feeds. 'I'll lose them from here, but I'll keep tracking their ID tags.'

'Understood. Keep me updated.'

Duncan kept his gaze fixed on the forested hill across the way. During his engineering of the compound, he had installed an additional precaution in case of emergency. He had sowed the island with napalm bombs. With a press of a button, he could burn the other island down to the dirt. At the moment he was tempted to do that.

Fry the whole place. Be done with it.

The security technician spoke again in his ear. 'The team has reached the tree blind where the broken camera was posted.'

Impatient, Duncan pressed his throat mike to open a channel to his team. 'Report in. What's going on out there? What did you find?'

The voice came back in a wary whisper. 'Camera's trashed. Looks like someone took a rock to it. Smashed it to bits.'

So he'd been right all along.

A mechanical glitch, my ass.

Duncan planned on laying into Malik once he got back to the villa. But that could wait. He didn't want his men out there any longer than necessary.

'Replace the camera,' he ordered. 'And hump your asses back here double time.'

'Will do.'

Before he could even sign off, the security nest cut in. 'Commander Kent, I'm receiving a distress call from a commercial charter boat. They're reporting an engine fire.'

He closed his eyes and sighed heavily.

Like I need this now . . .

He spoke into his radio. 'Where are they?'

'The beach patrol says the boat's about half a klick from the cove, blowing black smoke. How do you want me to respond?'

Duncan didn't like this. Warning bells rang in his head. He wanted to check this out himself.

'Hold tight before responding to the boat. I'll be right up.'

'Aye, sir.'

Duncan stared at the dark forest beyond the gate. The others should be heading back by now. The security nest could continue monitoring their status until they were safe.

He turned his back on other island and headed up the stone stairs toward the villa. He wanted to see this foundering boat for himself. By maritime law, they could not ban the ship from seeking shelter. To do so would only draw attention to the island.

Still, that didn't mean he had to roll out the welcome mat.

He touched his mike again. 'Tell the beach patrol to keep heavy watch on that boat until I get there. And order the gun battery in the crow's nest to maintain a fix on that target.'

During the construction of the villa, he'd had a M242

Bushmaster cannon built into a bunker atop the highest floor of the villa. It fired two hundred rounds a minute with the velocity to shred through armor. Might seem like overkill, but it was a reasonable precaution considering that the seas around here continued to be hounded by modern-day pirates, raiders who attacked small islands, pillaged unsuspecting estates, and slaughtered or kidnapped anyone unlucky enough to be around.

Duncan refused to be caught by surprise. If whoever was out there wanted to make trouble, he'd make them regret it.

Chapter 49

Five meters underwater, Jack sped above a line of reefs into the island's shallows. His fingers gripped the handles of a portable Mako underwater scooter and powered toward the shoreline. He adjusted the pitch of the unit's propeller to keep him a foot above the seabed.

To either side, Mack and Bruce paced him, zipping through the shallow waters. They all wore black neoprene wet suits. Each of them hauled oilskin dry sacks holding clothes and weapons, M4 carbines and H&K double-action pistols. Jack had also packed his Remington 870 shotgun.

He didn't hold out any hope that such firepower was sufficient for a full-out frontal assault. The weapons were meant as a last resort. This mission's success or failure hinged less on firepower than on stealth. To that end, Jack had coordinated with the Thibodeauxs' boat. The others should have raised a distress signal by now, drawing attention to the far side of the island while Jack's team snuck in the back door. As an added precaution, he had studied the satellite maps and opted to make landfall on the wooded island to the north. With the villa on the southern island, this smaller island would be less likely to be watched.

Or so he hoped.

Jack slowed his scooter as the seabed rose under him. Twenty yards off the beach, he powered the propeller off and let the scooter drop to the sand below. He carefully floated to the surface and peeked his mask above the surf to scan the shoreline. A thin strand of beach fringed a dark wall of forest, mostly palms and mangrove trees near the water with Caribbean pines and walnuts up higher. With the sun setting on the far side of the island, the woods were thick with shadows.

He watched for a long minute for any sign of movement. All seemed quiet.

Mack and Bruce joined him, hovering to either side. He shed his air tanks, weight belt, and swim fins. Holding his breath, he grabbed his dry sack, then signaled for the others to follow. With a kick of his legs, he propelled himself toward shore, staying underwater for as long as possible. Finally, with sand rasping the belly of his wet suit, he surged up and lunged for the beach.

In seven steps, he was out of the water and into the shadows of the woods. Bruce followed next, his lithe shape barely making a splash. He dove over the sand and rolled into the shadows on the right, not even leaving a footprint. On the other hand, Mack stormed the beach like an amphibious landing craft. He lunged out of the water and pounded low across the sand, hitting the woods to the left.

Once under shelter, they kept silent. Beyond their hiding places, the waves slowly washed away most evidence of their landfall.

Jack shivered as he waited. Now that he was no longer moving, his skull began to ache again. The smells of the forest filled his head: moldy leaf rot, wet sand, some spicy-scented flower. His feverish eyes burned, making even the shadows seem too bright. All his senses stretched outward, wary for any sign that their landing had been spotted.

But no alarm sounded. No shouts rose.

Satisfied, he motioned for the others to get ready. They stripped out of their wet suits and into rough duty uniforms in green and black. Weapons were freed; radios fixed to ears and throats.

Once outfitted, Jack lifted an arm and dropped it like an ax in the direction of the land bridge that separated the two islands. The bridge lay not far from the villa. Using the cover of this island should allow them to creep almost to the doorstep of the place.

From there, they would need information. He planned to ambush one of the outlying guards, to interrogate the man under threat of great bodily harm – a threat that would be realized if the man didn't cooperate. Jack had no time for subtlety. He intended to find out if Lorna was here, and if so, where she was being kept.

Jack again felt that bone-deep surge of fierceness. His vision narrowed as he headed into the dappled forest. His men moved silently to either side.

No matter where Lorna was, he would find her.

Lorna stood before a closed door. It read AUTHORIZED PERSONNEL ONLY. Malik swiped his ID card. Bennett stood behind her. They were accompanied by Lorna's assigned bodyguard, the redheaded Connor, who wore his usual hard scowl.

The guard posted himself at the door as the lock disengaged and Lorna and the two men entered a nondescript anteroom. A second door led into the next room, but it couldn't be opened until the first door was closed.

Like an air lock.

Malik turned to Lorna. 'What you're about to see may seem callous at first glance – but it is necessary.'

'In order to maintain their purity,' Bennett added.

Malik gave a half shrug. 'Or in other words, to isolate variables. To strip any possibility that contact with animal minds is contributing to the psychotic breaks demonstrated by the first generation of specimens. To that end, let me show you the second generation of our research.'

Lorna suddenly quailed against stepping across that threshold, fearful of discovering what new horrors lay hidden here. Malik opened the doorway – and Lorna was shocked to hear childish laughter, accompanied by the clapping of small hands. Music also wafted out. The theme song from *Sesame Street*.

The incongruity of laughter in this house of pain set her teeth on edge. Fear grew sharper inside her.

'Come with me,' Malik said, and led her inside.

Lorna had no choice but to follow, trailed by Bennett.

Malik continued his dialogue, sounding vaguely nervous, maybe even embarrassed. 'Though they're isolated here, we treat them very well.'

Lorna stepped into what could pass for an ordinary day-room in any preschool. A chalkboard covered one wall. Beanbag chairs dotted the floor in a rainbow of colors. Crayon drawings decorated a corkboard, and in a corner, a plasma television showed a furry puppet conversing with Big Bird.

But it was the children in the room who drew Lorna's full attention. Dozens of children sat on chairs or sprawled on rugs, raptly staring at the television screen. Each looked around the same age, or at least the same size. They stood no taller than her waist, but these were not toddling babies. Their fully developed features suggested maturity beyond their size. And from the downy fluff on cheeks and limbs, they were clearly related to the inhabitants on the other island. But rather than being naked, the children wore matching blue jumpers.

'How old are they?' Lorna whispered, choked by shock.

'From sixteen months to two years,' Malik answered.

As she stepped farther into the room one child turned toward her, then the others all swung to face her. It reminded her of the synchronization witnessed on the camera. Like a flock of birds startled into sudden flight or a school of fish turning on a dime.

She remembered Malik's term: a hivelike intelligence.

Was that the source of this behavior? She knew *flocking*

314

was still poorly understood. Some scientists wondered if there might not be some electromagnetic connection between birds in a flock or fish in a school, to get them to act so perfectly in unison. But the latest consensus seemed to suggest that each individual was responding to microsignals from its neighbors and responding in a preprogrammed fashion.

Looking at the behavior here, Lorna wondered if it might not be a combination of both.

The faces eventually swung back to the screen as a new song began to play on the television.

'They're innocents,' Bennett said. 'Kept isolated here from any corruption, bonding only among their own kind.'

Malik nodded. 'We're monitoring their IQ scores with nonverbal tests and watching for any signs of aggression. So far, their IQ levels are rising every week. And they've demonstrated no aggression. But that might be too early to judge. Aggression really only manifested after puberty with the others. Still, we're hopeful.'

'What are you going to do with them?' Lorna asked, fearful of the answer.

'As fast as they mature, we'll be collecting eggs from the older females in another six months. They'll be nearing sexual maturity by then.'

Lorna went cold, contemplating such a violation of these little ones.

'From those eggs, we're going to attempt to destroy the active sections of junk DNA that seems to be triggering these throwbacks, to try to breed it out of the next generation.' Malik rubbed his hands as if anxious to proceed. 'We're so close to a breakthrough that could change the world.'

Bennett nodded. 'That's why we could use your help.'

Malik concurred. 'Your expertise with the breeding of exotic animals and handling genetic material is perfectly suited to aid us in the last leg of our work.'

The subtext was plain: it was an offer she couldn't refuse.

315

Not if she wanted to live. But how could she agree? These were not exotic animals close to extinction. In fact, they weren't animals at all.

One of the children, a little girl, wandered from her bean-bag and lifted her arms up in a universal gesture. Lorna leaned down and picked her up. The child was heavier than she expected, thicker boned, but her tiny hand lifted, and the girl began to suckle a thumb. Her small head settled to Lorna's shoulder while bright eyes followed the alphabet lesson on the television.

(. . . *brought to you by the letter W . . .*)

Lorna could feel the child visibly relaxing. A slight tremble in her small body quieted with each breath. Lorna sensed the deprivation of these children, the lack of warm contact. It raised a question in her mind.

She glanced to Malik. 'What happened to this child's mother? To all their parents?'

Malik sought to assuage her. 'You've seen them. They're housed at the habitat. When we populated the other island, we separated the youngest specimens here. We've built this nursery with copper wiring in the walls to confine this group's neural network to this handful of rooms, to isolate them from contamination while their brains are still pliable.'

Lorna pictured the violence caught on video, of one of the hominids attacking a guard. By Malik's own admission, these weren't dumb animals. Though they didn't have the power of speech, they were plainly highly intelligent, communicating among themselves in ways no one could fully understand.

She began to suspect the reason for such an attack, for such savagery.

She was carrying it in her arms.

Maternal instinct was strong in most animals. In a communal setting, that instinct would be magnified. The loss of each child would be felt by the whole. Such abuse could drive them into a maddened state. Combine that with heightened intelligence – *growing every week,* according to Malik – the danger posed by the compound's inhabitants would intensify.

No wonder the security measures were so strict.

Heaven help anyone who set foot over there.

Five minutes after hitting the beach, Jack led his team through a grove of pines. He had quickly sought higher ground, but continued to parallel the beach as he circled toward the land bridge. In his head, he kept his position by fixing the sun's position, the angle and direction of shadows.

Still, he wanted to getter a better lay of the land.

Spying a limestone outcropping that might suit his need, he lifted a fist.

Mack and Bruce dropped into shadows to either side, rifles fixed to their shoulders. Jack clambered up the rocky boulder. Sunlight dappled its surface. For the first time, he had a good view across the island, all the way to the cove on the western side. He noted a white speck out there. It trailed black smoke against the setting sun. He hoped Randy and the Thibodeauxs had enough smoke canisters to maintain their ruse.

He turned his attention to the immediate landscape below. He spotted the spit of sand connecting this island to the other. A glint of steel concerned him. It looked like some barricade split the bridge. The structure hadn't been on any of his satellite maps, but the surveys had been old and the detail poor.

He frowned at the barricade but knew he had no other recourse. He would face that challenge when he reached it. Still, its presence nagged at him.

Why construct a barricade between the two islands?

Frustrated, he backed to the edge of the boulder, intending to hop down – when a stuttering spat of rifle fire erupted, exceptionally loud. From his perch, he spotted a flock of doves explode out of the forest, taking flight halfway between his post and the bridge.

317

He crouched, expecting the foliage to shred around him, believing he'd been spotted. But a moment later, the rifle fire turned into bloody screams. They rang out brightly through the air.

Then the screaming cut off with a note of finality. Silence followed, as if the forest were holding its breath.

Jack slipped off the boulder and back down into the shadows, keeping as quiet as possible. A cold certainty set in. He pictured the barricade. Something else shared this small island with them.

He didn't know what that might be, but he knew one thing for sure.

He was on the wrong side of that fence.

Chapter 50

Duncan leaned his fists on the curved desk of the monitoring station.

The security nest had been built into a bunker in the hillside. It offered immediate access both to the villa and to the subterranean lab. Behind him, bulletproof windows offered a sweeping view of the cove and the foundering fishing charter as it limped within a pall of smoke into their waters. It was not his most immediate concern. The gun battery atop the villa kept the boat under a tight watch.

Instead, his attention remained fixed to the dark screen.

He listened to the static in his earpiece, straining for any sign of his scouting party. The horrific screams over the radio still echoed in his ears. He couldn't tell how many throats issued those cries.

Were any of his men still alive?

'Play the tape again,' Duncan said.

The technician seated at the desk manipulated a toggle, and the dark screen fuzzed with a blur of brightness – then stopped on a crisp image of a freshwater spring bubbling out of the side of a forested hillside. Camera 4A had been positioned near the island's sole watering hole. It was one of twelve cameras posted at key positions, areas that offered the best vantage for observing the test subjects' daily routine.

Duncan's team had managed to install the new unit. The image wobbled as the camera was quickly positioned and secured. He caught a glimpse of an arm waved in front of the camera, testing its function.

Then the hand jerked back, and one of his men sprinted past the camera. His rifle was on his shoulder, his cheek pressed tightly to the stock. Though there was no sound transmitted over the camera feed, the gun rattled and smoked as it was fired. Then the man disappeared out of view.

A moment later, the image cracked and went black.

Duncan straightened, taking in a sharp, deep breath. It was more than his men's fate that worried him. He stared across the remaining eleven cameras. They displayed various views of the island: a crude latrine, a rocky ledge, a shallow cave, and three cameras alone focused on the main village habitat. It all looked peaceful, except there was not a single sign of any of the inhabitants. Their conspicuous absence left only one conclusion.

'They know about the video cameras,' he mumbled.

All of them.

His mind worried on that implication.

So then why only take out one camera?

The answer was simple enough. The bastards had set a trap intended to lure men to the site. But why? To exact revenge? He didn't think so. The act was too calculated, too purposeful. He pictured again the rattle of the assault rifle. Another possibility asserted itself and grew more certain as he considered it. The broken camera was not meant to lure men – but *weapons*.

Duncan shifted to a computer monitor. It displayed a map of the island. Tiny red dots moved in real time across the screen. They represented the tracking tags of the fourteen ape-men and the twenty-three other specimens. But none of those tags had come near the spring at the time of the attack. As he stared at the screen he noted several of the tags remained fixed in place, some in the village huts, two in the cave, the rest in the jungle.

320

Duncan reached out and counted the number of immobile tags.

. . . twelve, thirteen, fourteen.

The same number as the ape-men. That couldn't be a coincidence. There could be only one other explanation.

'They've removed their tags,' he said aloud.

'Sir!' The technician jolted and pointed to the live feed from one of the cameras. 'You'd better see this.'

Duncan joined him at the monitor. The screen displayed a view of a jungle clearing. As he stared he saw nothing at first. Then a shift of shadows at the edge of the glade drew his eye. Shapes crept through the forest.

Two, maybe three.

He squinted.

Were they the missing inhabitants?

Then one of the shadows slipped into a dappling of sunlight. The figure wore trousers, a camouflage jacket, and carried an assault rifle. At first he thought it might be one of his men, still alive. But the gear was wrong. Duncan knew all of the men who had crossed the bridge into that hellish place. This wasn't one of them. Someone else was over there.

He weighed the possibilities. Ever since the trouble in Haiti, raiders had been growing bolder in the region. Could that be who they were?

On the monitor, the mysterious party disappeared into the jungle.

'What do you want done?' the technician asked.

Duncan turned to the computer monitor. The chaotic motion of the red blips had stopped. As he stared they began to move again, all of them – converging toward the trespassers like a tightening noose.

His lips thinned with grim satisfaction. The fools had picked the wrong island to land on.

'Sir?'

'Keep monitoring,' Duncan said. 'This problem should take care of itself in a few moments.'

But it didn't address another worry. How the hell did a raiding party get onto that other island in the first place? Duncan swung to the arc of windows overlooking the sea. The smoking boat continued to limp into their cove.

That had to be the answer.

He'd heard of birds that would fake a broken wing to lure a cat away from a nest. The same was going on here. The distressed ship had been used to draw their attention, to get them to drop their guard.

Anger stoked to a burn deep in his chest.

Time to grind that bird under a heel.

'Call up the gunner in the bunker,' Duncan ordered, still staring down at the cove. 'Tell him to open fire on that boat.'

Chapter 51

Jack sensed them before he saw them.

He lifted a fist to stop his teammates. Over the course of the trek, he'd grown attuned to the forest: the hushed whisper of a sea breeze through pine needles, the briny scent of loam and salt, the pattern of shadow and sunlight. Then suddenly a change. A quiet crackling rose from the woods all around, like a smoldering fire sweeping down on them. Off the wind, his nose picked up a distinctly musky smell. A flock of small swallows burst through the branches to the left.

Something was out there and closing in.

Jack lowered to a wary crouch and swung up his Remington. He preferred to hunt with a shotgun in woodland conditions. In such tight quarters, the scattering punch of a shotgun served better than the precision of a rifle.

Mack and Bruce took up positions to either side. They kept their backs toward each other, weapons pointed out.

Jack searched the shadows. The rustling went immediately quiet, as if a switch had been thrown. He waited. It would be easy to attribute the noises to an overactive imagination, except that overripe odor remained on the breeze.

A prickling spread down the back of Jack's neck. He felt eyes upon them – many eyes, studying him as intensely as he watched the forest. As he strained all his senses, his headache flared and his vision tunneled. For a moment a strange static filled his skull, like his body were a radio tuner straining for a signal.

Then a cracking of branches exploded to the right. For some reason he knew to glance up. A shadow passed overhead and fell heavily down toward Jack and his men. They had to scatter out of the way. It struck the ground in the center of their group.

Blood splattered in all directions.

Jack stared, disgusted and stunned.

A headless corpse lay on the ground. The arms had been ripped off at the sockets, leaving only a torso and legs. Blood continued to ooze from the wounds.

What the hell . . .

He noted the black khaki camouflage uniform. It was the same gear as the assault team that had attacked ACRES. He turned his attention back toward the shadowy forest. The woods remained dead quiet, so silent he could hear the waves washing the beach off in the distance. The static in his head dulled to a low hum – but as he strained with every sense on fire, the buzz slowly grew in volume.

'Here they come,' Jack whispered to his men.

Lorna continued to carry the female child in her arms while *Sesame Street* played on the dayroom's television.

'So you think last night's attack was an attempt to reach the young ones here?' Bennett asked.

Lorna shrugged. 'Why else would they attack this island? You said they have plenty of food, water, and shelter. So why swim over during the night and ambush a guard on the beach?'

'You may be right,' Malik said. 'But that doesn't explain the hyperaggression displayed *before* we relocated the adults to the other island. This can't be all about the young ones.'

Both men turned to her. They focused a bit too intensely, as if expecting a solution from her, some insight into their problem. She knew if she failed to impress them, failed to

324

prove her usefulness, her days on the island would come to a swift end.

'These bouts of aggression,' she started. 'You said that the attacks came without provocation.'

Malik nodded. 'That's right. Last year an adult specimen was calmly completing an IQ test when suddenly he whipped around and mauled the technician monitoring the test. The specimen was, of course, killed in order to weed out the troublemakers.'

'And nothing provoked that attack?'

'Not that we could judge.'

'What about procedures done elsewhere in your labs? Specifically, painful tests?'

Malik rubbed his chin in thought. 'We do examinations all the time. I still don't understand your point.'

She again pictured the strange flocking behavior she had witnessed earlier. 'You said these specimens share a hive mentality? That *thoughts* are spread across their magnetic network. So why not *pain*, too? In other words, *what one feels they all might feel*. If that's the case, if you provoke one specimen, an entirely different one might lash out in a reflexive reaction.'

Bennett stared at Malik. 'Had you considered that possibility?'

'No, but it's an intriguing angle.' The researcher's eyes narrowed with contemplation, but he looked unconvinced. 'I'll have to review the records.'

Lorna pressed. 'You have to stop thinking of them as individuals. There is only *one* intelligence out there, spread fractally among the group. They are a single psyche stretched across multiple minds. And for years, you've been abusing that psyche, torturing it on multiple fronts.'

She stared at Malik, waiting for him to object to her assessment of his cruelty. His silence spoke volumes.

She continued. 'Under such prolonged and sustained abuse, is it any surprise you began to see psychotic breaks?

325

But you've been tackling this the wrong way. Trying to weed out this problem by culling only the violent ones. These breaks aren't arising from *individuals* in the group, they're coming from the *whole,* from the hive mind that you've abused to the point of psychosis.'

Bennett and Malik shared a worried look.

'So you're suggesting the entire hive mind out there might be psychotic,' Malik said, his voice cracking with disappointment. 'Driven insane.'

'Maybe even worse.'

'What do you mean *worse?*' Bennett asked.

'If what Dr. Malik described is true about their IQs, the entity you've created out there isn't just insane – but *brilliantly* insane. Beyond our comprehension, beyond rehabilitation. Pure rage and madness coupled with cunning and guile.' She shook her head. 'You've created a monster.'

Jack stared down the length of his shotgun at the woods. His skull felt as if it were on fire. The corpse behind him reeked of blood and bowel. Why had they tossed it at Jack's group? As a threat, a distraction? Then why didn't they just attack?

As he studied the forest he sensed them on all sides. Jack and his men were surrounded, trapped. He again considered the corpse, his mind working fast.

Why throw it here?

Then he suddenly knew. He glanced over to the body, remembering the rattle of automatic fire. It sounded like it had come from more than one gun. Whatever was out there had dispatched the trained soldiers as easily as swatting flies. If they wanted to take out Jack's team, they could do so just as easily. But instead they threw the body here.

And he knew why.

As a message.

Jack called to Mack and Bruce. 'Lower your weapons.'

To demonstrate, he dropped his shotgun from his shoulder,

held it at arm's length, and crouched to set it on the ground.

'Are you nuts, sir?' Mack asked.

'Do it. If you want to live.'

Mack grumbled under his breath but obeyed.

Jack knew the corpse was tossed here as a warning. To show that their lives were forfeit if they didn't surrender. He also sensed that whatever shared this island knew Jack's team was different from the commandos.

As the weapons were dropped, shadows shifted, and a shape slipped into view. Much closer than Jack had suspected. Only a couple of meters. Others stirred out there, too. Some larger, some smaller.

'Jack . . . ?' Mack hissed at him.

'Stand down,' he warned.

Mack complied, but he was not happy about it.

The shape moved closer. At first Jack thought it was a large chimpanzee or a small gorilla, but as it stepped into the sunlight it walked upright like a man. No shambling or knuckle dragging. It cocked its head as it came forward. Jack noted an ear was missing, leaving a long jagged scar down one side. This was no surgical wound, but one lost in combat.

As it stepped closer yet again its flattened nostrils flared as it took in Jack's scent. Naked, the creature was covered in fur – and blood. Though smaller by a couple of feet, its body was heavy-boned and layered with muscles. Jack suspected the creature could rip him apart with its bare hands.

But for the moment there was an uneasy truce.

Large shining eyes stared at him.

Jack noted the intelligence there. But there was no warmth, no welcome. Those eyes remained as cold as a winter star.

Jack's blood settled into the pit of his stomach as another realization struck him. He remembered Lorna's description of genetic throwbacks. He knew what faced him was not any animal – but was once a man.

Another of the creatures, his face knotted in a snarl of threat, appeared behind the first. He carried a lightweight assault rifle, likely confiscated from the dead body behind Jack.

To the left, a black-furred tiger shoved into view. Lips rippled back to reveal fangs as long as daggers.

All their gazes fixed on Jack.

The combined focus set his head to aching, his skull bones to vibrating. He had to resist pressing his palms against his ears.

The first creature came forward until he stood directly in front of Jack. He leaned closer and sniffed at his clothes. Hands reached up and gripped Jack's shirt. Fingers dug in, and the arms jerked wide, ripping open his shirt. Buttons went flying. With Jack's chest and belly bared, he felt exposed and vulnerable. The bandages that Lorna had dressed over his wounds stood out starkly against his naked skin.

Hands reached again and tore those away, too, taking with it some hair and a bit of scabbing. Jack winced but made no move to shove the other away. Fresh blood dribbled down his stomach.

To the left, Mack swore under his breath, his hands still in the air.

On the right, Bruce remained in a fixed crouch. A pack of small wolves faced his teammates. Jack saw Bruce's eyes dart toward the weapon on the ground.

'Don't,' Jack warned between clenched teeth.

Bruce obeyed, but his gaze remained fixed on the rifle, ready to leap at the first provocation. Jack couldn't let that happen.

The man-beast before Jack cocked his head and leaned close, sniffing at the trails of blood down his chest, taking in long deep breaths. His small head then tilted back, eyes slightly closed, as if tipping that scent deep inside him. Over the creature's head, Jack noted the others doing the same. Even the cat's eyes slipped to half-mast, as if taking in his scent.

For a moment a rich smell of blood filled his own nostrils, almost overpowering in its intensity. Then it was gone.

The examiner's face rose before him. Hands gripped his shoulders and dragged him down until Jack was nose to nose with the beastly form. Jack smelled its fetid body, noted each eyelash, heard the rasp of its breath. Fingers remained clamped on his shoulders. He felt the raw muscular power in that grip.

But it was the eyes that held Jack's full attention.

Pupils dilated as Jack stared. It was like peering down into a dark well. He sensed that the abyss had no bottom – but it was far from empty. Something strange stared back out at him.

The static in his head ratcheted up to a volume that threatened to crack his skull. It felt like his brain was trying to squeeze out his ears. As he rode a wave of agony his sight suddenly narrowed until he seemed to be hanging over that bottomless abyss.

He was trapped there for a breath – then the beast shoved him away, and Jack stumbled back into a tree. The pressure in his skull receded to a dull throb.

The creature turned and headed away. The other beasts swung like one body and vanished back into the forest.

Jack remained standing, trembling.

What the hell just happened?

The beast who had confronted him glanced back before disappearing. Cold eyes stared at him, then down to the shotgun at his feet. The message was clear.

Mack stumbled over to Jack. 'What now, boss?'

He crouched and retrieved his weapon. 'We go with them.'

'What?' Bruce asked, aghast. 'They'll tear us to pieces.'

Jack knew his teammate's warning was not without merit. For the moment he had passed some test of fire here. What that *test* was he didn't know – and passing it scared him as much as it relieved him.

But he was also under no delusion. This was no warm

329

welcome. They simply shared a common enemy. Nothing more. He remembered the coldness in that attention and knew that the uneasy truce would last only as long as this war.

After that . . . it would end.

'Let's go,' Jack said.

They hadn't taken more than a couple of steps when a rattling roar rose from the other island. Jack rushed forward to a break in the hillside forest. Through the branches, he got his first view of the villa on the other island.

From a concrete bunker atop it, the black snout of a massive gun smoked and chattered. But it wasn't aimed toward them. It fired toward the cove, still hidden out of sight behind the shoulder of the other island.

But he could guess the target of that savage barrage.

The Thibodeauxs' boat.

Chapter 52

Duncan stood before the arc of windows in the security nest. Overhead, the gun battery blasted away from its bunker. The chugging roar of the chain-fed autocannon rattled the bulletproof windows. Down below, rounds chewed across the water toward the smoking boat in the cove.

At the first sign of trouble, the fishing charter had opened throttle and shot toward the beach. Its bow lifted high, pushed out of the water by some powerful engines, more than expected from an ordinary fishing boat. This observation was further supported when the first rounds of the cannon pinged harmlessly off the sides of the boat.

The craft's hull had to be reinforced with armor plating. Gunrunners and smugglers often disguised assault craft as ordinary fishing boats. The villa's cannon could pierce light armor, even bring down slow-flying aircraft, but distance and angle fought against them.

Then something strange happened.

From the stern end of the fishing charter, a Zodiac raft dropped into the water. It shot away like a black rocket, riding two pontoons.

The Bushmaster cannon found its main target again and rattled the bow of the fishing boat. The armored craft heaved to the side, skidding sideways through the water, exposing its flanks while protecting the smaller raft. Rounds ricocheted off the hull – then moved higher toward the bridge.

Glass shattered from the ship's windows. Men flattened themselves to the deck.

Out in the water, the Zodiac hightailed it toward the northern edge of the cove. It bounced across the waves as guards along the beach opened fire. Return shots sparked from the raft, accompanied by the smoking trail of a rocket-propelled grenade. It struck the beach and exploded, throwing sand high and shredding a palm tree.

As guards scattered from the beach the pontoon boat continued its flight across the waters, looking like it was trying to circle out and head toward the sandy spit that connected the two islands.

Before Duncan could assess that threat, a greater concern arose.

A man, popping into view atop the bridge of the fishing charter, balanced a long weapon on one shoulder. He knelt down and angled the black tube of a rocket launcher toward the villa.

Motherfuck—

Duncan twisted away from the window as smoke blasted out the back of the weapon. A rocket roared straight at him – or rather at the gun battery above him. Either way, he didn't want to be here.

He dove toward the door.

Lorna stood frozen with Malik and Bennett in the nursery ward. The child in her arms clung to the collar of her blouse and trembled violently as gunfire rattled – then a gut-punching blast boomed down to them. Muffled by rock, the explosion still shook the walls.

Everybody held their breath, then the first child began crying. In seconds, it spread like wildfire among the children. A day-care worker – a round-bellied Chinese woman – tried in vain to console the group, but they refused to calm down. The girl in Lorna's arms buried her tiny face and continued to tremble.

'We're under attack,' Malik said.

'Stay here.' Bennett moved toward the door, but before he could take two steps, it banged open.

Connor burst into the room and crossed quickly toward them. 'Sir, are you okay?'

'What's going on?'

'Commander Kent radioed down. The boat in the cove opened fire on us. Believes they're pirates.'

Pirates? Lorna tried to fathom such a thing. She had heard stories from Kyle about roving bands of marauders who plied the Gulf waters and hijacked ships at sea or ransacked homes along the coasts. Even an oil rig in the Gulf had once been attacked.

Bennett continued toward the door. 'Take me to Duncan.'

'He said I should keep everyone here.'

'Bullshit. I'm not some child to hide in a hole.'

Malik joined his boss. 'If there's a problem, I need to get back to my lab. Secure our viral samples in case this problem escalates. If we lose those samples, we've lost everything.'

Bennett nodded. 'Do it.'

Malik waved to the day-care worker in the room. 'Come with me. I'll need a hand.'

Connor made a halfhearted attempt to block them. 'Sir.'

Bennett strong-armed the guard out of the way and reached the exit. 'Keep Dr. Polk here.' He glanced back to her. 'We'll continue our discussion as soon as this fire is stamped out.'

Malik followed his boss.

Connor stood for a moment, then cursed and stomped off after them. He didn't even glance back as he secured the door and left Lorna alone.

With the door sealed, the rattle of the raging firefight muffled to a dull popping. Still, she could tell it had begun to escalate. Alarm bells joined the cacophony, along with distant muffled screams.

What was going on?

She didn't know, but her mind fought for some way to turn this chaos to her advantage. If she could break out, reach a radio, maybe even a boat . . .

But what then? Even if she could get off the island, what hope was there to escape through pirate-infested waters?

As she held the child the others drew toward her like moths to a flame, needing reassurance, growing quiet. She had to protect them, but was there another way out of here?

With her heart pounding, she hurried to an open door at the rear of the nursery. She popped her head through, seeking some means of escape. Rows of raised cribs lined both sides of a long narrow room. Only these cradles were made of steel and had lids that locked.

Despite the danger, anger stoked inside her. How could anyone be this callous with these innocent children? Large moist eyes stared at her, tracking her as she searched the rooms.

Alone now, she no longer had to mask her emotions. Fear turned to fury. She used it, allowed it to spread like a fire through her belly. She had wilted under panic once before – but never again.

These bastards had stolen everything from her: her life, her brother, her friends, even Jack. This last thought sapped some of her will. If Jack could not stop them, what hope was there for her?

She searched the remainder of her confinement. Other than a small lavatory and bathroom, there was no other exit from the dormitory. She was trapped here. They all were.

Not knowing what else to do, she returned to the center of the room. The children gathered around her. Some clung to her legs, others sucked thumbs, a few softly sobbed. She settled to the floor with them.

A small boy climbed into her lap, joining the girl. The two clung to each other. The pair reminded her of the conjoined capuchin monkeys back at the lab. But she knew these two

– the entire group, in fact – were merged at a level beyond mere flesh. More children nestled around her. Every pop and rattle of gunfire trembled through the group like a pebble dropped into a pond.

She did her best to reassure them. She reached out and touched each one. Where contact was made, they seemed to relax. Caramel-brown eyes shone at her. Tiny fingers clung to her, to each other. They smelled warmly of baby powder and sour milk.

Despite her fear and physical discomfort, a trickle of peace spread through her. She couldn't say where it originated: from herself, from the children. It didn't matter. The peace inside her was not one of slothful contentment, but of determined resolve, a steadying of her keel.

As panic drained, certainty grew.

'We'll get out of here,' she promised, as much for her benefit as the children. 'We all will.'

But how?

Duncan's head still rang from the rocket impact. Blood trickled from one ear and down his neck.

Moments before the blast, he had run out of the security nest and dove into the limestone tunnel that connected the command bunker to the villa. He had managed to slam the door behind him as the rocket struck the gun battery in the upper bunker. Still, the concussion had blown the door off its hinges and tossed him down the tunnel.

With his eyes burning, he fought through the smoke and back into the security nest. Glass crackled underfoot. Half the windows overlooking the bay had shattered into the room. He found the technician in a pool of blood on the floor. Duncan checked for a pulse but failed to find one.

He crossed to one of the broken windows. The chatter of automatic weapons echoed up to him, punctuated by grenade blasts. He spotted the fishing charter in the harbor, half obscured by smoke. The firefight continued to rage between the boat and the beach. It was a hellish barrage. Tracer rounds flashed through the growing smoke. Screams rang out.

Still, he sensed the fishing boat was playing a game of distraction, maintaining a holding pattern out there rather than launching a full frontal assault.

But why?

Duncan turned to the nest of monitors. Most were dark, but a few flickered with grainy images. Movement on one drew his eye. He shifted closer. The screen showed the fence between the two islands.

Also something new.

The black Zodiac raft from earlier had beached itself nearby. A stray round must have shredded one of the pontoons, deflating it. The boat wasn't going anywhere now. The pirates were lucky to have made it as far as the beach – and luckier still to have missed the flechette mines buried in the seabed alongside the land bridge.

Closer to the camera, five men huddled by the fence. Nearby, two bodies lay on the sand in a growing pool of blood. From the black camouflage jackets, the dead bodies were Duncan's men.

Anger curled his fingers into fists.

Who the hell were these raiders?

One of the attackers shifted closer to the hidden camera. He momentarily turned his face into full view, shaded by a ball cap. A jolt of recognition shot through Duncan.

That ball cap . . .

He'd seen it before and its owner. Out on the bayou road. The Cajun in the Chevy truck. Duncan struggled to comprehend how that man could be here. It made no sense. He'd watched the truck dump into the Mississippi. Even if the man had survived the river, why was he here? How had he tracked Duncan to Lost Eden Cay?

Answers slowly sifted through his shock.

The Cajun had mentioned something about a brother

being at ACRES. That was why the bastard had been on the road so late, why he had stopped to ask for directions. If that bastard was here now, that meant someone else probably survived the assault on the lab.

Duncan realized he still hadn't heard from the soldier he had left behind to canvass the area and clean it up. Had he been captured, forced to talk? Duncan knew better than that. His men would never talk.

Regardless, these bastards had found the island.

They would live to regret that.

As his initial shock faded Duncan digested this information. He watched the Cajun tilt his ball cap and stare across the fencerow toward the other island, as if expecting company. Duncan remembered the armed figures caught on camera earlier. Clearly this team was attempting to rendezvous with the other, to join forces for a surgical strike, to sneak in the back door while the firefight raged out front.

But what was their end goal?

It wasn't a difficult question.

This had all the earmarks of a rescue operation.

Duncan unclipped his radio and called up his second-in-command. 'Connor.'

'Sir?' His second spoke rapidly. 'Bennett is headed up. I couldn't stop him.'

Duncan didn't care. 'What about the woman?'

'I've got her holed up in the nursery. She's not going anywhere.'

Not good enough.

'Go in there,' he ordered. 'Put a bullet in her head.'

Chapter 53

Lorna sat with the children as muffled gunfire continued. Trapped here, she had to bide her time. She didn't know which side of the firefight she should be rooting for: the devil she knew or the pirates who were attacking.

Suddenly all of the children went tense and glanced toward the dayroom's main door, as if responding to a signal beyond her senses. They were all on their feet at once, rising like a startled flock of crows.

Their manner set her on edge, their tension contagious.

A loud *bang* drew Lorna's attention to the exit. She recognized it as the outer anteroom door slamming shut.

Someone was coming.

The children retreated toward the back. She got caught in the flow of them and followed. Or maybe she was dragged. Small hands clutched her pant legs and drew her with them.

They reached the dark room with its rows of locking cribs. As they passed the threshold Lorna caught a glimpse of the inner anteroom door swinging open. But she didn't see who entered as she ducked away.

The apprehension of the children continued to keep her heart pounding, her senses sharp.

A voice called out. 'Where the hell are you?'

It was Connor. Something in his voice pushed her heart into her throat. Along with exasperation, she heard a distinct threat. The children continued to draw her away, as if they sensed the same, tapping into some empathic connection.

Lorna held her breath and continued with them. But there was nowhere to hide in the nursery, not unless she wanted to cram herself into one of the cribs.

At last, the tide of bodies reached the center of the room, and fingers released her. The children scattered in all directions, moving with surprising speed, obeying a cue beyond her. They ducked behind and under the heavy steel cribs.

Lorna followed their example, seeking what shelter she could. She dropped to a knee behind a crib but kept an eye on the doorway. A couple of children hid under the crib with her. They shifted their tiny bodies next to her, trembling with fear.

Connor crossed past the door's threshold and headed to check on the bathroom first. She saw his hand drop to a holstered pistol at his waist. His thumb broke the snap securing the gun.

'Don't make this any more difficult than necessary!' he shouted. 'Come out and I'll make this quick and painless.'

She remained where she was. It was all she could do. There was nowhere else to run.

Jack moved through the forest, heading down the hillside toward the sandbar that connected the two islands. Mack and Bruce continued to flank him. Farther out and ahead, he caught glimpses of shadowy shapes, some small, some large, a living mass flowing downhill, gathering momentum and growing in number. All headed toward the sandbar.

At last the forest broke apart into a scatter of palms and stretches of sand. Light shone brighter here, glinting sharply off the water as the sun sat on the horizon.

A figure detached from the shadows ahead. It was the creature who had confronted Jack earlier, distinguishable by his missing ear and scarred face. An arm pointed toward the open beach.

Jack shifted forward and joined him. He immediately recognized the source of the creature's distress.

A tall fence wrapped in concertina wire blocked the way ahead. Jack noted a generator on the far side.

Electrified, he wagered.

Movement drew his attention beyond the fence to the other island. Only now did he note the raft beached over there. Figures hid in the shadows on the far side – but were they friend or foe?

There was only one way to find out.

As he stepped into the open he noted smears of crimson across the sand on that side, like bodies had been dragged away. The plan of attack had been for Randy to rendezvous at the land bridge. The Zodiac looked like the one from the Thibodeauxs' boat, but it had been shot up.

Had anyone survived?

Jack moved from shadow into sunlight, exposing himself. He kept his weapon at his shoulder, wary, ready to leap back.

A call shouted at him. 'Jack!'

Randy stumbled into view across the way, waving a rifle over his head. Jack lowered his own weapon.

Thank God.

His relief was short-lived. A growling roar rose to the right. A small two-man jet boat tore around the shoulder of the island and shot toward the land bridge. The soldier in the passenger seat stood with an assault rifle balanced on the windshield.

The muzzle flashed, and rounds chewed across the sand toward Jack's toes. He fled back into the shelter of the forest. Across the fence, Randy did the same.

As Jack ducked away a second jet boat roared in from the other direction, joining its partner. The two boats – one on each side of the land bridge – sped back and forth, sweeping a tight patrol, making it impossible to pass.

As Jack stared at the two sharks out there, he felt his plan falling apart. Someone already knew about this attempted backdoor assault. They were dropping the ax, cutting off access, splitting their teams. The element of surprise was now gone.

That thought raised a new fear.

Lorna's survival depended on a speedy extraction. Delay meant death. His fingers tightened on his shotgun.

Was he already too late?

Lorna stayed hidden behind the crib. Fear sharpened her breathing. She heard Connor bang open the door to the bathroom off the dayroom, searching for her.

It wouldn't be long until he came to check in the nursery.

As she struggled for some recourse a squeal suddenly erupted out in the dayroom, bright with terror.

Connor cursed harshly. 'Fucking monkeys . . .'

Her heart clenched. The bastard must have found one of the children hiding out there. The squeal turned into a cry of pain. Beyond the doorway, Connor appeared again. He held aloft a small boy by his neck. The child struggled and strangled, legs kicking, his mouth frozen open in a cry of pain and panic.

Lorna felt the two children clutched to her side tremble violently, sharing the boy's terror and pain.

Out in the dayroom, Connor pointed his pistol at the boy's belly. 'Come out now, or I'll make this monkey suffer for you!'

Stunned by such cruelty, Lorna was too shocked to react.

Connor shifted out of view, still searching for her. 'Now or never!'

Lorna couldn't let the boy die for her. She had to stop this, even if it meant her own life. She began to push up – but small hands gripped hers and held her down. There was an urgency to their attention beyond mere fear of being abandoned.

They moved her hand to the legs of the raised crib. She

341

felt casters at the bottom, wheels to help rearrange the cradles as necessary.

It took her a moment to understand.

She flipped the locks on the casters and moved to the back of the crib. Pushing with her legs, she shouldered into it. It took some effort to get it moving. Constructed of steel – more a cage on wheels – the crib was heavy and unwieldy. Wheels squeaked, but she called out to cover the noise.

'I'm coming! Don't shoot!'

She dug in with her toes and maneuvered the crib out of its line and got it wheeling down the center of the room toward the door. She fought for more speed. As if sensing her need, small bodies crawled out of hiding and hurried to the crib. Hands grabbed the steel legs and helped her push with surprising strength.

A part of Lorna's mind struggled to understand. On her own, she would never have thought to use the crib as a battering ram. But fear was a powerful motivator, and necessity the mother of all invention. Run all that through the combined intellect of the frightened children and this means of defense arose.

As they worked together the crib sped even faster.

Connor appeared again, facing the nursery door.

Lorna shot out of the room with her battering ram, pushing with all her strength, a prayer frozen on her lips. Connor's eyes widened in surprise. Unable to get out of the way, he tossed the boy aside and fired wildly at her.

She ducked as rounds ricocheted off the crib's steel front. Then the battering ram struck Connor square in the chest. His body went flying, arms wide. He landed on his back, and his pistol skittered across the linoleum floor.

Lorna didn't stop. She rammed the crib forward, keeping its momentum going and smashed it into Connor yet again. As the front casters hit his sprawled body she heaved up and sent the crib crashing down on top of him.

She dove to the side and retrieved his pistol. It felt heavy and hot, but the weight helped center her. She kept it pointed at Connor, but he wasn't moving, except for a twitch in one arm.

She searched around.

It took her a moment to realize she was free – and armed.

The children gathered to one side, eyes wide upon her. She read the hope there, along with the residual fear. She couldn't abandon them.

'Let's go,' she said and headed toward the door.

The children flocked behind her, trusting her fully.

She prayed it wasn't misplaced.

Chapter 54

'What's your plan from here?' Bennett asked.

Good question, Duncan thought. He shook his head, still calculating, struggling to wrap his mind around the strange nature of this assault. He felt control slipping away from him.

Duncan stood with Bennett in front of the bank of monitors in the security nest. Someone had thrown a blanket over the dead technician's body. Another computer expert was attempting to bring up the other feeds. On the monitor in front of them, Duncan continued to watch video from the camera posted between the islands.

Two jet boats were patrolling either side of the land bridge. Duncan had ordered the boats into position after spotting the Cajun from the bayou. It was lucky he did. Moments ago he had watched a figure appear on the *opposite* side of the fence, stepping from the forest onto the spit of sand.

The impossibility of it still jarred him.

From the clothing and gear, it had to be one of the men he'd spotted earlier in the forest. Somehow the man had survived his overland route to reach the land bridge. How was that even possible?

An answer came as the computer technician slid out from beneath the console. He wiped his hands as he stood up. 'The computer should reboot the tracking software in a moment.'

As promised, a neighboring dark screen went blue, then a map of the other island pixelated into view.

'Give it a second to start picking up the tracking signatures,' the tech added.

As they watched, small red blips began to blink into existence as each tracking tag came online, marking the location of each animal over there. More and more bloomed on screen.

Duncan swore.

Bennett glanced to him, then back to the computer monitor. 'That can't be good.'

Rather than their usual random distribution around the island's landmarks, all of the blips clustered at the base of the land bridge. The entire menagerie had converged there. Duncan could only think of one reason why.

'They're going to try to break through the barrier.'

'And you don't know who that stranger is?' Bennett asked. 'The one out there with them.'

'No.' And the man's survival confounded him. 'But he's got to be working with that group from the Zodiac. I wager this is all a private attempt to rescue Dr. Polk.'

It was the only thing that made sense. Duncan had already explained to Bennett about the Cajun in the ball cap.

'If they had any real government backing,' Duncan continued, 'there'd be a stronger response. Warships and helicopters. In some ways, I think this is just a fishing expedition. To see if Dr. Polk is still alive. But who knows how long that will last? A government response could already be mustering.'

'What do you recommend?'

'A scorched-earth policy.'

Bennett's eyes widened. He glanced to Duncan for clarification.

'If these bastards know about Lost Eden Cay, others will, too. We've lost control. We're now too exposed. We have to accept that reality and deal with it aggressively.'

'How aggressively?'

'We evacuate, burn both islands to the bedrock, kill everyone still out there. Leave no trace. With no trail back to us, we can start again somewhere else. It'll be a setback, but we won't be dead in the water.'

Bennett sighed with a note of resignation. He turned to the blasted windows that overlooked the cove and mumbled. *"So the Lord God banished him from the Garden of Eden."*

Duncan pressed him. 'Sir?'

Another sigh followed. 'I see your point. We don't have any choice. After all the problems here, a clean start might be good. Malik is already securing the last of our viral samples and all his records. We can be ready and at the helipad in fifteen minutes.'

'Better make that ten,' Duncan warned.

'What about Dr. Polk?'

'I've already taken care of that problem.'

Bennett looked resigned, but he'd get over it. Duncan was paid big money to make the hard decisions and carry them out.

'What's the immediate plan of action?' Bennett asked, changing the subject.

Duncan nodded to the video feed. 'To close that back door. To make sure we have no more surprises during our evacuation. I have a team headed down to ambush the group from the Zodiac. The bastards will be pinned down against the fence and the jet boats.'

'What about the other side?'

Duncan stared at the cluster of red blips on the computer monitor. It was time to put an end to Malik's failed experiment, to raze it to the ground. As a precaution, he'd seeded the entire island with napalm charges. Over a hundred. The resulting firestorm would destroy all life in a matter of minutes. And anyone who tried to escape would be picked off by the sharpshooters in the jet boats.

Reaching into a pocket, Duncan removed a radio transmitter. He'd taken it from his office safe before coming up here. Two buttons glowed on the unit.

One was tuned to the buried charges on the other island.

The second would ignite a pair of massive bombs built into the infrastructure of the villa: one in the upper building, the other in the subterranean lab. With the blast equivalent to forty-four tons of TNT, the bombs would blow the top off the island, literally wiping it from the map.

But that would have to wait.

He flipped the trigger guard over the *first* button.

Bennett gaped at the transmitter. 'What? You're blowing up the other island *now*?'

'No time like the present.'

Duncan pressed the button.

That takes care of one problem.

Chapter 55

Jack felt the tremble under his feet. Then the blast hit him, sounding like the earth cracking behind him. He swung around to watch the top of the island blow away in a spiral of smoke and fire. More charges blew in a series.

Boom, boom, boom . . .

Eruptions of flames chased around the island in a descending spiral, adding to the hellish maelstrom. The firestorm continued to blast its way toward the beach. A tower of black smoke climbed into the sky. Jack smelled the distinct odor of napalm.

They're torching the place.

Mack shoved next to him. He had to yell to be heard above the continuing detonations. 'What now?'

Bruce took matters into his own hands. It was death to remain in the forest. The only escape lay across the land bridge. The man dove out onto the open strand, staying low. He blasted away at one of the jet boats, but the vehicles never stopped moving, swerving and spinning chaotically, making for near-impossible targets. Rounds that reached them merely pinged off their reinforced hulls.

Return fire peppered the shore. Sand exploded around Bruce – then a round hit his shoulder and spun him, blood spraying.

Crap . . .

A shift in winds blew hot smoke over their position. The

stink of napalm burned Jack's lungs. With no choice, he sprinted out of hiding toward Bruce. His teammate was down on one knee. Bruce shifted his weapon to his good shoulder and continued to fire.

Mack flanked Jack, shooting at the other jet boat.

Behind them, the firestorm swept toward the beach.

Each *boom* sounded closer.

Across the land bridge, Randy's group laid down a suppressive salvo, too, recognizing the danger Jack's team was facing. But they made no headway. Pinned down as they were from both sides, the stretch of sand was impossible to cross. They'd be mowed down before they could even reach the fence.

Jack grabbed Bruce, ready to haul him back.

But back to where?

As he turned, a charge detonated only a handful of yards into the forest. Trees blew high in a column of flame. The blast knocked Jack onto his back, scorching across him. His vision narrowed to a tunnel. He choked on smoke.

Mack barreled into him and rolled him into the water's edge as gunfire ripped across the sand, nearly taking his head off.

Half in the water, Jack recognized the hard truth.

There was no escape.

From the security nest, Duncan watched the napalm charges blast along the top of the island and spiral down toward the beach, razing to ash all in their fiery path. In engineering the demolition, he had timed the charges to blow in sequence, to ensure maximum incineration.

He smiled as he watched the trio of men struggle in the sand – trapped between flames and gunfire.

They were doomed.

Bennett stood at his shoulder, but he took a step back. He'd seen enough. 'Dear God . . .'

God had nothing to do with this.

The charges continued to explode into whirlwinds of flame, one after the other, adding to the conflagration, spreading relentlessly toward the water.

As he lorded over the destruction with a deep sense of satisfaction, he noted movement in the forest. Figures darted into view. From their naked shapes, they had to be his missing inhabitants. His smile grew harder. Apparently the forest had grown too hot even for them.

But they'd find no salvation out in the open.

Still, something about their manner jangled a warning. There were only four of them. So where were the others?

He leaned closer.

What were they up to?

Still seated in the water, half dazed, Jack noted movement at the edge of the smoky forest. Four figures stepped into the open. They split into pairs and headed to either side.

Each pair hauled a sling of woven palm fronds between them. The slings were weighted down with black metal canisters that looked like small pony kegs. Each pair swung their slings and tossed their cargoes high into the air.

The canisters toppled end over end.

One toward each jet boat.

As they flew, the entire bestial force burst out of the forest and onto the bridge: men and women, massively muscled cats, vicious packs of wolfish dogs. Some creatures Jack couldn't recognize. One giant loped past him, knuckling on pairs of curved razor-sharp claws. Others followed, streaming past.

Behind the force, the last of the napalm charges reached the beach and exploded in a wall of flames. Jack rolled into the water to keep from burning. Twisting, he watched one of the flying canisters fall toward the jet boat. The nimble craft sped clear.

But accuracy wasn't necessary.

The canister exploded in midair.

Jack heard a matching blast behind him.

Fiery napalm washed over the sea and flooded the jet boat. Men screamed as they became living torches. Jack swung around to discover the other boat burning, too.

Impressed, Jack sat up in the water. The creatures must have dug up two of the napalm charges near the beach, waited until the timed series of blasts got close enough, then flung the bombs so they'd blow on cue.

But not all of that dark army escaped unscathed.

Lagging behind the others, a tiger burst out of the blasted forest. Its body was on fire, trailing flames as it ran. Blind and enraged, it flew straight at Jack.

He dove under its claws, coming close to getting eviscerated.

The fiery cat splashed deeper into the shallows – then the water exploded under it. The cat's bulk got tossed high, shredded apart within a column of seawater and blood.

A sting burned Jack's left arm. A slivered blade protruded from his biceps. He recognized the shrapnel. A flechette. The bastards had mined the waters, too.

Jack yanked out the sliver and hobbled to his feet, weaving and unsteady. They had to keep moving. With an open furnace burning behind him, Jack crossed to his teammates. The back of Mack's jacket was a charred ruin. Bruce's left arm dripped blood.

But they were alive.

Jack pointed after the bestial pack. Gunfire erupted there, coming from the trio of assault weapons they carried. Electricity sparked from the fence – then the gate fell open.

At last the way was open.

Duncan went cold as he watched the dark army flood across the land bridge. He could not believe what he'd just witnessed. The bastards had taken out his men with his own napalm charges.

Half awed, half horrified, Duncan watched as one of the ape-men raised an assault rifle and fired at the camera.

The monitor went black.

Duncan turned to Bennett.

The older man had gone pale as a ghost. 'There's no stopping them.'

'Makes no difference,' Duncan assured him. 'They'll find no refuge here. We stick to our plan. By the time they force their way through our lines, we'll be long gone.'

'What do you mean?'

Duncan picked up his transmitter from the table. One button had gone dark, but another still glowed, waiting to explode the massive bombs buried here.

'I'll set the villa to blow in half an hour,' Duncan said. 'That should give you time to collect Malik and get to the helipad. I've already alerted the pilot. He should have the rotors spinning by the time you get to the hilltop.'

The older man still looked stunned, but he was no wilting flower. Bennett's gaze focused again. He nodded.

'Do it.'

Duncan lifted the transmitter. He set the timer for thirty minutes, then flipped up the trigger guard. With his finger hovering over the button, he stared again at Bennett.

One last chance . . .

As answer, Bennett swung toward the door and headed out.

Satisfied, Duncan pressed the button.

There was no turning back now.

Bennett stopped at the door. 'What about you? Are we holding the chopper for you?'

'No. I'm going to make for the seaplane.'

Duncan had one last issue to address. Through the blasted window, the firefight between the fishing charter and the beach continued – but it had devolved into furious spats. He couldn't risk the boat escaping the coming detonation. It was time for this war to go airborne.

'What about the rest of the island's personnel?' Bennett asked.

Duncan was glad the two were alone at the moment. He needed all his forces to remain here until the last moment, to keep the beasts at bay long enough for them to make a clean escape.

Bennett continued to stare at him, waiting for an answer. He gave it to him. 'We can always hire more men.'

Chapter 56

Lorna ushered the last of the children through the anteroom that separated the nursery from the main lab complex. It acted like an air lock, requiring three trips to get all of the children through.

Scared while separated, the children required constant consoling and reassurance. She understood their acute distress. According to Malik, the nursery area was shielded with copper wiring in the walls, to insulate the nascent intelligence from contamination. So each time she left a group outside in the hallway and went into the nursery to fetch the next set, the hive bond between them was momentarily broken, severed by the copper shielding. She could only imagine the terror if half her brain were suddenly cut away.

She eventually got them all back together.

United in the hallway, they clustered even more tightly, needing contact, both physical and mental.

Still, they dared not linger any longer than necessary. Lorna removed the pistol from the waist of her pants. She had to find her way back to the main lab, then from there to the villa.

'Hush now. Stay with me.'

She headed down the hall with the children in tow. Wary of the new surroundings, they moved as if on ice, unsure of their footing, not trusting it would support them. Some of them had probably never been outside the nursery.

Still, the group traveled in silence, as if sensing the danger.

She traced her way back as best she could recall. The nursery was buried in the deepest level of the lab complex – to further shield the children with natural rock, but also to limit access only to those with the highest clearance. She was grateful for that.

With the war going on, no one seemed to be here.

At last she reached a familiar set of steps. She held up a hand for the children to wait at the foot of the stairs while she investigated. Moving as silently as possible, she crept up the steps to the landing above.

The passage at the top ran straight past the surgical suite where Lorna had first seen one of the hominids. At the end of the hall should be the main lab.

Muffled voices reached her. Her fingers tightened on the pistol. How many were in the lab? If it was lightly manned, she might be able to force her way through at gunpoint. She would have to try. The only way to reach the villa and escape was through Malik's lab.

No matter the circumstances, she had to move fast.

She waved the children up to her. 'Hurry now.'

The group scurried up the steps and poured into the hall with her – but something went wrong. The first boy up the stairs suddenly winced and clapped his hands over his ears. Then the others froze, too.

She knelt among them. 'What's wrong?'

The children remained in frozen postures of pain and fear.

She didn't have time for this. She had to get them moving. Bending down, she scooped a small girl out of the group and stood up. Rather than melting into her like before, the girl remained a hard knot in Lorna's arms.

She had no time to discern the source of their distress. She crossed down the hall with the girl. The others followed, but a low whine escaped them, like steam from an overheated kettle. Hands remained clamped to ears.

What was bothering them?

Out in the woods, Randy held his brother at arm's length. 'Christ, Jack. You're as hot as a streetcar in July. And you look half dead. No, I take that back. You look full-on dead.'

Jack didn't argue. His vision remained pinched. His head throbbed with every ragged beat of his heart. But more disturbing was that both of his hands had gone strangely numb.

But at least he'd reached the main island.

And with allies, too, as strange as they may be.

'What's wrong with them?' Kyle asked.

Lorna's brother stood a step away with one of the Thibodeaux brothers. T-Bob had come with Randy, while Peeyot remained on the fishing charter. Kyle clutched his cast against his chest. It had been wrapped in duct tape to keep it dry, and he carried a Sig Sauer pistol in his other fist. From the way he held it, he was familiar with the weapon.

Two other men – black Cajun cousins of the Thibodeauxs – also hid in the forest. The pair shouldered shotguns and had hand axes tied to their belts.

All eyes focused on the beasts hidden in the shadows with them.

'Why did they all just stop like that?' Kyle pressed.

Jack stared around. The sun had sunk into the horizon, leaving the woods dark. Firelight from the burning island behind them flickered into the edge of the forest, dancing shadows all about.

Still, he could easily pick out the one he had come to mentally call Scar, the apparent leader of this dark army. The normally animated figure had frozen in place – as had all of them, man and beast.

Moments ago, Jack and Randy's teams had joined forces in the woods. After dealing with the initial shock from Randy's men, Jack had wanted to keep moving, to maintain the momentum of their overland assault. But the entire dark army had simply stopped in their tracks, frozen in various positions.

Scar stood with his head cocked as if he were listening to a song only he could hear. The same seemed to be true of the others.

Before Jack could fathom what was going on, Scar suddenly turned to him, studied him with those cold black eyes, then without any signal, his entire group set off again.

Before leaving, Scar acknowledged one other: a fellow man-beast, a one-armed figure who was scarred even worse than their leader. He looked older, and most of his disfigurements were linear, suggesting the scars came from surgical experiments. Jack also noted a saucer of metal strapped to his chest like some thick crude shield.

Scar touched the other's shoulder. They gazed at each other – then the one-armed figure turned and ran off into the jungle in a different direction.

Without any other explanation, Scar continued up the wooded slope.

Beasts both small and large spread out in a wide swath, covering the hillside. Four cats flanked to either side, a phalanx of wolf-dogs led the way, and the giant slothlike creature loped to one side. Jack also noted for the first time a trio of black foxes the size of Dobermans. These last moved so swiftly they seemed more shadow than substance.

The trio vanished into the woods.

Along with the beasts, a dozen of Scar's men and women kept pace, carrying crude weapons: spears, cudgels, stone axes. Three of them also bore automatic weapons.

Jack followed behind the group, trusting they knew the way better than he did. But that path would not be easy.

They'd traveled less than thirty yards up the hill when a barrage of gunfire shredded the forest ahead. The muzzle flashes lit up the shadows. Tracer rounds speared through the dark woods.

An ambush.

Bodies got cut down near the front, torn nearly in half.

A round burned past Jack's ear.

He dropped to a knee, taking shelter behind the trunk of a tree.

A step away, Kyle tackled Randy to the ground – and not a moment too soon. A grazing round tagged the bill of his ball cap and flipped it off his head.

Randy cursed as Kyle rolled off him, but it wasn't directed at Lorna's brother. 'That was my favorite hat.'

'I'll buy you a new one if you'll just shut the hell up,' Kyle said.

Randy glanced over to the kid, as if truly sizing him up for the first time. More rounds tore over their heads. The pair crabbed sideways to a rocky outcropping and took shelter there together.

Jack had lost sight of Mack and Bruce, but a raking spat of return fire from nearby suggested they were okay. Jack lifted his own shotgun, ready to charge up the hill.

Then the screaming started.

Indifferent to their own safety, the dark army hadn't slowed. They used the dead bodies of those in front as bloody shields and overran the snipers' positions. Even more disturbing was the eerie silence of their attack.

Gunfire escalated, taking on a panicked note.

A rock came rolling and bouncing down the slope. As it passed Jack's position he was horrified to see it was a helmeted head.

Then as suddenly as it all started, it was over.

The army flowed onward, drawing Jack and his group in its wake.

'Keep going,' he called out. 'Stay with them.'

They moved up through the slaughterhouse. Blood turned the ground to mud. Some soldiers still lived. A few attempted to crawl away, missing legs, dragging entrails.

A frightened soldier leaned against a tree, half his face gone; he pointed a pistol at them and kept squeezing the trigger, but he was out of bullets.

They hurried past him.

After a minute Jack began to stumble and trip, his legs full of lead. His breathing grew ragged and hot. But rather than growing numb to his surroundings, his senses remained strangely sharp.

He smelled the sweet dampness of a flower he brushed against. He heard the crunching snap of pine needles underfoot. Even the twilight forest seemed too bright to his eyes.

Then, after another ten yards, the villa appeared ahead. They took up wary positions at the edge of the woods, and Jack studied their target.

With all of its lower windows sealed behind steel shutters, the villa looked like a fortress under siege. A bunker near the top was a blasted ruin. Teak furniture on the open patios had been chopped to kindling by machine-gun fire from the Thibodeauxs' boat.

Scar suddenly appeared next to Jack. They eyed each other. Again Jack felt like his skull was splitting in two. Scar reached to Jack and gripped his forearm. The gesture seemed like both a thank-you and a threat.

Jack understood.

They'd both reached their goal.

After this final assault, all bets were off.

Chapter 57

Lorna kept the children lined along one side of the hallway. She edged up to the set of swinging doors that led into the main lab room. Voices reached her.

'How much time is left?'

Lorna recognized Malik's accent. She also heard the panic in his voice. She used the tip of her pistol to ease open the door and peek through.

Bennett stepped across her view, his back to her. He kept his voice low. 'Less than twenty minutes. So hurry up.'

Malik stood by a bank of computers. He was shoving hard drives into a metal suitcase. A portable Dewar flask for transporting cryogenic samples stood next to it.

'What about the rest of my team?' the doctor asked.

'Expendable,' Bennett said, his voice pained. 'That's why I sent everyone out. We keep this evacuation on a need-to-know basis.'

Lorna struggled to understand. Why were they leaving? Why this sudden urgency? She attempted to fold this new reality into her plans of escape. Could she somehow use this to her advantage?

Bennett checked his watch. 'Pack up everything and let's move.'

Malik snapped his briefcase shut, passed it to Bennett, then grabbed the cryogenic bottle from the tabletop. 'We have to get these viral samples into a secure lab within twelve hours or risk losing everything.'

'Understood. We'll make arrangements en route.'

They turned and headed toward a far door, but it was not the one leading into the villa. An 'Emergency Exit' sign glowed over the doorway.

Where did it lead?

As if hearing her question, Malik asked, 'The tunnel to the helipad, is it secure?'

'It's out of the direct line of fire. And the pilot is armed.'

Lorna stayed hidden. For the first time since her arrival here, hope bubbled through her. *There's another way out!* If she maintained a safe distance and followed them out this back door, she could take the children into hiding in the woods and wait for this war to end.

But her luck wasn't holding.

A harsh voice barked behind her. She turned to find a stick figure of a man standing by the entrance to the surgical suite. She recognized the technician, Edward, the one who had drawn her blood, injected her with hormones. She also recognized the rifle pointed at her.

'What are you doing here?' he called out loudly. He eyed the kids and kicked the closest one. 'Drop your pistol and move into the lab.'

Lorna had no choice. She let the pistol clatter to the floor. The children came rushing up to her. She backed through the swinging doors into the main lab.

She turned to find Malik and Bennett stopped and staring at her.

'Dr. Polk?' Bennett said, his voice full of surprise, suspiciously so. Lorna noted a flinch of guilt pass over his features.

Malik's eyes widened upon seeing the clutch of children sticking close to her legs. 'What luck.'

Bennett glanced to him.

'I could use a couple of these specimens,' the doctor explained. 'They'd be perfect seeds for the new facility.'

Lorna's stomach sank toward her feet. She'd delivered them straight into the hands of the monster.

Edward pushed into the room behind her. He had confiscated her pistol and pointed it at her. He took in the scene with a glance: the briefcase, the Dewar flask. His eyes flicked up to the emergency exit sign.

'Where are you going?' he asked.

Malik took a step forward, crouching slightly with a hand on his hip. He eyed the remaining children, as if trying to pick out a ripe melon. 'I won't lie to you, Edward. You deserve at least my honesty. The island is going to blow up in about seventeen minutes.'

Edward stumbled forward. The tip of the pistol wavered with his shock. 'What?'

Lorna felt equally stunned. She now understood their furtive urgency.

'Don't worry,' Malik said. 'Your work won't be in vain.'

Edward swung his pistol toward the two men. 'Take me with you.'

'I'm afraid that's not possible. No room. Especially now. We need these specimens.'

Malik straightened from his crouch. A tiny pearl-handled pistol had appeared in his hand as if by magic. He pointed it at Edward's face and fired.

The shot was loud, stinging her ears.

Edward fell backward, tipping like an axed tree.

Even Bennett gasped at the cold-blooded murder.

Malik turned to his boss, but he kept his pistol aimed at Lorna. 'We could each take one specimen. A breeding pair would trim at least a year off our new start-up.'

Bennett checked his watch, knowing he had no time to argue. He growled, 'Pick which ones and let's go.'

His gaze briefly brushed across Lorna's. The guilt that had flickered before now shone steadily. Lorna suspected he normally kept himself above such dirty work, purposely diverted his eyes from the bloody reality of this project. But such innocence was no longer possible.

The same couldn't be said of Malik. Working in the trenches from the start, he was covered in blood up to his elbows. 'I'm afraid we'll have to leave you here, Dr. Polk. You'll have your freedom for' – he checked his own watch – 'another fifteen minutes.'

Malik bent down and grabbed a boy by the arm and dragged him into the air, carrying him like a sack of groceries. 'We'll need a female, too. Take that one.'

He pointed his pistol.

Bennett bent down and gently scooped the child in one arm. His gaze fixed to Lorna. 'I'm sorry.'

As they backed away a massive explosion ripped through the space.

The blast lifted her off her feet and tossed her backward. She slid across the floor. A flaming book tumbled past her nose, trailing ash. More debris blasted into the space. She fought to raise up to an elbow.

Children had been blown to the far wall. Bennett and Malik lay sprawled facedown.

Lorna searched around for a weapon.

Edward's body had rolled against a table. There was no sign of her pistol, but his rifle was still tangled over his shoulder.

If she could reach it –

But Malik was already pushing up off the floor.

Bennett heaved over to his back. He had sheltered the girl with his body and still clung to her.

Lorna began to sidle toward the rifle – when something massive bounded out of the fiery doorway and landed in a crouch. She stared in disbelief at the monstrous tiger. The beast roared, black tongue curled, exposing saber-sharp fangs.

Malik scuttled away like a crab.

Bennett froze in place only yards from the monster.

Lorna recognized the tiger from the video feed on the

other island. The psychotic bunch must have broken free of their prison – and plainly had come for revenge. She now understood why Bennett's group was blowing this place to kingdom come.

More shapes piled in behind the first, pouring out from the short tunnel that connected to the villa. Flames and smoke obscured their shapes, but some walked upright on two legs.

Off to the side, Malik had backed to the emergency exit. He had somehow kept hold of the Dewar cryogenic flask. He hugged it to his chest and dove out into the tunnel.

Bennett was trapped, pinned down by the monstrous army.

One of the hominids came forward. He was missing an ear, and his face was massively scarred. Lorna recognized him from the video feed. He had been the one with the pregnant female, the one Bennett had named Eve.

That would make him Adam, she thought.

He came at Bennett with a long spear.

The man didn't bother to move or struggle. There was nothing he could do.

Then the children suddenly rushed forward, moving like a flock of starlings protecting a nest. They piled on top of Bennett, joining the girl in his arms and shielding his body with their own.

Adam stood over them. More hominids appeared behind him.

Through the doorway, a heavily muscled shape bulled into the room, knuckling on claws. A giant sloth. They'd gone extinct ages ago. The genetic throwback settled to its haunches. Fur along one flank had been burned to the skin and still smoked.

Its large eyes scanned the room, then joined the others in staring down at the knot of children.

Bennett finally sat up, as confused as Lorna at the behavior of the children. The young ones continued to stand between the monsters and the man.

All their small eyes locked gazes with the elders.

A silent negotiation seemed to be under way.

Then voices echoed from the demolished doorway. Half deafened by the blast, she couldn't make out the words, only that it sounded like English.

Another figure stepped through the smoke on two legs.

Only it wasn't a hominid.

Lorna choked on her shock, at the impossibility of it.

She struggled to her feet.

'Jack . . . ?'

Chapter 58

Relief welled through Jack as he heard his name called out. He blinked tears from his stinging eyes and stumbled farther inside the room. It looked like some mad scientist's workshop. Flaming debris dotted the floor and curled smoke into the room.

Jack squinted, straining – then spotted a figure rising from the floor.

Lorna . . .

He rushed toward her.

She came at him.

Reaching her, he crushed her in his arms. He took her scent deep into his chest. Her heartbeat pounded against his ribs. Her cheek, tender and soft, nestled against his neck. He needed to make sure she was real and not a feverish delusion. He clung harder to her.

But she broke the embrace too soon, fighting him in desperation. Her face stared up, wide-eyed and full of worry. With his shirt ripped open, she placed a hand against his bare chest. Her palm was ice against his skin.

'You're burning up.'

He took her hand down and clasped her fingers. 'Just a fever. Flu. Doesn't matter.'

She didn't look convinced. But for the moment she had a larger fear. Her fingers tightened on his hands.

'Jack, the island. They've planted bombs here. Set to blow

in another ten minutes or so.'

He tensed, picturing the exploding napalm charges. So it wasn't just the one island. The bastards were cleaning house and burning all bridges behind them.

'We have to get off this island,' she said.

He took her by the hand and led her back toward the door, but more of Scar's forces had piled into the room, blocking the way out.

Jack stepped forward and confronted him. He had to get the message across. 'We must go!' He waved an arm toward the door. 'Now!'

Scar ignored him. His gaze remained fixed upon a cluster of children standing in the room. The brood stared straight back at him in a silent war of wills.

Jack didn't have time for this.

He stepped between Scar and the children.

Finally, the man's eyes snapped angrily in Jack's direction. Agony ripped into Jack's skull. Gasping, he blacked out and fell to his knees. Fleeting images flashed through his head: a spray of blood, a flash of a scalpel, a cinch of leather straps, a splay of a dissected body.

With each image came a bolt of pain.

Then he felt his body tugged to the side. The pressure in his head popped and drained away. His vision returned.

Lorna knelt beside him. 'Are you okay?'

Jack touched his forehead, expecting to feel shattered bone. 'I think so.'

He looked up. Scar had returned the full brunt of his black attention upon the group of kids. Jack recognized a hard truth. Whatever truce had existed between them before had ended.

He turned to Lorna. 'They're not going to let us go.'

Malik wheezed as he ran up the last of the steps. A doorway opened ahead, brighter than the dark tunnel. As he fled toward his salvation he clutched the cryogenic jar tightly to his chest. After Saddam firebombed and bleached the original source, this was the last of the virus supply.

With it, I can start again. With or without Bennett.

From this frozen seed, whole armies could be born.

And it didn't matter *who* financed his work. There would always be governments willing to pay the price. If not the United States, then another country. And as a free agent, he could command any price.

Reaching the tunnel's end, he ducked through to the outside.

The sun had set, but the western skies still glowed a deep orange.

The helipad sat atop the highest point of the hilltop. A circle of asphalt, painted like a yellow bull's-eye, held back the forest. He sprinted toward it along a crushed stone path. Even from here, he heard the low drone of the helicopter's engine. As he topped the rise he spotted the rotors spinning.

He reached the asphalt and called for the pilot.

A man in a flight jacket stood on the far side, staring down at the beach. He flicked away a cigarette with a flash of ash, turned, and crossed briskly to the chopper.

Malik met him at the open door.

'Where's Mr. Bennett?' the pilot asked.

Malik put on his best face of concern and regret. 'Dead. Caught in an ambush.'

The pilot glanced toward the tunnel as if wagering if he should confirm the story. Malik made an overly grand motion of checking his watch. 'We're down to less than ten minutes. We either go now or never.'

With a concerned glance at his own wrist, the pilot finally nodded. 'Load up. I want to put some distance between us and that blast.'

Malik climbed into the backseat while the pilot settled behind the stick. In seconds, the engine roared, and the blades cut faster through the air. With a lurch of his stomach, the skids lifted off the asphalt.

Simply breaking physical contact with the island calmed Malik's hammering heart. He cradled the frozen prize in his lap and stared out the window. Trees dropped away under him. The expanse of the sea spread wide with all the promise of the world.

He allowed a smile to form.

The pilot called back, shouting to be heard. 'What's that smell?'

Malik didn't know what he was talking about. He sniffed deeply, fearing a gas leak or maybe smoke. They didn't have time for a maintenance check.

'What are you carrying?' the pilot yelled. 'Smells like an animal took a dump back there!'

Brought to his attention, Malik finally noted a rank smell. He had failed to distinguish it earlier, too accustomed to the odor. He smelled it all the time down in the labs. It got into your clothes, hair, even your pores.

He sniffed at his shirt.

It was freshly laundered.

As he lifted his head the odor grew stronger. It wasn't coming off him. Fear swamped over him.

He swung around to the small storage space behind his seat. His heart pounded as he peered over the edge of the seat.

A bestial face stared back at him with a savage leer. The creature had crammed itself into the tight space. It must have climbed aboard when the pilot was out smoking. Malik noted the old surgical scars – but also the disk-shaped object strapped to its chest.

A flechette mine.

A year ago, Duncan had tested the blast effect on a male specimen who had dared to punch one of his men. Malik had seen the body afterward. All the flesh had been shredded off the bone – and according to Duncan, the specimen had lived for a full minute afterward.

Horror filled him.

'No,' Malik begged. 'Please . . .'

As the creature smiled coldly, a hand lifted to the center of the mine and pressed the trigger.

Lorna heard a distant explosion. At first, she feared it was the island blowing up. But nothing worse transpired.

We should have at least eight minutes, she estimated.

But what were they going to do with those last minutes?

Standing with Jack, she continued to watch the silent war being waged between the children and their elders. She didn't understand it, but she suspected the two intelligences – one nascent and pure, the other tortured and broken – fought for dominance. Or maybe it was something less brutal, a probing for compatibility. Having grown apart, maybe a merger wasn't even possible.

What would it be like to experience this reunion, to see your children again, but be unable to connect at that deeper level?

Finally, some impasse broke. One of the children reached and took hold of Bennett's hand. The older man stared down at the small form. His face was bloody, his nose broken when he hit the floor.

Moving with that strange flocklike synchronization, the children suddenly stepped forward and openly confronted the larger mass of beasts and men. The young ones looked unnaturally calm, joining hands in a web that Lorna knew went beyond flesh.

Lorna helped Jack to his feet as the mass of children brushed up to her. A small girl extended a tiny hand. Lorna took it, but she kept a grip on Jack's fingers, too.

Taking a cue from the children, Lorna allowed herself to be led toward the army massed at the door. The one she named Adam stood his ground.

Then a child in the lead – the tiniest boy from the looks of him – reached out toward the scarred figure.

Adam looked down. A mix of grief and agony played

across his face. Instead of taking that hand, he danced back as if fearing the boy's touch.

But for whose safety: his own or the children's?

Following Adam's example, the wall of beasts parted and opened a path out of the room. They were being let go . . . or maybe cast out. Either way, the tiny boy took the lead, and the children headed out, drawing Bennett, Lorna, and Jack with them.

Within a few steps, Lorna found herself back in the villa's study. It seemed like days since she had last passed through here.

More of the beasts took refuge here. But they allowed the group to pass unmolested. Moving on, Lorna spotted a group of men farther down the hall. One of them broke away and ran toward her.

'Lorna!'

She could not believe it. 'Kyle!'

After seeing Jack, she had hoped her brother might still be alive, but she had been afraid to ask, fearing the answer.

Kyle shoved Jack aside to hug her. 'Don't ever do that again.'

She wasn't sure exactly what *that* was, but she nodded. 'I promise.'

Over Kyle's shoulder, she watched Jack cross to his own brother. He spoke rapidly, gesturing. Randy stiffened, twisted around, and headed off with the others toward the front door. One of the men already had a radio at his lips.

Jack returned to them, stepping quickly. 'T-Bob is radioing for more pontoon boats. They'll meet us at the beach. We'll have to hurry if we're going to outrun the explosion.'

'Explosion?' Kyle asked.

Rather than explaining, Jack swung away. As he turned he lost his balance. She reached for him, but he tilted and crashed headlong to the floor.

'Jack!'

She rushed to him, dropping to her knees. She had known

something was wrong. While holding hands, Jack had been trembling, quaking with what appeared to be microseizures. She already feared the worst.

Kyle helped turn him over.

Through his burning skin, she felt tremors rising up, growing worse. His muscles quivered and spasmed. His eyes had rolled back into his head. Whatever last reserve he had been riding had finally given out.

She laid a palm on his cheek. With her touch, his eyes snapped back into view. They focused weakly on her. His lips moved. She leaned closer to hear.

His breath brushed her ear. His words were few.

'Tom's gone.'

She pulled back, at first not understanding this reference to his younger brother. Then she saw something in Jack's eyes, something that perhaps had always been there, something she had tried best not to see, dismissing her own feelings as echoes of another boy, another love.

Tom's gone.

A tear rolled down from the corner of his eyelid. He had wanted to get this out before it was too late. Perhaps to say even more.

'Jack . . .'

But he was already gone. His eyes glazed as his body lifted up in a backbreaking arc. His limbs contorted into a full-blown seizure.

Lorna sprawled on top of him. 'Help hold him down.'

Kyle grabbed his head. Two men ran up in gear that matched Jack's.

'What can we do?' the larger of the two asked.

Bennett answered from two steps away. 'Nothing.' His eyes met hers across Jack's quaking body. 'I've seen it before. Too many times. He's infected.'

Lorna had suspected the same when she first hugged Jack. She remembered Malik's description of the protein found in the blood and saliva of the genetically altered animals, how it self-replicated, crossed the blood-brain barrier, and burned through the cerebral cortex like a wildfire.

'There's no hope,' Bennett said.

She wasn't going to accept that. She stood up and pointed an arm toward the door. 'Get him to the boats.'

'What are you going to do?' Kyle asked.

Lorna turned and headed back toward the labs.

Bennett called over to her. 'No one ever survived.'

Lorna ran back through the gauntlet of beasts.

Bennett was wrong.

Someone had survived.

Chapter 59

Under a pall of black anger, Duncan hiked toward the isolated deepwater cove. A boathouse sat over the water, and a rocky quay ran out to the moored seaplane, a small Cessna workhorse. The setting sun had turned the cove to hammered bronze.

Far from the fighting, the peace of this small oasis calmed him, helped him put his thoughts and plans in order.

He carried a backpack filled with cash and gold coins that he'd taken from Bennett's safe. He'd planned on safeguarding it until they were all back in the States.

But those plans had swiftly changed.

As he had trekked over the ridge from the main cove to this smaller one, he had watched Bennett's helicopter take off from the hilltop. Satisfied that all was secure, Duncan had continued down – then seconds later, a resounding blast had echoed over the island.

He had turned in time to see the chopper tip on its nose, stirring up a cloud of smoke. Debris rained down, trailing fire. Then the helicopter plummeted in a death spiral and crashed back to the hilltop.

The site continued to glow like a warning beacon in the night.

Duncan understood that fiery message.

It was over.

Bennett and Malik should have been aboard that flight,

along with all hope for restarting the Babylon Project. He didn't know why the chopper blew: a grenade, another rocket, or just an unlucky spray of bullets.

It didn't matter.

Duncan took the new reality in stride. He was a survivor and had the scars to prove it. With over a hundred grand in cash and gold on his back, he'd start over. He had originally planned to use the seaplane to bomb the fishing charter. He even had a satchel bomb slung over his shoulder.

As he reached the rocky shore he let it drop, abandoning it. It no longer mattered if the other boat escaped the coming detonation. He would be long gone before any word reached the outside world.

All that concerned him now was getting the hell off this rock.

He crossed toward the stone quay, picking up his pace.

He still had five minutes. Plenty of time to fly out of the cove and beyond the blast radius. But he didn't want to cut it too close.

He reached the stone jetty and hurried down it.

But as he neared the boathouse something raised the hairs on his neck. He stopped. As if knowing the trap had been sensed, a sleek shape stalked from behind the boathouse. It stood as tall as his waist. Black fur bristled down its back, ending at a bushy tail. Orange-red eyes glowed at him.

Duncan recognized it as one of the giant foxes from the other island.

Black ghosts, one of his men had named them.

He reached to his belt and pulled out his pistol, refusing to give in to panic. He aimed and fired. But the monster lived up to its nickname and flowed to the side.

Rounds sparked off the stone.

Duncan backed away, but there was no safety in that direction. The island was about to blow. He stopped. His brain urged him to run at the beast, emptying the clip at it. He had to reach the seaplane. But his heart quailed against running *at* the carnivorous beast.

Sweat beaded, and his hands grew slick.

He had no choice.

Duncan steadied his pistol with both hands, arms straight out. Bunching his legs, he sprinted straight at the monster. He squeezed the trigger again and again.

Some rounds missed, but a few struck home.

A front leg shattered under a bullet, lurching the beast to the side. Another round blasted through its left ear. Yet another struck it square in the chest. The beast toppled over on its side. He didn't stop firing. He emptied his clip into it.

Duncan continued at full sprint, ready to hurdle the body.

From there, it was only steps to the seaplane.

Then something heavy struck him from behind and sent him crashing headlong into the stones. He took the brunt of the fall on his shoulder by turning at the last moment. A large shadow bounded past him.

Another of the foxes.

He immediately understood their hunting strategy. The first fox had been a decoy, allowing the other to take him down from behind. He stared at his attacker as it loped and turned toward him.

Duncan discarded the one clip and slapped in another.

But he had learned his lesson.

He remembered there had been *three* foxes on the other island.

He whipped around and found the last fox standing directly behind him, eyes shining. It lunged before he could fire. It bit into his wrist. Bones crunched. The pistol dropped from his fingers.

Duncan punched with his free arm.

But the beast had latched on hard.

The second fox joined the attack, running up and snapping like a bear trap onto his leg. The two monsters then backed in opposite directions, stretching him like a wishbone. His shoulder and hip joints screamed as the ligaments in the sockets tore. They were trying to tear him apart.

Again he was wrong.

A shadow loomed next to him. It was the third fox, still alive. It limped on its three good legs. Blood flowed from the gunshot wounds.

He realized the tug-of-war was not meant to tear his limbs off, but to hold him steady.

The third fox snarled, baring sharp teeth as long as fingers.

No . . .

It dove into his exposed belly. Teeth ripped through clothes, skin, and muscle. Then burrowed deeper. He felt teeth *inside* him.

They were going to eat him alive.

But yet again he was wrong.

The fox backed away, withdrawing its muzzle, soaked in blood. But the beast hadn't come out without a prize. It retreated step-by-step, dragging out a loop of intestine, relentlessly gutting him. Agony and terror welled up.

Duncan finally understood the truth.

There was a horror beyond his worst nightmare.

The foxes hadn't come to eat him.

They'd come to play.

Chapter 60

Lorna burst out of the villa and sprinted across the patio toward the expanse of beach. She had found what she needed in the lab. Behind her, the strange army of beasts followed, as if drawn by her urgency.

She spotted the others at the water's edge.

Two Zodiac rafts floated in the shallows. Children were being loaded into the boats while Jack's two teammates hauled his limp form.

Was he still alive?

She ran faster, knowing time was running out.

As she reached the edge of the beach something snagged her wrist and hauled her around to stop. All that kept her on her feet was the viselike grip on her arm.

The scarred male hominid had hold of her. She tried to yank her arm away, but his grip was iron. He twisted her around. She was ready to scream for help – when a shape stepped from behind a flowering bush. It was another of the hominids. The female. Her breasts were huge, her belly still big. Only she carried an infant in her arms now, a newborn from the look of it. She had swaddled it in a banana leaf.

It was Eve's child.

The woman had given birth.

The female came to her and held out her baby. Lorna shook her head, not understanding. Eve came closer, pushing the baby into her arms.

'No . . .'

The male shoved Lorna roughly from behind.

Eve's eyes pleaded with her.

Lorna finally raised her arms and took the child. Eve turned and hid her face in her mate's chest. He waved Lorna toward the beach, toward the boats.

They wanted her to take the child.

She backed a step, shifted the tiny baby under one arm. She motioned to them. 'Come with us.'

Her plea fell on deaf ears. The pair retreated together, back toward the forest. The other beasts followed.

Lorna stumbled after them. 'It's not safe! Come with me!'

The male turned and snarled at her, making it plain the discussion was over. Eve glanced back before vanishing into the shadows. Tears flowed down her face, but Lorna also read the peace in her expression.

There would be no changing their minds.

'Lorna!' Kyle had spotted her and waved. 'Hurry up!'

With no choice, Lorna cradled the child to her bosom and ran for the rafts.

Kyle waited and helped her through the shallows. He frowned at her burden. 'Is that a baby?'

Lorna ignored him. She waded over to Jack's boat. Half the children were there, along with Bennett. She passed the child up to the older man as she climbed into the boat with them.

Bennett lifted a questioning eyebrow.

'Eve's child,' she explained.

Bennett's eyes widened as he glanced down at the baby. The other children gathered closer.

The Zodiac's pilot gunned the outboard engine and tore away from the beach. The other raft followed. The water in the cove was as smooth as glass. The boats took advantage and gathered speed, shooting across the surface.

The fishing charter had already begun steaming away and had almost cleared the cove.

Lorna turned to Jack's sprawled body. The larger of his two companions sat with his slack form in the bottom of the boat.

'He's still breathing,' the man growled. 'For now.'

She placed a hand on Jack's shoulder. Even through his clothes, she felt the feverish heat of his body. He continued to quake under her touch, locked in a continual seizure. It was burning him up.

Before she could get a better assessment of his condition, a rumbling shook across the still waters of the cove.

'Hang on!' the pilot yelled.

Lorna turned as the villa blew apart, shattering outward in a massive explosion, most of it vaporizing into a thick black column of smoke. The column pushed high into the sky, glowing at the core with hellish fires. A hot wind washed over them as they raced away.

But it wasn't over.

A secondary blast erupted, even stronger than the first. The entire top of the hill blew off this time, shoving the smoky column higher, curling it into a fiery mushroom cloud. Debris pounded into the water, some boulders as large as minivans. But the two rafts had fled far enough away. All that reached them was a large swell.

It picked up their boat and sped them even faster out to sea.

Lorna continued to stare as the island burned.

She finally turned to the pilot, fearing for Jack. She had never taken her hand off him. 'I need to get him over to that ship.'

What she intended was too dangerous to attempt here.

She prayed it wasn't already too late.

Bennett stared over at her. 'What are you going to do with him? Like I said, no one's ever survived.'

'Duncan did.'

Bennett was taken aback by her statement.

Lorna needed to talk it through. 'You said he was

attacked back in Iraq, by one of the earlier incarnations of these altered forms. But he survived. So what made him different?'

Bennett shook his head.

'You told me Duncan's injuries were so severe that he spent a week in a *coma*. That's the difference. This deadly protein hyperexcites the brain. So the only way a brain could protect itself during such an assault was to turn itself off until the infection ran its course. I think that's why Duncan never got sick.'

Bennett frowned. 'Then what are you going to do with Jack?'

Lorna took a deep breath and stared over at the larger boat. Stating it aloud made it seem insane, but she had to face it.

She turned to Jack and answered Bennett's question.

'I'm going to send him into a medically induced coma.'

Chapter 61

'You're going to do *what* to my brother?'

Randy's voice cracked with disbelief.

Lorna followed Jack's body down into the ship's hold. Mack carried him in his arms. His other teammate was receiving first aid for a bullet wound. The captain had offered Lorna the use of his cabin.

Randy dogged her steps. As Jack's only kin here, she had confided in him. He had a right to know, but from his terrified expression, maybe such honesty wasn't appreciated.

'I'm going to drug him,' Lorna said. 'Send him into a coma and keep him there until a medevac helicopter arrives.'

The ship had already radioed for help, but it would take hours for anyone to reach them. Jack would be dead by then. She had confirmed the prognosis with Bennett. Once the seizures started, patients died within the hour.

It had to be attempted.

Randy reached to his forehead, as if looking to adjust a ball cap that wasn't there. His eyes shone with worry.

Kyle followed behind him. 'My sister knows what she's doing.'

Randy turned on him. 'She's a vet!'

'And a darned good one!'

They reached the captain's cabin. Mack manhandled Jack inside.

Out in the hall, Lorna turned to them. 'Randy, you should

stay out here. I promise I'll do everything I can to save him.'

Randy faced her, balanced between fury and fear. He lunged at her. She took a startled step back. But he only grabbed her in a bear hug.

'Take care of my little brother,' he whispered in her ear, biting back tears. He straightened. 'I know there's bad blood between our families. But Jack trusts you. So I do, too.'

Lorna nodded.

Kyle took Randy's shoulder. 'Wanna beer while we wait?'

Randy sagged, nodded, and turned with Kyle back toward the stairs.

Lorna joined Mack in the captain's cabin. The big man had Jack sprawled across the bed.

'Need a hand?' he asked.

'I could use the company,' she said, smiling wanly, not wanting to be alone.

He sank to the bed beside Jack's head. She placed the drug bottle down on the bedside table. It was labeled *sodium thiopental*. She had taken it from the Malik's surgical supplies. It was a common anesthetic used in animals, and considering Malik's research, she knew the lab would have a supply.

But she intended to do more than just anesthetize Jack with it.

For years, thiopental had also been used by medical doctors to send patients into an induced coma. Though the drug propofol was employed more commonly today, thiopental was still useful in cases of brain trauma or swelling. The drug triggered a marked decrease in neuronal activity, which was the effect Lorna needed most right now.

Jack's brain was on overdrive.

She had to turn that engine off.

Working quickly, she prepped Jack's arm and established a tourniquet. Ready, she picked up a syringe that she had preloaded with the thiopental.

She met Mack's gaze over his body.

'You can do this,' he said.

Swallowing back her fear, she inserted the needle, aspirated blood to make sure she had a good stick, then released the tourniquet.

Slowly she pushed the plunger and sent the man she was growing to love into a coma.

Half an hour later, Lorna stood on the stern deck of the ship. Mack continued to watch over Jack. She had needed to get some air. At least for a minute. Her body trembled with exhaustion and stress.

Standing by the rail, she took deep breaths and stared out at the dark sea. Stars glistened overhead, but the moon had not yet risen.

The scratch of a match made her jump.

She turned and found Bennett seated on a deck chair. Lost in her own thoughts, she had failed to see him in the dark. He brought the match to his pipe. The tobacco glowed ruddily as he puffed it to life. He stood up and joined her.

'How's he doing?'

Lorna sighed. 'I don't know. His fever's dropped. The anesthetic has quieted his spasms. But I don't know if he's still even in there. He's been seizing for a long time.'

Bennett exhaled a stream of smoke. 'You're doing all you can do.'

They stood quietly for a long moment.

She needed to change the subject. 'How's the baby?'

'Sleeping. We found some formula. The captain's wife has a four-month-old. Lucky for that.' Bennett turned to her. 'Eve's baby is a little girl, by the way.'

'How about the rest of the children?'

'They're all sleeping in there with her. I think they recognize one of their own and want to welcome her into the fold. Or maybe it's just plain childish curiosity. Hard to say.'

Silence stretched again, but Bennett was full of questions.

'Why do you think Eve gave her up?' he asked.

Lorna had pondered the same question. She couldn't say

for sure, but she could guess. 'I think it's the same reason they let us go . . . or rather let the children go.'

'What do you mean?'

'The baby's pure. It's neural net is still infantile. I think back at the villa the older ones recognized that the children were equally uncorrupted. In that moment of confrontation, the two hive minds met. One was pure and innocent, while the other had been tortured into psychosis. I think the older hive mind recognized that the younger ones were lost to them, that they could only offer poison and pain.'

She remembered the agony and grief in Adam when one of the little ones had offered his hand.

'So they did the only thing they could,' she said. 'As a final gift and sacrifice, they let them go.'

'What about afterward? Do you think they knew they were going to be killed?'

She pictured Eve's last expression. It had been full of peace and acceptance. 'I think they did.'

Bennett spent a long introspective moment with his pipe. He finally got around to the true question that had been troubling him.

'Why did they protect me? It doesn't make sense. The monsters were going to kill me.'

'You may know that answer better than I.'

He stared at her. Tears glinted in his eyes. He needed some direction. She didn't know if he deserved it, but she took her example from the kids.

'They protected me, too,' she said. 'Though they can't bond to us as intimately as they can with each other, I think they possess a strong sense of empathy. They sensed something in you worth saving.'

'But what could that be? All that I did . . . all that I turned a blind eye to . . . and sometimes not even a blind eye.'

He shook his head.

'I don't know. I can't read your heart. But maybe they recognized the possibility of redemption in you. And amid all that bloodshed, they couldn't let it be destroyed.'

Bennett turned from her. He covered his face with his hands. His shoulders shook.

'What have I done?' he sobbed softly.

'That's just it. It's not what you did, but what you have yet to do.'

As those words passed her lips she took them to heart herself. For so long, she'd let her past define her, isolate her, keep her trapped in a limbo of her own guilt. No longer. Jack's last words came back to her.

Tom's gone.

It was time for her to truly see that, to act on it.

She prayed she still had the chance.

Chapter 62

The uptown campus of Tulane University rose amid clusters of turn-of-the-century mansions, magnolia-shaded parks, and college housing complexes. It was only a short ride on the St. Charles streetcar from Lorna's Garden District home.

Still, for the past three days, she seldom left the neurology department on the fourth floor of the Tulane Medical Center. She paced the hall outside the room, anxious for the neurologist to finish his exam.

Jack had been airlifted here from the Thibodeauxs' fishing boat. Lorna had gone with him during that flight, explaining to the doctors about his treatment. She glossed over many details but was honest about his condition.

Half the hospital departments had been through Jack's room. Once here, he had been switched to a propofol infusion to maintain his coma, his EEG was monitored around the clock, and his body was hooked to a battery of equipment.

But today was critical. The doctors had been weaning him off the infusion all morning, slowly allowing him to wake while closely monitoring his EEG for any sign of continuing seizure activity. So far so good. But a bigger question remained.

What was left of Jack?

The neurologist seemed confident that there was no permanent brain damage, but after such an injury, he could make no guarantees. Jack could remain in a vegetative state or fully recover. But the doctor had warned that the more likely result was somewhere in between.

So they waited.

Randy sat down the hall with Jack's mother and father. Kyle had gone down to the cafeteria to fetch them all more coffee. None of them had slept. In the trenches these past days, they had all grown closer.

During their vigil, Lorna had finally shared the whole story of that night with Tom, of the loss of her baby, the attempted rape, Jack's rescue, and its tragic conclusion. Once she started, it had poured out of her. There had been many tears, on all sides, but in the end, just as much healing.

'You were just a child,' his mother had said, taking her hand. 'You poor thing. Such a burden to bear all these years.'

The door to the room finally swung open, and a cluster of white coats and nurses flowed out. The neurologist came over. Lorna tried to read some clue from his face. Jack's family joined her.

'We've taken him off the infusion,' the doctor explained with a sigh, 'but we're going to maintain a low-dose benzodiazepine drip as he wakes. We'll also be monitoring his EEG and vitals.'

'Can we sit with him?' Lorna asked.

The doctor frowned at the large group. 'One at a time.' He admonished them with a finger. 'And not for too long.'

Lorna turned to the family.

Jack's mother patted her arm. 'You go on in, dear. You're family now, too. Besides, if my boy wakes, he should see a pretty face first.'

Lorna wanted to argue, but she allowed herself this moment of selfishness.

She hugged Jack's mother, then hurried through the door. Inside, a nurse stood by a bank of monitoring equipment. Lorna crossed and sat on a bedside chair. She had spent the night in that same seat, holding Jack's hand, talking to him, praying.

She stared over at his pale face. She watched his chest rise and fall. Lines and tubes ran from under his sheets to machines that beeped and blinked. She leaned forward and took his hand.

'Jack . . .'

His hand twitched – causing her heart to jump. But was it in recognition or were the seizures starting again? Fearful, hopeful, she stood up, still grasping his hand. She leaned over him and stared down.

His chest rose heavily, then he sighed out loudly.

His lids fluttered open, but his eyes remained rolled back.

'Jack,' she whispered down at him. She placed her other palm on his cheek. 'Please . . .'

He blinked slowly – once, twice – then she found him staring back up at her. 'Hey,' he whispered groggily.

She squeezed his hand. 'Hey yourself.'

A ghost of a smile shadowed his lips. They just stared at each other. His eyes seemed to drink her in. Then his fingers tightened on hers with surprising strength. His expression became a mask of regret.

'What I said before . . .' he said coarsely, his voice raw with exhaustion and maybe something more.

She stopped him. She understood the guilt buried in those two words.

Tom's gone.

It had haunted both their lives, but it was time to free that ghost.

She leaned down, brushed her lips against his, and whispered into his breath. 'But we're here.'

Chapter 63

Three months later, Jack was speeding down the waterway in his cousin's airboat. The wind whipped his hair. His only companion, Burt, sat in the bow, his tongue lolling, his ears flapping. Jack guided the craft with deft ease and a light touch on the stick. He sat high in the pilot's chair. The height allowed him to see over rushes, reeds, and bushes.

It felt good to get away from the city, from the station house. He was also tired of needles, rehabilitation appointments, and psychological tests. Besides a residual numbness in his left hand and the need to take a low-dose anticonvulsant tablet once a day, he had fully recovered.

Still, the best therapy of all could be found out here.

As the midday sun glared off the water he took a deep breath of the rich bayou air, heavy and humid, redolent with brackish water, yet sweetened by sedges and summer flowers.

As he raced deeper into the swamplands he again appreciated the stark and primeval beauty of these wide and trackless lands. He watched white-tailed deer bound away from the roar of his boat's propellers. Alligators slipped deeper into nests. Raccoons and squirrels skittered up trees.

Rounding a bend, he slowed the airboat and let the engine die.

He needed a private moment to collect himself.

He let the boat gently rock as he listened to the life around him. Some considered the swamps to be a desolate and quiet place. That couldn't be further from the truth. He closed his eyes, taking in the buzz of gnats, the chorus of frogs, the distant bark of a bull gator, and woven throughout it all, birdsong from hundreds of warbling throats.

After the events of last spring, Jack took moments like this to stop and appreciate the wonders around him. It was as if he had new eyes. In fact, *all* his senses seemed sharper. Not because of any residual effect from his illness, but simply because of his renewed appreciation for life.

This particular moment was especially significant for him.

His life was about to change in ways he couldn't imagine, and he needed to prepare for it. But he also sensed the pressure of time.

Lorna was waiting for him – secretly summoned out here under mysterious circumstances – and he dared not keep her waiting any longer than necessary. She still had much work to do over at ACRES as the new facility was under construction.

'Better get going,' he said to Burt.

His hound thumped his tail in agreement.

Taking a final deep breath, Jack started up the airboat's engine and shot down the waterways and channels. It was a maze through here, but he knew the way by heart. Skirting around an island, he reached a channel that ran straight toward a large log home, newly rebuilt after the fires.

He flew straight for the pier, then, at the last moment, angled the craft broadside and raked the bow to a perfect stop alongside the dock. A familiar round shape dressed in coveralls and an LSU ball cap rose from a chair and helped him tie off the airboat.

Burt bounded onto the dock and greeted him like an old friend.

''Bout time you got here, Jack. Your little filly was growing restless. Thought I might have to tie her down.' With a final tug, he cinched the mooring rope to the pier's stanchion.

'Thanks, Joe. Where is she?'

'Where do you think?' He waved beyond the log home, to the grounds of what was formerly known as Uncle Joe's Alligator Farm. 'She's off with Stella and the kids.'

*

Lorna stared in amazement at the sight. She never grew tired of it. She stood on the observation deck above the spread of ponds and elevated walkways. A glass of lemonade sweated on the log rail. Below, children ran and played, bounded and jumped. Several hung from trees.

The ponds no longer held any alligators. They'd all been moved, including Elvis, who now was a star attraction at the Audubon Zoo in the city. To support his acquisition, a major marketing campaign was under way. Its slogan could be found emblazoned on billboards, buses, and streetcars all across New Orleans. It was only two words: *Elvis Lives!*

Stella climbed the steps with the youngest child in her arms. Only three months old, the girl was already walking on her own – though she plainly still liked to be carried.

'Eve is getting heavy,' Stella said, hiking the child higher in her arms.

'I can see that.'

'We're weaning her off the bottle like you suggested, but she's fighting it.'

'They always do.' Lorna smiled and nodded below. 'I have to say, you're doing a great job. They all look so happy.'

Stella matched her grin. 'Oh, they have their usual scrapes and bruises like any kids, but I've never seen a more loving bunch. You should see how they dote on Igor, Bagheera, and the two little monkeys. They keep stuffing them with treats.'

Lorna laughed. She had never doubted the brood would find a good home here, but she was surprised how quickly they had adjusted to their new environment and circumstances.

Before leaving the Thibodeauxs' boat, Lorna and the others had made a pact to keep the existence of the children secret – at least until they were strong enough and the world ready enough to handle such news. The Thibodeauxs had proved skilled at getting the children through the bayou in secret. No one appeared to be any the wiser, and when it came to keeping things hidden from sight, there was no better place.

Lorna had only confided in two others – Carlton and Zoë – knowing she'd need their help in establishing this secret sanctuary. It had been an easy sell. ACRES had been started to protect and nurture endangered species.

Lorna watched the children play.

Was there any species more endangered, more at risk?

To help matters, the project had the backing of an open checkbook from a silent partner.

After reaching U.S. shores, Bennett had turned himself over to the authorities. He did not hold back, exposing all the crimes done in his name, opening the balance sheets to Ironcreek – but as promised, he had remained silent about the children. He told authorities that the facility on Lost Eden Cay had been a viral lab undergoing human trials, that a weaponized organism had gotten loose, and that it became necessary to burn it all down.

Afterward, Bennett had been moved to a high-security facility while he assisted the Justice Department in rooting out other guilty parties both within the government and out in the private sector. His testimony continued to shake up Washington.

Hopefully for the better.

But Bennett's largesse didn't end there. Through the use of dummy corporations and financial channels that made Lorna's head spin, he secretly financed both the rebuilding of ACRES and the establishment of this secret sanctuary.

Lorna understood the motive behind this generosity.

Bennett had started down a path to his own redemption.

If she ever doubted it, she only had to turn around. At Bennett's personal request, a message had been carved into the lintel above the new home's doorway.

Matthew 19:14

She had to look up that particular Bible verse. When she did so, it left her smiling. She found it entirely fitting.

Let the little children come to me, and do not hinder them, for the kingdom of heaven belongs to such as these.

Lorna stared across at the joyful play and youthful innocence. Her smile grew as she took it all in. While this might not be Heaven, it was definitely a little slice of Eden.

Footsteps sounded behind her.

She turned to find Jack crossing toward her, Burt trotting at his side. The shock must have been all over her face. She hadn't known he was coming.

Stella retreated toward the house with Eve in her arms.

Jack took her place. He was dressed in a crisp black suit, his hair wet and combed back, like he'd just stepped out of the shower – though he still had a day's worth of stubble over his chin and cheeks.

She was confused. 'What are you doing here?'

He lifted his arms to encompass this new Eden. 'Where better than *here?*'

She still didn't understand. 'For what?'

As answer, he dropped to one knee.

Epilogue

Spring
Baghdad, Iraq

Two young men hurried through the Al-Zawraa Gardens toward the main gates of the Baghdad Zoo. The smaller of the two sped ahead of his older brother. He called back impatiently.

'*Yalla!* Come on, Makeen!'

Makeen followed, but with less enthusiasm. He had no particular desire to ever set foot in the zoo again. The place still haunted his nightmares. But many years had passed. He had a girlfriend, a job at a video store, and hoped to save one day for his own car.

Yet, more than all that, today was his little brother Bari's sixteenth birthday, an auspicious day. A party was planned in the park later. His mother had spent the past week preparing this birthday picnic. The apartment still smelled of baking bread and cinnamon. With the promise of a full stomach, even nightmares lost their power.

Bari hurried through the gates. His younger brother showed no hesitation. Over the years, Bari often visited the new zoo, but whenever Makeen tried to talk to him about what had happened, his brother said he didn't remember. And maybe he truly didn't. Bari hadn't seen the monster, not up close, that black beast of *Shaitan*.

Even to this day, Makeen sometimes woke with his bed-sheets tangled, soaked with sweat, a scream trapped in his throat, picturing eyes aglow with a smokeless fire.

As he crossed the gardens he lifted his face to the sun and burned away such dark thoughts. On a bright morning like today, amid the bustle of the early-morning visitors, what was there to fear?

He found Bari dancing at the entrance. 'You move like a constipated camel, Makeen. I want to see the new baby chimp, and you know the crowds gather later.'

Makeen followed. He didn't understand his brother's love for all things furry, but on this special day he'd tolerate it.

They wound through the various exhibits – birds, camels, bears – and headed straight toward the chimp enclosure. He strode quickly with his brother, matching his stride. Thankfully their path did not take them past the old lion cages.

Subhan'Allah, he thought to himself. *Allah be praised*.

At last they reached their destination. The monkey-and-ape exhibit had been refurbished after the bombing. It was a popular site. After the war, a few escaped apes had been recaptured and returned to the new exhibit. For Iraqis, such continuity was important. It held special significance for the besieged city, a symbol of recovery and stability.

So the birth last year was doubly special.

An older chimpanzee – one recovered in the streets – had given birth to a baby, a child born bald. It had caused a media sensation, declared an omen of good fortune.

Makeen didn't understand that.

Even a year later, the naked chimp continued to draw large crowds.

Bari hurried to a separate entrance off to the side. It led into a small nursery ward.

'Over here, Makeen! I can't believe you've not seen it!'

Indulging his brother's enthusiasm, he walked into the enclosure. A short hall ran past a cage enclosed behind glass. At this early hour, they had the ward to themselves.

With his arms crossed, Makeen stared into the exhibit. A fake tree sprouted from a sandy floor, its limbs draped in ropes, tire swings, and woven slings.

At first, he failed to spot the star of the exhibit.

Then something as black as oil dropped from above and landed in the sand. With its back to the glass, it looked like a tiny bare-assed old man. Its skin was all wrinkled, like a suit cut too large.

Rather than being charmed, a wave of revulsion swept through Makeen.

The creature held a long stick in front of it and beat at the sand.

Bari got excited. 'Look how close it is. I've never seen it up against the window.'

His brother rushed forward and placed a hand against the glass, trying to have an intimate moment with the chimp.

'Get away from there!' Makeen yelled, louder than he intended, allowing his fear to ring out.

Bari turned and rolled his eyes. 'Don't be a *shakheef*, Makeen.'

The creature ignored them both and continued to dig at the sand with his stick.

'Let's head back to the gardens,' Makeen said, moderating his tone. 'Before Mother feeds your picnic feast to the birds.'

Bari sighed with much exaggeration. 'There's so much more to see.'

'Another day.'

'You always say that,' he said in a heavy sulk and headed off.

Makeen remained a moment longer. He stared at the small chimp, struggling to calm his heart. What was there to fear? He moved closer to the window and looked down at what the creature had drawn in the sand.

With its stick, it had scratched a series of numbers.

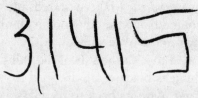

3,1415

Makeen frowned. Clearly it was mimicking something it had seen. Still, a shudder passed through him. He remembered reading in the local newspaper about how quickly this chimp was growing, how it had escaped its first cage by stacking boxes to reach a grate. It had even fashioned a crude spear by chewing a tree branch to a sharpened point.

As if sensing Makeen's suspicion, the chimp swung around and stared him full in the face. He fell back. The naked visage was terrifying to behold, like a wizened black fig come to life with fat lips and huge yellow eyes.

That gaze locked onto him.

Makeen gasped and covered his mouth. In those yellow eyes, he recognized a familiar and frightening sheen of intelligence, aglow with a black smokeless fire.

He stumbled back in horror.

As he fled, the chimp's lips curled into a hungry smile.

Baring all its teeth.

Author's Note to Readers: Truth or Fiction

I always try to root my books in the real world while dabbling in topics that intrigue me. So I thought I'd take this moment to draw the line between truth and fiction in this novel. So here we go:

Baghdad. One of the seeds for this story came from reading a book about the efforts to rescue the Baghdad Zoo following the Iraqi war. The zoo was badly damaged during a firefight between American forces and the Republican Guard. Afterward, there was extensive looting, and many of the animals escaped into the city. If you'd like to read more about the harrowing efforts to protect the zoo and rebuild it, check out *Babylon's Ark* by Lawrence Anthony with Graham Spence.

ACRES. Lorna's place of employment, the Audubon Center for Research of Endangered Species, is a real facility, located in a remote location alongside the Mississippi River. It's not open to the public, but you can read many details about the staff's wonderful efforts to preserve endangered species on the Internet. They do indeed have a 'frozen zoo,' where genetic material is stored in an effort to help sustain and protect this fragile heritage. And the researchers there have been doing cutting-edge work into cloning as a means of preservation. Of course, all the characters depicted in this book are fictitious, and I've taken great liberties in regard to the floor plan of the actual facility.

All Creatures Great and Small. The claims concerning animal intelligence, especially in regard to parrots, may sound far-fetched, but they are based on facts. A great book in which to read about this subject is *The Parrot Who Owns Me* by Joanna Burger. You'll be amazed. Also the hunting habits of jaguars are based on real science, and all the details about the human-animal bond discussed in this novel are true (and we're learning more and more about this astounding connection every year).

Genetics. All the chromosomal details are accurate, including the fact that geneticists have discovered old pieces of viral code in our junk DNA. But what about 'genetic throwbacks'? Is such a thing possible? If you have any doubts, check out this article about a snake born in China with a fully functional reptilian leg growing out of its side: *http://www.telegraph.co.uk/earth/wildlife/6187320/Snake-with-foot-found-in-China.html*

Fractals. This subject fascinates me. And I've barely scratched the surface in this book about the subject. Fractals are found everywhere, and to better visualize and to understand the full extent, go seek out a PBS *Nova* special titled 'Fractals: Hunting the Hidden Dimension.' Also, the details regarding the power and growth of 'fractal antennas' are real.

All Things Brainy. It's true that all animals – including humans – have strange magnetite crystals seeded throughout their brains. Scientists believe that they are still used for migration in birds – but why do we have them? I had to explore this further. As to Jack's blood-borne illness, I based his infection on *bovine spongiform encephalopathy* (mad cow disease). This scourge is caused by a self-replicating protein called a *prion*. It crosses the blood-brain barrier and triggers madness. Of course, I just juiced up that protein for this novel. Also it's a small detail but true: the human brain does continually produce about twelve watts of electricity, enough to power a flashlight.

Things That Go Boom. All of the weapons depicted in this book are real, including flechette mines and Gar's wicked AA-12 combat shotgun. To witness the latter in action, there are many videos on YouTube.

War Room. The JASONS are a real think tank who advise the military. They did indeed produce a paper recommending that the U.S. military invest greater resources into 'human performance modifications.' They suggested further research into drugs, genetics, and the neurological fusion of cybernetic computers, all in order to manipulate the human brain and produce better soldiers. Also, the abuses related about private defense contractors are real and currently under investigation. Similarly, these corporations have been moving into scientific circles, including establishing labs outside the United States to circumvent laws and oversight.

Location, Location, Location. If you couldn't tell, I love New Orleans. I've visited the city at least a dozen times – both before and after Katrina. I tried to be as true to as many details as possible. I've visited alligator farms, toured the bayou by airboat and canoe, walked on floating islands, and talked to people about their lives. Cajuns have a rich and colorful culture, and I tried to capture it all as best I could.

So go visit New Orleans. Have Sunday brunch at Commander's Palace. Enjoy beignets and chicory coffee at Café du Monde. Take some of the great tours offered (to the Garden District, to Oak Alley Plantation, or my personal favorite, a ghost tour at night). Stop by the Garden District Book Shop (one of my favorite places to browse).

Take a ride on a St. Charles streetcar. Have your palm read by candlelight in Jackson Square. And don't forget to visit the Audubon Zoo . . . throw Elvis a marshmallow for me. Lastly, don't miss a chance to experience one of America's premiere landscapes: the swamps and bayous of the Mississippi River delta. Who knows what you might discover out there, hidden beneath the shroud of Spanish moss and towering cypresses?